# THE
# BIG
# LAW

# THE BIG LAW

## A NOVEL

# CHUCK LOGAN

HarperCollins*Publishers*

HarperCollins books may be purchased for educational, business, or sales promotional use. For information please write: Special Markets Department, HarperCollins Publishers, Inc., 10 East 53rd Street, New York, NY 10022.

FIRST EDITION

*Designed by Kris Tobiassen*

Library of Congress Cataloging-in-Publication Data

Logan, Chuck, 1942–
    The big law : a novel / Chuck Logan. — 1st ed.
        p.   cm.
    ISBN 0-06-019133-3
    I. Title.
    PS3562.04453B54   1998
    813'.54—dc21                                                    98-29852

98 99 00 01 02 ❖/RRD 10 9 8 7 6 5 4 3 2 1

*For Kelly Logan*

**December 11; 11:33 A.M.**

The box came in the UPS morning delivery at the rear entrance of the Warren E. Burger Federal Building at the corner of Kellogg and Robert, in downtown St. Paul. It measured eighteen inches by sixteen inches, and was six inches deep. It weighed about twelve pounds. A red label slapped diagonal to the address announced: CONTENTS REFRIGERATED. A retired cop in a security company blazer manned the guard station. He placed the box on the X-ray machine belt.

First, the label caught his attention.

Then the quilt of mismatched stamps. And the address: "*For* FBI Special Agent Lorn Garrison"—like real personal. And the office number of a federal and local joint task force investigating narcotics traffic in the county; it was an office number not given out to the public. Very alert now, he ran the box and focused on his video monitor.

He was trained to look for five objects inside packages: detonators, power sources, switches, chemicals, and wires that connected them.

He saw shapes in the monitor screen that could be all five. He stopped the conveyor, picked up his phone, and alerted the main security office. In a calm forceful voice, he ordered everyone in the immediate area to exit the building.

People spilled into the intersection of Jackson and Fourth Streets, among them a supervisor in the IRS offices. He'd heard someone at the guard station say the word *bomb*. So he called his office on his cell phone and said, "I think there's a bomb." Other office workers lined up to use his cell phone and notify their offices.

In sixty seconds the stairwells thundered with people whose imaginations thundered with visions of Oklahoma City. There was still no official order to evacuate. Hundreds of federal employees were now out stamping in the cold on Jackson, Fourth, and Robert Streets and on Kellogg Boulevard.

A photographer for the St. Paul paper, returning from an assignment, drove down Fourth Street, got stuck in a crowd of people milling in the intersection of Fourth and Robert, and asked what was going on.

"There's a bomb scare."

The photographer called his photo desk and omitted the word *scare*. Then he left his car in the middle of the street and jockeyed for a good shooting position. He conjured an image of the building perfectly captured at the precise moment it collapsed. He saw it in his mind's eye and also on the covers of *Time* and *Newsweek*. With equal clarity, he saw his photo credit. Only one thing bothered him. The cruddy overcast day had wet cement for light. He loved to light and pose everything just so. How do you pose a building?

All over downtown, phones and pagers buzzed. Fire trucks rolled. Police barricades went up.

At 11:40 the FBI office at the building formally requested the St. Paul Police Department's bomb squad to investigate a suspicious package. They checked the switchboard and the mail room. There had been no bomb threats. They held back on the order to evacuate.

The city did not have a dedicated bomb unit, but in fifteen minutes, two pickup squad members arrived in the white "ice cream truck" with their bomb disposal wagon in tow. At twelve noon they took control of the site. After confirming that everyone was out of the rear entry area, one cop remotely toggled a wheeled robot down the truck ramp. The other cop Velcroed on ninety pounds of Kevlar navy blue armor, inserted a thick steel chest plate in the suit's breast pocket, pulled on a sloped visored helmet, activated the internal cooling system, struggled into a pair of cumbersome mittens, and clanked through the door.

If this was the big one, the suit would maybe allow the coroner to have an intact corpse to poke. The guy wearing the suit knew this.

He approached the X-ray machine and made a visual inspection. Two shadows on the video screen caught his attention. The detonator cap was inert, missing a portion, and the connecting wires were, in the lingo of his dark trade, "shunted," meaning crossed. Not an open circuit.

In case the bomb squad was having a bad day, the creator of the apparatus had stuck thin lead foil strips on the "explosive" bundle to painstakingly spell out: SMILE IF YOU EAT SHIT.

"Bomb hoax," the bomb tech radioed his partner.

But, following procedure, and just in case, they remotely disrupted the package. The man in the suit used a sixteen-foot pole with a pincer to move it off the X-ray machine and place it on the floor. Then they toggled in the robot and blew the box apart using a twelve-gauge water cannon on the robot's arm.

After the robot's video camera inspected the debris, the man in the suit went in again, made a visual sweep, and issued an official all clear. He paused in the doorway and removed his helmet. A knot of fast-moving men left the police cordon and approached him.

Perusing the stern faces and spit-shined wing tips, the bomb cop queried, "You FBI?" The agents nodded. "Who's Lorn Garrison?" he asked.

"I'm Garrison," said a tall, saturnine senior guy. Maybe fifty-five.

The bomb cop handed Garrison a sopping wet portion of cardboard with the address on it. Expressionless, he said, "You've got mail."

Garrison peered through the door at the scattered box. A white cloud seeped from some of the debris.

Garrison sniffed. "Is that smoke?"

The bomb cop shook his head. "Vapor. It's safe—physically. I don't know about psychologically."

The agents exchanged glances. Going in, Garrison tapped his finger on the typed return address on the crumpled wet cardboard that bore a St. Paul postmark, dated yesterday:

ALEX GORSKI
3173 HARRIET PLACE
ST. PAUL

One of the agents groaned; he had installed two electronic receivers, a camera, and a telephone tap at that location two weeks before and had been monitoring it ever since. Gorski was a key informant who had been recruited in New York, and then moved to

Chicago. Garrison had brought him to St. Paul on a special assignment involving a huge shipment of powdered cocaine.

St. Paul was small-time to Garrison, compared to Atlanta and New Orleans. But it turned out to be the big time for Gorski, who had disappeared three days ago.

Garrison cautiously skirted the pieces of the box and its strewn contents. His shoes made soggy squeegee crackles and pops. The device had been packed in those green Styrofoam peanut things, and they were everywhere. As was a coil of wire. A taped bundle of double-A batteries. The switch still had a price sticker on it from Ace Hardware. Ditto for the small digital clock.

The white vapor seeped from chunks of dry ice in a large transparent plastic bag that spilled from a cedar cigar box. The foil message was intact on the side of the box.

Garrison did not smile.

His attention was riveted to a reddish gray oblong shape jammed in the bottom of the bag. It reminded him of something he had last seen back home, after Thanksgiving on a shelf in his refrigerator. The chemical ice steamed on exposure to the air.

Someone behind Garrison gagged and cleared their throat.

"Steady," said Garrison. He took a ballpoint from his coat pocket and poked the bag open more.

Several chunks of dry ice oozed out onto the terrazzo floor. So did a slightly blackened, intact human tongue trailing tentacles of ligament.

Garrison carefully removed his suit jacket and laid it on top of the X-ray machine. Then he leaned forward to inspect the shriveled organ lying on the cement floor in a clutter of fuming ice. As he squatted to make a closer examination, a young agent stifled a gag reflex and muttered in back of him: "Jesus, they *cut out* his tongue?"

Lorn mentored the younger man without turning. "You're a city bo—" Garrison paused and enunciated clearly. "City *guy*, aren't you, Terry?" Terry was what they used to call a high-yellow Negro back home in Kentucky. His hair was tinged with a reddish hue, and he had orange freckles. Garrison reminded himself. You hadda watch it these days.

The younger man shrugged. "Yeah, so?"

"If you were country, you'd know your organ meats better. That tongue was ripped out, root and branch. See the ligaments there. It's a message."

"Alex Gorski's talking days are over."

"That's a roger."

"You ever have anybody send something like this to the office before?" asked Agent Terry.

"No," said Lorn Garrison as he stood up with the careful posture of an athletic man past a certain age. He cocked an eyebrow at Terry. "But these Russian guys aren't your normal hoods, now are they."

There was an attempt to squash the "tongue rumor" through all the agencies involved in the event, but—something like this—people were bound to talk, and by happy hour, the word started to crackle. The routine story about the bomb scare was spiced with an uncon-firmed rumor about enclosed body parts delivered to the FBI. CNN picked the story up from local TV that night, and it appeared, page one, in both the Minneapolis and St. Paul papers in the morning.

The local FBI was furious, and no one was more pissed than Lorn Garrison, who was three months from retiring to his home county in Kentucky and running for sheriff. Some sumbitch was sticking their tongue out at the bureau, and they would pay.

Interstate 35 started in Laredo, Texas, curved up the breadbasket of the country, ran a few blocks past the St. Paul Federal Building and ended, 144 miles north of St. Paul, in Duluth. Beyond Duluth, North 61 was the only road in and out of the North Shore of Lake Superior. Mileposts commence at the Duluth city limits and pace Highway 61 for 150 miles, northeast, to the Pigeon River on the Ontario border. Some locals hold to the notion that you leave the climate and culture of the lower forty-eight behind when you pass through Grand Marais at Milepost 109. North of Grand Marais, the terrain was claimed by loggers, trappers, dog mushers, and Indians who fancied they would be at home on the Alaskan frontier.

This rocky wilderness shore also attracted pilgrims like Phil Broker, who grew up here, left twenty-five years ago, and had returned for the winter.

Broker decided that his baby daughter, Kit, would learn to walk north of Grand Marais. And she had. Now she had seen her first wolf, a little past Milepost 127.

Except the spot this wolf picked to cross the road was occupied by a speeding pulpwood truck that chopped him, dragged him, and rolling-pinned him flat.

Broker, driving home from his weekly grocery shopping at the IGA in town, saw the truck swerve, straighten, and roar past. A hundred yards later, he stopped the green Cherokee Sport, got out, and stared at the mature black wolf, its dusty gray fur presented with the usual roadkill trimmings. From her car seat, fourteen-month-old Kit watched, big gray-green eyes under a flip of copper curls.

Not like her stuffed Wolfie toy, not like the friendly talking wolf on *Sesame Street*.

And not like Daddy, with his shaggy black eyebrows that grew straight together above his olive-gray eyes, who growled "Grrrrr" when she pulled on them.

Just the thing they leave out of the children's books—real dead. And now, he thought, she gets to see the inside and the outside at the same time.

It should have been a Daddy thing: her first wolf, first deer, first bunny, glimpsed in the cathedral hush of snow-draped balsams or out on the frozen lake—*Shh, quiet, see it, there, that shape against the snow*. But there wasn't any snow, and Christmas was two weeks away.

The freeze clamped down each night and lost its edge by afternoon. No ice jostled the shore. No crystalline lattices tethering the ledge rock with abstract webs. The forecasters on Duluth TV swirled their hands around Arctic air masses, the West Coast storms. They predicted an unusually mild season.

It was the year of El Niño. The year his daughter turned one. The second year since the adventure, from which he and Nina had returned rich, pregnant, married. And the second year since he'd quit police work.

The year Nina went back to the army.

Along with the weather, his personal world was upside down. His wife traveled "down range" to Bosnia, where she ran an MP company stationed in a grim haunted town outside of Tuzla called Brcko.

While Nina chased Serbian war criminals, he got stuck on stateside baby watch, changing diapers. So he'd brought Kit up here, to the old home ground, to teach her Daddy things on the bedrock of the Canadian Shield, the oldest exposed granite in the world.

Broker stared one last time at the pile of mangled fur, then walked back to his truck, got in and said, "How you doing, Kit, we're almost home." Kit, very involved in an Arrowroot animal cookie, said nothing.

Broker put the Jeep in gear, continued up the road and scanned the sodden brown birch leaves that carpeted the forest.

Kind of hard to teach Kit to be a hardy survivor—a Broker—if winter wouldn't come.

He turned off at a weathered sign that spelled BROKER'S BEACH
RESORT and drove down the access road. A natural amphitheater hol-
lowed the granite bluff and overlooked a cove. Resort cabins were
tucked into the stone terraces. All closed now. Electricity and water
turned off. His folks, who ran the cabins, were in Arizona for the
winter. Just him and his daughter staying in his lake home on a point
that formed the south arm of the cove.

He turned his truck and backed up to the porch. As he unstrapped
Kit from the car seat and placed her on the porch, the phone rang
inside. He ignored it, popped the rear hatch, and began lining up bags
of groceries. Car to porch. Then open the door and ferry them to the
kitchen. All tasks were modified and extended by the factor of mind-
ing Kit. The ringing stopped.

He worked one-armed so his other arm could anchor her. He hovered in his task, ready to pull her back from a fall, or from digging in
one of the bags. Or from sticking something in her mouth.

As he transferred the grocery bags, he talked in a calm voice.
"Careful. Look out for the edge." Specifically, he meant where the
top porch step dropped off. But his intent was larger, to sketch an
awareness of boundaries. And of dangers, which, as a former cop, he
saw everywhere. "Easy," Broker said endlessly. "Watch it. Look out."

He unlocked the door and ferried bags into the kitchen and placed
them on the table. Kit charged from the table to the door and back
with more speed than balance.

The phone started ringing again. He continued to ignore it, busy
tucking half gallons of milk and frozen baby food in the fridge. Four
rings. Let the tape pick it up. He paused. It could be his folks or Nina
calling long-distance. Better check for messages. He left the groceries
and went to the phone. Kit stood at his knee, squinted up as he
picked up the receiver, watched him tap in the voice mail code and
listen.

She cocked her head, furrowed her brow, pursed her tiny lips. This
was the first time she had seen her dad's face go tight with surprise.

The woman's voice was clenched, almost wrung dry of personality. But he knew her immediately. Only one woman called him
"Phil." They'd been married a long time ago, before he had grown
into "Broker."

"Phil, Keith's got himself in a lot of trouble and I need your help."

The single, cryptic sentence seemed to exhaust her. Caren, his ex-
wife, mumbled her number and hung up.

Tom James had faithfully reported the news for twenty years and was forty-one when he started craving sugar in the morning. It was right after his wife left him, not long after he was demoted to the East Neighborhoods Bureau of the St. Paul paper.

He ripped the wrapper off his second Snickers and washed it down with black coffee.

Tom read a lot. Because he was a writer he was skeptical of what he read—unless he wrote it, in which case he never tired of reading it. But he was quick to see where a descriptive scenario could be applied broadly to enhance his copy.

Looking out over the newsroom this morning, he had the unsettling experience of applying a descriptive scenario to his own life. Last night he'd read a *Newsweek* article about serotonin, the neurotransmitter your body produced or didn't produce—according to the article—depending on your relative social status. If you were on top of the heap, looking down, you had high levels of serotonin in your system and all the zillions of little chemical tabs and slots aligned and inserted just fine. You were therefore calm, alert and easy to get along with. Like he was, last year, when he was a general assignment reporter.

But if a general assignment reporter's fortunes went down in the world—if he were exiled to a suburban beat of endless school board meetings—his serotonin levels would crash and he would suffer depression, aggression and surges of impulse. And in—say—the smug eyes of the twenty-four-year-old Hispanic female-type person who now sat at his old desk in GA, he would be a loser. He'd have to get his serotonin levels adjusted, in prescription drug form. With Prozac. Tom looked around. He figured that half the over-forty newsroom staff was sucking down Prozac.

Tom finished his Snickers and gulped his coffee. No Prozac for him. Male Prozac users paid for the chemical illusion of well-being with impotence. And that was just about the only part of his life that still worked.

One newspaper era had ended. Another had begun. In between yawned a tough-luck chasm into which he was slipping inch by inch.

When he started at the paper in 1978, the slot man on the copy desk wore a green visor and smoked a cigar and nobody had heard of serotonin. Depression was an economic condition best cured by the unconditional surrender of Germany.

Back then, more than one desk drawer contained eighty-proof refreshment, and some of the women still wore slips, nylons, and two-inch heels. Deadline sex was banged out standing up in the stairwells.

Now the office was carpeted, smoke free, sexless, and passive as a monastery staffed by eunuchs. People over forty, especially white male people over forty, were feeling like endangered species. More specifically, Tom James was feeling especially vulnerable.

Yesterday, because he was still on probation, he had not been allowed to work the bomb scare story. While everyone else ran around the federal building, he had been sent out to suburban Cottage Grove to interview a man who had strung ten thousand lights on his home for his Christmas display.

"Oh, oh," cautioned gray-haired, forty-five-ish Barb Luct, the reporter who occupied the next desk. "Here she comes."

*She* was Molly Korne, from Georgia—aka Cottage Cheese Knees— the new managing editor. Korne was single and childless. A dedicated corporate nun. Also loud and egg-shaped, with a bizarre predilection for miniskirts that showed off her triple canopy dimples.

Barb leaned over and whispered behind her hand. "Kim heard her bragging in the elevator to some guy in Advertising, how she's going to fire someone, just to show who's boss."

Howie Norell, at the desk on the other side of Tom, piped in. "I heard she ordered all the supervisors to rank their staffs in order of who's the most productive."

"Story quotas are next," Barb warned darkly.

Tom nodded. But his eyes swept along the floor, locked on the open bottom drawer of Barb's desk and saw her purse in the shadows. Open. And amid the cosmetic clutter his eyes fixed on the plump luster of worn leather. A succulent green ripple of bills sprouted from the wallet like new lettuce.

Barb got up and went to the LaserJet to retrieve the story she had just printed. Tom leaned forward, swept his right hand over the drawer and lifted two twenties. As his eyes came up level, he saw Korne rolling her folds toward Neighborhoods, like a predatory ball of suet.

He tucked the two bills in his jacket pocket—something he would have never done a year ago, but he'd had a bad night at the casino, and he was in between paychecks, hurting for gas and lunch money. He didn't approve of petty theft and was furious that he had been reduced to it. But what really filled him with self-loathing was the realization that the only way he could reliably support himself was to show up in this office every day and do what he was told.

By someone named Molly Korne.

Tom watched her coming and felt a powerful nostalgia for the days when descriptive adjectives like *fat* and *ugly* were still vital engines of the language. She swatted her accent at the aging Neighborhoods reporters. "Wasn't for the Newspaper Guild y'all wouldn't be here." She grinned, waited for a reaction and then said, "Just kidding."

Tom removed his horn-rims and cleaned the lenses on his tie to avoid her judging eyes. The new corporate style was subtle, couched in team rhetoric. It barely masked Korne's need to manipulate, control and dominate. According to a book Tom had just read by the leading FBI profiler, these were the same impulses that motivated serial killers.

Korne moved on, to the Metro desk, and Tom watched a group of young reporters chirp around her, their smiles so wide and needy that Tom half expected to see a worm appear between her curved teeth, which she would plunge down the nearest gullet. There was an African American, an Asian, one Native American and one Hispanic. Only the Asian was a male. All were in their twenties. Look at them grin. Tanked with serotonin.

Then his sugar binge flamed out and left his mouth coated with a lumpy metallic taste—like discovering a well-worn bit between his teeth. Dig in. Hunker down. He had twenty years at the paper. Ten more would fully vest his retirement. That would still leave fourteen years until he could collect a pension. He looked around. Twenty-four more years of this?

The phone rang.

He picked it up. "Tom James."

"You know the bomb thing? It was an inside job," stated an electronically distorted voice. "Guess who the FBI is looking at?"

"Huh? Who?"

"Keith Angland."

The line went dead. Tom immediately punched in *69. The phone company tape informed him his last call was from an unlisted number.

He didn't move for a full minute. Angland. The infamous Narcotics lieutenant who was rumored to have called the new liberal St. Paul police chief "nigger lover."

And who refused to deny it when confronted by the press.

Tom had met him. He'd done a feature story about Angland's wife last August. He glanced over his shoulder. His supervisor, Ida Rain, was away from her computer.

The tip was off his beat, but—Wow.

His eyes roved the newsroom and settled on Korne, who was now employing her terroristic smile to motivate the Copy Desk. Individual threads on her lumpy wool skirt popped in his vision. He'd read about this adrenaline enhancement, an acuity that men of action experienced.

It was risky.

Thirty-three days ago he had wagered his November rent money on one hand of blackjack at the Mystic Lake Casino. And won. He'd tried to repeat the performance with his December rent three days ago and lost.

He had two Snickers bars in his stomach. And two stolen twenty-dollar bills in his pocket. What would it be like to bet his job on one story?

Purposefully, he stood up and walked across the newsroom, steering past the gaggle of loud young reporters. Their chatter dipped as he went by, as if they'd suddenly encountered a funeral cortege and remembered their manners.

He continued on to the desk of Layne Wanger, the cops reporter. Wanger, fifty-five, reflected light off his bald head, steel-rimmed glasses and starched white shirt like a death ray. Wanger was working on the "tongue" story. And he was in a foul mood. Nobody would confirm the rumor.

Tom smiled. Wanger would kill for the tip he had just received.

"Yeah, Tom, what is it?" Wanger banged keys hunt and peck and kept his eyes pinned on his computer screen. Wanger considered Tom harmless. Possibly tragic. Tom had the physical persona of a handsome cocker spaniel, eager but needy; his manner elicited Samaritan impulses from total strangers. It was his most lethal tool as a reporter.

"Last summer I did a story on this cop's wife," Tom began.

"Huh?" Wanger continued to type.

"Keith Angland's wife," said Tom.

Wanger paused. "What about her?"

"I did this story about her restoring an old Victorian house in Afton and I'm thinking about a follow-up. But her husband's still in hot water, right?"

Wanger pushed his glasses up on his nose. "I'd back off on the wife."

"You would, huh?"

Wanger spun in his chair and gave Tom his full attention. "There's talk his marriage is in the toilet with his career. I hear he's been drinking."

"Ah, I see what you mean," said Tom. But Wanger had already rotated back to his screen and had resumed banging keys.

Briskly, Tom continued into the lobby, went up the stairs to the next floor and into the library. Without speaking to any of the staff, he walked directly to a file cabinet, paged through the As until he found Keith Angland's photo file, tucked it under his arm and walked from the library.

He returned to his desk and picked up his assignment—a meeting of the Woodbury school board that was to discuss the school lunch menu. Right.

Tom pulled on his coat. The Neighborhoods bureau hunched over their keyboards like turtles, heads pulled into their shoulders. Ida was still out of sight. Good. That woman had radar like a bat and would pick up on his mood change. Avoiding eye contact, Tom strolled from the newsroom.

He purposely did not take a company car.

Sometimes, like now, he imagined himself walking in spotlights. Like when he first pushed through the doors of a casino with money in his pocket and knew that somewhere in the smoky room, among the swirling gaming lights, he had just locked eyes with Lady Luck.

**4**

U.S. 94 going east out of St. Paul looked like a dirty, frozen kitchen sink. Twelve degrees packed the cinder clouds. No sun, no wind and no snow. Tom tensed behind the wheel, running bald tires, ready for a skid. Invisible black ice vapors coughed from thousands of tailpipes and shellacked the frost-etched asphalt. Not the time to get snared in a fender bender.

Questions.

Bomb hoaxes and rumors of human tongues. The feds had denied that a tongue was found in the fake bomb. But Wanger was taking the rumor seriously. So how in the hell was St. Paul Police Lieutenant Keith Angland mixed up in mailing tongues?

And . . .

Who leaked to him? Probably the FBI. Sending him into the grass to thump around and scare out some snakes. Because he'd been to the house, had interviewed the wife.

Whoever it was, they didn't know he had been canned from GA and wasn't supposed to cover federal investigations. Tom was on a short leash, but fortunately, he licked the hand that held the leash.

He pulled his nine-year-old used Volkswagen Rabbit to the shoulder, cranked open his window, flipped on his company cell phone and punched in numbers.

"Ida Rain." She answered on the first ring, her best husky telephone voice.

"Ida, it's Tom. My car quit on me. I won't make the school board meeting." He held his phone out toward the whooshing traffic. "It's the battery. I need a new one," he said, lowering his voice, "you know, like you told me when it barely turned over this morning," he added.

"Okay," she said quietly, "I'll cover for you. You think you'll have it fixed by tonight?" she asked with a hint of amusement in her voice.

"Sure. See you." He smiled. Lick lick. Ida would look out for him.

He rolled up the window and shivered. The Volkswagen had one of those famous no-heat German heaters. The company leased new Fords that had good heaters but also radio antennas, and Keith Angland might spot it lurking around his house.

Tom palmed the manila envelope on the seat next to him: *Angland, Keith. Lieutenant, St. Paul Police.* The library had filed the house feature about Angland's wife in his envelope. Photos fanned out under his fingers. Angland took a good picture, and he'd been in the paper a lot the last few years. Various awards. Honor graduate, FBI Academy. But those accolades came under the old police chief.

He put the photos aside and consulted his *Hudson's Street Atlas* to refresh his memory of the location—an address on a gravel road along the St. Croix River in the quiet community of Afton.

He pulled back into traffic, drove east, sorted the pictures of Angland's wife out and left them on top of the pile. Tom believed a wife would talk when a marriage was going down, even a cop's wife. You just had to catch them at the right moment, be a good listener and have patience to wait for the verbal slip that, with the right coaxing and pleading, dropped a detail on which a story could turn.

The wife's picture cut a rectangle of green whimsy against the winter day, taken against a sweep of summer sunshine and foliage.

Tall and outdoorsy, tanned tennis legs in cutoff jeans, she wore a work-stained pebble gray T-shirt on top, *Architectural Digest* blazed in script across the front. Hands on, when she had to be. But Tom pegged her as more comfortable in a dress and makeup, flipping through swatches of drapery and wallpaper.

For the camera, she had arranged a row of tall window frames on sawhorses and was removing layers of old bubbled paint with a putty knife. A red bandanna turbaned her tightly curled dark hair.

He fingered another picture, the family shot, that showed her with her husband. No kids. No pet. Keith Angland resembled a blond, two-hundred-pound falcon instantly ready to tuck and dive after a mouse in a square mile of cornfield. His eyes were intense hazel, he had a cleft in his chin and all the ruddy skin on his body looked tight and hard as the skin stretched over his high Slavic cheekbones. He'd have a radioactive ingot of testosterone for a heart.

In contrast, the wife's vivid features harked back to a pretelevision beauty that Tom associated with old black and white movies on big screens; when theaters were temples, not cineplexes, and filmmakers used close-ups of faces to carry whole scenes. Hers was heart shaped, with protruding expressive eyes and a classic profile that evoked the Spirit of Westward Expansion Pointing the Way on a WPA mural in a post office. Straight, tall and brave.

A poster wife for Keith, the tough guy cop.

Caren with a *C*.

Tom turned off the freeway and went south on Highway 95. He came to the tiny collection of storefronts clustered around a frost-burned, desolate park. Afton, Minnesota. He checked the *Hudson's* again. A secondary road paralleled the river and passed through stands of oaks that still clutched brown leaves. He located the house and trolled by.

Once he'd owned a garage full of tools and woodworking manuals. He knew a little about old houses. He'd always dreamed of getting one and fixing it up. But his ex-wife, who didn't want to live in a cloud of Sheetrock dust, nixed the idea. So they lived cramped with two kids, a dog and a cat in a rambler in Woodbury until Shirley filed for divorce and took the kids to Texas last year. Woodbury was a first-tier bedroom community to St. Paul. Afton lay twenty minutes and several steep income brackets to the east and was, by comparison, country living.

The Angland house was roomy and old enough to have a stairway off the kitchen for the servants. It had bird's-eye maple on the ground floor. And a mansard tin roof and a square turret topped by a delicate scrim of blackened metalwork.

The house sat on a big lot back from the road overlooking the water. Last summer, the peeling paint had been seaweed green. Now that paint was gone. The wood siding had been sanded, but only half the surface had been sealed with primer. It gave the structure a mangy, deranged aspect that was amplified by missing sections of gingerbread trim. A scaffold, fouled with frozen leaves, leaned, stranded, against a wall.

Work interrupted; that could signal a marriage on the rocks? And other homes on this road had put out wreaths, boughs, and strings of lights. The Angland house displayed no holiday garnish.

No one seemed to be home. No lights on. The windows winked, cold black rectangles, a hundred yards off the road, behind a screen of red oaks. As he drove past, he rolled down the window and inspected the cobbled drive next to a back door. Empty. Garage doors closed. Keith would drive an unmarked Ford Crown Victoria from the police motor pool. He saw Caren in a sports utility or maybe a small truck.

In back, a patio hugged the bluff. A stairway descended to the water, the rails silhouetted against the iron and brown hedgehog of the Wisconsin river bluffs. The nearest neighbors were a quarter mile in either direction, separated by brittle regiments of standing corn.

A long gust of cold wind swirled up from the river and rattled the cornstalks. Closer in, curled oak leaves skittered down the cobblestone driveway like hollow scorpions.

There was no place for him to hide his rusty blue Rabbit near the house, so he drove on, turned and waited at a bend in the road.

Staking out the house was a long-shot gamble. People were naturally defensive at the threshold of their castle. Angland could be home, his car out of sight in the garage.

He needed Caren to go out, on an errand, to the grocery, to the bank. Then he would slide up and start a conversation to test her mood. If he saw the right signals, he would put his questions.

But right now it was just cold. Should have made a move ten years ago, when he still had the legs. Someplace warm. His breath made a chalky cloud. Not a very big one. Was that really the size of a lungful of air?

A measure of his life.

Tom hugged himself and looked around suspiciously. Other measures, the numbers, were never far away. He kept them at bay by staying busy, by keeping on the move. Now he was stationary, and he imagined them creeping out from the cornfield. A picket line of strident dollar signs circled him and banged on his car.

The rent.

Two augured-in VISA cards.

Sears, Dayton's, and Target. His ex-wife had run them into the ground just before she filed for divorce. Tom had taken them on as part of the divorce agreement. Another price of freedom.

The big-hit child support.

The car loan for this piece of junk. Insurance.

All the numbers merged into one monthly figure that exceeded, by many hundreds of dollars, his salary.

His blackjack strategy having failed, he'd have to skip out on his rent.

Possibly he could move in with Ida Rain.

If he moved in with Ida he could pay down the credit cards. But Ida didn't need a roommate. She didn't appear to *need* anything. She was thirty-nine, never married, a confirmed femme solo and a very thorough lady. Other women at the paper bought whistles when one of their coworkers was attacked in the ramp where they parked. Ida bought a hefty, five-shot, .38 caliber Smith & Wesson Bodyguard model revolver with the recessed hammer and a two-inch barrel. She took a police course of instruction and learned how and *where* to shoot it: "Three shots, center mass." In her thorough way, Ida had "taken him on" in every sense of the phrase, as a reclamation project. It was a problem. When her concern left her body, it was compassion and affection. When it touched him, it became control.

Tom shivered.

Jesus, it was cold.

Thirty-four icy minutes later a set of low beams swung down the gloomy gravel road and a bronze-colored Blazer turned into the driveway. Hatless, coat unzipped in the hard wind, Caren Angland got out and walked stiffly to the back door. Tom watched lights switch on, marking her progress through the first floor.

Ten minutes later, the back door opened again and she stepped back out. Now she wore faded jeans and had exchanged the long coat for a green and black mountain parka. She still wasn't wearing a hat. She paused to test the lock on the door, then got in the Blazer.

He trailed her back through Afton, north up the highway that skirted the river and connected with I–94. Short of the interstate, she turned left up a gravel road that wound through a tract under construction where fields and rolling woodland were losing to tiny plots with huge new wood frame homes.

For the second time he saw a sign that advertised HANSEN'S CHRISTMAS TREES—CUT YOUR OWN TREES. Caren turned at the sign. Tom smiled. She was going to get the tree.

The access road curled into a miniature evergreen forest and ended in a rutted dirt lot. Caren parked the Blazer and got out. Tom remembered her face as bright, casting light. Now it was drawn, pale, a little puffy. She walked past Tom's car to the shack where a sign explained that Hansen loaned you a small saw to cut your twenty-five-dollar tree. On a very cold afternoon, she was the only person in the field not wearing a hat or gloves.

Tom bypassed the shack and trailed her into the fir, spruce, and pine.

Two dozen people wandered through the trees. A third of the shoppers towed preschool children who looked like characters from the Sunday comics, bundled in floppy fleece Jester caps, scarves and mittens. Frosty captions of breath stuck to their faces. Families. Mom, pop and kids doing the ritual. In some cases it was just pop and the kids. There were several solitary men, so Tom didn't stand out. Caren Angland was the only single woman.

The other people circled, fluffed gloved hands at the boughs, and debated. Not Caren. She walked directly to a tall, long-needled white pine.

Tom slid through a thicket of shorter spiky firs and paused to watch her stoop and begin to trim away the lowest branches, better to get at the trunk.

He browsed toward her, turned, inspected a tree. When their eyes met briefly through a tunnel of pine needles, he looked away.

Awkward embarrassment. Caren's eyes paused for a beat, assessing him for threat.

She saw a man of medium height, in his late thirties, early forties, who had once been good-looking behind his plastic horn-rims, but had stopped taking care of himself. His baggy tan parka came from the United Store. Wrinkles overwhelmed his corduroy suit. Galoshes, a purple wool knit cap with a Vikings logo and cheap leather gloves completed his wardrobe. The clothes wore him, and with his tousled straw hair, fleecy mustache and soft blue eyes he had the rumpled persona of a perpetual graduate student who'd have stains on his tie and who toiled slowly after obscurities in a too-fast world. English lit. perhaps.

Harmless. A Minnesota Normal.

Through the screen of pine, his eyes swung back and caught the corner of her glance. He smiled self-consciously. "Can't make up my mind. Every year I do this. And then somebody else gets the best trees."

Polite, crisp, she replied, "It's early. There's still a good selection."

He nodded. "Last few years I went with balsams. But now they strike me as cramped and uptight."

"Scotch pine is a nice tree," said Caren. "Problem is they drop their needles in three weeks." Her saw made a pile of damp white dust as she efficiently cut through the base of the tree. Resin dripped in the minty air. A smell like turpentine.

Tom took a step closer and cast a sentence calculated to hook a raw nerve. "You seem to know what you want."

The tree fell over. There was more room between them. And for the first time she had a clear view of his face, and Tom saw she recognized him.

For a spilt second her eyes shot pain. Tom was encouraged, thankful that Christmas was a vulnerable time for troubled people.

But she recovered smoothly. "Now what?" she mused in a calm resigned voice. "Tom James, isn't it?" She glanced around. "Are there more of you?"

"Just me." He took off his gloves, pulled out his wallet and handed her his card. As she took it he saw that she had skinned her knuckle cutting down the tree. A bluish patch of torn skin the size of a dime stood out on her cold-chafed right hand. Blood started to well up. She ignored it, and a red trickle curled between her fingers and crept down her palm.

She studied him. "You're not interested in house renovations today, are you?"

"I'm sorry to be asking you this, Mrs. Angland, but is the FBI investigating your husband?"

"Fishing, Mr. James?" She raised an eyebrow.

"Tom. And the FBI's doing the fishing, wouldn't you say?"

"I didn't say."

"So you're not denying it?"

She sighed: "Have you considered getting a real job?" She bent to get a grip on her tree. Tom stepped forward.

"Let me help you," he offered, reaching. They tugged at the branches, and he lurched. His shoe shot sideways on a patch of ice beneath the pine needles and he slipped. She thrust out both hands and gripped him above the elbows and steadied him.

"Careful, Tom," she said tartly.

He nodded. "Look, I don't like this any more than you do." He went in his pocket, took out a handkerchief and dabbed at the blood.

The small succor of concern seemed to affect her all out of proportion. "I didn't mean to be rude," she said, her eyes darting. For a second Tom thought he saw an opening. A centipede of adrenaline scurried up his spine.

He glanced around. People and kids shuffled in and out of the trees. No one looked threatening. The Christmas trees stirred. The wind whipped up. For the first time in a long time he noticed the loud silence of the racing winter sky and was thrilled.

A drop of blood seeped between her fingers below the handkerchief and dotted the coarse green feathers of pine boughs at her feet.

Her contradictory energy struck him. So competent and hardy, so heedless. No hat. Bare-handed. But little stabs of dread.

Ten years ago he would have desired her. Ten years ago he thought anything would have been possible. Now, he quietly resented her. There had always been a net beneath her. She'd never known what it was like to be a paycheck away from disaster. She had never had to work for idiots. She was attractive. She was connected. She was fair game in open season.

And she was good, and she was hiding something.

But his face remained full of patient, plodding sympathy and understanding. She kicked the Christmas tree, laughed, looked up at the clouds. But she kept her thoughts to herself.

Tom's hands hovered, trying to time her mood swing and step in.

Then she withdrew again. Businesslike, she took hold of her tree and dragged it toward the parking lot.

Tom called after her. "You can reach me anytime. All the numbers are on the card. Work, home, pager . . ."

She ignored him and plodded on, exertion showing in a flame of white breath.

Tom, shivering with cold and excitement, noticed the left sleeve of his jacket and removed his glove to touch a dot of her freezing blood.

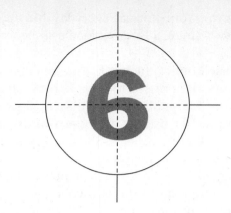

Caren's world was as shrill as the bottom of a pie tin. Road, traffic, sky—the colors ran together like water over metal.

She had been warned. Don't go abruptly off the medication. Last night, numb after watching the news, she'd found herself staring at a documentary on the Discovery Channel about African lions hunting. Lionesses, really. She had watched them cull an impaired zebra from the herd and drag it down. She'd thought, aha—that striped pony quit taking her meds.

Therefore vulnerable. And the guilt made you slow. But it was being bad that made you stick out from the herd so the lion noticed you. Like a smell.

Tom James, the reporter, was an unlikely lion, but he'd been hunting and he'd noticed *something*. Keith had started to stink, and the jackals were gathering out there. She hadn't expected them so soon.

She wasn't ready. Talking to him at Hansen's, Caren had thought: This is what a drunk feels like, trying to act sober, attempting to walk a straight line.

The drive home exhausted her.

Keith's car was skewed, blocking the garage. She braked so hard she stalled the Blazer. Her breathing problems, which her doctor called anxiety attacks, but she knew to be mortal fear, now formed a hard crust around her throat and chest. The pressure suggested apt images from old movies; gangsters from Chicago used to take you for a boat ride. Stick your feet in a washtub and mix it full of cement. Tell jokes while it hardened and then they'd heave you overboard.

Just grin it down. Your normal everyday, "Hi, honey, I'm home, how was your day?" smile. Just download a smile from the old smile server.

She forced herself out of the truck. The tree had to be dealt with. A habit of normalcy she refused to part with. As she untied the tree from the top of the Blazer she saw Keith's shadow shimmer in the living room window. Her usually firm grasp went butterfingers. The eight-foot pine rolled to the cobbles. She left it where it fell. Last year at this time lights were strung on the eaves, around the windows.

Keith, smiling, had tossed strings of purple lights in the oaks. They'd walked on the road in the crunching snow and looked back and seen the trees float under the stars like Picassos dashed out with a child's sparkler.

This year there were no lights. The tree lay abandoned near the freeze-burned lawn, and it looked like the week after Christmas. The edges of Caren's lips curved down, but she had to force a smile.

It turned out she didn't because, when she entered the house, she heard Keith's footsteps going down the stairs to the basement, then she heard the pop of the TV come on. She spied a beer bottle cap and the torn carton of a microwave burrito dinner on the counter. The microwave door was ajar.

She scooped the mess and deposited it in the trash. Carefully, she closed the microwave. Touched up with a damp dishcloth. Clean up. Make nice. Hide his empty whiskey bottles in the recycling bin.

Denial and avoidance. Passive aggressive. Words you volleyed in counseling. Like throwing Ping-Pong balls against those hungry lions.

They wore the house like a Victorian straitjacket and always kept at least one room between them. On the inside, all the snaps and buckles were accurate. This was the second big house she had remodeled. She ran her hand along the purple wallpaper she'd chosen for the hallway, just to see if Keith would notice the morbid pattern.

Decor for *The Addams Family*.

Except there was no family, just Keith and Caren. Unless you counted Paulie Kagin. He was family. From Chicago.

Don't worry, Keith had assured her. *I'm* using *them*.

Then it was, don't worry, I won't spend the money.

All of a sudden it had turned into killing people. Caren knew in detail what the news reports only hinted at.

She knew it all.

Now she had to do something about it.

First she had to stop taking the pills.

The pills had combed it smooth in the beginning. Let her live with it. Like floating.

Duty didn't float. It thudded through room after empty room.

A wall of drawers rose in the hallway by the front door and she took an old wooden footlocker from one of them. It looked like a pirate chest, and it had been dented and scarred when her mother passed it down to her when she was six, in Williston, North Dakota.

Just now it reminded her of Phil Broker, who'd become a sort of pirate.

She carried it into the living room and placed it on the floor, where the tree should go, in front of the broad bay windows. Through the side panel of the window she could see the tree, out in the cold, abandoned on the cobbles. The room was boxed by horrible Prussian blue wallpaper. Gothic rockets in a turgid sea. She had taken her pills and papered the walls with signals of distress.

She sat down on the shiny hardwood planks, opened the trunk and removed a cardboard box. Inside, stacked with care, were tiny handmade Christmas tree decorations that fit in the palm of her hand.

The pills she had taken for the last six months had magically dried her tears. Now, in the absence of the antidepressants, the vast cloud of accumulated tears condensed in her head and began to drizzle. Hot wet streaks burned down her cheeks.

This is really crazy, Caren. Thoughts wouldn't balance on her head. They fell off. A jumble of blocks.

With difficulty, she placed them in order. She. And her first husband. Made the decorations. Up north, on their first vacation. The year they were married. In a storm of sawdust, delicate designs had come from Phil's rough hands like intricate charms. Hers incorporated beads, fabric and feathers. Arts and crafts class.

Phil, the rustic, turned out diminutive stars, moons, suns, trees and animals on his band saw. She made angels. She selected one of the awkward angels and placed it on a wide plank called a king board. She had learned about king boards from Phil. In colonial times the best lumber went back to England, and it was illegal for a colonist to own a "king board." The crafty Americans used the wide boards as flooring in their attics where the redcoats didn't inspect.

Her angel, with its rosy cheeks and misshapen wings, was meant to hang and not to stand, so it toppled over on the king board.

The sound of a roaring crowd carried up the stairwell from the basement. Tapes of old college games. Keith, the Minnesota Gopher quarterback, was throwing touchdowns down in the dark. Keith would never find the time to make a tree decoration. But, unlike Phil, he could plan a Christmas party down to the last detail that the mayor of St. Paul would attend.

Not this year.

A telephone was the only other occupant of this hollow room, and it coiled on the floor like a plastic tapeworm. That phone weighed fourteen years of living. That's how long it had been since she'd left Phil Broker, to marry Keith Angland, who had once been Phil's partner and then, his boss. She'd deserted Phil because he wasn't going anywhere and sure-footed Keith was.

She stared at the phone and squeezed an angel in her right hand and made a wish that the phone would ring. That Phil would call. That he would come and give her some help.

He'd come if he really knew. But for now, because she had been vague, he wouldn't trespass. She'd been vague because she kept hoping Keith would pull it out of the hat at the last minute. Do one of his famous scrambles.

But the federal building story changed all that.

She didn't trust anyone Keith worked with. There was too much money involved. So it had to be Phil. He'd been off the job for two years. Independent now. And if she'd missed something, he would spot it. So she'd have to take what she had to Phil. And when the time came, let him—as they quaintly put it—drop the dime.

He was up there, alone with his baby, while his damn Amazon child bride was off playing St. Joan in Bosnia.

God. Edgy Phil with a kid. Round with paternity, padded with much laughter. She tried to imagine him smiling. She bet he'd gained weight.

She knew the baby was a girl—Caren flinched as her muscles curved in and stabbed her, in both breasts and in her belly. Her imagination ambushed her with a detailed blueprint of the flawed eggs lined up in her ovaries, racks of them, drawing lots to see who would take the Kamikaze trip down the red rapids this month.

Dammit. Leaving that message was the hardest thing she'd ever done in her life. Breaking the vows. Going outside her marriage. No, it was just the first step in the hardest thing. It was going to get much harder.

Something had to be done about Keith.

She shut her eyes and prayed: Please call. Don't make me do this alone.

Going west on U.S. 94, the automatic pilot grabbed the wheel. Tom resisted the first pull, steered straight. The next tug came at the southbound exit for U.S. 494. He beat that one, too. Ten minutes later, as the spire of the state capitol marked the horizon, the impulse snuggled up again. This time, seduction was fast and total; he drove past the downtown St. Paul exits and continued west on 94 until it branched and he took 35E south. The Rabbit knew the way. Get off on County Road 42, turn west, and then it was eight miles to the Mystic Lake Casino.

Working through the turns, his pulse quickened: Eagan and Prior Lake—the crossroads. Casino to the left. Racetrack to the right. He turned left, passed the frost-rimmed rock-landscaped entrance to the "Wilds" golf course. A few miles later, the casino rose like a squashed modernist wigwam from a sea of parked cars.

He turned into the lot, left the rusting VW, squared his slumped shoulders and walked through the tinted glass doors. Mystic Lake was roomy and clean, without the sweaty opium den feel of smaller casinos. Showroom bright, a cherry Acura gleamed on a dais. *Win me.* He inhaled the signature incense of cigarette smoke entwined with the loopy rush of calliope music spiraling off the slots.

With childlike faith, he let it all surround him like the pulsating heart of an immense plastic toy. It reminded Tom of his deceased mother's living room in Bayport, Minnesota, in the shadow of Stillwater Prison, where his dad had worked as a guard. After Dad died, she'd draw the curtains and recline like a silent movie star on the couch in front of the TV, sucking on Winstons that protruded from a slim cigarette holder. *Wheel of Fortune* flickered on the screen. The volume was turned all the way up.

Mom died before Minnesota legalized gambling. Her one trip to Vegas with her chain-smoking girlfriends was her preview of heaven.

All he had was the two twenties he'd lifted from Barb Luct. Start small. Play his way up to the blackjack tables. Hell, go to the nickel machines if he had to.

*Just show me some magic.*

When his stake was minimal, he always started on the same machine, an Atronic game scrolled with bright symbols of heraldry and knights in armor. A bank of them nested between quarter keno and across from a row of deuces wild poker. *Camelot* combined interactive video with the slam-bam spin of a slot. Three pay lines rotated icons on the drum. Shields, castles, crenelated pennants, number sevens, battle-axes crossed on shields; the usual arcana of the one-armed bandit. But there were also progressive symbols; when an archery target appeared on one line the play moved to a new screen on which two knights squared off in an archery contest.

Choose left or right.

Two helmets on one line moved the play to a jousting tournament.

Three swords in a row summoned the test of Excalibur and the stone.

Blackjack was cold sober business. You had to count. You had to mind the rules. But this game, with its colorful marquee of castles and armor, took him back to the realm of childhood wishes. He stepped up to a machine like a knight errant confronting a squat Sphinx.

Am I worthy. Judge me. If he pulled the sword from the stone on his first pass Caren Angland would call him up. He would write the biggest story of his life, and they'd have to take him back on general assignment.

He would only use the money he had in his pocket. Promise.

But soon the two twenties he'd slipped from Barb's wallet were gone. Then all of his pocket change. He had to amend the rules. Just this once.

At the check-cashing booth, he slapped down his last piece of plastic, a MasterCard to which he'd transferred all his other balances; 5.9 percent APR, no finance charge for twelve months.

The circuits rejected $100.

"Fifty," he told the bored clerk. Fifty also drew a pass. Probably the clip of the service charge exceeded his credit limit.

"Forty." Forty went through.

With two more twenties he returned to his machine, fed an Andy Jackson into the slot. Eighty credits electronically clicked up on the screen. Coolly, after toying with him, the machine gulped down the eighty. His hand shook, sweaty, as he tendered the second bill into the electronic maw.

An ascending stream of chimes erupted in back of him. Big winner. Coins steadily clinked, little silver hammers striking base metal. Other people were winning.

*My turn, dammit.*

Like mockery, from across the vast room a PA voice complimented Tony Lofas of Grand Forks, who had won twenty-three hundred dollars on Dollar Double Diamond.

The drum in front of him cocked and spun and cocked and spun and nothing matched up. Change the pattern. He cashed in his few remaining credits so he could feed the coins manually into the slot on every play. Soon his stake had shrunk to a pile he could hold in the palm of his hand. More slowly, the quarters dropped down the cool steel gullet. Grimly, he plugged in three of his dwindling quarters, selected the center line and spun the drum.

The clamor, the cheap electronic champagne bubbles, the needy human press all around, receded. Tom was alone, locked in the slot.

Three swords in a row.

A trumpet fanfare. A new display magically swam up from the electronic alchemy. A forest grotto. Two princes stood on either side of a sword plunged to the hilt in a huge rock.

The prince on the right was short and dark, with a sinister, spaded black beard and red and black livery. Tom favored the younger man on the left, who was blond, broad-shouldered and clean-shaven. Like he might look if he got in shape. Tom even had a lucky nickname for Mr. Left. The pillow talk nickname Ida whispered in the dark.

"C'mon, Danny," he chanted under his breath as he keyed the left button.

The blond prince reached forward, and for a beat, his hand paused on the hilt. Then, effortlessly, with a smooth confident kingly sweep of his arm, he drew the sword from the stone and held it triumphantly over his head to a cloudburst of special effects.

Thunder pealed, lightning bolts electrified the display. The boulder pulsed red as a living heart. A crown appeared on the winner's head. A regal purple robe draped his shoulders. Sparkles of anointing energy closed the circuit between Tom's rapt face and the screen.

A scroll above the stone announced *You WIN 1000.*

Only quarters, not dollars. But it was a jackpot. Someday he'd have this feeling in Las Vegas or Atlantic City. And it would be thousands and thousands and thousands of dollars. "Yes!" affirmed Tom James. He punched the cash-out button and listened to the abundant shower of falling silver.

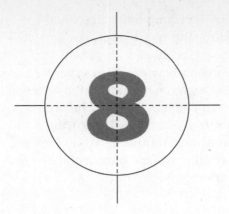

8

All of his adult life, Broker despised and avoided working routines. Most of his sixteen years as a cop he'd spent undercover, preferring the solitary risks over paperwork and a predictable schedule.

Lone wolf, they called him. Misfit.

As he removed gobs of clean baby clothes from the drier and stuffed them into a plastic hamper, he mused that his life resembled the baby socks he held in his hand: turned inside out.

Patiently, he hauled the basket into the kitchen, wiped down the table and began to fold the clothes. His muscular hands were thick-veined, knuckle prominent, turned on a lathe of heavy labor. Of physical shock. They dipped into the laundry basket like the jaws of a steam shovel, extracted a tiny white Onesie undergarment and gently smoothed it on the table.

Old habits from the army; get out the wrinkles, make uniform folds. Precise little stacks. Socks, sleepers, Onesies, miniature pastel T-shirts: all lined up like a toy vision of peace.

Friends urged him to take on a housekeeper/nanny when his folks went on vacation. But he insisted on doing all the cooking and cleaning himself. After two weeks solo in babyland he was amazed at the sheer volume of work his sixty-five-year-old mother had put into taking care of Kit.

Going on week four, he began to accumulate low-grade resentments. Every itty-bitty sock he turned into its mate was another tiny contention against Nina, who had left him alone with a child.

Because she insisted on pursuing her career.

Soon he'd have to build a whole new wall of shelves to house his hoarded arguments. Petty. Broker caught himself. Like his curiosity about Caren's odd phone message. Keith was in trouble. Well—good.

He did not take malicious pleasure in others' troubles; but Broker was not surprised that Keith Angland had stepped into it. News traveled the cop grapevine.

Keith's famous control-freak thermostat went haywire after he was passed over for the second time on the promotion exam for captain. His sour grapes took the form of racial slurs hurled at the new police chief.

So Broker could imagine the depth of Caren's agony; Keith had become a loose cannon. Probably the mayor had expunged them from his Christmas party short list.

Still, he was curious. And she had sounded overwrought on the phone message. Too embarrassed, maybe, to talk to her circle of friends, most of whom were police wives.

So call good-old, regular baby-changing Broker in his new life up in the north woods. Broker, never a womanizer, was too steady and old to draw any romantic inferences from the call. She probably wanted him to lobby old colleagues on Keith's behalf.

Of course, he decided not to pursue it—but—if she called again and actually spoke to him, he would give a good listen. It was just that he had trouble taking Caren seriously after she married an ambition-driven bastard like Angland.

He folded a pink T-shirt with Pooh Bear on it and placed it on top of the T-shirt stack. With his palms, he plumped the edges of the shirts so they made an even line. As he reached for a Polarfleece jumper, he did admit to a small amount of satisfaction that Caren would turn to him. Vindication, maybe.

In the middle of this thought, the phone rang. He reached over, plucked it off the wall mount, and when no one said anything for the first few seconds, he thought, uh-huh, her again, working up the spit to finally make actual contact. And he said, "Is that you, Caren?"

The silence stretched out a few more seconds and then a clear chiseled voice, pitched between surprise, pique and command assurance, stated with great emphasis: *"What?"*

The connection from Tuzla was like right next door.

"Jesus, Nina?" he blurted.

"Check me if I'm wrong, but you did say Caren—as in wife number one?"

Broker's explanation sounded lame. All true, honest, but lame. "That's right. She called and left a message on the machine. I thought you were her calling again."

"Hmmm," observed Nina eloquently.

"Yes, I agree," said Broker. Then he waited to see if she would take it further. When she didn't, he asked, "How are you?"

"Fair. How's baby?"

"Every day she looks more and more like Winston Churchill."

"I miss that fat little kid, I really do."

"I know you do."

"Okay, look, it's five in the morning here. I've been on patrol for six days and I'm beat. Thing is, I weaseled a leave over Christmas. I'm attending a conference stateside . . ."

"What kind of conference?"

"Sorry."

He understood. Not a secure line. The meeting probably dealt with NATO ratcheting up the pressure on nabbing war criminals. It had been in the news.

"How long can you get away?" he asked.

"I'll come in Christmas Eve and leave on the twenty-eighth. Best I can do."

"Sounds great."

"Broker, you spent a mint on that house and we still don't have a computer. E-mail would be a lot easier for me here than finding telephone time."

Broker frowned. "I hate computers. Bad enough I have the TV. Besides, I like hearing your voice."

"Gawd. I married an analog cavefish. Caren, huh?" she needled.

"Knock it off," he protested.

"Kiss Winston for me. See you. Love."

The connection ended. Broker hung up the phone and sat down in the chair next to the table. He leaned forward, rested his elbows among the mounds of infant clothing. Mild rebuke knocked the idle kinks out of his thoughts. Foolish, daydreaming about Caren Angland and her social turmoil when Nina had been soldiering in the snow.

He carried the folded clothes to Kit's room, crept in and piled them on her dresser. On the way out, he checked her, bathed in the soft night-light. Definitely Churchill, painted by Rubens. Carefully, he pulled the door shut behind him.

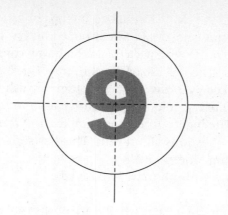

Tom had not been given a house key. Ida showed him where she kept one hidden for emergencies, under a flowerpot to the side of the house, next to the garage. But he thought it best to knock. The door of her bungalow in the quiet neighborhood of Highland Park swung open. She wore a long-sleeved pearl sweater that buttoned to the throat. A long, slim gray wool skirt reached down over leather boots.

Her naturally wavy shoulder-length auburn hair was replicated in her thick arched eyebrows. The eyebrows framed intelligent brown eyes set wide over smooth cheekbones. A narrow slightly crooked nose. And then—the generous lips teed up on that chin she got from the Wicked Witch of the West in *The Wizard of Oz.*

With a firm grasp on the curious power of her physical presence, Ida Rain disdained wearing all but the barest touches of makeup on her unlined face.

How long could she go on like this. Renouncing age. One more brutal Minnesota winter. Two. Eventually she'd crash on the far side of forty, snowflakes would stick to the corners of her eyes and crack into crow's-feet. She'd shed smiles and store hurt between the pages of her heart like pressed nettles.

But tonight her husky voice, like her hair, was gorgeous. An editor to the core, she cut straight to the nut graph: "You didn't really have battery trouble today."

Tom grinned and spread his hands.

"You're on to something, aren't you?" She reached over and lifted his left hand and inspected it with a cool thumb and forefinger. "And you went out to celebrate." She rubbed the tips of his fingers and came away with a light gray metal talc. She dropped his hand. It was her way of letting him know she'd suspected, and had now confirmed, that he'd been to the casino. The residue of the coin tray. He resented her knowing smile and cocked eyebrow. He'd forgotten to wash his hands.

"Sally, in the library, told me you snuck a file out of the building. Keith Angland. The bigmouthed cop. I talked to Wanger, and he said you were asking questions about him. This has something to do with the federal building, doesn't it?"

"What makes you think that?" he toyed.

"The timing."

News was their inky Spanish fly. Curiosity itched in her voice. "You're off your beat," she probed.

"Just checking something out," he said tightly.

She waited for more, and when she saw that it wasn't forthcoming, said, "You'll tell me first."

"Of course."

She nodded and with a brief knowing smile allowed a beguiling tease to swing in her voice. "Just watch your step, Danny."

They laughed at the same time, which they took as a good omen.

"I won. Get your coat. We're going out to eat tonight. I'm buying," said Tom.

*Danny.*

*Going down for the third time, Tom had felt someone firmly take his hand. Ida. Quietly, they dated. Ida suggested that he try writing fiction to diffuse his funk about being transferred down to the burbs. Writing a novel was every reporter's daydream, so he dusted his off and put a few more hours into two chapters about a private eye who had been a reporter. He gave his PI the name Danny Storey. Ida liked the character's name but critiqued his story line as improbable and convoluted. After a few discussions the two rough chapters disappeared into the desk drawer in her study in the four-season porch off the living room and were forgotten.*

*Except in her bedroom in the dark.*

*Calling him Danny was her foreplay spoof in bed. For all her powers of observation, she had no idea how deeply the name goaded him or how severely he had come to hate the boundaries of his life. How he resented needing her to keep his job.*

Later, after dinner, after they returned to her house, she undressed in the ritual darkness. It was also in this darkness she moved her damn pistol around, like a pea under a shell—from her purse to the bed table drawer, sometimes even under her pillow. He waited and thought: she was the face of realism. Hold on to realism and it will save you from desperation. You will make do.

After you were with Ida awhile you lost your bearings. Was she extremely beautiful or disfigured? Certainly she was old-fashioned, a Freudian machination straight from a Hitchcock film. Stylishly repressed, precise; the best-dressed woman in the office.

But in the dark . . .

Like a guerrilla army, she owned the night. Her queen-size bed rustled with satin sheets, the air was moist and humidified, there were lotions, knowing fingers. She'd evoked in Tom something his pallid ex-wife of twelve years could never comprehend. Something called good sex.

Then Tom and Ida had joined hands and skipped over the slim, but unforgettable, margin that separated good sex from great sex.

"Can't we leave the light on?" he asked.

"Why?"

"I want to see you do things. In the dresser mirror."

"No lights," said Ida.

"Never?"

"Not tonight. Sometime, maybe."

"When?"

"When you tell me what you've got going."

"No. Oh." *Yes*. Some light, faint slivers, eked through cracks in doors, glowworms of moonlight noodled between the drapes and windowsills. Just enough to make her out, subtle and expert. Silky smooth white muscle, rising. Tongue out. Red Joker's grin.

"C'mon, tell me what you're on to . . . ," she whispered.

They practiced together, keeping up their skills. Grouping the thrills in tidy clusters. Better together in practice than they would be in real life because they were not each other's first choice.

They took turns pleasing each other. When her turn came round, she sighed:

"Yes, Danny, *yes*."

He held on. Shut his eyes. Pretended. She was Caren Angland and he could hit the jackpot and win the Pulitzer and he was someone else—the Danny of their closet rapture.

His orgasm flamed in deep space. Elated and sad and lonely, he held realism in his arms, and in a moment of pure hell, he knew this was as good as it was ever going to get.

At 4 A.M. Phil Broker and his daughter slept on the Lake Superior shore, twenty-two miles south of the Ontario border. Two hundred seventy miles to the south, in Highland Park, Tom James snored in the soothing bondage of Ida's satin sheets. Twenty miles to the east of Ida's bed, the black water of the St. Croix River slid between rippled sheets of ice, below the Angland house. On the second floor, behind her locked door, Caren lay on top of a down quilt, rigid as a crusader chiseled on a medieval tomb.

She wove tiny threads of hope in the dark. At the last possible moment Keith would catch himself and pull back from the edge.

The phone rang. Keith's bed squeaked in the separate bedroom down the hall. He lurched awake. Thump, his feet struck the polished floor.

Slippers slapped down the hallway past her doorway and descended the stairs. Sounds. Light switches. More footsteps.

Ten minutes later, headlights swung through her windows. Tangled shadows from the oaks spooled across the wall above her headboard. The lights switched off. The antique door knocker on the front door rapped three times.

Downstairs, the door opened. A brief muffled conversation carried up the stairwell. Women circle and embroider their communication. The two male voices dumped their load of subjects and verbs like bags of sand. The door slammed.

In the crash of the shutting door Caren felt the jolt of his anger gather primal force. He was cold gravel and ice, a fast-moving glacier who took the stairs two at a time. The knob on her latched door rattled. When she didn't respond, he hit the door with his heavy shoulder.

The door splintered on its hinges. "God, you make me sick," he hissed as he pushed through the broken door. His breath smelled meaty with whiskey and rage. He wore his old Minnesota Gophers warm-up, with untied Nikes on his feet. Shoelace tips whipped the floor.

He pulled her off the bed, pushed her down the stairs into the kitchen and shoved her in a chair.

He was madder than she'd ever seen him. Her fear was emotional, psychological, moral. She still clung to the one truism that summed him up: He was the ice man, capable of anything except losing physical control.

Keith ran a hand through his thick yellow hair, a vain gesture she had once thought attractive. Now she shuddered when he pointed to a black and white photograph that lay on the kitchen table. Her. Hands out, steadying Tom James in the Christmas tree lot. The photographer had caught the moment so it almost looked intimate. She was impressed how fast they'd had the film developed.

"So now you're having me followed," she said.

"Not me. Them." The words dropped from his lips. Clink-clink-clink, like three stacked coins.

The kitchen closed in around them, a silent aviary of tile, stainless steel and polished wood where unanswered questions came to roost.

Even now, if only he'd drop his damned arrogant front, she'd reach out to him. Try to understand. But he was too brilliant. And now he'd been seduced by the darkness of his own big dumb shadow. Destiny was too kind, but not too strong, a word for him.

"I have to know. Did you change or were you always like this?" she asked.

"What? What?" Not even language, just an angry grunt.

His eyes tracked around the kitchen and everywhere they touched she could imagine the red rampage of a laser, which, like Keith himself, was precise and destructive.

She raised her hand to shade her eyes against a glare, but the cold December dawn gave no light. The room was barely lit by a fluorescent bar over the stainless steel range. The hollow glare was in her head.

The slight movement tripped a hair trigger in him. His left hand whipped out—his hard cop's hand with his shoulder behind it like a leg of beef—and the heel of his open hand caught her alongside the right cheekbone and sent her sprawling from her chair onto the hardwood floor.

Caren Angland was forty-one years old and she hadn't been struck in the face since grade school. Lights went tilt in her head. Not just pain. Something fundamental broke.

"Low impulse control," she said, a stand-up girl through the sting of tears and a bloody nose. During their early years, when he was a ball of fire working the streets, he'd regaled her with stories about how blunt and obtuse the "assholes" were. How they'd go from zero to sixty on the stupid accelerator at the drop of an insult because they had low impulse control.

He shook the picture at her and rolled his eyes. "Tom James? He's an idiot. They used to call him One Call James at the courthouse. He'll print anything."

Caren's smile. White teeth outlined in blood: "He asked me if the FBI was investigating you?" Her eyes focused through a knotted veil of pain and gave him such a look he should die right there.

"That little bastard," muttered Keith, his voice vacant, trapped, fatal.

You dumb shit, she thought. Looking Medusa in the eye and you don't know it. You're stone. You're dead. *Drop.*

How fickle the passion was that once wore the decorous chains of loyalty and commitment, and yes, love and sacrifice and everything they put in vows to make them stick. How agile it turned a somersault and bounced up spitting poison.

He ignored her and stalked from the room, slapping the picture against his thigh.

How one-pointed and inelegant was hate—now that she held it, unsheathed, in her hand. "You're going down, fucker!" she screamed after him, through the open front door, into the night.

Mad. When the growl of his car had faded down the road, she stood in front of the bathroom mirror, applied pressure and then packed tissue in her right nostril. Swelling and discoloration had already blurred the contour of her right cheek. She'd have a raccoon eye before lunchtime.

The battered face, by itself, was enough to cost him his job.

Stay mad. While she waited for the slight bleeding to staunch, she opened her prescription pills and methodically dropped the blue caplets one by one into the aqua-tinted toilet water.

The psychiatrist who prescribed the antidepressants was a nice St. Paul liberal with Inuit stone sculptures on her desk. She believed in small dark corners in your past, and she'd kept probing for one in Caren's. Caren had played along, looking for that faraway dark little corner when really she was stuck all alone in the echoing rooms of this big, pitch black house with Keith, who was playing Faust.

Dr. Ruth Nelson would have probably liked the Faust reference. She might have thought it an apt metaphor for the concessions her clients made to keep up in the 1990s. It would have been easier and cheaper if Caren had just told her, "Look, I was bad."

Dr. Ruth believed in "disorders"; certainly she didn't believe in evil. Or that the devil could sit in Caren's basement in the form of Paulie Kagin and Tony Sporta from Chicago.

Caren tugged at her wedding ring. Wanting it off. Swollen knuckles, water retention; it stayed. She flushed the toilet, turned and trekked through the blue rooms, up the stairs, stepped over the broken door into her bedroom and stripped off the now blood-dotted T-shirt she'd worn to bed last night. She pulled on jeans, a lined denim jacket. She resolved to keep it simple.

She had to warn Tom James, the reporter. She had to go to Phil Broker and tell the truth. Get his advice about what to do next.

Take her lumps.

But Phil would be standoffish. Keith and Phil disliked each other, but they had history, all the way back to that bad night on St. Alban.

She needed an intermediary. And this brought her back to Tom James. They could help each other. She could get him out of harm's way and whisk him with her up north. He could make the approach to Phil and explain it all. She could give James the information. The story.

Find a way to make it *his* story. That way, she could stay out of the loop. That might work. A standing wave of dread rose up and mocked her. She ground her knuckles into her swollen face to freshen the pain. Pain revived anger and anger conquered fear.

Better now, she went downstairs to the tool drawer in the breezeway, to the garage, and took out a cordless screwdriver. On the move, enjoying the sensation of motion, she made sure a Phillips driver was in the head. On the way down the stairs to the basement she tested the battery.

*Whirrrrr . . .*
*Shouldn't have hit me, Keith.*
Uh-uh.

So she stepped right up to the wall in Keith's paneled den, under the indifferent glass eyes of the stuffed whitetail and the stuffed ante-lope. He'd left room up there between the deer for her, the stuffed trophy wife. She removed the screws that fastened the vertical slats of stained boxcar siding.

Time to get the "bricks."

When she had yanked out six of the boards she could see the suit-case sitting in its nest of studs and sawdust. Compact square vinyl, the bag weighed almost fifty pounds. *Twenny bricks* Tony Sporta had said. *That's ten packs to a brick, that's a hunnerd to a pack.*

Tony talked like that, swallowing his consonants. Keith's new partner.

*That's a hunnerd hunnerd dollar bills to a pack.*

Give the bag to Phil, Keith's *old* partner, and let him hand it over to the feds. Keith'll love that.

She trundled it out into the den and carefully replaced the siding. A minute with the vacuum erased any evidence of sawdust on the shag carpet.

Caren, five nine and strong, dragged and bumped the case up the stairs and down the breezeway. She opened the garage door, and the bluish predawn air flooded in, pristine as a new beginning. With bent knees, she stooped and heaved the suitcase into the back of the Blazer.

She returned to the basement and entered the laundry room. There, between the washer and dryer and the water heater, the par-tition didn't go all the way to the ceiling. An unfinished spot that Keith had masked with imitation planters.

She reached behind the dryer, pulled out a leather shoulder bag that contained a Panasonic video camera, and popped out the tape. She had warned Keith. If he wouldn't do something. She would. He thought her threats were just more of her "blue room syndrome." So . . .

Caren's home movie featuring Keith Angland playing Faust, meeting with "Them."

She'd just positioned the camera on top of the partition between the planters where it commanded a view of the whole den. She'd turned off the camera light, put in a thirty-minute tape, and when the time was right, just let it run. The thing was virtually soundless.

On her way to the garage she picked up an overnight bag she kept packed in the hall closet. Toiletries and a change of underwear. Just in case.

She tossed the bag in the car, turned and squared her shoulders. She craved a cigarette. Not a physical need, but a dramatic urge. There were no cigarettes in the house.

She went into the kitchen, opened a cupboard and picked at a bag of chocolate truffles. She took one bite from the candy and set the remaining half down on the counter.

Deep breath. As a girl, in Lutheran Sunday school, she'd been taught that God never tests you beyond your strength. She shut her eyes, tried to remember. Corinthians something. Too far away now.

Most people are tested in little ways. So they talk to friends. If the test is moderate to serious, they may need a lawyer. Real trouble, they call a cop.

C'mon God, who do you call if the trouble is your cop husband?

Not fair. Being tested this hard. Her jaw trembled with emotion, thinking; Dad must have felt like this when all those Germans came at him out of the black winter forest.

Because he didn't run, he made a difference. A man wearing a VFW hat said that at the funeral.

Stay mad.

She jammed numbers into the kitchen phone. First ring. She shut her eyes. Her lips moved silently. Second ring.

"What," Phil Broker's voice, drugged from deep sleep.

"It's me," said Caren, and it was as if just a few feet separated them across a dark room. Despite the hour and the bruised pain, she lightly touched her hair with her fingertips. Smiled. Which hurt. This was so crazy. She wondered if he ever thought of her. But his voice dispelled that fantasy quickly.

"Caren," he said, flat, direct.

The new wife was younger, vital—shot people in Bosnia with machine guns for all she knew. They had the kid. God.

"I'm in trouble," she said with a tone of rising alarm just ahead of a wall of tears.

"Calm down." Concern in Phil's voice sounded like a stallion stamping, impatient to be harnessed; moving him to old familiar ground, to the thing he loved most—a crisis. She knew that about him and counted on it now.

Panic caught at her throat. She blurted: "I'm leaving him, Phil. He hit me."

Broker asked, "Is he there with you?" She didn't answer. "Caren?"

"I'm here. He's gone now."

"Walk away. Get out. If you really want to pull the plug, call 911. Get some people around you."

"Aw God, I'm so damn fucked up."

"Just leave. Get in the car and drive." She didn't answer right away and his voice sped up. "You still there?"

And she finally said it. "Phil. It's *real* trouble. I need help. I need to get someplace safe. I need to *talk* to you about what to do."

One second ticked. Two. He decided, "C'mon up."

"You sure?" Some hope.

"Get moving. If you need some help getting out I can call—"

"No caveman stuff, okay?" Getting stronger.

"Okay. Just do it."

She thought of the reporter, James. People had already been hurt. Gorski had been hurt dead. She didn't want James on her conscience. Tried to picture him. A nebbish, in need of a haircut, with glasses, soft blue eyes, a soft mustache and his rumpled corduroy soul.

"I have one stop to make first. I might bring somebody." She hung up before he could respond and retrieved the card from her parka and punched in Tom James's home phone number.

11

Broker stared at the telephone on the bedside table and tried to change the subject, which was difficult when you're having a conversation with yourself.

Kit stood up in her crib, through the connecting doorway, hands on the rail, doing chubby knee bends. She watched him, smelling like cow pie. Big X-ray eyes. With her ears like radar dishes and a fresh new mind that absorbed everything.

Like him thinking—the first time he saw Caren she was standing in a Macalester College gym with a dozen other neighborhood women. Broker, the bad street cop, was there to teach a class in self-defense. To his hot young eyes she'd looked good enough to be in Hollywood. But she didn't go to Hollywood. She stayed in Minnesota and kept marrying cops.

Broker rubbed his eyes. Zombie Daddy. He went to Kit, who had begun to cry, placed her on the changing table and changed a three-wipe pooper, dusted on powder, strapped on a dry Huggies and snapped her back into her sleeper.

Then he walked with his baby on his shoulder.

Thinking.

Caren. Coming here. Today. Into his new world of diapers, cleaning, cooking and folding baby clothes. Not to mention . . .

Nina, who watched him from a framed photo on the bedside table with her smiling Pict princess smile and her freckles like Scotch-Irish war paint under a fur cap. Camouflage fatigues, a flak vest and a pistol belt strapped around her waist. Black camouflage oak leaves fastened on her collar. Major Mom.

Broker grimaced and said to his wife's picture, "I said I'd give her a good listen. Okay?"

Then.

Keith, you idiot. Domestic assault. There's that new law. They'll take your gun away, son—they'll put you out to pasture answering phones and force you out of the job.

Serves you right for being smart enough, or dumb enough, to steal my wife.

Ex-wife, Broker reminded himself.

*Sonofabitch hit her, she said.*

Some buttons still lit up.

It took him half an hour to get Kit back to sleep. Then he pulled on his Sorel boots and a jacket and stepped out on the front deck. Unseen, Superior heaved and splashed behind a curtain of fog. Lots of things were up and moving out there in the fog. Like Caren. And if she was coming, Keith wouldn't be far behind.

Tom abandoned Ida to the mysteries of the curling iron in her steamy bathroom and went home to clean up. Grumbling at the cold, he kicked his VW along Shepard Road, skirting the Mississippi River bluffs. Dawn spiked the eastern horizon, bitter as flint roses.

Disheveled, his hair uncombed, he tramped up from his parking garage and waited as a load of scrubbed office worker ants unloaded from the elevator. He rode up to the fourteenth floor, walked to his door, stooped, picked up the morning paper, turned the key and went in.

As he tossed the newspaper on the table, a large manila envelope slid out. The business card was fastened by a squeeze-clasp: THE FEDERAL BUREAU OF INVESTIGATION. SPECIAL AGENT LORN GARRISON.

He grabbed the envelope, tore it open and pulled out an eight-by-ten glossy photograph of himself and Caren Angland talking over a horizontal Christmas tree at Hansen's Tree Farm.

Oh boy.

His hand went to his phone. Heard the interrupted tone. Message. He tapped in the code for his voice mail. Caren Angland's voice, tight, shaking: "Take some precautions. Keith knows that we met and he's acting very . . . crazy. He hit me. Call me immediately." She left a number.

Tom punched in the number and Caren answered on the first ring. "Mrs. Angland? It's Tom James. I just got your message. Are you all right?"

"No. Where are you?"

"My place at Kellogg Square, downtown."

"Go someplace where there are other people, don't stay alone," she cautioned.

"What's going on?" A cold shiver wrinkled his scalp.

"If you want a story, I've got one. But I can't talk on the phone. Where will you be in two hours?" She sounded mad. Mad was good.

Tom's blood pressure climbed a red inch up the roots of his hair. "At the paper."

"I'll pick you up, out front. Don't tell anyone you've talked to me. Two hours exactly." She hung up.

He'd barely replaced the receiver in the cradle when three emphatic raps sounded on the door. Caveman knuckles. Angland? Jesus. Could be. Tom stood rooted to the carpet, paralyzed by stage fright. "Who is it?" he croaked.

"Lorn Garrison, FBI." Southern inflection twanged like a thrown knife.

Oh boy. Sweating, giddy, Tom turned the knob, opened.

Lorn Garrison filled the doorway. He had pale blue eyes, a long pouchy face and a tobacco smile under a brown felt hat from a departed era.

A big guy with a badge and a gun, like Angland; six two, solid, with a white starched shirt riveted to his barrel chest. He wore a heavy olive drab trench coat over a houndstooth sports jacket, a burgundy tie, dark slacks and glossy black wing tips. Fifty plus and fit.

He extended a calloused, manicured right hand. "Lorn Garrison, good morning Tom, glad to meet you." Garrison wagged Tom in his big hand. "Can I come in?"

"Ah, sure. Can I see a badge?"

Garrison flipped open his coat. A badge and ID card were clipped on his belt, along with the patterned grip of a holstered automatic pistol back there. "I'll skip the foreplay," said Garrison. He nodded at the glossy photo. "If you're smart, you'll share some information."

"You were following me?" Tom flushed, gulped the words.

The agent stifled a smile. His practiced eye toured Tom's grim efficiency apartment. The chairs and table were cheap seconds from a Futon factory. Unpaid bills cascaded off the desk next to his cheap computer. Garbage wasn't emptied. Flies buzzed.

Tom took a deep breath and ran his hand through his frizzed hair. With more precision, he said, "You were following her."

"And we have no idea why she'd reach out to someone like you. Enlighten us."

"She didn't approach me, I went looking for her," Tom insisted.

"Sure, Tom. We all got to protect our sources. So what'd she say?" Garrison loomed over him.

"Let me see your badge and ID again," demanded Tom.

Garrison placed his broad hand, palm out, on Tom's chest and plopped him back and down onto the couch. "Listen carefully. We checked. You're on probation. You're one fuck-up from being tossed out of your job. How you got on to this, I have no idea. But here we are. Now, you can be stupid, in which case you'll be subpoenaed to appear before a federal grand jury, or you can be smart."

Tom uncluttered his mind of sticky impediments and conceits like the First Amendment, confidentiality, fairness, ethics and the public's right to know. He cleared his throat. "What happens if I'm smart?"

Garrison's eyes were as sympathetic as an empty patch of prairie sky. "You maybe get some attention, you know, get to be the hot shit reporter you've dreamed of being your whole ordinary, messy little life." He thumped his knuckle on the picture on the table. "So what'-daya say."

*You get some attention.*

Jackpot cherries. All lined up. He didn't even hesitate. "I just talked to her on the phone, when you knocked on the door. She's scared. She wants to meet. She says she has a story."

"Good." said Garrison. He patted Tom on the shoulder. It was patronizing. Tom didn't care. He smelled a deal.

Garrison smiled. "How'd you like exclusive rights to a story that would get you out of the doghouse."

Tom sat up straighter. His chest puffed up. "Try me," he said.

"Can you swim, Tom?" asked Garrison.

"Sure," said Tom.

"I hope so, because the water's about to get real deep."

"Go on," said Tom.

"Two days ago the federal building emptied out because of a bomb scare. That package was addressed to me, personally. What do you think happened?"

Tom shook his head. "The bomb squad called it a hoax. There's a rumor about a tongue being in the box the bomb came in. But nobody can confirm that."

"Not rumor, fact. A male human tongue. They ran tests on it at the lab in Quantico. The return address was the home of a key undercover informant who disappeared three days before the bomb hoax."

"Why was it addressed to you?"

"To send me a message. I brought the snitch into town to do a special job. We're assuming his forwarding address is the bottom of the Mississippi."

"This is St. Paul. Not New Orleans," Tom thought out loud.

"Same river, except up here it freezes over," said Garrison.

Tom asked dryly, "What was he working on?"

Garrison smiled. "Revealing the identity of a dirty St. Paul cop who's helping certain people set up a narcotics distribution network in Minnesota."

"Angland," Tom said. *By Tom James.*

"Don't jump to conclusions, we need proof," warned Garrison, "not talk, not allegations—evidence. Now I know," Garrison paused, "it's a privileged relationship. The sinner and the priest, the dying man and the doctor. The pissed-off wife and the reporter. The problem with pissed-off wives is pissed-off husbands can throw their testimony out of court because of this thing called spousal immunity."

"What's your point?"

Garrison shrugged. "You go off half cocked and print something you could prejudice an investigation," cautioned Garrison. "But if you help us get the whole thing, you can have the story from the inside. Right now, we're curious what his wife knows and if she's willing to talk to us."

Tom asked, "These certain people—are they local drug dealers?"

"No. They're serious organized crime. International."

"So this is dangerous," said Tom. He stood up straight, like brave.

"Very. You still interested?" Garrison watched with dubious eyes.

"Absolutely. Is there any other press on to this?"

"Nope," said Garrison. "Just you."

"Keep it like that and you have a deal," said Tom. He extended his hand. Garrison shook it.

"Look," said Tom, "I don't mean to be rude, but I haven't cleaned up yet and I have to get to work."

Garrison worried the inside of his cheek with his tongue. He tossed two more business cards on the table. "I'm always in touch with that number," he said. "I can get back to you in ten minutes any time day or night. Let us know the second you connect with her."

"I understand," said Tom.

"Do you?" speculated Garrison. "There's some real nasty people mixed up in this. If Caren Angland knows something and is willing to talk, she doesn't want to be on the street. You might impress that on her."

"I hear you." Like a hole card, he held his knowledge of Caren's alleged beating by her husband close to his chest.

"I sure hope so," said Lorn Garrison.

Tom took his time. Leisurely, he slow danced in the shower with The Dream Story that could whisk him to the Pulitzer mezzanine where the suits were all tailored and the elevators were marked *Washington Post, Los Angeles Times* or the *New York Times.*

Tom understood that, beneath their trappings of arrogance, law enforcement and journalism were privileged systems of barter and gossip. To catch a big story or a big crook, somebody had to squeal on someone.

So who tipped him.

Maybe some disgruntled cop who'd worked with Angland. A black cop, maybe, angered by Angland's outrageous remarks. Maybe Garrison himself, grabbing at straws.

His doughy image in the steamed mirror was an argument for a haircut, for exercise. He saw himself, ten pounds lighter, with a razor cut. He removed his glasses. Contacts maybe. Yeah.

The problem was how to control the story. The *Minneapolis Star Tribune*, unlike the anorexic St. Paul paper, would throw money and bodies at something like this. The TV stations would hold high carnival.

Twenty minutes later, Tom floated into the newsroom, more buoyant than he'd been in years. He smiled so broadly at Ida Rain she barely contained a blush. He sat down at his desk. Barb Luct wasn't in yet. Magnanimously, Tom slipped two twenties from his Mystic Lake winnings into her bottom drawer.

Outside, another dark, snowless Scandinavian day tapped on the sixth-floor newsroom windows and invited suicides to jump. Inside, Tom struggled to keep from grinning. Call Rush Limbaugh and spread the word. Another overforty, not-quite-dead white male was getting a second wind.

He imagined Caren Angland in a black dress. A tight black dress. With blond hair and wet red lipstick. A Raymond Chandler fantasy. Very much in trouble. Coming to him.

In real life, Tom had to read his E-mail. Sometimes he read Ida's E-mail. Figuring out passwords was a little game he played.

First message. From Ida Rain, being fussy and vertical on the job. Much different from horizontal Ida. Real earth-shaking stuff. *Re: yesterday's school lunch program story, which you missed. I never got anyone out to cover it so make a call and do it on the phone.*

Another great assignment. Out to lunch by *Tom James, staff writer*. He disliked his name. *Tom* and *James*. Like two first names, as if he didn't have a proper last name. His middle name was Shelle, no help there. He'd changed his byline to his initials, T. S. James, for a while.

His colleagues started calling him "Tough Shit James," so he tried Thomas, but it sounded stuffy. Tommy came off weak.

So he was back to Tom.

He checked his wristwatch again. She'd be out front in about half an hour. His briefcase was ready to go. Pads. Pens, tape recorder and cell phone all charged up.

Look busy. No distractions, then, just get up and make his move. The only reason to be in the office was in case she called with a change. Ida's back was to him, perfect as a page out of *Vanity Fair*; herringbone belted jacket over black slacks. She'd kill him if she knew. God. The FBI. International crime ring.

Keep busy. He drummed his fingers on his desk and turned to his keyboard. His cursor pecked through the files and selected the one titled Names. He scrolled through notes and pages, revisiting old lists of outlaws. His eyes strained the words for textures. The power of the sounds we call each other.

Take Jesse James . . . if his name had been Tom, he'd probably have been a bank clerk. But Jesse—see, it all changed.

William Bonney.

Ma Barker.

Clyde Barrow.

John Dillinger.

Cole Younger.

Pretty Boy Floyd.

Those people *knew* from childhood they would lead dangerous lives. Just the sound of their names was like hearing a dare and a taunt.

And what about Charles Starkweather. No office job kissing politically correct ass for that bad boy. That name had big wrists and big shoulders and was plain scary as an ax handle stained with blood and left out on the frozen prairie.

Starkweather would cut Ida Rain in half and throw the top away. Tom paused. He conjured the image of Caren Angland's top on Ida's bottom. Ouch.

After outlaws came monsters. He put the name Donner at the head of this list: a place, a family, a particularly evocative American moment. He'd never met anyone named Donner. Just as he'd never met anyone named Hitler.

But Bundy was a common enough name.

The monsters didn't have the statuesque phonetics of the outlaws. Ted Bundy sounded normal. Dillinger sounded like bare knuckles.

Charles Manson.

The monsters did not answer to their names. Their directions came from a chat room on the moon.

He'd studied his lists of names until he created one for a fictional hero and alter ego: *Danny Storey; gambler, lover.* Private eye. He whispered it out loud. The sound fit magically in between the outlaws and the monsters. It sounded decisive. A good name for today. That's when the shadow blocked the overhead fluorescent light, fell across the screen, and a violent kick jarred his chair.

## 14

A sour blast of whiskey breath announced Keith Angland, who bristled over Tom, big as the FBI man, Garrison. But no smooth manner, no manicure. Angland was dressed in dirty blue jeans, scuffed running shoes and a thick charcoal wool sweater under a long dark wool overcoat. His cheeks were flushed and gritty with bronze stubble. Uncombed hair. Wraparound sunglasses hid his eyes, doubling his menace in the December gloom.

A photo dropped from Angland's hand into Tom's lap. Jesus. More Tom and Caren among the Christmas trees. Tom experienced the disturbing sensation that his spine had turned to ice and was going to slide out his bottom. But this was his ground and Angland was the invader. He struggled up from his chair, licked dry lips, pushed his glasses up on his nose and challenged in a cracked voice:

"Are you being investigated by the FBI?" In his peripheral vision, Tom caught general motion—reporters' heads jerking up like alerted deer.

Angland's lips curled in contempt. He sneered and heaved Tom into his computer, a chair clattered over. "Stay away from my wife, you fucking hamster."

Shocked stares crisscrossed on them from all over the office.

Ida Rain was quick, out of her chair, moving to confront Angland. But Molly Korne was quicker, appearing out of nowhere. She placed her knuckles where her hips should be if she had hips and announced, "You can't come in here and treat my reporters like this."

Angland held out his left arm like a bar and firmly moved the women aside.

God. Everybody was watching them. Him. So Tom stepped protectively in front of Ida and Molly and blurted, "Leave them alone."

Standoff. Time for dozens of reporters and editors to engrave Angland's demeanor on their memory and for the slow ones to be informed by the fast ones as to his identity. Angland jerked a thumb toward the lobby. "Outside," he ordered.

"Okay," said Tom, warning Ida and Molly with his eyes that it was all right. It wasn't of course. It was like a movie. On screen, they walked from the silent, stunned newsroom.

Angland rolled his shoulders when he walked, top heavy, like a siege engine. At six foot one and two hundred pounds, he was made for contact: a hitter, a shooter, a man catcher. Tom was a soft five foot ten. Like a male movie star, he was shorter than he saw himself on the screen of his mind.

They went through the lobby, through the fire door, into the stairwell. Angland turned, grabbed. A seam in the armpit of Tom's shirt ripped as Angland mashed cloth in his fists.

Tom wanted to protest. There were rules. The main rule was that the reporter was not supposed to get involved. He wasn't supposed to get hurt. That happened to *other* people.

Angland bounced Tom off the tile wall, hard. He removed his sunglasses and tucked them in his pocket. He had long, blond eyelashes. Booze robbed him of his bird-of-prey edge, gave a puffy bovine quality to his brawny face. Tom could imagine him snorting, sleeping in hay.

Pale yellow eyes. Insane fires trapped inside ice. Pores and whiskers like a cratered forest. His lips curled back in a contemptuous grin that showed predatory canines.

"Stay . . . away . . . from . . . my . . . wife," he repeated.

"NO!" Ida's voice caromed off the stairwell tiles. She stood in the doorway. Her wide eyes fixed, determined. Angland shrugged, drooped a shoulder in a deceptively fast, short movement and punched Tom in the stomach. Then Angland sauntered down the stairs as Tom sagged, gasping against the wall. Ida rushed to him. "Tom?"

"I'm all right," he wheezed.

"Is that?"

"Angland. The cop. He's out of his gourd. Don't worry," said Tom.

"Are you kidding? I'm calling security."

"No. Let me handle it."

Ida touched his cheek. "Are you sure you're all right?"

"I'm fine. Do me a favor."

"Okay."

"Go in. Get my briefcase and jacket from my desk. I don't want to go back in there right now."

She spun on her heel and left the stairwell. She returned in less than a minute with the briefcase and the coat and the picture Angland had dropped. "What's going on? Is this woman his wife?" she asked,

"Not now."

"Why are you supposed to stay away from her?"

He snatched the picture and started down the stairs, one arm clamped to his aching stomach. She matched him, step for step.

"Where was this taken? When? Who took it?"

Tom couldn't tell. Was she jealous? Was it the newsie smelling blood? Two flights down, three, and the questions kept coming.

"Is this personal or is it a story?"

Tom paused. For the first time in his life the words bounced funny and he wondered—why were they separate issues? He put a hand on her shoulder, "Look, Ida, I don't know what I've got, as soon as I do, I'll call. Stay near the phone. If I have what I think I have, I'll need your help." He continued down the stairs.

Without missing a beat or a stair, she said, "What do you think you have?"

"Ida, please."

She switched gears, tried for levity, "You said that last night. Hey, Danny boy, tell me."

He ran ahead, through a door, into the lobby, past the guard desk and out the front entrance onto Cedar Street. "C'mon, you can trust me," Ida persisted, pacing him. Then, "You *have* to trust me, I look out for you."

He spun. "What's that supposed to mean?"

"Easy," she tried to calm him. "It just helps to have an extra set of eyes go over—"

"You think I can't handle it myself?" Getting angry.

Patiently, she said, "Tom, I think you're going through a rough time in your life and you just . . ."

The gray Subaru station wagon pulled out of traffic and almost hopped the curb. Caren dropped the passenger side electric window.

At first he didn't recognize her; a scarf was tied over her hair and she was wearing sunglasses. The attempt at disguise dramatized his excitement. Ida tugged at his coat sleeve. "Is that . . ."

Caren pushed open the passenger door. Tom jumped in. "Are you all right?" she asked. One second Ida was framed in the open window, the next, the tires squealed and Ida disappeared.

The upholstery smelled showroom fresh. The floor carpeting was immaculate. She had folded the backseat down to make space to accommodate a big suitcase. She'd rented a car. Disguised her appearance. Packed a bag.

"Keith came by the office with a picture," he said tersely.

"Did he hurt you?"

"Tried to play tough with me . . ." He rubbed his sore stomach, then stopped in midsentence, caught in a slow-motion plunging sensation. Caren's right cheek was *beat up* beneath a layer of cosmetic base. She got rubber leaving the curb, ran a red light turning left on Fourth Street and then, another one turning left onto Minnesota. Tom grimaced, opened his briefcase, removed Garrison's picture and looked at the two photos side by side.

He held them up. "Two pictures?" she said.

Tom held one up. "They were following you yesterday. An FBI agent gave me this one, this morning." That made her dip one corner of her glasses with a finger.

"FBI agent?" she repeated. "You called the FBI?"

Tom shook his head. "They visited me. They've been watching Keith and you." He held the pictures up side by side. "You notice anything?"

She shook her head, now concentrating on weaving through traffic. She went for a full count on run red lights and accelerated down the ramp onto Interstate 35E.

Tom explained. "I'm in the foreground in this one. You're in the front in the other."

"So?"

"Two cameras. On either side. Somebody, besides the FBI, was taking pictures of us."

Caren stared straight ahead. "What'd you think? This was about Keith stealing a piggy bank? People are *dead*." She stepped on the gas, and Tom braced his hand on the dashboard. Be nice if there was a mute button on the world, he thought, so he could tap down his rising vertigo.

Deadline pressure was one thing. Dead people was another.

And raw fear was something else. Until this morning it had lurked on the streets between the safe buildings of his life.

"Is someone following you right now?" he asked, looking around.

"Not anymore. I did the old serpentine car switch in the Hertz parking garage. Keith showed me how—the prick. He learned it at the FBI Academy."

"Did he do that to your face?" Tom asked.

"Yes he did."

Tom's thing was talking and writing. He drew the line at physical violence. He thought of Lorn Garrison. Big hands and shoulders—as big as England's. Lorn had a gun. Hell. Lorn was federal. He had the marines. He turned and looked back at the skyline of St. Paul dropping below the horizon. "We're going in the wrong direction. We should go to the FBI," he stated.

"There's somebody I have to see first," Caren said doggedly.

"Who?"

"My ex-husband."

"Why?" Tom's voice strangled. Ex-husband? The situation took a sickening pulp fiction plunge.

"Because he can protect us and I need his advice."

"About what?" Tom yelled.

"What do you think? About what I should *do*," she yelled back.

"No you don't." Tom dug out his wallet. He held up Garrison's card.

"I can call the guy who was at my place this morning. Right now, on my cell phone. He's ten minutes away, day or night, he told me."

"But then I wouldn't get to see Phil."

Tom stared at her, confused.

"Look," she explained. "Once the feds see what I've got they're going to stick me in protective custody. Before that happens I want to talk to Phil, I want to make sure what I have. And he'll know the best way to negotiate."

"Negotiate?" There was something wrong here. Some imbalance.

"Yes," said Caren brightly. "Because I might be looking at Witness Protection."

"That's forever." Tom's head snapped to the left, alert.

"So is turning over a federal informant to the bad guys. Where do you think that goddamn tongue came from." She pounded the steering wheel with both fists so hard her sunglasses fell off. "And . . . he *hit* me."

"Jesus." He reached to steady the wheel. Her swollen cheek pulsed. Her eyes were . . . fury. "I think I'd better drive," he said.

Caren ignored him, set her jaw and stuck her glasses back on. "You don't rat out brother cops for money, that's basic . . ." her voice trailed off.

Tom mumbled, "I don't get it, you know this how?"

"It's on tape. I filmed it," said Caren.

"Filmed what?" Tom's voice broke. *A tape.* The media's Holy Grail. Tom actually put his hand on his chest over his banging heart. My God. A tape. I'm going to be on *Larry King Live.*

"What Keith did. Why the feds are after him." She jammed her hand into her purse and withdrew a compact plastic cassette. "Right here. If it's all right with Phil, you can give it to the FBI."

*On tape.* Independent confirmation. No hearsay. To hell with spousal immunity. "What's on tape?"

"Keith ratting out an FBI informant, taking money from some guys who run rackets in Chicago. They're opening up a dope business here and Keith gave him the keys to the state. Check it out," said Caren grimly. She slung her head back, indicating the cargo area to the rear. "That suitcase is full of money they gave him, packets of hundreds. It was in our basement."

"Stop the car!" shouted Tom, transfixed.

She pulled over onto the shoulder, worried he might be sick. He was out before the wheels stopped rolling, walked to the rear, and oblivious to the traffic rushing by, tried to open the hatchback. Locked. Impatiently he waited for Caren to come around and unlock the rear hatch. He lifted it and climbed in with the suitcase and seized the handles in both hands. Heavy. His heart fluttered. It could be fifty pounds. His fingers flew over the clasps and clicked them open.

Caren hugged herself. A semitrailer rocketed past. Blasted her two inches sideways.

Tom opened the bag and—*Aw God*, Sweet Jesus, look at that—row after row of currency. A solid wall of hundreds, two feet square, in crisp packets. Pounds and pounds of hundred-dollar bills.

He was just a gentle tug of a man. He'd spent his life quietly pulling on loose threads and hoping one of them would lead to a big fish. Until this moment. What a mighty urge came over him—to reach out and *grab*. Thank you, God. Here was Moby Dick. He leaned over, pressing his hands down on the dollars, feeling the dense little ridges comb his fingers. He slammed the case shut and they got back in the car. The classic questions pranced before his eyes. Who-what-where-when-why-how.

Only then did he realize that he had taken one of the bills. He turned it in his fingers. Ben Franklin's subtle smile gazed enigmatically up at him. Questioning.

"So, who's your ex-husband?" he asked, more calmly.

"He's"—she paused—"married to Nina Pryce."

Tom sat up. He never forgot a name he'd read in a headline. "She's the one . . . the army, some stink from Desert Storm?"

"That's right, the one with the Joan of Arc complex. The first woman ever to pee standing up." Etched acid diction.

"So, ah, what's he do?"

"He has this chair at his kitchen table. When you're in trouble you go sit there and explain it to Phil."

"I see," said Tom dubiously.

"No you don't."

"Where's he live?"

"Right now he's up on the North Shore. Past Grand Marais."

Tom tried to gauge her. An ex-husband suddenly waiting in the wings had an uncertain edgy feel. On the other hand, Grand Marais was the end of the world, and that gave him time to think about the best way to orchestrate . . .

The story, he reminded himself. All that money and he'd actually touched it. Right back there.

"Are you . . . involved with your ex-husband?" he asked.

She actually blushed. Horrible to see under the swollen bruises. "Phil. God no. I haven't seen him in years."

"Does he know we're coming?"

Caren nodded. "I called him and told him I was in trouble." Her lower lip began to tremble. "I told him Keith hit me."

Every time she mentioned being hit she trembled with anger. She shouldn't be driving. He should get her off the road. The safe thing would be to call Lorn Garrison right now. Jesus Christ—he had a tape.

"Once we get up north you'll give me the tape?"

"Right. I want you to crucify the sonofabitch."

Really should wait. But he couldn't resist it. He flipped open his cell phone and punched Ida's number. He recalled this vintage news-room poster, a guy in a 1940s hat—like Lorn Garrison's hat—with a press card stuck in the band, talking on an old-fashioned pedestal phone—Hiya doll, gimme rewrite.

"Ida Rain."

"Ida, it's Tom," he tried to sound brisk, but he could hear his voice puff up importantly. He twirled the hundred-dollar bill in his fingers as he spoke.

"Jesus, you all right?" She didn't hide the concern in her voice. Then she yelled, "It's Tom, it's Tom."

Tom imagined the whole newsroom alerted at the mention of his name. Converging on the phone. Everybody talking about him.

New voice. "Hey, Tom, how're you doing, man?" said Bruce Weitling, the city editor. More words in the greeting than he'd spo-ken to Tom in the last year.

"I'm on to something really big here, Bruce . . ."

"We're starting to appreciate that. The guy who gave you a hard time this morning. He's Angland, right? Mixed up in some kind of FBI investigation? We called the feds already and they were very cool, like, what ever gave you that idea?"

"No. No. No calls. I want to work out some ground rules. First, it's exclusive and copyrighted . . ."

"Tom, c'mon back to the office and we'll talk. We need you to work the phones and brief Wanger and Kurson."

"Hey, *screw* that. This is my story." Tom was incensed. Cheryl Kurson was just a kid. A *girl*.

"Sure it is and your name will be on it. We just want to field a full court press, if it's big."

"No," said Tom calmly. *Mine. Dammit. Mine.*

"What do you mean, 'no'?" Bruce's voice was ruffled, indignant.

Tom punched off the phone. Caren was watching him, so he shrugged confidently. "They can wait. Let's go."

Caren nodded. "It's a six-hour drive to get north of Grand Marais."

"Good," said Tom. He could use the time to think. Distracted, he started to slip the bill into his pocket, but she was still watching. Quickly, he tucked it out of sight, in the glove compartment.

**16**

Broker eyed the clock, pictured Caren on the road and envied Kit her world of friendly talking puppets and animals. She was watching them now, stamping from bare foot to foot as credits rolled on the television screen. *Sesame Street* ended with a furry monster tribute to the number nine. Kit poised, defying gravity, pitched slightly forward.

The theme music for *Barney and His Friends* came on.

"Oh-oh," she announced with a judgmental furrowing of her eyebrows and forehead. She weighed twenty-one pounds, and a third of that was baby fat. He wasn't kidding Nina, their kid was a diminutive Churchill, sculpted in pink dough, crowned with copper locks.

What if Nina's lean, mean tomboy gene skipped a generation?

"That's right, a *big* oh-oh," Broker said as he handed over her reward, an Arrowroot cookie strictly forbidden by Major Mom before afternoon.

Their secret.

Since Kit, there were rules in the house. No smoking and no profanity. So he spelled out the curse: "Ef-You-See-Kay Barney and the yuppie puke he rode in on." He knit his own thick eyebrows and improvised on his favorite line from *The Treasure of the Sierra Madre.* "We don't need no stinking purple glob of fat."

He disliked Barney with a savvy passion he reserved for all the forces he intended to arm his daughter against. He'd seen fat, jolly, beady-eyed slugs like Barney operate around kids before. And he thought that the corpulent reptile was a fitting mascot for America at the end of the twentieth century. Like half the country, the lizard was an overweight blimp; and he mouthed the kissy-ass victim-speak that was smothering the culture like a tree cancer.

Broker pointed the clicker and punched *Washington Journal* up on C-SPAN. Brian Lamb appeared, sturdy as the smiling Quaker on the oatmeal package on the kitchen counter. Broker put Kit's high chair next to the kitchen table and ladled oatmeal into two bowls. Daddybear bowl and Babybear bowl. He blew on hers to cool it, then placed it on a Winnie-the-Pooh place mat on the high chair tray. Hoisted her into the chair.

He told her, "Right now life looks like all fun and games with Grover and Elmo. But what they don't tell you on *Sesame Street* is it can get rough out there. People who don't eat their oats grow up weak." He held up a spoonful of oatmeal for her edification. "Kit, listen to Daddy: The weak die."

*Ring.* Broker eyed the phone. Malignant plastic intruder in his house. He ignored it, sliced a banana in Kit's bowl.

*Ring.* It was going to be a soap opera and he hated soap operas. Throw in stubborn people like Caren and Keith who had a knack for fighting dirty and *soap opera* translated to "domestic" on a police blotter. Messy, probably dangerous.

Caren, always popular, managed never to have friends. And Keith was, unfortunately, the smartest pompous asshole Broker had ever met. Always popping up where you'd least expect him.

*Ring.* He sprinkled cinnamon onto the oatmeal, stirred it with the baby spoon. *Ring.* The phone was an arm's length away on the kitchen counter. It was inevitable, so he picked it up and reminded himself. Be cool.

"What?" he said in a resigned voice.

"Broker? Yeah, this is kind of awkward, it's Keith . . ." Like real concerned.

"Been a while," said Broker.

Silence. Then:

"It's Caren. She's in trouble. Need some help. She's in a real mess with this reporter from the St. Paul paper."

"Yeah? . . ."

"I think she might be headed your way."

"Oh yeah?"

Keith's voice lost its veneer of concern. "What it is—she called this number this morning."

"What gives you that idea?"

"I pulled the phone records."

"Did you hit her?" Broker asked, striving to keep his voice level.

"So she *is* headed there. Yeah. I slapped her. Mistake on hindsight, but there was provocation." Keith sounded like he was padding a police report.

Broker grimaced. "Give her some room to cool down. You too."

"I'm looking for my wife, not half-assed advice from you." Keith hung up. Caller ID registered an Amoco station. Probably already north of the Cities, on the road. Bastard always was sure of himself.

"Shit."

Kit, wearing oatmeal all down her chest, stared up at him with saucer eyes and a truncated brow. Soaking up prickly new nuances and adrenal grace notes. Anger.

Broker mumbled, "You're probably going to get to see your first fistfight."

"Chit," trumpeted Kit. She hugged a floppy, stuffed yellow dog that wore a sombrero, a serape and a beard of oatmeal. When you pressed the toy's tummy, it played a zoned-out version of "La Cucaracha." A present from his folks.

Besides no swearing and no smoking, there was no hitting in Broker's house. So he needed help to referee Keith and Caren. He picked up the phone and called a friend, Jeffords, in Grand Marais. Good. Jeff was in his office.

"Jeff, it's Broker. I have a touchy situation coming my way this afternoon. Ah, Keith Angland and Caren are having a mean fight and she's on her way here. No kidding. I'm serious. . . . She says he hit her . . . Yeah . . . I know. Haven't seen either of them for years. Must be bad if she's running. Yeah, guess he finally came apart. Nope. Keith just called and said she's got something going with a reporter. So it could be that again. Who knows? But they're both headed this way. If he goes crazy on me I have the baby here. No. Hey. Okay. I doubt they could be here earlier than noon. Okay. Appreciate it."

Broker hung up the phone and lifted his daughter out of the high-chair. "Looks like we're going to have a party. Uncle Jeff is coming over too," he said.

Tom Jeffords had copped with Broker in St. Paul, part of the free-wheeling rookie "big five" that had included Keith, before he became a power-hungry asshole, and J. T. Merryweather and John Eisenhower. Jeff was the Cook County sheriff.

Caren staring straight ahead, tugging on her wedding band, driving eighty-five miles an hour.

"What's Broker like?" Tom tried again.

Thoughtful chevrons creased her forehead. "He never grew up. He's an . . . adventurer, I guess." The creases deepened. "He and Keith were partners for a while, way back, when Phil was a St. Paul cop. Then Keith used to be his boss. It's like—Keith loves giving orders. And Phil hates taking orders. And Keith was always trying out new approaches to improve Phil's attitude. And then there was me."

She smiled gamely. "They don't really like each other much. Funny thing was, they made a hell of a team."

Quite possibly she was impaired. Concussion perhaps. Out on the road, alone with him. With a priceless tape and at least a million dollars. Spiraled off on a tangent, reliving her first marriage.

"Is he still a cop?" he asked.

She shook her head. "He got rich. His folks have this cabin resort in Devil's Rock, he plays at managing it sometimes."

Tom cleared his throat. "Is he quick-tempered? Calm?" Armed? Dangerous? Still in love with you?

She removed her sunglasses, inclined her head and searched for words. "He used to watch that Robert Redford movie—*Jeremiah Johnson*—over and over. Every year, just before deer season. It used to drive me nuts."

"Be serious."

"I am. It drove me right up the wall, every November." She cranked her neck and stared at the rearview mirror. "I hope nobody is following us. Something bad always happens at the end of a car chase."

"So, does he know about . . . the stuff on the tape," Tom thought out loud.

"Not yet. I need you to act as go-between? To, you know, set up a meeting. Let him know it's serious and not just some dumb fight I'm having with Keith."

Tom stared out the window at the toothpick wreckage of a cornfield. A woman has a fight with her husband. The husband hits her. She runs for help to her former husband. The two husbands dislike each other. The only thing they agree on—being cops—is that they hate reporters. Tom could wind up being a lightning rod for all the hot emotions zigzagging around. She could be dissembling—it could be a romantic triangle that involved at least one alleged murder, some crooks, more than a million bucks and an FBI investigation.

What if Caren and Keith made up? It could happen. They'd have this tearful and probably sexually very hot reunion. Then Keith would get up, take a leisurely Clydesdale pee, and make Tom James disappear along with the guy whose return address was on the bomb hoax.

They wouldn't let him write his story and this was for keeps. *Jesus, Tom. You're too far out in front of this thing. You could get yourself killed.* Something new in the shudder of fear beckoned him. Held him tight. The excitement.

And then, a cool, veteran insight squinted down twenty years of seedy crime stories—*I'm not the logical person to get killed, am I.* Tom savored the dizzy drama, almost out-of-body, looking down, watching his own thoughts. Plans were forming.

*Plans.*

He began this way, in a dry voice. "Pull over. We have to talk."

She slowed and then turned off on a wide portion of shoulder. Tom said, "It's the money in the back. If there are bad guys and they follow us, we need to hide it."

Her brow furrowed. She removed the glasses. "Not exactly secure back there, is it?"

"No it isn't."

"So," she said with aimless practicality. Her attitude was strong on mission and weak on details. Clearly she needed help.

But then . . .

There was Ben Franklin's enigmatic smile.

He fixed his vision on a line of spruce across the road. A flock of crows detached from the trees and rose in a black scatter against the wool sky.

"A murder of crows," said Caren.

Her words yanked the hair on the back of his neck up on end. He jerked around and faced her.

She shrugged. "My dad used to say that, back in North Dakota. There's probably a dead deer over in those trees."

"We could put the tape in a luggage locker in Duluth, at the airport. And hide the money somewhere," he suggested.

Caren considered, nodded. "Makes sense."

"Where can we hide the suitcase? I don't want to be seen dragging it into a public place."

She mulled his question. In less than a minute, she had an answer. "Keith's dad has an old hunting shack up the Witch River trail, just past Lutsen. He moved to Florida after Keith's mother died, but he keeps up the taxes on it. There's a filled-in cistern back in the woods. We could put it there."

"Good," said Tom, who didn't have a better idea. It would have to do. He opened his door. "Take a break. Let me drive the rest of the way," he said equably. They traded places, and as he put the car in gear, his eyes beheld the wheeling turmoil of the crows.

Two tense, mostly silent, hours later they arrived in the port city of Duluth. Tom knew the area and drove to the airport. Caren didn't even blink when he told her to change seats and drive the car around the parking lot and pick him up at the terminal front entrance. He quickly found the security lockers, put the tape in one locker, dropped coins in a second locker and left it empty. He ducked in the gift shop to buy a Minnesota highway map.

Outside, feeling more confident, taking control, he climbed back in the car and handed Caren the key to the empty locker. Then they studied the map. She pointed to a local road, just past Lutsen. The turn off for the cabin.

They left Duluth and headed up Highway North 61. What if, he thought. *What if I was alone in this car?* Like the land, his thoughts changed, becoming rougher, wilder. Fields and oak trees were left behind. Granite-toothed hills and pine trees overlooked the road. *What if she just disappeared?* Superior paced them, an endless stampede of whitecaps.

They stopped in Two Harbors at a Holiday, so Tom could buy some industrial-size black plastic garbage bags and a roll of duct tape. Caren bought a pack of Marlboros and returned to the car. Tom went to a public phone on the wall next to the fruit display. He stared at a pyramid of oranges, took out Garrison's card and called the FBI office in St. Paul.

"Garrison's not in," said the agent who answered.

"Tell him it's Tom James. I'm with Caren Angland and we're in danger. I'll call back in an hour. Make sure he's there." Tom saw it developing as a classic plot, not a news story; feed Garrison the broad details to start, save the best for last.

Back on the road, in motion. Was he reporting it? *Or was he living it?* He stepped on the gas.

Signs: CASTLE DANGER, GOOSEBERRY STATE PARK. BEAVER BAY and SILVER BAY, where immense chalk clouds balanced over hulking relics of the iron mining industry. The road was narrow, two lanes curling and dipping.

Getting remote, wilder.

Tofte, Lutsen, and then Caren showed him where to turn on the gravel road that twisted up a ridge. A small sign with the number 4. Away from the familiar highway, even with the windows up, and the heater on, Tom could hear the trees groan in the wind, an eerie sound that disturbed his city-trained ears. And he could feel the deep-woods chill. At Caren's direction he slowed and then stopped. A dark narrow lane carpeted with pine needles wandered into the trees. The access was barred by a logging chain strung between two pines.

Caren got out and felt around the roots of one of the chained trees. She held up a rusted Sucrets tin. Opened it and took out a key. Tom forced the rusty Yale lock open and dropped the chain. Drove in. Put the chain back up.

Tom checked the deserted road. Just the low howl of the wind, the heaving pine crowns. Alone.

A hundred yards up the bumpy track they came to a sagging cedar plank cabin on a boggy pond. Caren's expression fit right in; it was the most desolate place Tom had ever seen.

The cistern was another hundred yards from the cabin, in thick undergrowth and jack pine. It took Caren half an hour to find it. Stonework from another century jutted from the moss and pine needles. Rusted sheets of buckled metal bolted to gray wormwood heaped over the sides. A mattress spring. Orange, flaking refuse; decaying tin cans.

Back at the car, Caren stood hugging herself in the cold while Tom dragged the suitcase from the cargo hatch. Acting as if he were checking the locks, he slipped his hand in, pulled out a packet of bills and stuffed them into the zippered, inner security pocket of his jacket.

All right, Tom. You just crossed the line.

Feels . . . *alive.*

Then he doubled and redoubled garbage bags over the luggage as protection against water damage. When he finished, he secured the bundle with loops of duct tape.

Carrying the suitcase on his shoulder, he was soon sweating and dizzy from exertion. She tapped him on the arm and spelled him with the bag. Amazing. She wasn't even breathing heavily.

Aerobics at the spa. Gym rat.

At the cistern, he carefully rearranged the rusty mess to make room for the bulky package. Then he eased the bundle into the cranny he'd prepared and placed layer after layer of corroded debris over it. The frozen ground was stiff as steel. They left no footprints. He took this as a sign.

As he used pine needles to scrub the rust off his hands he wondered if he could find the place in the dark. He'd counted his steps back to the cabin. One hundred and six. When he emerged from the trees he took a visual fix on a wind-damaged birch tree to the right of the cabin. If he stood in front of the birch, the direction to follow through the trees was two o'clock.

He realized he was staring at Caren's back as she huddled in her baggy denim jacket, smoking a cigarette. He tapped her on the shoulder and put his hand out for one of her cigarettes. He tore off the filter and lit it with her plastic Bic.

First time in ten years he'd had one. He inhaled. Breathing poison felt right. Hot little sparklers of nicotine sizzled in his fingertips. But then—no. Smoking was backsliding, one of Tom James's weak habits. He was moving away from Tom James. Moving fast. He stamped the cigarette out on the cold ground.

They were all alone out here. He looked at his hands, which were nicked, raw and bleeding slightly from working at the cistern. The slight labor had raised several blisters.

Weak. But getting stronger.

Back in the car, Tom wrote down the exact mileage on a business card as they turned onto the gravel road. He made another mileage notation when they reached the highway. For a minute he studied the intersection, sketched a collapsed billboard for a landmark. Then he dropped the car in gear and drove north toward Grand Marais, and beyond it, Devil's Rock.

Kit was down for her nap. The dishwasher and the clothes drier hummed their safe lullabies. Stacks of clothes were folded with precision in two plastic baskets next to the kitchen table. Morning chores were done. That wasn't true. With Kit, the work never ended.

When he and Nina had gone off to take on the world, she had quit the army, had been a grad student at the University of Michigan, Ann Arbor. When they got back, she was pregnant and he thought . . .

He paused. Aired out the resentment. Moved on.

Banks of thermal windows lined the lakeside wall. A desk. Low shelves full of books. Gathering dust, except the ones about child rearing . . .

The window casements still smelled of new maple and cedar. The whole house smelled new. Like Kit smelled new.

Like his life did.

An olive drab, rectangular metal box sat on his desk, the shape and cover latch identifying it, to a veteran's eyes, as a fifty-caliber ammo can. But this one was outfitted with a cedar liner. Broker ordered it out of a catalog, full of cigars, from a warehouse in North Carolina. He popped the lid, removed a corona and snipped it in half with a guillotine cutter he carried in his pocket. He put half back in the box and stuck the other half in his mouth.

He patted his stomach where it strained slightly against his waist band. Off cigarettes for six months. Eight pounds over his best weight. He had been through hundreds of cigars and a lot of frozen yogurt. He had yet to light one of the cigars.

He mulled over them, rolled them in his lips, then clipped off the end when they started to get soggy and chewed them and cut them down to a nub. An interim step. Insurance against reaching for a cancer stick in times of stress.

Like now.

It would be all right. Jeff would be here. Steady Jeff.

Seventeen years ago—God, that long—they'd all been up here, cases of beer, steaks. Steelhead fillets from the nearby Brule River on the grill. Sleeping bags lined up on the plank floor of the then one-room cabin. Jeff, Keith, John Eisenhower, J. T. Merryweather. Wives and girlfriends. Caren laughing.

Rookies. Crazy brave. Run every red light in town to be the first one to get shot at.

Pieces of Caren lingered, literally. Nina had unearthed artifacts during her pregnancy, as she and Broker emptied out the old cabin in preparation for the wrecking crew—a cup with a lipstick mark on the rim, a slinky, black knit dress stuffed in the back of a drawer. Nina in her eighth month, at first self-conscious, then bewildered that her body could swell up like special effects. Not the best time for her to find old snapshots of lithe, sable-haired Caren.

In the female hierarchy, Nina disapproved of Caren, whom she saw as a woman who attached herself to men. To Nina, Caren's home remodeling business was an affluent hobby. Not serious work.

Nina's current idea of serious work was to parachute into Belgrade and personally arrest Radovan Karadzic.

A car swerved off the highway at reckless speed and interrupted his rumination. Broker moved through his house, toward the sound of frozen gravel ricocheting across the hardpack. The gray Ford Crown Victoria drifted in a four-wheel, controlled skid around a turn and down the driveway.

Unmarked cop car. Keith had gotten in front of her. Broker watched his former friend, partner and boss snap the big car out of the slide, rock it to a stop, roll from behind the wheel, cross the drive and trudge up the porch steps. Broker met him at the front door.

Behind the menacing sunglasses, Keith's features twitched like mummy ribbons coming undone.

He was an inch taller, thicker and had a gregarious side; he would look at home at a prayer breakfast, something Broker could never do. He'd been to the FBI Academy. Broker always suspected there was an uptight fed inside him, filing applications in triplicate, trying to get out.

The grievance list was long; Keith had made Broker's life miserable until he left the St. Paul Police Department and went to the BCA, Bureau of Crinimal Apprehension, to get away.

He'd hunkered down in his new life, within walking distance of the Canadian border, and now here was Keith, coming up his steps. But not the old control-freak Keith; this Keith was a shiver of barely contained fury. Broker opened the door.

"C'mon in. No sense freezing," said Broker in a calm, almost inaudible voice. He noted Keith's sloppy appearance, the underscent of alcohol layered by Certs.

So the stories were true.

Keith reacted with caution, knowing that voice and the trip wire tension it conveyed. He nodded, removed his sunglasses and swung his head. Fatigue threaded his eyeballs, bloody wires around the jonquil iris. A day's growth of rust-blond beard roughed his jaw. "Christ, I was hoping she'd be here. She shouldn't be driving the way she's fucked up."

"Getting hit can do that to you," said Broker.

Keith looked away. His eyes tracked the high-beamed living room, the blaze of new wood, skylights—and stopped on the fireplace. Broker's one indulgence, a fearsome, coiled gilt bronze dragon's head, an actual hood ornament off a tenth-century Viking long ship, weighing over a hundred pounds, was bolted to the chimney over the mantel. Attracted, Keith walked to the serpentine metalwork, reached up and clasped it in both hands, like a derelict Norseman making a vow.

He rubbed his bleary eyes. "God. What'd this set you back?" Looked some more. "Place looks like a goddamn mead hall now." Frowned. Curled his lip. "You still don't own a computer." He pointed to the brightly colored plastic baby toys heaped in boxes by the Franklin stove. "Where's the kid?"

"Sleeping."

"Nina?"

"She's overseas, Keith."

Keith grimaced. He pointed to the table. "Can I sit down?"

"Coffee?" asked Broker.

Keith nodded and went for a chair. Broker walked to the kitchen counter and the coffeemaker. They moved with decorum, walking on eggshells. Broker returned with two coffee cups. Another car came down the drive.

Keith came around in a half crouch. Then he collapsed back in his chair when he saw that it was a tan on brown county sheriff's Bronco. Sheriff Jeffords got out of the truck wearing a patrol belt with a full load. Keith swung his eyes on Broker.

"Sorry, Keith. I thought we might need an umpire," said Broker, waving the big lawman in.

"Great, Jeff," said Keith. "Another fuckin' runaway to the fuckin' woods."

Jeff was six two, weighed 240, had sandy iron hair and quiet brown eyes. Banded in a cold leather gun belt, he creaked when he walked into the room. "How you doing, Keith?" he asked as he padded to the coffeepot.

"Not so hot," said Keith.

"You know," said Jeff, giving him his chilly lawman's eye, "they got this new law for cops. Pop your wife and it's domestic abuse and you lose your right to carry a gun. You heard of that new law, Keith?"

Keith sagged and reached in the pocket of his overcoat. He pulled out an empty plastic pharmacy bottle and placed it on the table with a decisive click. "I found it in the bathroom this morning. Empty. Couple of pills were in the toilet bowl."

Broker reached over and read the prescription aloud: "BuSpar."

"Read the rest of it," said Keith.

"Caution: Do not stop taking this medication abruptly without consulting your physician." Broker and Jeff exchanged glances.

Keith reached in his other pocket and brought out a mangled photograph. He tossed it on the table.

There was a slight, but tribal, tightening of jaws all around. Quietly, with distaste in his voice, Broker said, "Who is he?"

"Tom James. Reporter for the St. Paul paper." Keith expelled a lungful of air.

"And . . . ," said Broker.

"And"—Keith strained his breath between clenched teeth— "Caren has a borderline personality disorder. She's been seeing a shrink for a year . . ."

Two vertical worry marks deepened above the center of Broker's thick eyebrows.

"She's anxious, depressed," explained Keith.

Broker looked away. "Caren and I didn't agree on a lot of things, but she was always resilient."

"The strain got to her," said Keith, looking him straight in the eyes.

"The strain, huh?" queried Broker. Time slipped, missed a beat. It seemed they'd had this conversation before.

Keith exhaled. "Yeah. Of living with me." He nodded at the empty pill container. "She quit taking the medicine four, five days ago and went totally snake shit."

"What about the reporter?"

Keith muttered under his breath. His eyes swung, trapped. "The little creep is witch-hunting me. I'm real quotable these days."

"We heard," said Jeff.

"Well, it must have been a slow news day because he came out to dig some dirt. And the shape she's in . . ." He shook his head. "I just lost it. Went after both of them. This time it's my job. The press'll blow this thing way out of proportion."

Caren said she might be bringing someone. Broker took a breath. Hit an air pocket. Why bring a reporter? Great. Caren would show up. His kitchen table would be an autopsy slab for dissecting a failed marriage and Keith's dead career. "Who took the picture?" he asked.

Keith looked away. "I followed them, I wanted something, to get in her face."

"Besides a fist?" asked Broker.

Leather hitched. Jeff shifted from boot to boot.

"What happens if you stop taking the pills suddenly?" asked Broker.

Keith enunciated in a weary voice. "Overreaction to stress. Violent mood swings." Then, with elaborate precision, he quoted, "A propensity to misperceive reality."

The ex-husband's resort was just minutes up the road. Tom really wished Caren Angland would just disappear in a puff of smoke. Presto. Go back for the suitcase, cross the border into Canada. No more Ida Rain sending him to school board meetings. No more child support payments.

But the fantasy was full of holes.

Caren faced away, her forehead leaning against the window. He touched the money packet next to his chest—saw himself walking into a casino in Vegas with that wad in his pocket.

"Turn in up there," she said suddenly. A bridge, a sign: BRULE RIVER. The trees opened. Another sign. NANIBOUJOU LODGE AND RESTAURANT. The structure had the obtuse shape of an ornate barn roof rising out of the ground.

Tom turned down the driveway. Wooden lawn chairs froze on a stark band of cobble beach; under a slag sky, six-foot Superior breakers auditioned for North Atlantic surf.

"I'll stay here, you'll go ahead to talk to Phil," she directed.

"I will?" But the fact was, he liked the way it gave him some control, keeping her separate from the ex-husband. Letting him lead the play. He drove on, turned and parked the car; they got out, and Caren laughed as they walked to the office.

"What? he asked.

"Personal joke. I'll tell you sometime," she said.

"Tell me now."

"Okay. This lodge is where Keith and I *started*, I guess you could call it. Later, he brought me back up here, to propose to me."

Tom stopped and cocked his head. "He drove all the way up here to propose?"

Caren shook her head. "There's a waterfall up there in the park." She pointed to the ridge across the road. "That's where." She yanked at her wedding ring. The knuckle was really swollen, agitated by her constant worrying at it. The ring would not come off.

"Try some soap," he suggested.

They entered and she asked the man behind the counter if she could get something to eat. The clerk stared at her bruised face; the sunglasses and scarf, given the time of year, were a gruesome costume. He told them the kitchen was closed until supper time. But she could get a cup of coffee.

Caren said that would be fine.

The dining room dwarfed them—towering stone fireplace, soaring walls and ceiling. Flamboyant reds, oranges, yellows, greens swirled around Tom; the batik, cutwork and quilting of an immense pagan fun house.

Wild, like his thoughts.

"North Woods baroque," quipped Caren, joining him. "It's Cree, the designs." Then in a more serious voice: "Let's go outside. I want to use your cell phone to call Phil," her voice accelerated. Breathy.

*Like a teenaged girl*, thought Tom.

Outside, they stood in the lee of the wind. She tapped the numbers and all of her tension drained out in a loud hopeful, "Phil?"

Keith Angland slapped a US West printout on the table. Not a regular billed account. A copy a cop could get pulled in a hurry. He pointed an accusing finger at an underlined number. Acid voice, "C'mon Broker—she called you this morning. What'd she tell you?"

"That you hit her, Keith. So I told her to get clear."

"Clear up here, huh?" Keith pushed the sheet of paper in Broker's face. Broker swatted the accusing hand aside. The phone sheet fell to the floor.

Jeff stood close, striving for an impartial expression, with his heavy hands on his hips and his weight poised on the balls of his feet.

When the phone rang, Keith and Broker were speaking at once and pointing fingers. Broker stepped over to the wall phone under the bulletin board next to the kitchen cabinets, picked up the receiver and barked, "What?" Then he sagged. "Aw, Jesus."

"What you got going on behind my back, asshole!" Keith seethed, suspicious. He lurched up, banged the table and crossed the room in long strides. Broker sagged, exhaled. It was going to hell. Keith grabbed at the phone. Broker sidestepped, still holding the receiver to his ear.

Caren's voice, in the handset, said, "I need you to look at something."

"Not now," said Broker tensely.

"Caren, goddammit, where are you?" yelled Keith.

Behind a closed door, the baby cried.

"Oh my God, he's there. Did you tell him I was coming?" Caren's tiny voice whined inside the plastic.

"No. Wait," Broker addressed them both. Caren on the phone and Keith, who was dancing in front of him. Jeff shadowed them, his large square hands held up, signaling for calm. In the bedroom, Kit began to cry in long rolling sobs.

"Keep him away from me," shouted the tiny voice. "He'll kill me." A male voice came on the line. He was shouting too.

To quell the riot breaking out in his house Broker slammed the phone down on the hook and turned to face Keith.

Four miles away, Caren blurted: "He's there, Keith is." She pressed the telephone to her chest.

Tom took a deep breath, grabbed the phone and yelled, "This is Tom James. I won't let her near that guy, is that clear?" The line went dead.

She hugged herself, rocked in place.

"That's it," said Tom. "It's FBI time."

"Just don't tell them where we are until I get to talk to Phil. Okay?"

"Uh-uh. I'll handle this from now on." In the cold wind, his fingers left dots of sweat on the square number pads when he touched them.

"FBI," said a mechanical male voice.

"Lorn Garrison."

"Agent Garrison is in a meeting—"

"Listen, it's Tom James. It's about Keith Angland. It's urgent, goddammit!"

Garrison was on the line immediately, "Tom, it's Lorn. Did you put some reporters on us this morning?" First-name basis.

Tom overrode Garrison's question, "You want Angland?"

"What've you got?" asked Garrison. The patented, low-key all-purpose FBI question.

"A home video of him and some people. His wife made it. Like Rodney King." Tom's sentences were breathless. Run-on.

Garrison came back fast, chiseled. "What people?"

Tom covered the handset and asked Caren. "What people?"

Caren grabbed the phone and blurted, "Keith gave Paulie Kagin and Tony Sporta a picture of Alex Gorski posing with some FBI guys and a pile of confiscated cocaine. Kagin gave Keith over a million bucks. It's on videotape and the sound is good." She handed back the phone, turned to the cedar shake wall of the lodge and hid her face in her hands.

Tom took a deep breath while Garrison's voice hockey stopped, changed direction and lost its sandpaper grit. And its distance. Tom knew that agents were trained to negotiate with tense people on telephones. "Tom. Are you all right?" Good buddies all of a sudden. Real concerned.

"I'm with her. Angland roughed both of us up this morning."

"You have to be careful. If it's Paulie Kagin, he's real bad news. Where are—"

"We took off. We're up on the North Shore."

Garrison yelled, not into the receiver: "Get onto the flight lines. Find me a chopper, ASAP. National Guard, Army Reserve." He turned back to the phone and said to Tom, "Where's this tape?"

"We put it in a secure place. Look, I gotta figure a few things out. I'll call back when I feel safe."

"Wait. We got these calls from the paper. Tom . . . are you working on a story?"

"Lorn. That wasn't me. Angland marched into the newsroom this morning and pushed me around in front of the whole staff. I'm working on staying alive. Can you get up to Grand Marais? We're just north of there, at the Naniboujou Lodge. Angland's up here and the sonofabitch is after us. We may be moving around, so I'll have to call you from my cell phone. Stay in contact with this number, will you?" his voice pleaded. Then he thumbed the power button and extinguished the conversation.

Twin jets of fear and excitement propelled Tom past the lodge, out across the broad back lawn. Superior snapped at the beach a hundred yards away. Sleety spray pecked his face. Slowly his breathing returned to normal. Caren moved to his side.

"You can see a hundred miles. It's so big," he said softly.

"Actually about fifteen miles, then the horizon falls away. You know, the curvature of the earth."

She spoke matter-of-factly. Smart. Probably valedictorian *and* homecoming queen. Tom felt a powerful resentment. The only reason he was remotely close to these events was because he'd once written about something she'd done.

"The water's real cold," he said in a distracted voice.

"Stays about thirty-four degrees all year. Bodies don't float. Water temperature is too low for decomposition. They stay down."

Violent waves smashed the shore. Not as violent as the scenario he was trying to concoct in his mind. All the icons dropped in place, almost in perfect sequence. He faced her. Saw the wind strip away her flimsy scarf.

*Lady Luck with a black eye.*

The angry husband had a motive to shut her up. He had struck her earlier in the day. The motel clerk, if shown a photograph, would testify to the damage on her face.

She'd told her ex-husband of the attack, that she was leaving Angland and felt the need of his protection.

She had assured a member of the press she had an incriminating tape of her husband's collusion in the disappearance and alleged death of a federal informant. Now the FBI knew of the tape and were in motion. That left one thing.

He spun and asked point blank, "Does Keith know you have the money?"

She shook her head no. "It took me a week to find where he hid it after I first saw the tape." She studied his face and asked, "Are you all right?"

"I was just thinking how it isn't a story for me anymore. It's a tragedy happening to some people."

"That's an odd sentiment for a reporter."

"I don't feel like a reporter right now, Caren." He studied her beautiful, bruised face, saw how it was chilled by the wind, almost like a carved ivory brooch.

Or a death mask. How would it look under a million tons of Lake Superior ice water? Effortlessly, he sketched the rough headline: "Dirty Cop Kills Wife Who Helped Indict Him."

But he didn't know how to make that happen. He tried to imagine himself holding her under water, out there, in that violent surf. Hell. She was stronger than he was. And that would still leave him walking around, the last person to have knowledge of her whereabouts. The loose end. Loose ends get yanked on, they could braid into a noose. An exercise in fantasy.

Still—almost perfect.

He turned and faced south; every atom in his being was drawn to the hidden cash. Magnetic greed. But it was probably dirty. Easily traced. Still, there were ways to pass cash. He'd written about it.

But not without accomplices. Not in large amounts.

The fantasy was coy, danced close, then moved off like a third person and pranced on the frozen grass. It handled her all over and she didn't know it.

He still had the story. With a resigned heave, he turned to her. "Do you really need to talk to Phil? The FBI will be here in a couple of hours."

Caren nodded her head vigorously. "I want him to know that I'm doing the right thing for once. And, I don't know—maybe I need a lawyer. Ask him what he thinks about the Witness Protection Program."

Tom could still experience a piercing moment of compassion for her. "People like you don't go into Witness Protection. It's for crooks."

"Then what happens to people like me?" she asked in a flat doomed voice.

They looked at each other, out of words. Tom had the impression they'd arrived at a place off the map of their lives. They turned back toward the warmth of the lodge. Inside, Tom said, "Okay, I'll go talk to him. Where is he?"

"Keith's there," she cautioned.

"I'll just have to deal with it."

She scanned his face dubiously. "Broker's Beach is about four miles up the road on the right. There's a sign. You can't miss it."

He left her sitting at a table, alone, with the ornate hall surrounding her like a gaudy broken heart.

Tom drove to Devil's Rock, which was nowhere. Just a sign. He pulled over to the side of the road fifty yards from the faded sign for BROKER'S BEACH RESORT—CLOSED. He took the packet of bills from his pocket. It won't be missed, he told himself. He slipped off the rubber bands that secured the ends. Broke the paper strap.

The hundreds fanned in his hand. He counted, thinking there was nothing that couldn't be fixed by money. That buried suitcase contained enough to manufacture a whole new life.

The count was one hundred. He'd never felt so strong, lifting $10,000 with one hand.

Except Caren knew where it was hidden. She would gush it all to this Broker guy. Maybe she had a count and would figure out the packet was missing.

A hundred hundreds and that was just one. The goddamn bag weighed almost fifty pounds. And now he'd have to put it back.

Looking up and down the empty stretch of road, he was stricken. What a wild desolate place this was. It wasn't fair. Being this close. He stuffed the loose bills in his jacket pocket. Angry now, Tom stabbed the gas and turned down the entrance road to the resort. The only satisfaction left was seeing the look on Keith Angland's face when he told him his wife had ripped off his money. And the FBI was coming for his ass—*and all because of me—Tom James.*

The gray Subaru pulled into the drive and parked alongside the county Bronco, Broker's Jeep, and Keith's Ford. Broker watched a pasty guy in a baggy brown parka get out—longish hair, mustache, glasses, the same guy in the picture lying on his kitchen table.

A chair tipped, slammed against the plank floor. "Hey! What's going on?" Keith was on his feet.

Everybody was moving. Broker pointed to the picture, out the window, said to Jeff, "That's him, he's traveling with Caren." Kit had quieted. Now she began to cry again in the bedroom. Keith yanked open the door. Jeff stayed with him step for step.

Broker was torn. One step forward and two steps back. He confirmed that Caren was not in the car. The old Broker would have Keith on the ground by now. Jeff yelled over his shoulder, "Stay clear." The new Broker went for the baby.

Outside, Tom James slammed the car door, looked around and pulled up his collar. Resort cabins, bleached by cold, with shuttered windows, hunkered in a rocky cove. A county sheriff's Bronco, the big unmarked Ford, and a green Jeep were parked in front of a large cedar-plank home, out on a rock promontory.

Lake Superior lashed the shore. Spume flew ten feet. The air turned to shadow. Even Tom, an inside city dweller, could feel the storm charge jitter in the swirling clouds.

The door to the house opened and Angland pushed through it. A tall husky uniformed cop strode after him. Seeing the tough hick lawman provided instant comfort as Angland bore down on him. Shouted:

"Where is she, scumbag?"

"Guess what, Angland, it's FBI time," Tom shouted back in a shaky voice, trying to stand his ground. The wind whipped the words away.

"Hey, fuck you," seethed Angland, and Tom saw that he was working himself into a jerky Samurai rage, like an actor in a Japanese movie. The uniformed cop threw out a restraining arm. Angland put both his palms out, warding off the cop. "Stay out of my personal life, Jeffords," he warned.

*Personal.*

The word tattooed into Tom's brain. They still thought it was personal. Keith was fooling them. Oh boy. Caren hadn't told them about the real reason . . .

A lean, dark-haired man with striking black eyebrows strode out on the porch, holding a toddler bundled in a blanket. Another tough hick. The uniformed cop swung his eyes to the man on the porch and called, "Stay there, Broker."

In that instant, when the cop's eyes were averted and he took a step back toward the porch, Tom and Keith were alone.

Tom sneered at Angland, wanting to wound him. The words shot out, "Hey, tough guy. Guess what—she's got your dirty mob money."

For a second, Angland did nothing except tabulate behind his cold eyes. Then his face curdled. "I'll kill you sonofabitch!"

Before the cop spun back around, Tom's wild glance locked with the hard-eyed gaze of the man on the porch. He had seen the exchange with Angland and was now scrutinizing Tom. But then the cop lunged and threw his arms around Angland's shoulders. Broker sprinted, baby in arms.

"Hold her," he yelled, holding the baby out as he pushed Tom toward a door in the side of the garage, opened it and thrust him and the kid through. "Stay put."

Inside, a woodstove, wood shavings curled on the floor. The walls held racks full of woodworking tools. The kind of shop Tom once dreamed of having. The kid squirmed and started to cry. Tom ignored her. Voices surged outside. He went to the door, to watch the fight develop in the yard.

All big guys, in their forties. Tom sensed their slight caution, past the straight-ahead fury of their youth. Broker waded in and hooked one of Keith's legs with his ankle and swept him off balance. But Keith, light-footed, recovered, shook them both off and went for Broker. And Tom saw that it was definitely Japanese movie time, the way they puffed up with macho-strut and put on their bad Kabuki scowls. Wow. These two guys really *hate* each other.

*Fighting over Caren, maybe.*

He tensed forward, eager to see two men their age fight. Especially these two. But then he became aware of the weight of the toddler in his arms—she had stopped yowling.

And plunged her plump hand into his pocket and now was fascinated by the fistful of hundred-dollar bills mashed in her small but strong fist.

"Hey, you little shit," protested Tom.

As he shifted the baby's weight to reach with his other hand, the kid thrust the hand up and out, throwing open her fingers. Bills erupted and fluttered all around. The kid squealed, distinctly, "Pretty-pretty."

Unceremoniously, Tom dumped her on the cold cement floor and stooped to gather up the cash. She shook off her blanket. Damn. The kid was quick. She snatched a loose hundred. Tom tried to grab it back.

The bill ripped. Instantly, Tom matched the torn halves. Christ, the whole middle was missing. Fast as a little mongoose, the fat kid stuffed the missing portion into her mouth. Tom was totally flummoxed, squatting, stuffing money back in his pocket with one hand. Bills everywhere.

He spotted an empty air mail envelope under the workbench, seized it and shoved money in as fast as he could. Didn't want them loose in his pocket. He crammed the envelope in his jacket, yanked the kid up in his arms and tried to get a finger in her mouth. Good luck. Little piranha had teeth. Then he did and . . .

Ow, shit! Fucking kid bit him.

From the corner of one wild eye, through the door window, Tom saw the big county cop interpose himself between Broker and Angland. He grabbed each of their collars in a slab hand and pushed them apart. Tom turned back to the kid.

The kid glowered, jaws clamped obstinately shut.

Christ. Frustrated, angry, Tom shoved. The kid plopped over on her butt. Amazing. Damn kid got up and faced him. Good. She was chewing. Go on, you little shit. Swallow it.

Outside, the two overforty gladiators backed off, and Tom saw that the concern on all the faces was intimate. Local. Not the kind of cop masks you'd expect when capital crimes and federal agencies were waiting in the wings.

*Dumbass hicks. They don't know. They don't know.*

Tom grabbed the kid and shook. When she started crying, he got a finger in her mouth, swept around, trying to avoid her six or seven teeth. Nothing. She had swallowed it.

Relieved, Tom patted her. "Nice baby," he said. Outside, the tough guys performed a face-saving male dance of heavy breathing, straightening their clothing, running their hands around their belts and hitching up their pants. He opened the door and stepped out onto the porch.

"Okay," Keith was saying. "Just keep this guy away from Caren."

Tom couldn't resist. He pointed his finger. "He beat her up. He beat her up." *Nah nana nah na.*

Keith started to come at Tom again, and the big cop snared his right hand in a hold Tom recognized—from a police manual—as an arm bar. He levered Keith to the ground.

"You're real close to an assault charge here, Keith," the cop admonished with massive understatement.

Tom marveled at them, caretaking that fucker Angland. Cops. Buds to the bitter end. He reached back into the shop, swept up the bawling kid, and hugging her before him as a shield, stepped toward Keith. Tingling. It was jazz. He was improvising. He loved it. "Lock him up, he's a wife beater . . ."

A moment passed during which Keith made signs he had stopped resisting. "I'll take Keith back in the house," the cop said. "You talk to this one."

Keith muttered but jerked his head in agreement. The cop eased back on the arm and Keith stood up and swatted rusty, frozen pine needles off his overcoat. He turned and walked back to the house with the cop.

The baby stopped crying. Little eyes cranked saucer huge, bulging up at Tom.

Tom grimaced and held the kid at arm's length. Damn bugged-out eyes annoyed him, so he turned the kid to face away. Kid was a little too cute. His own kids at this age had faces like cold macaroni and cheese. Like Caren. Like Keith. Even the ex-husband, the Marlboro Man. All of them. They were all somebody.

And this snotty little kid would grow up to be like them. Should drop-kick the little brat into the lake.

Broker snatched his child back and hugged her close to keep her warm.

Tom held out his hand. "I'm Tom James with the—"

"I know who you are," snapped Broker. "Where's Caren?"

Tom appraised Broker at close range. Midforties, 180 pounds packed long and tight into a six-foot frame. His spare face was a study in edges. His black eyebrows grew in a bushy line across his brow and lent a lupine intensity to his gray-green eyes. And hard. Not health club hard or even street hard. Harder than that—working outside in all weather hard. And still acting like a cop, because he had that barely concealed cop expression, the physical smirk he and all his cop buddies reserved for civilians and especially for reporters: *I've forgotten more about real life than you'll ever know, asshole.*

The wind reared off the lake, and Broker, who wasn't wearing a coat, instinctively stepped into the shop. Tom followed him, cleared his throat and said, "I just wanted that moron to know I'm not afraid of him."

Broker's gaze did a slow burn over Tom's face. With his free hand he reached out and thumped Tom on the chest. "Where's Caren? Why'd she drive all the way up here with you?"

Tom shook his head. "Uh-uh. Not till he's gone."

"How is she? Is she acting strange?" Broker demanded.

"She's strung out. Who wouldn't be . . ."

Broker reached in his pocket and pulled out a plastic bottle with a pharmacy label. He thrust it at Tom. "Keith says she went off these all at once. Which is dangerous. So quit dicking around and *tell me where she is.*"

Giving orders. Tom grimaced, hating the authority implicit in the man. He took the pill bottle and turned it in his fingers. It explained a lot. He jerked his head toward the house. "What about Angland?"

"That's the county sheriff in there with him. He'll escort Keith to the county line and send him home to cool off."

"You're going to let him go?"

Broker's squint was like a beagle sniffing. "Does Caren want to charge him?"

"She . . ." Tom couldn't say it. He had come to deliver a message, and now he couldn't. All he saw, thought, felt, was: the Money. And he liked it, Keith being on the loose . . .

"She what?" Broker took a step closer. Razor-slit eyes, real skeptical. "What kind of trouble is Keith in? That would send a reporter on a field trip?"

Tom fought for control of his features. "How long will Angland be here?" he muttered.

"That's up to the sheriff."

"Okay. I'll call back, and if he's gone, I'll tell you where she is."

"Who made you stage manager. And who said you could leave," said Broker. Dead flat voice. Arrogant cop's eyes.

The baby was still staring at Tom with those X-ray eyes. Baby cop's eyes. She squirmed, trying to twist from Broker's arms, trying to get down. Eyes getting bigger and bigger. That's when Tom saw the object of her struggle. A hundred-dollar bill lay on the floor an inch behind Broker's right boot.

"C'mon, we're going inside for a little talk," said Broker turning, moving to the door. Tom dropped to one knee and scooped up the bill. Eyes darting, he checked the floor. Clean. Rising up, he came level with the damn kid, looking over her father's shoulder. Saw him take it but she couldn't do anything about it.

*Can you, you bug-eyed little shit.*

Now the damn kid's face was beet red, swollen; she was holding her breath. Going out the door, Tom and Broker sensed it at the same time. She was *choking.*

"Kit!" shouted Broker. Scary fast—this whole other set of scary reflexes kicked in—he hurled her belly-down into his left hand and smacked her hard on the back with his right. At the third hit, she gasped, coughed and expelled a wad of drool-wadded paper onto the floor.

"What the hell?" Hugging his gasping daughter, Broker stooped. Poked at the expectorated mess. Picked it up.

Tom walked stiffly past him in a controlled panic. All he could think was: have to get out of here. Jesus, right there, Ben Franklin's smiling face oozed in Broker's fingers.

The baby, her airway clear, screamed.

Broker, perplexed, concerned for the child, hugging her, shot out his free hand and spun Tom around by the shoulder.

"How the hell did she get this?" he demanded, brandishing the wad of chewed paper. It fell away as Broker's hand hooked at Tom's collar.

Tom tried to sidestep. Broker blocked him. Tom tried to run, but Broker closed the distance, tightened his grip on Tom's collar. Slam. Tom's back hit the side of the workshop.

He met the suspicion in Broker's eyes honestly, with a look of trapped hatred. He had the distinct impression it was a face that Broker had seen before.

Guilty of something.

"What's going on?" Broker demanded; fast eyes, fast study. His strong hand twisted on the collar, shutting off wind.

The baby screamed. Tom wanted to scream. Then somebody yelled, a hoarse male voice, furniture tipped over; trouble, inside the house. Broker released his grip and turned.

"Don't move," he ordered. But he had started to jog toward the sounds of struggle in his home. The second Broker's back was turned, Tom ran for the car as fast as he could.

Broker had to let James go. All hell was breaking loose in his house. Running, hugging Kit, half thinking: Choking. Really shook him. She was still panting, gagging, trying to catch her breath. The protective instinct fired afterburners more powerful than adrenaline. It was . . .

Just powerful. So powerful he . . .

Heard Tom James's car door slam, engine start. Gravel clattered off car doors as James peeled up the driveway. Keep going. Jeff was in trouble.

He vaulted the steps and stepped into the empty living room. Stopped. The odd quiet set his neck hair on end. Then he heard a muffled thump from the bathroom. At the same time he felt the draft from the ajar door leading to the deck.

Clutching Kit to his side, he threw open the bathroom door and— aw Jesus—a very angry Jeff sat, arms extended behind him, cuffed to the water pipe under the sink. He had a washcloth stuffed in his mouth.

Broker yanked out the rag. Jeff yelled, "I don't believe it. He's nuts. He pulled his weapon the minute we got inside."

Keith's car door slammed in the yard. Kit began to cry louder.

"Shit," hissed Broker. "Where's the key?"

"They're *his* cuffs. He's got the key."

The Crown Victoria's engine revved. "Shit," said Broker again, tensing. Maybe he could run down Keith before he made the road. Then what?

Kit held him back. The fear leaped again when she turned bright red in midwail, holding her breath. Not choking, scared.

Jeff studied Broker's turmoil. "Let him go. Leave it to us." He bounced on the floor, furious. "Call 911. Give them Keith's car."

Goddamn fucking kid. How was he going to explain the money in her mouth? Tom rotated the pill bottle in his fingers as he drove. Side effects. Had his own side effects to worry about. There could be a regular landslide of side effects. He crushed the plastic bottle in his fist and slammed the debris on the dashboard.

Tom winced, remembering Broker's suspicious eyes, questioning the piece of currency, putting it together. Tom and money.

*I'm going to get caught.*

Just say I took some of the money to show the FBI. That might work. All that buried money. He almost cried. Okay. Get past it. Needed Caren now, to vouch for him.

He parked the station wagon in front of the motel office, headed into the dining room. The clerk called to him.

"She isn't here. She said to tell you she went for a walk."

Tom was confused. "Where? It's freezing out."

"In the woods, up the ridge."

"Great." Tom grimaced. Finding people in the woods was not his specialty. "Did she say where she was going?"

"She uh, went up the trail to the Devil's Kettle. It's a waterfall a little ways up the Brule River."

"Waterfall?" Tom was incredulous.

"It's pretty unusual, mysterious actually," said the clerk. "Half the river disappears in this enormous pothole. Over the years they've run experiments. Dumped in red dye, bobbers, hundreds of Ping-Pong balls. None of them were ever seen again. It's bottomless."

"Where's this trail?" Tom sagged, resigned.

"Right across the road. There's a path this side of the bridge. Otherwise, you go in through the park. It's clearly marked, can't miss it." The clerk pointed.

"Okay," said Tom. He shook his head to clear it. His hand squeezed the shape of the cellular phone in his jacket pocket. "Do cell phones work up here?"

"Have to be on top of the ridge. There's a new tower they just built."

He opened the door and stepped outside. Roiling clouds grumbled, tiny snowflakes zipped, stacks of urgent whitecaps ripped across Superior. Across the road, the ridge rose in ominous pine thickets, black and green, like serrated teeth.

"Thunder snow," offered the helpful clerk. "Something you don't see very often." Tom nodded as he handled his cell phone, making sure the battery was socked in tight. Sheets of icy wind sheared off the lake. Shivering, he stuck his hand in his pocket and felt the locker key.

He wanted to kill her, of course. And her crazy ex-husband. And the damn kid. But he needed her. To explain the money.

With a rueful smile, he realized he hadn't thought about the story for hours.

He pulled on his light gloves. Should have brought mittens. Couldn't find his hat. Not dressed warm enough but he had to get it over with. He got in the car, drove it to the end of the drive and braked out of habit, to check both ways.

The growl of the big engine preceded the speeding Crown Vic. Keith Angland skidded around a turn and came straight for the Subaru.

Seeing that car coming directly at him, Tom panicked. He kicked open the door, jumped out and darted across the highway. Where's the damn trail? Running. Found it. Cold air seared his lungs. But he kept going through a knee-deep slush of frozen grass until he'd gained enough high ground to overlook the highway through a break in the trees.

Saw Angland park at the lodge, hurry into the office. He came out a minute later at a dead run, jumped back in the car and came up the drive, heading right for the spot where Tom had disappeared into the trees.

Tom gripped the cell phone in his pocket. Call for help. But he couldn't move, paralyzed by fear. Angland was loose. After him.

But then—

A hot, loud cheer shoved aside the detached, reasoning voice that had guided him through twenty years of journalism. *Take a chance, Tom.*

Angland was after *them*. Terror whittled his imagination to a lethal sticking point. He saw the way out.

What if Keith threw her in a frozen river and she drowned?

It would be his word against Angland's. But he had the tape. *Got to try.* Angland was out of his car. Three hundred yards away. Tom sprang forward and ran for his life, up the trail, into the spiky black forest.

The wind swung an ax. Frozen sweat clicked in his hair. Snow pecked his face. He shuddered, hunched his shoulders, gasped for breath, and his lungs crunched the ice-cold air.

Tom didn't care. He prayed to his Jackpot God: Please, let me have this one thing and I'll never ask for anything else.

Signs. C. R. MAGNEY STATE PARK. To his left, a deserted campground, some brown buildings, a footbridge across the lower stream.

The trail skirted the edge of a river gorge carved through raw rock. Curtains of mist twinkled in the chill air. From the corner of his eye he saw rushing brown water, dirty ivory froth, curling between ice swirls.

All uphill, tricky footing on ladders of landscape timbers furred with frost and frozen mist. Brilliant green mats of Arctic moss bunched in crannies. Weird trip roots. Rocks. He paused. Gulped air. Heard—brush crackling behind him. With a sob in his lungs, he bolted on.

The low subterranean grumble of surging water animated the canyon. His breath came harder. His calves burned. His thighs burned. Up more slick-timbered stairs. A sign. DEVIL'S KETTLE. Arrow to the right. Running now, along the lip of the gorge, the ice-choked river a hundred feet below. Down. Up again. Then he was slipping and falling down the longest cascading flight of rugged wooden stairs he had ever seen, out in the middle of nowhere.

With a silent pop—the ice gray day mushroomed into Snow City.

Tom's white tortured breath exploded. A million snowflakes filled the world and dropped a gauzy net of sticky flakes. Every surface—coated. The mangy undergrowth had its Cinderella moment, transformed. Delicate white-encrusted coral lines graced the hillsides. Even Tom was struck with the gentle sorcery of first snow.

Soon a white, soft silent cushion absorbed the thud of his shoes. All he heard was the blast of his own breath. And the muted torrent up ahead. Then he breasted the slope, passed an observation platform of stout timbers and saw the falls below. The Brule growled, hidden beneath a petticoat of ice that pitched down a fifty-foot drop.

Granite boulders divided the river into two channels. To the right, the solid ice sheet masked the falls. But on the left the ice was open. The left channel spun on the brink, spiraled in a tight roller-coaster turn and boiled like a runaway black sprocket between the glassy skirts. Down, out of sight, into a granite cavern.

Seeing it, Tom believed it was bottomless.

And he saw Caren. A pale, blue denim figure poised—dangerously—on the huge slippery boulder that divided the river. He saw how. She'd crossed an ice bridge that linked smaller boulders to the shore. Through breaks in that ice Tom could see the streaking white water mark the velocity of the current as it rammed the boulder. Bareheaded, ghostly in the thick snow and mist, snowflakes sequined in her black hair, she stared into the exposed pothole.

Intent on the raging water, she tugged at her wedding ring.

Tom threw one look over his shoulder. Nothing but the snow and trees. He scrambled down the slope to the ice bridge and forced himself to cross it fast. She saw him then and stopped tugging and held up the ring hand for his inspection.

"He proposed to me here, you know," she yelled in a hollow voice. Tom James couldn't hear. He was dizzy with the power of the place. The moment.

"I talked to Broker, he doesn't think you should go into Witness Protection. He has a better idea," he shouted.

She smiled. Beamed. "How is he? Does he look well?"

"He gave me something for you." He wondered if it hurt, her face beat up like that and smiling so much.

A crooked trident of chain lightning connected the snowy forest to the Armageddon clouds. Thunder ricocheted off the boulders. Dazzle. Witchery. The snow was a frenzy of drunken killer bees.

"Thunder snow," yelled Caren happily.

*Magic.*

"Yes." Tom floated. Maybe the boulder pulsed red beneath them. *Act.*

For the first time in his life, he experienced the electric current of perfectly merged thought and action. Rockets ignited in his arms. Fired into his hands. He extended his arms stiffly, almost ceremonially, and felt the jolt of her sternum under his palms. Wide-eyed, in total surprise, Caren flew backward. For a second, her shoes slithered for purchase on the lip of rock. No blood, no struggle, no mess. Almost an accident.

Her jacketed arms protested in manic circles. Her feet pumped in a desperate uphill sprint through midair. The eerie scream ended abruptly when she was sucked out of sight in the blowing snow and the wind, into the foaming pit.

*Holy shit!* "I did it," crowed Tom James.

Time spun its wheels, grinding adrenal sparks that wove him a hot new skin. His right fist extended over his head. He half expected more waves of thunder and lightning.

Huh?

She was still screaming? Over the sound of the wind and the water. Tom felt the surge of new survival instincts. He turned. And hey—it wasn't her screaming . . .

Through chattering fevers of snow he saw Keith Angland, overcoat flapping, sprinting down the trail. A berserker's rage quavered from his hideously open mouth.

Angland's powerful quarterback's right arm shot out and threw sparkles from a black pistol. Particles of granite spattered Tom, beads of blood bloomed on his right wrist, stinging through his glove.

A fast zipper of wet, red hurt slit the trouser along his left calf. He growled, amazed, baptized and born again in a fiery Jordan of pain.

Common sense jerked him. He ran like hell.

Instead of chasing him, Angland went to the spot where Caren had stood on the snow-swept boulder. Tom watched, panting, from the trees and waited to see if Keith would continue the chase. He took off his gloves, pressed them against the wet rip in his trouser leg.

Angland scrambled out of sight, down into the ice-girded rock face around the pothole. Tom was paralyzed with doubt. What if she hadn't gone in? Was down there, and Keith was going to her.

No, no. He'd seen her disappear.

After a full minute, when Keith didn't reappear, he shook off the shock and staggered through the stunted pines, marveling at the brilliant, delicate red stipple of his own blood on the fresh new snow. Smeared on his bare hands. Thinking clearer now. Being shot would make it more believable. Still had the magic going for him. He circled back around the falls, emerged from the pines and started back down the trail, lurching alongside Keith's faint filling-in shoe prints. It was time to do some reporting.

He took out the cell phone and called 911. Nothing happened. Get higher on the ridge. Ignoring the pain in his leg, he scrambled up the slope, slipping and falling, crawling on all fours. Finally he stood above it all, under the furious sky. He called again. A voice answered. "Help!" he screamed. "He killed her. He pushed her in. He shot me."

"Where are you, if you're calling cellular I can't track you," the urgent controlled voice said back.

"In the woods. In the woods." Despite the throbbing pain, Tom covered his mouth with his shaking hand to keep from laughing. In the woods. What a great 911 one-liner in northern Minnesota.

"Where in the woods?" yelled the voice.

Tom James collapsed in the snow and realized he couldn't remember the name of the river rushing in the gorge below him. The clerk had said . . .

"Sir. Sir . . . ," squawked the telephone in his bloody hand.

"There's a waterfall up a trail from the highway," he blurted.

"What waterfall is that?" The operator came back.

For the first time, Tom registered the reality of the wound in his leg. His own blood was leaking from his body. The new, hot, runny adrenaline garment he'd discovered deserted him in the cold wind. A hydraulic press squeezed his lungs. Shock. He began to shake. Then, like a miracle, he saw two tiny police officers below him, running in the snow, coming up the lower trail.

"I see them," he yelled into the phone.

One carried a long gun in both hands, swinging in front.

He disconnected 911. With great concentration, he pulled out his wallet. His numb wet fingers fumbled among the business cards. He found the one he wanted, stabbed the number in the phone, and as it rang he laughed, giddy. It was perfect after all.

"FBI," said the cool omnipotent voice from faraway, inside a marble air conditioner.

"It's Tom James," he gasped. "Angland killed her. He shot me. Where's Garrison." Tom heard them tipping over chairs. Yelling.

"Wait one," shouted the agent in a controlled voice. "I have to patch you through. He's in Duluth."

Time plodded. Tom watched the cops climb. Maybe a minute. C'mon. C'mon.

Garrison's voice was on the line. "Right here, Tom. Tell me exactly what happened and where you are."

"There's cops coming. I think I'm all right."

"Who shot you?"

"Angland. He went crazy. Wait, uh, get ahold of the sheriff's department in Grand Marais . . ." Tom could hear background commands.

Garrison said, "Tell me where you're hit."

"Leg. below the knee."

"Is the blood seeping or pumping?"

"No, no, don't worry. Not that bad. Not that. Look we gotta . . ." Tom swooned and woke up a second later coughing snow.

"Steady," said Garrison.

"I'm good. There's cops. Hey. The tape?"

"The one Angland's wife made?"

"Right. Listen, we gotta make a trade. Got her killed. It's not safe for me."

Garrison talked to somebody, then he came back up. His voice had changed. Closer somehow. Real focused. "We're in contact with the sheriff's department in Grand Marais. Angland assaulted the county sheriff. They say they have a deputy and a state patrolman climbing some trail looking for you and Angland's wife. They saw the cars and talked to a motel clerk. Wait. They say they heard shots."

"That's me, that's me." Tom vigorously nodded his head.

"Where's Angland, Tom? I can patch it through and alert the officers. He's up there armed, right?"

"Pushed his wife. Went down into this waterfall thing. He's not up here now. I think it's safe." The two cops were about two hundred yards below him. Tom heaved to his knees and waved.

Garrison was off the line for a moment. Then back. "The cops see somebody above them. A tan parka. If it's you, wave one hand slowly."

Tom grinned, raised his right hand with the phone and slowly swung it back and forth. Beauty queen wave.

"Okay," said Garrison. "They have you. Hang on."

"I want a trade," insisted Tom. "I just saw him kill his wife, man.

They'll get me if I give you that tape." Tom's voice rose hysterically, a quavering shout that tumbled, echoing against the snow-draped pines. The cops below him reacted, crouched. One of them raised the shotgun.

"Easy, easy," said Garrison. "We can protect you."

"Bullshit, you can protect me. This is big. I want to go away. I want a deal."

There was a moment of silence. "He wants the Program," stated Garrison, as if he were inspecting the thought coming from his lips. Words were exchanged in the FBI office far away. Garrison said carefully, "If what you have is good, it can be arranged."

"No, no. I want it all spelled out. In writing and notarized. You fuck people all the time in Witness Protection."

"Calm down, Tom. We'll take care of you."

Tom swooned again. "Promise," he said in a thready voice.

"Absolutely, I promise," said Garrison.

Tom blinked. The cops were just yards away. One was square, muscular, with a neatly trimmed black mustache. Same uniform as the county sheriff's, at Broker's house. He carried a crackling radio. The other wore highway patrol maroon and had the shotgun. Tom transferred the phone to his left hand and grabbed his leg and felt the blood go warm and sticky between his freezing fingers. With a groan he pitched forward. His victorious smile wore a beard of sticky white snow.

Then the county cop was bending over him, turning him, doing something to his leg where it hurt. Cutting his trousers. Some bandage. The other one squatted with the shotgun, peering into the woods. The first one finished tying on the compress and gently took the cell phone from Tom's cramped fingers.

"Deputy Torgerson, Cook County," he said into the phone. "We have him. Right. Not bad. Flesh wound, left calf, just broke the skin. Shock. No sign of Angland or the woman. We have backup coming. Thank you much for the assist."

Tom pawed feebly for the phone. The deputy handed it to him.

"Garrison," Tom said softly. Dreamily.

"Right here."

"If I go into Witness Protection can I choose my own name?"

And Lorn Garrison laughed, a discharge of tension. "Well, as long as it's, you know, ethnically compatible. Can't be Gomez." Har. Har.

An idle snowflake landed on the tip of Tom's nose.

He composed the lead to the biggest story he would never write in his life: *St. Paul Police Lieutenant Keith Angland, the target of an FBI investigation, apparently killed his wife, Caren, because she was threatening to turn an incriminating videotape over to federal authorities.*

Perfect. A million bucks for seed.

He offered a muffled laugh to the beautiful chaotic snow. Gomez. That's funny, Garrison. Then he raised his bloody hand to his mouth and it tasted like the sea and tears and dirty pennies. He licked his lips and smiled.

*It was going to be great.*

# 23

"Pretty. Pretty." Kit, her choking episode forgotten, jumped on the porch. Her first real snow floated down with indifferent wonder. Cheryl Tromley, the closest neighbor, hovered in the cabin doorway.

"Pretty. Pretty." Like Caren's epitaph.

Cheryl had to come over on foot because her car was in the shop. Jeff and Broker rushed through changing the rear tire on Jeff's Bronco. Keith. Bastard had punctured tires on both their vehicles.

Jeff didn't have spare manpower; he'd flagged his men to the Kettle. Now he placed and hoisted the jack. Broker cranked off wheel bolts and replaced the spare while a stoic cop voice crackled over the police radio.

"That's what the wounded guy said. She went in the Kettle. Angland shoved her."

Broker compartmentalized, functioned. But he was hearing and seeing through a constricting tunnel. He spin-tightened the wheel bolts. James shot. Caren gone. He and Jeff had misread it. Let it get by them.

Their eyes met. Silently blamed themselves. *Our fault.*

And Caren. Gone. Broker blinked. The word formed in his mind: *Gone.* Sucked down into crushing turbines of ice water. Drowned. The oxygen exploded to jagged crystals in her lungs.

Stopped. Ended. Dead.

Jeff ratcheted down the tire jack and kicked it away. He slammed Broker's shoulder. "C'mon, c'mon." Broker snugged up the bolts, flung the tire wrench and scrambled into the passenger seat.

The cop on the radio kept talking in an eye-of-the-storm Chuck Yeager voice that reminded Broker of the army: Keith had climbed down into the Kettle spillway and clung to the icy rocks next to the pothole. In a bizarre turn, James had been in cell phone contact with the FBI field office in Duluth.

"I told her to come here and I left her out there alone with that idiot James," said Broker. He trembled at a sudden chill. "There's something wrong about that guy."

"We'll question him, hold him if I have to," said Jeff, driving in a controlled fury, wearing steel bracelets that Broker had nipped with a bolt cutter. He expertly corrected a four-wheel skid. Bad snow and he was doing sixty. He reached behind the seat, pulled out a wool blanket and shoved it at Broker. "Wrap up."

"What?"

"Cover up. You're in mild shock."

Broker threw the blanket over his shoulders, shook his head, disbelieving. "Keith's capable of a lot of things. But not killing Caren. Not up there. Christ, he *proposed* to her up there."

"Keith's a bastard," Jeff reminded him.

"Right. A cold, *efficient* bastard. This is too sloppy, especially with a doofus like James for a witness."

Jeff ground his teeth. "James could be confused."

Broker nodded. "Maybe they got into it again, struggled and Keith's pistol went off. Caren got in between and slipped. That's plausible in this weather."

"Doesn't add up. Kit choking," said Jeff. Broker had told him about the incident. "What happened to that piece of money?" he asked.

Broker grimaced. "Dropped it. Now with the snow . . ."

"Worry about that later. One thing at a time," said Jeff. More radio traffic. They listened to cop blank verse and tried to piece it together.

A highway patrolman responding to Broker's 911 call had spotted Keith's Ford and James's station wagon at the lodge across the highway from the park. While he waited for backup, he'd grilled the Naniboujou clerk. That's when James's 911 call came into the dispatcher, in Grand Marais. But James hadn't given them a location. By then, two cops were headed up the ridge acting on the clerk's story.

And suddenly, the FBI pops up on the phones, into their radio net and are in phone contact with James. They worked a radio relay with the officers through Grand Marais.

The feds threw a long shadow of big-time, big-city trouble across Keith Angland.

The state trooper and a Deputy Torgerson found James, wounded, on the trail. Torgerson had put a call into Devil's Rock First Responders when he went in after James. The medics came in by a shorter back road and stretchered James out. Angland was now the focus of the rescue. Possibly injured, suffering shock or remorse, stuck down on the lip of the Kettle. The only qualified police climbers were hours away in Duluth or up in Ontario. No time. The medics had brought a rope. Torgerson, who had a lot of water rescue time in the coast guard, went down after Keith.

James was already en route by ambulance to the clinic in Grand Marais when Jeff wheeled into C. R. Magney. Cruisers from Cook and Lake Counties and the state patrol were slewed at odd angles, motors still running. Silently rotating police flashers lashed the thickening snow and streams of exhaust. Lurid swipes of blue and red.

Before they had time to get out, the radio crackled. "At the Kettle, say again," said Jeff.

"Jeff, we got him out. Lyle's about froze. We're bringing them out the back way, by the gravel pit."

Jeff keyed the mike. "Meet you there." He wheeled the Bronco into a fishtailing U-turn and aimed back for the highway.

"But I don't want anything for the pain," insisted Tom James, who had avoided physical pain all of his life and now was catching up fast. Tom made the doctor nervous; the way he sat up, supporting himself on his hands, staring at his bare legs stretched out on a gurney in the Sawtooth Mountain Clinic. And the way he held his coat in a death grip in his bloodstained hand.

The doctor removed the soaked compress the paramedics had tied on his left calf. Angland's bullet had gouged a small trench from the fleshy muscle. There was enough concavity for him to see tiny bits of veins in the welling blood, threads from his pants.

"I'd better freeze it," the doctor said. "This is going to hurt when I clean it out."

"No," said Tom. He stared into the doctor's blue eyes and saw them waver ever so slightly. Sweat formed on the physician's upper lip. Tom had a sudden insight that the doc was uneasy, working on someone who wasn't numbed.

More new knowledge.

"Tell me everything you're doing," said Tom.

"What?" said the doctor, blinking sweat.

"I want to watch," said Tom.

They hauled Keith Angland out strapped in a Stokes rescue stretcher. He still wore the sodden dark wool overcoat under a blanket. Ice polyps swung in his blond hair thick as Popsicles. With his arms crossed rigidly across his chest, he looked part embalmed pharaoh, part demented yeti.

Snow blazed point blank. A group of cops huddled to form a windbreak for Lyle Torgerson. Out of stretchers. Lyle had to walk. "Damn tricky," Lyle chattered from his blankets.

"What happened to his pistol?" asked Jeff.

"Dropped it in the Kettle," said Torgerson.

"He say anything?" asked Jeff.

Torgerson shook his head. "Just keeps staring at his hand."

Broker envied him. Growing up, he'd always wondered what it would be like, going down there into the Kettle.

Broker knelt to the stretcher. "Keith, what happened?"

Keith stared. Jellied eyes. His face looked like something bird-eaten and dead a month on the beach. Broker looked away, but an eloquent controlled horror in Angland's fixed gaze seduced him back.

"Keith, it's all right. We got you . . ." Jeff's voice startled him, jogged his memory. Broker remembered a steamy afternoon in thick brush near Cam Lo; a soldier desperately trying to carry water to a buddy in his bare cupped hands.

Keith protested with a violent wrench of his ice-fringed head. Like burned-out stars, his eyes sought out Broker. Then he collapsed back into the blankets. One of the paramedics said, "We better look at that hand."

"Huh?" Broker grunted.

"His forearm and hand's all fucked up." The medic peeled back the blanket, eased up Keith's sleeve. Broker grimaced. The claw marks started halfway up Keith's inner left forearm and ripped down into his palm. Curls of flesh more than an inch deep, exposing muscle and tendon shriveled in gruesome ripples. Then Broker saw the shreds of red flesh splayed under Keith's fingernails.

"Jesus, Mary, and Joseph," muttered Jeff. He crossed himself. The medic felt for leverage on the clamped fist. Dead fingers, white as folded piano keys. The medic bore down with both hands. Finally the stiff fingers parted.

Broker studied the pattern of the wounds and revisited the fatal undertow in Keith's eyes. Then he lowered his gaze to Caren's gold wedding band, imbedded in a thick paste of blood in Keith's shredded palm.

Speechless, Broker and Jeff exchanged grim stares. Then, quickly, they helped load Keith in the waiting ambulance. As it pulled away, a cop waved Jeff to a county cruiser. Broker followed, heard the radio squawk:

"Jeff, you gotta get to the clinic fast. We been invaded," yelled Madge, the Grand Marais radio dispatcher.

"Define . . . invaded," gasped Jeff.

"Feds."

A black helicopter had landed in Grand Marais, smack in the parking lot of the Sawtooth Mountain Clinic.

On the way in, the dispatcher debriefed them. The invaders were FBI, agents from St. Paul and Duluth. The chopper was Army Reserve out of the Twin Cities, up at the Duluth Air Base for winter ice testing.

As the caravan from the Kettle drove up the Gunflint Trail, they saw the Blackhawk, dark and sleek, props drooping in the moderating snow like a steel dragonfly.

Two FBI men stood guard at the helicopter. The side hatch was open, and Keith, on the stretcher, was visible inside. Like a Praetorian, one of the feds held an Uzi at port arms across his chest. The other held a small radio. The freezing mob from the Kettle got out of their cars and started toward the helicopter. When the fed with the Uzi stepped forward, Jeff, incensed, withered him. "Point that thing down range, sonny, or you're under arrest."

Helicopters. State-of-the-art weapons and communications gear in plain view. Broker and Jeff exchanged squints. The feds loved this. Called it going "high profile."

"Who's in charge?" demanded Jeff.

"Garrison. He's inside," said the Uzi holder.

They went inside. Nurses and orderlies stood in the corridor by the reception desk, stymied and blinded by a blaze of FBI badges. When Doc Rivard started out to check Keith in the chopper, one of the feds accompanied him.

"Wait a minute, hold on you," yelled Jeff at the agent.

"FBI. Outa the fucking way," the agent stated coolly, holding his badge up.

Jeff ripped off his fur cap and flung it on the floor. "My county, goldarnit. Nobody move."

"Yeah," said the very worked-looking state patrol trooper who'd partnered with Lyle Torgerson up to the Kettle.

"Yeah," chattered Lyle Torgerson, throwing off his blankets.

Five more feds came down the hall in a pack, surrounding Tom James, who sat in a wheelchair. They were configured in a politically correct tartan that looked like big-city America slouching toward the millennium. One black, one Chicano, one Asian woman and two white men. Broker had always disliked government types and considered them beyond pigment and gender. Their pinstripes were branded clear through their skin and onto their internal organs.

James sat mum, clutching his brown parka in his arms. He'd been hastily outfitted from the clinic lost and found. A blanket was thrown over his shoulders, old felt boot liners on his feet. A blaze orange wool hunting cap on his head. Bare shins—one of them tightly bandaged—showed below his hospital gown. Broker was stunned to see a sturdy armored vest Velcroed around his torso. The feds formed a human barrier around him.

"What the heck?" Jeff pointed at James and thrust out his chin.

The Head Fed was a rangy six-foot-two silverback in a dark gray wool suit, a metallic silk gray tie, and two-hundred-dollar shoes. Well preserved, midfifties. His creased tanned face was out of place in winter. He affected a brown felt 1940s hat, the brim turned down over one eye.

Looking more like someone who drew his pay from Allan Pinkerton than from Louis Freeh, he said, "Hi, boys." Out came the magic badge. "Lorn Garrison, Special Agent, temporarily working out of St. Paul. Who are you?" Easy smile over an easy southern accent. The motley crew of freezing Cook County lawmen appeared to amuse him.

Jeff, hands on hips, blocked their path: "What are you doing?"

"James is a federal witness. And I'm taking Angland in for probable cause. Exigent circumstances," said Garrison evenly. He withdrew a folded sheet of paper from his suit coat pocket and slapped it into Jeff's hand. "And if that doesn't cool your jets, here's a writ of habeas for them both, signed by a federal judge in Duluth an hour ago."

"Bull," protested Jeff, "Angland is my prisoner and James is *my* witness."

"Don't look like you booked Angland yet to me," observed Garrison. "Read that piece of paper and be warned."

Broker lunged forward and grabbed at James's throat. "Where'd my kid find a hundred-dollar bill to choke on, you fucker?" James shied away, terrified. The biggest fed jumped forward.

But the powerful hands that spun Broker out of the way were Jeff's. "You're a civilian, Broker; stay clear," he admonished.

Garrison pointed at Broker. "Who's this?"

"He's with me." Jeff was mad.

"You better get him, and yourself, under control," advised Garrison. He narrowed his eyes. "This is federal business."

"Get off it," stated Jeff. "We've just had a woman maybe murdered and you're taking my witness and my suspect."

Garrison whipped out a cell phone and consulted a small note pad. "It's Jeffords, Sheriff right? End of the World County. Nowhere, Minnesota."

Jeff waved his arm. His cops surged forward and took a blocking stance across the hall.

Garrison smiled tightly. "Sheriff, have you ever talked, person to person, with Janet Reno." He poised his finger over the phone buttons.

"Oh, *c'mon*," protested Jeff.

"I shit you not, pardner," said Garrison offering the phone to Jeff.

The silence in the clinic hallway sharpened the contrasting parties to the lopsided standoff. One side shivered from the cold with icicles literally dripping from their noses. The other exuded steely-eyed imperial high confidence. Warm and dry, they were organized in a wedge formation around James and the wheelchair. The agent who stood next to Special Agent Garrison wore body armor under her London Fog trench coat and rested an Uzi automatic on her hip.

Jeff stared at the legal writ in his hand. He knew the judge who had signed it. Garrison, sensing an opening, closed up his phone and moved closer. "Look, I don't like it either, hotdogging it in your jurisdiction," he temporized.

"The law—" Jeff insisted.

"C'mon, Jeffords. There's the law and then there's The Big Law, know what I mean." He wrote a number on a card and handed it to Jeff.

"I'm going to want to interview him," insisted Jeff.

"Sure, that's my direct line," said Garrison. "Call me in St. Paul."

They were done in. Out of fight. And the feds had the writ, signed by a judge. Exhausted, battered by the cold, sniffling and red faced, they stood by, numb, while the feds formed a human shield around James and rushed him out the front door. The doctor came into the ER, shivering. "The one in the chopper has frostbite on his fingers. He has to get to a full-care hospital. Either they take him or we call Lifelift out of Duluth."

As the person formerly known as Tom James rolled past them he couldn't resist flipping Broker the bird and sneering, "Give my love to your fat little kid."

"I told you," Broker seethed to Jeff between clenched teeth.

"I heard it," said Jeff.

When they hoisted Tom into the helicopter, he saw Angland and had a moment of fright, fearing Angland would accuse him, blab his version. Wrapped in blankets, Angland's eyelids just fluttered. Possibly sedated, he didn't seem to know where he was.

Tom leaned back, savored the moment. He'd never been in a helicopter before. Guns. Radios crackling. Sizzling circuits. *Star Wars* lights winking on the control panel. All to guard him. This was like . . . Tom Clancy.

**25**

Tom had wind in his hair, playing chicken with the world, driving a coast-to-coast convertible orgasm.

He had his own call sign: Tango. If he stepped outside the secure house, Lorn keyed his little black radio and said, "Tango is walking in the campus. Look sharp up on the ridge."

Juice.

How had he lived his life without it. Now he saw the world through the eyes of a tiger. Like in the poem. Stalking the burning night.

His posture changed. The strength of his grip. The way he walked would change too, when his leg healed. He was becoming A Force to Be Dealt With.

And he was gambling for high stakes, stringing a U.S. attorney along to make a deal, betting on the outcome of a videotape he had never seen. The clock was running. Keith Angland was in St. Paul Regions Hospital, under guard, recovering from hypothermia and frostbite. Tom had given up the locker key; an agent from Duluth had retrieved the video and was en route.

He needed that tape to be as good as Caren said it was; so he could get his deal before Angland starting talking. If the tape was good, Tom could deny anything Angland said.

C'mon tape.

Tom had one real worry. Broker, the suspicious bastard. What if Angland talked to Broker? Could Broker and that North Woods sheriff find a way to screw up his deal?

His flesh wound, just a deep scratch, was his proud badge of courage. It had been cleaned and freshly bandaged by a doctor earlier in the morning. The medic said he could walk on it if he used common sense. Garrison kept him under guard, at a safe house tucked into the river bottom at the base of a wooded bluff on the Wisconsin side of the Saint Croix River. They were about five miles south of the Hudson Bridge. Afton, Minnesota, was just across the thin ice. Tom searched for Caren Angland's house, a toy cube in the distance, against the gray mist of the Minnesota shore.

Two agents stood guard on the cabin's first floor, trading off with two more who had cold duty in parkas, pile caps, and mittens with the trigger finger cut out so they could handle scoped rifles in the surrounding woods.

The house was stocked to accommodate a family, so Tom found needle and thread in his room. The first night he carefully unraveled the lining to his parka and tucked the hundred-dollar bills around the hem. Slowly, carefully, he resewed the lining. The insulated padding disguised the paper and camouflaged the rustle.

Now. Get rid of the envelope he'd used to hold some of the bills. He went into the bathroom. About to tear it up and flush it. Then he noticed the return address.

MAJOR NINA PRYCE
OPERATION CONSTANT GUARD
APO AE O9787
CJCMTF (CAMP McGOVERN)

That, he thought, might be useful. He tucked it in his pocket. Broker and his kid presumed to rob his glory. His desire to strike back at them was a flaw that would get him in trouble. It flared up once an hour.

"Control that," he muttered aloud. First get your deal.

Waiting.

Lorn allowed him to check his voice mail at his apartment. Every TV station in town, plus CNN, had logged in, plus the *Minneapolis Star Tribune* and the *Duluth News Tribune*, the other two big papers in the state. Some messages he saved to listen to over and over. Others he erased. The one from Layne Wanger he saved: "Hey, Tom, sure would like to talk to you," etc. Sprinkled between the business calls were hushed inquiries from Ida Rain:

"Tom, if you hear this please know that I understand how difficult it is for you to communicate right now. How is your leg? We're all so proud of you. Just let me know you're all right. Love you. Ida."

God. He curled his lip. Listen to her. Bubbling with . . . pride. She was probably yakking to everybody in the newsroom how she'd been intimate with Tom James. *Hi Ida. Bye Ida.*

Erase. Erase.

When he wasn't monitoring the calls he read about himself in the papers. The story was still sketchy. Mainly it came from the Cook County sheriff, Tom Jeffords, because no one else involved would talk to the press. In Jeffords's account, Tom assumed the role of mystery witness and victim in the events at the Devil's Kettle that resulted in the alleged murder of Caren Angland and the arrest of her husband by the FBI. Tom had been whisked into hiding by the feds because he was involved in their chain of evidence against Keith Angland.

But the feds had taken Angland into custody for racketeering, not the murder of his wife. It was a trade-off. The feds could use the RICO statutes to ask for stiffer sentencing than the state could, even under its first-degree-murder statute. Proving first-degree murder against Angland would be difficult.

And the feds weren't going to share their witness.

Jeffords put it this way: "All parties assume Keith Angland killed his wife, but without a body, a witness, a weapon, or any material evidence other than a 911 tape that doesn't mention Angland by name—it falls in a legal crack—technically, no crime was committed. We have to carry Caren Angland as missing, presumed dead."

No crime was committed.

More magic.

The safe house was outfitted with a computer, printer, and copier-fax. Happily, the computer was on-line, so Tom could browse the Web. Mainly, he scouted out information on the Witness Protection Program. Or WITSEC, as Lorn referred to it.

He didn't really need to bone up on WITSEC. He'd read a book about the U.S. Marshals Service in the last year, and he had a funda-mental knowledge of the program.

If the tape was good, he'd have no problem getting in.

He'd be all right. Just had to be patient and *don't do anything dumb*. That's how most people got caught. They did something dumb.

Tom's dumb hang-up was a recurring fantasy. He imagined Broker's chubby baby, now big as a cow, sitting in the woods, at the cistern where he'd hidden the money. One by one, she ate the bills.

That's really dumb, Tom, he told himself. But every hour the crazy image rolled by, like a goddamn crosstown bus.

He found himself wondering if the kid was precocious and could communicate with her father. Tap her foot like a trained pony. Tell him what had happened in the workshop.

Broker had put his hands on Tom's throat, wanted to hold him on suspicion.

There it was again. Baby Huey, eating his money; crapping green like a goose.

Broker wouldn't be so tough if he weren't worried about his kid all the time. Cops were weird about their kids. He'd done a story on a cop once who got in trouble for running background checks on the boy who was dating his daughter.

He was somebody now. He didn't have to take shit from hicks. Maybe write a little something. Send a note to the fancy pants wife in the army, too. Give her something to think about.

Don't mess with Tom.

Tom opened a new file and began to play with words. Not the straightforward AP style that characterized his reporting. No, this was a mood piece. This was twitchy.

Send a little love note to Broker. And the wife.

Just a page to keep him up nights.

Only mail them if he got into the program.

His fingers flew over the keys, inspired. He went over it a few times, hit the spell check, polished here and there. He scrolled to a clean screen and typed *Phil Broker, General Delivery, Devil's Rock, Minnesota*. Then he typed the wife's military mailing address. Quickly, he printed out the sheets.

The desk contained basic office supplies, which he took to his room, along with the printed material. Using a Kleenex to mask his fingers, he folded the sheets with the writing on it and slid them in envelopes. Then he used a scissors to cut out the addresses. The desk drawer had a Glue Stic, which he used to affix the addresses to the envelopes. There was also a roll of first-class stamps. Recently purchased. Madonna and child. The stick'em kind. No need to lick. Carefully, again employing Kleenex, he stuck one stamp on Broker's envelope, eight on the other.

Now he just had to wait until he could sneak them in the mail. He slipped the envelopes into a copy of *Newsweek* and tucked them under his mattress.

Lorn Garrison sat across the kitchen table, rolling a blue tip safety match in his lips. Ex-smoker. He watched Tom read the stories about

Caren's death and Angland's arrest for the tenth time. Then he leaned over, gathered all the sections and piled them in the wood box. A Franklin woodstove, fire blazing, sat on a pedestal in the center of the room. Lorn bunched one of the sections and tossed it into the flames.

"A little advice," he said. "Our recommendation carries a lot of weight with the U.S. attorney when he makes his decision to put somebody in the program. But the final say is up to the Marshals Service. And they are real sticklers for detail.

"If the marshals see you drooling over your press clippings, they'll figure you've got an ego connection to your past. They won't take a chance on you. Catch my drift."

"Good point." Tom nodded. But he resented the agent messing with him. He asked, "How long since you quit, Lorn?" The agent narrowed his eyes and Tom smiled. "Your fingers are still stained yellow from nicotine. Camels? Unfiltered Luckies? Pall Malls?"

"Pall Malls," said Lorn. "And it's fourteen months." The agent cleared his throat. "This time."

Tom hobbled to the windows and wondered if he could get Lorn Garrison to smoke a cigarette as part of his deal.

Whole pack. One after another.

Tom found it interesting, setting up housekeeping with FBI agents. They had been distant figures when he was a reporter. Their personal manners were always obscure behind a tightly controlled official screen. Now he saw them in a relaxed state. Because the safe house was remote, it was easier to do their own cooking than order out. Surprisingly, the laconic Garrison turned out to be the chef.

This afternoon he planned to make spaghetti. He had slipped a red apron over his pinstripe shirt. And, as a concession to static duty in the safe house, he had removed his tie. The apron bulged over the big pistol on his hip.

Seeing him standing there, wincing a little as he methodically sliced onions, reminded Tom of a scene in *The Godfather*. Cooking for an army of hoods who had gone to the mattresses.

"What kind of gun is that?" asked Tom.

"Pistol," corrected Lorn patiently.

"Okay then, pistol."

"Forty caliber."

"Why not a nine millimeter? I thought everybody used nine millimeters?"

Lorn looked warily from side to side, a conditioned reflex. "Nine millimeter is for pussies," the agent said phlegmatically.

Tom grinned. Lorn was the kind of material that would make a great color piece on the changing of the guard at the FBI. Probably shook J. Edgar's dainty little hand when he received his badge. Wonder if he's ever thought about that dainty little hand buttoning on a dress. But that was too over the top for Garrison. That would probably get Tom knocked on his ass. So he pursued the gun talk: "Why for pussies?"

Lorn smoothly moved the sliced onions aside with the edge of a long butcher knife and assessed a green pepper. "'Cause it's a woman's gun. Light, to fit in their nice little hands. Not too loud. Not too much recoil. Makes tidy little holes. You know; like we don't really want to hurt anybody." A serpent of mannered distaste coiled in his border state accent.

"Can you carry any kind of gu—pistol you want?"

"Forty cal. is the current policy."

"But if you could pack anything you wanted, what would it be?"

Lorn set the knife down and wiped his hands on a dishtowel. Then he carefully unbuttoned his cuffs and rolled up his sleeves. His forearms were heavy, thick with black hair, liver spots, and freckles. A fading blue tattoo in the shape of a globe, anchor and eagle showed just below his rolled cuff.

"Forty-five." Lorn was emphatic.

"Isn't that kind of dated?" observed Tom.

"Yeah," Lorn grinned. "Make a hole in you the size of this." He held up a gnarled right fist.

"You've actually seen that?"

Lorn Garrison's piercing eyes passed right through Tom for a second and then he turned back to his knife and cutting board. Tom thought, So you've seen people shot. Big deal. I've *been* shot. And I've seen Caren Angland try to fly.

Tom stood up. "I'm going out for a walk. The doctor said it was okay if I take it easy."

"Take Terry. Just stay down near the shore," said Lorn.

Before he left, he couldn't resist dialing up his messages one more time. The first saved message was from Ida. "If you need to talk, Tom, I'm always here . . ."

He tapped number three twice, which speeded up the message, then he erased it.

Agent Terry was a scrubbed, light-skinned black guy with freckles. Real in-shape. Like Tom was going to be when he became Danny Storey. They were about fifty yards down the beach, making slow progress through driftwood. Tom marveled how fluid his imagination had become. He fantasized Ida Rain's flawless body, naked and head-less, skipping in the cold. Conversationally, he asked, "Hey, Terry, you ever screw an ugly woman?"

Terry quipped, poker-faced, "When I was a little kid I remember seeing a few ugly Negro women. As I got older I might have seen one or two plain black women. But now, I know for a fact, there is no such thing as an ugly woman of color—so you must be referring to white women."

Tom grinned. "But if you wound up with an ugly one—you think making her wear a mask would improve things?" For the rest of the walk, Tom gave Ida back her head—because she gave such great blowjobs—but he made her wear a mask.

After their walk, Tom asked Terry how he stayed in such good shape. So, downstairs, Terry changed to a sweat suit and showed Tom the calisthenics routine he used on the road. It involved stretching, push-ups, crunches, a jump rope and weights. Terry was coaching Tom through the exercises, a little impressed because Tom was taking notes, when cold gravel scattered outside. The agent from Duluth wheeled up to the house with the tape.

Lorn, Tom, and Agent Terry gathered before the TV/VCR in the living room. Front row seats. The others sat in back. Terry inserted the tape in a Play Pack cassette and pushed it in.

"Okay," said Lorn. "Let's see what you've got."

Terry thumbed the remote. The blinds were pulled. A pack of Red Hot Blues corn chips was open on the coffee table. Diet Cokes had been set out.

The mosaic of static on the screen transformed into a basement still life featuring a couch, a coffee table and an easy chair. One minute passed. Two. Garrison cleared his throat. Tom began to see himself employed by Prison Industries at Stillwater Prison. As Garrison started to turn to Tom—

*Keith Angland walked onto the screen followed by a short older man. Keith sat on the couch against a background of dark paneling. His knobby elbows jutted from a polo shirt and rested on his knees. He smoked a cigar. So did the husky balding man in a cardigan who took the chair across from him. The older man had a scarf thrown shawl fashion around his throat and shoulders. Little white numbers ran in the corner of the screen establishing the time and date.*

*A bottle and glasses sat on the coffee table between them. Angland poured two shots of clear liquor and they downed their drinks. The other man set down his glass, leaned forward and placed his hand on Angland's shoulder. "Fuck 'em. What did they do for you. They never appreciated you. It's hard, I know, Keith. But you're doing the smart thing," he said in a gravel voice.*

"Bingo, that's Kagin," said Lorn quietly.

*On the screen they made small talk. Then they both stood up. Caren's ghost appeared. Her fixed smile looked like a still photograph pasted in the animated footage. She had on the same fashionably baggy denim jacket she'd worn on the day she died.*

Terry shook his head sympathetically. "Goddamn man, goddamn," he said softly.

"Shhhh," said Lorn.

*Voices bantered, tinny amateur audio.*

*"I'm going to Hudson. Do you need anything special?" she asked.*

*"Nah, we're good," said Keith.*

*Caren departed, and they made more small talk, about remodeling basements. A third man entered the frame. He was heavyset, with ringlets of dark hair, and he wheezed when he said, "She's gone."*

*"Bring it in," said Kagin.*

*The third man continued to wheeze as he hauled a large suitcase onto the carpet in front of Angland.* The same suitcase Tom buried in the woods.

*The older guy, Kagin, chided the Wheezer. "Shit, Tony, you're outa shape, ain't that fuckin' heavy."*

*"Twenny-five bricks is always heavy," protested the Wheezer.*

"Bricks?" said Tom aloud.

"Shhh," said Lorn again. But he came forward in his chair and reached for the telephone.

*On-screen, the wheezing man popped open the suitcase and proceeded to stack compact bundles on the coffee table. "Your five," he said to Kagin. "Rest is for you," he said to Keith. "Now who's the rat?"*

*While Kagin stacked the money bundles into a gym bag, Angland reached down and flipped a magazine open on the coffee table. He tossed some papers to Kagin.*

*A photograph. Stapled sheets of paper.*

*Angland explained. "Transcript of the wiretap the task force put on your organization." He tapped the photograph. "I told you not to do any business with this guy on his phone line, or in his living room."*

*Kagin picked it up. "Alex, Alex." He pursed his lips and shook his head sadly.*

Lorn was talking on the phone in high spirits. "Sharkey, Yeah. I'm watching it. Forget Angland. Grab your dick, boy. This is Chicago, big time. I got Kagin and guess who? Only *Tony fucking Sporta* giving a suitcase full of money to Angland for Gorski's ID. I shit you not. They are dividing it up before my eyes."

Tom listened to Lorn with one ear and the tape with the other. *On the tape, Kagin studied the picture. "Who are these other guys?"*

*"FBI agents," said Angland.*

*"And they pose for pictures like this, huh. Lookit them. All grins, like they shot a big deer or something?"*

*"Right. Celebrating after taking down a big score. Except it's a lot of product, your product they confiscated in Chicago. Before I threw them some curves."*

*"An' we 'preciate that, Keith, all you done. Shepherding through those three shipments," said Tony the Wheezer.*

*And Kagin, still staring at the picture, shook his head. "Somebody should tell those guys it's not real smart to be taking pictures," he grumbled.* Lorn and Terry exchanged incredulous expressions and burst into laughter.

*On the screen, Angland said, "They first squeezed him in Brighton Beach. He was stooling on you regular in Chicago and kept doing it when you brought him up here."*

*Kagin said, "This is all good stuff here. But before the others will accept you, you gotta take a blood test." He tapped the picture with a stubby finger. "If you're coming in with us, you gotta whack this creep."*

*Angland shrugged. "Understood. I'll handle it."*

"Bingo," crowed Lorn. "Tom, buddy, you just swept the Oscars."

Tom grinned. Best Actor.

*On the screen they were now talking about money.*

*"It's hunnerd percent pure. No fluorescent, unmarked; it's all washed through the Red, White and Green Pizza chain in Illinois, Iowa and Michigan," said Tony Sporta.*

"They just opened up here," blurted Tom.

"Yeah," said Terry. "We think that's their distribution network for powdered coke. They did it that way in Jersey."

"Shhhh," said Lorn.

*"You count it all yourself?" asked Angland.*

*"Shit no," said Kagin. "We run it through a currency counter and weigh it. Ten bricks is what—Hey, Tony. What is ten bricks?"*

*"Twenny-two pounds. Ten thousand one-hunnerd-dollar bills is twenny-two pounds; pile about thirteen inches on a side and four and a half inches deep. That's ten bricks," wheezed Sporta.*

*"Yeah," said Kagin, with a profligate wave of his palm. "We only handle fifties and hundreds. The fives, tens and twenties we burn. Just not worth it at this level."*

*"Burn. No shit?" said Angland.*

*"Yeah, I got this fifty-five-gallon drum at the summer place I got on Lake Michigan. You know. Roast wieners. Have a few beers. I'll show it to you when you come down to Chicago to pick up your next load."*

*Angland poured another round of drinks. Kagin opened a slim portfolio and slid sheets of paper across the coffee table. "This is where the niggers are shipping that crack bullshit to in St. Paul out of L.A. and Detroit. You go bust their animal asses. Make you look good at work, eh?"*

*"This is fine, thanks," said Angland, carefully folding the sheets of paper.*

*"Good," said Kagin. He coughed and waved his cigar. "Let's go up for some air, huh—my eyes are burning up down here."*

The three men walked off screen. Tom stared at the couch, the table, the paneled wall and the suitcase full of money. "Twenny bricks" remained in the suitcase. According to Sporta, that was forty-four pounds of hundred-dollar bills. *Two million dollars.*

Tom squirmed in his chair and crossed his legs. He was actually getting a hard on. Terry stopped the tape and thumbed rewind. Lorn was saying, ". . . and bring some equipment so we can copy this thing." He turned, one hand over the receiver and spoke to Tom. "Sharkey says you done good. I got a feeling you're flying first class."

Tom endeavored to look like a dutiful citizen. Lorn was back talking to a U.S. attorney in charge of a midwestern task force.

"Tony doesn't have Kagin's balls. He's too old to do more time. He's got a bad ticker. He definitely could flip. Come over here and have a look at this thing. Get a search warrant for Angland's house to see if that money is still there. Right. See ya."

An hour and a half later, Tom watched a dozen justice department attorneys huddle around the VCR after viewing the tape. A crew was making duplicates. The Minnesota U.S. attorney was there grinning his slightly bucktoothed grin. But Joe Sharkey, the prosecutor out of Chicago, was the one cloud walking.

Sharkey was the man to make the deal. Short, intense, with pinstripes on everything he wore, including his socks, he strutted, with his thumbs hooked in his pinstriped suspenders. The other suits in the room congratulated him in awed voices, "Joe, this is a career-defining case."

Sharkey set his narrow jaw in his knife-edged face. And he'd say, "If Sporta flips on Kagin, we'll be into the Italians *and* the Russians. Jesus . . . they'll have to build a whole new Marion, we'll get so many bad guys."

The lawyer gave off an unholy glow, like, boy, am I gonna look good at the press conference when I spring this one. Already dreaming of a corner office at Justice.

Tom continued to stand quietly, meekly, reverently. Until finally, the attorney let Lorn Garrison lead him across the room to meet the man who delivered the tape into his hands.

"Homage is due," said Sharkey, throwing a wiry arm over Tom's shoulders and hoisting his can of Coke.

"Here, here," saluted the room full of feds.

The attorney smiled broadly. "You want to disappear, Mr. James— shazam. I personally sprinkle you with pixie dust."

"But I still have to pass with the Marshals," Tom wondered aloud.

"Hey, you're not some bottom-feeding thug," said Sharkey. "The tape is pure platinum. You're going to be flying up there right behind the pilot, trust me. You're gone."

Tom smiled modestly.

*Twenny bricks.*

That night Agent Terry escorted Tom back into St. Paul, so he could remove clothes and toilet articles from his apartment. When Terry used the bathroom, Tom slipped into the corridor and dropped his letters down the mail chute. Then Tom packed a single bag and never looked back.

Shazam.

*All his life he had come up here and watched the Devil's Kettle lash the Brule in an endless crack-the-whip against the granite walls, then disappear into the depths of the earth. It had always been a mystery. As a little boy, he believed a monster lived down there, thrashing in the raging current. When I grow up, he'd told himself, I'm gonna catch that monster.*

A clump of iris turned black on the snowy rock in the center of the Brule River. The rock overlooked the pothole and was assumed to be the place where Keith Angland threw his wife to her death.

Or, more accurately, to the first stage of her death, mused Broker as he rehashed the conclusions he and Jeff had aired earlier today. He stood on the observation platform over the Kettle, rolling an unlit cigar in his mouth.

Apparently she didn't go in all the way, so Keith had to risk his own life, climb down, and shove her the rest of the way, inch by inch, while she clawed his arm to bloody ribbons.

Of course, given the terrain and the weather, this method of coup de grace virtually insured he would need assistance to climb back out. That, or take his chances getting down the icy cascade, then off the partially frozen and extremely treacherous river.

No one seemed to remember that Keith had a weapon. Even though he'd shot James. If he was so bent on killing Caren, who was clinging to the rocks about thirty feet below, why not lean over and squeeze off one or two rounds and let gravity take it from there. Keith had a basement full of marksmanship trophies.

And why would Keith shoot a reporter and then let him get away? Keith ran marathons. James was the original couch potato.

The theory Jeff and Broker suggested was more plausible: a confused struggle in the snow on slippery footing. But two of the parties to that scenario had survived, and neither of them would talk about it.

Broker rotated his neck and shoulders. Working out the tension. You gave up this line of work, remember, he told himself.

*And then—the FBI touches down like a tornado, sweeps up Keith and James, and disappears. They don't even interrogate Jeff or me. If I was working this case I'd damn sure want to know why Caren would drive three hundred miles to see an ex-husband she hadn't spoken to in five, six years . . .*

Broker was finding his way out of the wind tunnel of shock and remorse. Hearing old music; the compulsion to solve something. Two days in a row he had left Kit with Jeff's wife, Sally, and had climbed the trail up to the Kettle.

A lot of people were making the trek. A few were gawkers. But mostly they were women paying their respects. After Duluth television sent a remote team to film on this spot, women came to lay flowers. The story rolled down a familiar nightmare alley—abused wife dies at the hand of her violent husband.

The reporter had done her homework and pieced together a story from interviews with cops and medics who had been involved in the rescue at the Kettle. She depicted Caren running for her life from her current husband to the protection of her previous husband. The TV bullshit incensed Broker deeply.

Especially the nuance of unrequited romance that connected him to the story like black crepe crime-scene tape.

The first night was the worst. Caren visited his sleepless thoughts as he lay awake listening to the rise and fall of Kit's breathing in the crib next to him. He imagined Caren, perfectly preserved, in a time capsule of ice water, deep within the granite folds of the earth, or five miles out, gently turning in the crystalline bowels of Superior.

Her blue lips stuck on the request: *Phil, I need your help.*

But then, he could reduce it to a much simpler, visceral knot in his stomach: Kit turning blue, choking, and that smug weasel, James, knowing why.

The feds pulled a curtain of official silence over the death at Devil's Kettle. After a few calls to the federal prosecutor in Minneapolis, Hustad, the new Cook County attorney, saw it was futile to build a case against Keith Angland. Tom James was unavailable, held incommunicado in federal custody.

The word drifting up the cop jungle-telegraph to Jeff was: Witness Protection for James. Caren's death was lost—but not forgotten, the feds insisted—in the shadow of something big.

The story rolled from Duluth downstate and washed against an official stonewall at the FBI and the U.S. attorney's office and lost momentum. After a few days, the pilgrims stopped coming to the Kettle. Caren's story, like all news stories, ended.

America shopped toward Christmas. Life went on at the decibel level of a radio commercial written for third grade comprehension.

Sound bite metaphysics.

Caren was dead.

Shit happens.

Blip.

Unconcerned, the Kettle sucked the Brule River underground as it had done since the glaciers piled up the ridge, too powerful and unapproachable to give up its secret.

Broker walked back down the trail, rolling his shoulders, working out the kinks. He snipped a soggy inch off his cigar and stuck it back in his mouth.

Jeff called that night: Quick, turn on the tube. Duluth. Channel 13. With Kit under his arm, Broker tapped the remote. The opaque gray screen turned into the Minneapolis U.S. attorney. He stood at a podium in front of a phalanx of Cheshire-smiling feds. He said that Caren Angland had not died in vain. She had provided taped evidence—through the intercession of Tom James—to a federal investigation. Based on that evidence, her husband, Keith, was being questioned by a federal grand jury for conspiring to murder a federal informant.

The conference veered out of control when the U.S. attorney confirmed that, yes, a human tongue had been delivered in a fake bomb to the FBI office in the St. Paul Federal Building a week ago. He termed this "a taunt from the Russian mob." He added that the presumed-dead informant's name and return address were on the package. And that the man's car and some of his clothing had been found in the Saint Croix River, near Scandia, Minnesota.

Testing at the FBI lab in Quantico, Virginia, confirmed that the tongue belonged to a male.

Then the U.S. attorney introduced a federal strike force prosecutor, a dapper, short man named Joe Sharkey, from Chicago. Sharkey explained that Keith was just one target of his investigation, and a minor one. A Chicago mobster captured talking to Keith on Caren's tape had copped a plea and turned federal witness.

"How big is this?" asked a reporter.

"Big as Sammy Gravanno. We're looking at an interlocking case involving the Italian and Russian Mafias."

The report added a local follow-up, querying a spokesman for the St. Paul Police Department about Keith Angland. "That's a federal matter, no comment," said a dour department media representative.

As soon as the report ended, Jeff called back. "Holy cow. Keith trafficking in human tongues? Two flavors of Mafia? She ever mentioned a tape?" he asked.

"This is the first I heard," said Broker.

"She must have wanted you to see it. Why?" asked Jeff.

"Don't know. But James does. He knew about the tape. He had to be talking to the FBI. How else could they come out of nowhere so quick."

"And I was right there, big as a barn, wearing a badge. If I'd of known what kind of danger Caren was in . . . ," mulled Jeff.

"Probable cause, at least," said Broker.

"You bet. I'd have cuffed Keith before he cuffed me. And I would have put some people around Caren—fast."

"But you couldn't, because we didn't know where she was."

"James could have told us. But he didn't," said Jeff.

"Yeah, I think maybe he started out working on a story and ended up working on something else," said Broker.

"Like what?"

"What did Kit choke on?"

"Hmm . . . ," said Jeff.

"It's about money," said Broker.

The books were all read. The tippy-cup finished. He sat in the rocking chair with the weight of the child on his shoulder. Her vulnerable breath rose and fell against his throat, magically clean and innocent. Broker rocked and thought.

On a night fourteen years ago, in this very room, which was smaller then, just a shack, Keith Angland showed up to go hunting without his gear. No rifle, no hunting clothes.

*"The strain is getting to her, you working all this hairy undercover stuff. You're never there. You never talk to her."* And finally. *"I love her and you don't,"* he'd said. *"What you love is the action."* And he'd been right. Then.

In fourteen years, the world had turned upside down. Keith had been too rigid to bend with the times. He had cracked wide open and madness and murder had gushed out. And Broker . . .

Broker rose slowly from the rocking chair, carefully balancing the sleeping baby on his shoulder, and walked the length of the spacious living room to the windows overlooking the lake. The cabin where he and Keith had their showdown over Caren was now a three-bedroom lake home.

And it did resemble a mead hall, complete to the detail of the snarled dragon's head over the fireplace. One huge high-peaked room, pinned with beams, sited parallel to the shore. The wall that faced the lake was all thermal glass, banks of windows. Opposite the windows three bedrooms and a bath. The tall fireplace dominated one end of the long room, an open kitchen filled the other. He'd never used the big fireplace and was saving that for Christmas. Kit's toys, books, and a rocking chair sat next to an old Franklin stove raised on a dais of tile between the living room area and the kitchen. Where they lived, by the fire.

His hideaway.

By recent occupation, Kit's father was, by some accounts, a pirate.

Now, like a pirate, he brooded from his granite point, down on the rising northwest wind that herded white-plumed six-foot waves into his rocky cove. When the lake whipped up, he fondly remembered illustrations in romantic books for boys: Robert Louis Stevenson's *Kidnapped* or *Treasure Island*. Wind-swept crags. Tempest seas.

Another issue Caren had with him. Never growing up. Chasing adventure.

Two years ago, he had done exactly that. Now he paid his bills with a MasterCard drawn on a bank in Bangkok. For runaround cash he used a VISA attached to a numbered account at the Deutsche Bank in Hong Kong. Funds seeped via electronic interbank transfers into his account in the Grand Marais Bank, always less than $10,000 a transaction.

Rebuilding this house called for real money, so, last year, he'd declared a half million in taxable income. Broker's nest egg was a ton of Vietnamese imperial gold bullion and ancient Cham relics, tucked in a bank vault in Hong Kong.

Broker had found it, dug it up and smuggled it out of Vietnam. His treasure hunt had also turned up a mate. And a child. Had bought him freedom. Room to get away. But it hadn't stopped the world from coming in on him.

He carried Kit to her crib, gently lowered her to her blankets and stuffed animals.

What the hell. A man should be able to handle whatever was in front of him. Kill an enemy, field dress a deer, fix the plumbing, read a rectal thermometer and stay up, worried, all night, with a croupy baby.

Back in the kitchen, he glanced at Nina's picture pinned to the bulletin board. *You stayed on the Widow Maker without getting bucked off, this is your life.*

Across the length of the dark living room, the dragon glinted in tightly wound contortions against the chimney stones. *And this too is your life.* And there was room in his life to find out what really happened out there at the Kettle. He owed Caren that much. Two men could tell him: Keith Angland and Tom James.

But the privateer in him counseled that something vital had been missing from the feds' news conference: Buried in this tragic human riddle there had to be a hell of a lot of money.

In the morning, after Kit was changed and fed, he dressed her in layers of Polarfleece, mittens, a scarf, hat and stuck her feet in lined, black rubber boots decorated with raised reliefs of chunky dinosaurs.

Outside, the day was overcast, crisp. They barely cast shadows. The thermometer on the porch pointed to twenty-six degrees. First, he carried her through the motions of filling the bird feeder with sunflower seeds.

"Dees," piped Kit.

"Right, gotta feed the dees." She liked to watch the chickadees zoom around the feeder he'd planted outside her bedroom window.

Then, he opened the door to the workshop, let Kit waddle inside, shut the door, turned on the light and checked the bench and the floor for stray pieces of hundred-dollar bills.

Nothing.

Squatting, he tugged Kit's scarf down, so her face was more than an eye slit and said, "I don't suppose you want to tell me why Tom James gave you a hundred-dollar bill to choke on, do you?" Kit exuded a trickle of foggy breath. He picked her up and carried her outside.

"Okay. Here's the thing. I dropped that chewed lump of money around here just before it snowed and we're going to find it. Ordinarily, I'd shovel the snow, but today we're going to do something different."

Broker went into the garage and returned with a regular rake and a leaf rake. Kit sat down and began pawing at the snow. She raised a snowy mitten and tentatively touched it to her red tongue.

Broker raked; he figured the piece of currency would look like a clip of frozen broccoli.

"I don't really expect to find it. But if I did find it, and if I find Tom James, I'd show it to him and ask him how he thinks it got stuck in your throat."

Kit pushed another handful of snow at her mouth. Broker paused and studied her round face.

"It's called making a start," he explained. There was a person in there, but some of the books said kids didn't have memories from this age. She wouldn't remember choking. She wouldn't remember Tom James.

When her mother came home at Christmas she probably wouldn't remember her, either. At least not right off. Broker went back to sifting and searching with his rake. Kit continued to eat snow.

That's how Jeff found them when he drove up. He got out of his Bronco and said, "Why didn't I think of that instead of spending five hundred bucks on a Toro."

"Very funny."

"I give."

"This is where she spit out that hunk of hundred-dollar bill."

Jeff squinted. "As I recall, you were the lousiest investigator of the bunch. What you were good at was letting Keith talk you into carrying a raw steak into a den full of starving lions. That was more your speed."

"I wouldn't have lost it except I had to run in the house when you started yelling."

Jeff cleared his throat, walked over and picked up Kit. "This kid is freezing to death. Her lips are blue."

"Don't change the subject. She's tough. Just eating snow."

"So, what if you find it?" asked Jeff.

"It's money."

"Well, sure it's money," said Jeff.

Broker stopped raking and stood up. "Keith is accused of doing some heavy-duty crime. Where's the motive? The Mafia doesn't give out merit badges. It had to be for a lot of money."

"Hmmm," said Jeff.

"And what did Kit choke on?"

"I can only handle one hypothetical at a time," said Jeff. He turned, walked with Kit in his arms along the house, down to the end of the point. High waves had swept the snow from the ledge rock. Garlanded with lichens, the shiny black granite gleamed like the skulls of sperm whales. Broker came up behind him and said, "We have to find James."

"We, huh?" Jeff repositioned Kit in his arms and said in her ear, "Once, a long time ago, your great-grandfather and my grandfather had a fishing boat and they shipped out of this cove. It was during Prohibition and times were pretty rough. Sometimes your great-grandfather would talk my grandfather into sailing their boat up to Canada, to Thunder Bay, and picking up a load of contraband whiskey. Then they'd land it here and sell it to people who'd drive up from as far as the Cities.

"They didn't smuggle all the time, just when times were hard. 'A little here and there,' Grandpa used to say. And it was always the Broker who talked the Jeffords into going on the little adventures. Like what your dad is trying to pull on me right now. That's how it goes, Kit. North of Grand Marais."

He turned to Broker. "So where should *we* start?"

Broker smiled. "People will talk to you. You have such an honest face. And nobody has ever heard you swear. Make some calls. Find out what's on that tape."

"I can do that," said Jeff.

Down the street from Grand Marais's one stoplight, Cook County housed its sheriff's department in a flat-topped, one-story cement bunker made of opaque glass brick and dirty cornmeal-colored cinder blocks. Like *Truth or Consequences*, the other tenant of the building was the Municipal Liquor Store.

Broker, with Kit slung in the crook of his elbow, walked under the stark sign that said COOK COUNTY LAW ENFORCEMENT, opened the door and entered a grim antechamber. Wanted posters hung on a bulletin board. A brochure on a plastic chair invited: *Join The Border Patrol.*

The smudged wall of bullet-proof glass that fronted the dispatcher's station was the only window you could see through in the whole place. An exhausted plastic Christmas wreath drooped in one corner of the window.

Madge, the robust dispatcher, buzzed him in. He handed Kit to her. "Teach this kid to type will you, she needs to learn a trade to fall back on."

"So you already got her college picked out, eh?" asked Madge.

"You kidding. She's going to be a waitress in Two Harbors. Probably marry some strong-back guy who cuts pulp and lives in a trailer. That way I don't have to waste money on piano and ballet lessons."

He continued down the cramped corridor and entered Jeff's office, which looked more like a storeroom: secondhand steel desk, industrial shelves piled with equipment and stacks of cardboard boxes.

A topographical wall map of Cook County filled an open space between the shelves. The crude poster on the wall behind Jeff's desk was an early-generation computer graphic stamped out of a dot-matrix printer, the images formed by overprinted letters in the shape of a scoped rifle. The slogan under it announced:

LONG DISTANCE: THE NEXT BEST THING TO BEING THERE
RAMSEY COUNTY SWAT

But Jeff never had the spit-shined swagger required for extended SWAT work, and the poster was more joke than nostalgia. Notations and telephone numbers were slowly filling it up.

"God, at least paint this place," said Broker.

Jeff grunted. "Why? The county board will only send over buckets of puke yellow paint. All they seem to have."

"So what happened?" asked Broker.

"John Eisenhower says hello."

"How is John E?"

"Keeping the beds in his new jail full. Keith's in one of them."

Washington County Sheriff John Eisenhower had this new, over-built, twenty-first-century jail in Stillwater that boarded a lot of high per-diem federal prisoners.

Jeff said, "John E feels lousy about Caren. Like everybody. He also said he talked to the marshals who brought Keith over. And this marshal said he talked to an FBI guy who talked to a lawyer in the U.S. attorney's office who saw the tape."

"Ah," said Broker.

"Yeah, well; it's two million bucks. The guys on the tape gave Keith two mil. Hundred-dollar bills in a suitcase. Keith apparently has been running interference for huge cocaine shipments. He also gave them a picture of an FBI snitch who'd penetrated the Russian mob. And Keith's on the tape saying he'll get rid of the snitch. That

Gorski guy. The one the feds say had his tongue mailed to the Federal Building. Good sound, clear pictures. Caren hid a video camera in her laundry room pointing out to Keith's den in the basement."

"Anybody hear what happened to the money?" asked Broker.

"Nope."

"Anybody have any idea why Caren was coming to see me with the tape?"

"No again."

A cry in the hall interrupted them. Madge walked in and handed an aromatic Kit to Broker, who still had the diaper bag over his shoulder. "Sorry," said Madge. "Don't do diapers at work." She left the office.

Broker laid Kit down on Jeff's desk, removed her boots, snow pants, unsnapped her Onesie, positioned a fresh Huggies under her and pulled the tabs on the sodden one she was wearing.

"Fierce green poop," admired Jeff.

"Peas. She ate a lot of them last night."

"Or Kermit the Frog met an awful fate in there," said Jeff.

Gingerly, Broker tucked the overflowing diaper into a plastic bag, put it in the diaper bag and rigged Kit's clothes. Then sat her on his lap. She grabbed the first thing within reach, a Vietnam Era forty-millimeter grenade launcher round, used as a paperweight.

"So, what about Tom James?" asked Broker.

Jeff cocked his head to the side. "You remember that agent who ran the show up here, Garrison?"

Broker nodded. "Old-style G-man."

"I called him up, and he's at least up front about it. He says, 'Oh yeah, that guy. We don't have him. Don't even need him for chain of evidence. This Sporta flipped. And Sporta live on the stand is better than some tape. We turned James over to the U.S. Marshals Service.'

"So I call the U.S. Marshals in Minneapolis, and these guys have no sense of humor at all. They just say, 'We're not authorized to discuss our caseload.' They gave me the number of their PR office in DC." Jeff exhaled. "Sounds like James went through the looking glass."

"Funny, don't you think? Most reporters would kill to write a story like that. He goes into Witness Protection."

"Most reporters don't stop a bullet. Maybe getting shot made a believer out of him," said Jeff.

Broker scratched his chin. "But how the hell did a zero like James get on to Caren in the first place?"

"Don't know."

Kit dropped the grenade round. As it clattered to the floor, both men flinched. Broker picked it up, handed it to Jeff, who put it out of sight, in a drawer.

Broker sat up in his chair. "That gray Subaru Caren drove up here. What happened to it?"

Jeff shrugged. "Towed it in. Have it parked out back. Hertz is supposed to send somebody to pick it up. No one showed yet. Probably the holidays. Never got the keys." Jeff opened his top drawer, dug around, held up a door slip.

The station wagon was just outside the back door. Jeff inserted the slip and unlatched the driver's side, reached over and popped the passenger door. Broker placed Kit in the back and began looking into cracks, under seats, feeling in the cushion crevices in the seats. Shards of Caren's pill bottle were scattered on the floor carpet. He picked up a triangle of plastic with the prescription label attached. Read the doctor's name: Dr. Ruth Nelson. Slipped the label in his pocket.

Jeff opened the glove compartment. "No way," he said.

The unwrinkled hundred-dollar bill lay on top of a neat plastic folder containing rental information. Jeff removed it and showed it to Broker.

"This James guy seems to leak hundred-dollar bills," said Broker.

Tom traveled in a black velvet casket. That's what the inside of the U.S. Marshals Chevy van resembled; it was totally masked with black material to shut out light and sound. Part casket, part birth canal. Tom James was going to burial. Danny Storey was being born.

Lorn Garrison and Agent Terry had said good-bye and wished him luck. The farewell was hasty, the agents were rushed; off to join the raid being mounted against Red, White and Green Pizza Parlors throughout the Twin Cities.

Tom was touched when Agent Terry gave him his bag of workout equipment. The canvas satchel contained hand weights, leg weights, a jump rope and two hand squeezers. Tom sat in the plush van and pumped a hand spring in each fist until his forearms ached.

Two U.S. marshals were driving him to his intake interview. They were polite young men with short haircuts, of a lean body type; ex-military, Tom thought. They didn't wear suits like the FBI but dressed like normal people, except for the big Glock pistols under their jackets.

The van's front seat was sealed off from the locked rear compartment physically but not visually. The marshals sitting in front could watch Tom through a pane of two-way mirror. Tom had a low camp bed, magazines, a CD player, earphones and a rack of CDs. A plastic cooler was stocked with ice and cans of pop. At intervals a hatch would slide open next to the mirror and one of the marshals asked how he was doing. Did he need to use the john?

They obviously knew the stretch of road because they always asked him when they were close to a rest stop.

At supper time, they consulted Tom about what kind of menu he preferred, but he had to eat it, take-out, locked inside the van. Later, when they stopped at a motel, the van pulled up right next to the door; the marshals stood on either side, and Tom stepped from the vehicle to the door.

They stayed in the same room. Tom asked and was told this was normal procedure until he was out of the "Danger Zone," a radius of unspecified miles around the Twin Cities. Just as well. Had he been left alone he would have used the phone. To call Ida Rain. Just to hear her voice and fantasize a little. Then hang up.

He could wait.

In the morning, Tom showered and then inspected his slack body in the mirror over the sink counter. He couldn't do anything about the flab immediately. But, on impulse, he shaved off his soft-looking mustache. He left his glasses off. First thing he'd ask for: contacts.

Starting to change. To emerge.

Before they got back on the road, one of the marshals opened a large first aid kit and changed the dressing on Tom's leg. As he removed the old gauze pad, he remarked how well the wound was healing.

The other marshal told Tom how lucky he was. Catching a clean flesh wound like that.

Tom kept a straight mild face, inside he growled all over.

*Lucky.*


Finding the hundred-dollar bill in the Subaru was a single puzzle piece on a bare board. But Jeff and Broker agreed; quiet, ordinary Tom James was starting to cast an unclean shadow over Caren's death.

Jeff tucked the bill into an evidence bag and, assuming the State BCA was handling the Angland investigation for the U.S. attorney, called the crime lab in St. Paul.

"Nah," said a forensic scientist. "The feds are hogging the show, routing all the good stuff—like the famous tongue—through their lab in Virginia. So call them."

Jeff did. Garrison wasn't in the St. Paul office. An agent listened, consulted a supervisor, then told Jeff they'd send some agents up to collect the car. He could send the bill certified mail. Jeff said he would, hung up and turned to Broker, "There. Now, go home, and remember, you're a civilian. Have Christmas with Nina."

Broker drove back to babyland and spent a quiet night cooking, cleaning, bathing and putting Kit to bed. A rising wind woke him before dawn. He was up, refreshed, focused. Barefoot, he padded the plank floors of his living room, chewing on a cigar. Coffee water heated. A soft plague of gray snow blotted out the dawn. He couldn't talk to James. But maybe he could talk to Keith.

*"Dada Dah Da*

*"Dada Dah Da . . ."*

Kit announced herself upon the morning with authority, hurling "Cucaracha Dog" out of her crib. Broker's day began; remove diaper, take shower, dress her. As he spooned oatmeal, he started a list of "things to do for Christmas":

Buy a tree.

Buy Kit a sled.

Get Nina a present.

He'd considered writing her a letter explaining Caren's death and Keith's arrest. But he figured she'd be in transit, working through echelons between Bosnia and the States. She'd call when she got situated. He'd tell her then. And she'd be home in less than a week.

The dishes hummed in the dishwasher. The clothes were folded. The weekly menu posted on the refrigerator had Tuesday and Wednesday marked off. Today, Thursday, was cabbage soup. When Kit was down for her nap, he walked through the trickling snow, up to the road, to get the mail.

He opened his mailbox, scooped the letters and walked back, sifting through the junk, put the propane bill from Eagle Mountain Energy under his arm. Inspected a beat-up envelope.

No return address. The address caught his attention—printed, cut out and pasted on the envelope—was imprecise: General Delivery, Devil's Rock. The mail sorter in Grand Marais had penned in his route number.

Postmarked four days ago. From St. Paul. Lost in the Christmas rush. He tore the flap. At first, he thought it was a homemade Christmas card. Desktop format, in stanzas, like a poem. Words like fishhooks ripped his eyes:

*What does Daddy fear the most*

*Crib death right off*
*sneaks into daddy's head at least once every day*

*tiny nostrils plugged. A faceful of blanket.*
*Cats they say can steal baby's breath*
*half a handful of air to stop the tiny pink lungs.*
*so put crib death up there on the top of the list.*
*And Kitty Cat*

*There's choking. All those things that lay about can find their way into*
  *baby's mouth. Pennies and buttons and pins and pills.*

*germs*
*poisons*
*cellophane bags*
*the fall down the stairs.*
*the lake is never far away.*
*cars jump the curb*

*Hey, daddy; who watches baby when you sleep?*

A hard shuffle stirred in his chest, a stamping, like impatient hooves. Broker had always had a reverse nervous system. He descended now into that cool practical chamber where he kept the men he'd killed. Very calmly, he harnessed the surge of anger and continued to read:

*is he can he will he be*
*strong enough to protect baby*
*every second of every minute of every day*
*from bad men lurking and dogs who foam and bite*
*from black widow under the pillow and invisible visitors in the night*
*poor baby*
*doesn't even know she is alive*
*she doesn't even know how easily she can die*
*soft and fragile tiny breaths*
*tiny ears that don't understand*
*bump bump bump in the night*

*which tree is Wile E. Coyote behind today*
*do crosshairs tickle copper ringlets*
*how hungry is the cold lake water*
*how cruel and hard the rocks*

*or the fire that burns*
*or the glittering eyes of five hungry rats*
*needle teeth and beady eyes and greasy whiskers*
*chew chew chew*
*through the tender flesh, the soft red muscle and tendon and ligament*
*    until they seize on a shiny clip of bone*
*snap it and gobble marrow that's soft butter yellow*


*daddy daddy, I don't even know what is destroying me*
*I don't even know that this is pain*


*daddy daddy*


*Be seein' you*


Broker took a deep breath to center himself. He looked around. Sky, water, trees, house. All clean and smoothed by the new snow. Familiar, reassuring. His safe place.

His eyes settled back on the sheet of paper.

Not somebody from the past he'd put in jail. Most of those guys couldn't write a complete sentence. He'd been up here for five months. The reference to choking. Cold water. Rocks. And how did the writer know Kit had copper ringlets?

Because he had seen them. Even touched them. Because he had held her in his arms.

Like with the hundred dollars in the rental Subaru, Broker's intuition was immediate: James, dropping crumbs of money behind him all the way into the maze of the Federal Witness Protection Program. Now this.

*Giving him the finger again.*

Slowly, Broker walked a circuit of his home. The house occupied a finger of granite with sloping boulders on two sides and a cobble beach descending in front, facing the lake. The approach from the highway was screened in old red and white pine, smaller evergreens, brush.

The summer cabins were shuttered, locked. Cheryl and Don Tromley, the closest neighbors, were half a mile away. The only visible habitation was a new log cabin, set on another point, a hundred yards to the south. A doctor from Chicago had built it. A rental. A black Audi had parked there, with skis on the roof, for three days.

He'd glimpsed a young couple coming and going in cross country ski togs. Saw their lights at night. Smelled their wood smoke.

He had sited his house for maximum appreciation of the lakefront. Defending it against attack had not been a consideration. Distance, geography, weather—they were supposed to provide that margin.

Should have a dog. His folks had a hell of a dog. But a guy named Bevode Fret had killed it almost two years ago.

Then.

He stopped himself. If it was James, and he was processing into WITSEC, he was far away, under heavy security. There was no immediate threat.

By overreacting, he was doing what the "writer" wanted him to do. Getting angry, on the verge of calling the FBI, demanding to talk to Agent Garrison and accusing him of harboring a dangerous nut. And he had nothing but intuition to go on.

In which case Broker would sound like a talk radio conspirator. And that's how he would be remembered if he contacted them again. No. He had to cultivate a good relationship with Agent Garrison, or someone like him. Because they had the forensics to check this letter and envelope against every printer that Tom James had been near while in their safekeeping.

But first, there was something he had to try. He went in the house and called the Washington County sheriff, John Eisenhower, in Stillwater. John's gatekeeper, Elaine, answered.

"Broker, how are you? Just terrible about Caren Angland, just terrible. And we have the bastard who did it in our jail."

"Pretty ugly. Is John available?"

"No, he's at this state gang task force planning session in St. Paul. What's up?"

"Ask John if he can get word to Keith Angland, see if Keith will put me on his visitors list."

"Oough, sounds nasty; what are you, working again?"

"Thinking about it."

He hung up and carefully slid the letter and envelope into a Ziploc bag and slipped them into his desk drawer.

He'd used up the early afternoon. Soon Kit would be awake, and he hadn't started supper. He resorted to the freezer and the microwave. When Kit woke up and was changed, he opened frozen packages and zapped them while she stumped back and forth in front of the fireplace.

She had found a Magic Marker and streaked her face with blue scribbles. "Puf," she shouted. The word they'd worked out for the dragon head on the chimney. "Puf," she shouted again, doing a stomp dance. The blue markings on her face and her fierce lumbering gait gave her the aspect of a midget Maori warrior.

Watching his baby cavort, Broker considered the mind that would write such a letter. Then, practical; the food was getting cold. He washed Kit's face and stuffed her in her high chair. Sitting side by side, Broker watched his daughter eat, oblivious to the creepy vibrations squirming in his desk drawer.

"The thing about Tom James is he looks so harmless. He's the kind of guy they write commercials for."

"Spa Ga," said Kit. Her word for *spaghetti*. She waved her spoon back and forth like a windshield wiper. Most of her microwave spaghetti was down the front of her bib. By curling her wrist back and down, he was able to scoop a spoonful off the bib and guide it toward her mouth. It was not to be. The windshield wiper motion took precedence over hunger and an orange meatball flew into Broker's lap.

"Looks can fool you. Sometimes the most dangerous guy is a gifted amateur. They don't react according to pattern. They make it up as they go along. Do you think James could be like that?"

Kit began banging on the high chair tray with her spoon. Broker took the spoon away and pushed her tippy cup into her red-orange sticky fingers.

"So it's like this. Daddy knows there's something there. I'm looking right at it, but I can't see it. There are times the best way to find what's missing is to *not* look for it, to kind of look away. Then you might catch it, all of a sudden, from the corner of your eye." Broker acted out his words, with dramatic hand gestures, pointing to his eyes, turning his head. Kit slurped her milk.

"So we won't bother Uncle Jeff about the bad letter we got today. We'll put it away for a while. And when Mommy comes home we'll talk to her about it, because she's got a mind like a steel trap."

For all his attempts to downplay the sick letter, Broker found himself holding Kit constantly for the rest of the night. Making himself into a bunker of love, muscles and vigilance.

He lingered over a bath, washing her until she was on the verge of wrinkling, apologized profusely when the shampoo nipped her eyes. After drying her off, he rubbed her down with lotion, taking care to massage each finger and toe. Then he dressed her for the night in a fresh green sleeper with a moose on the chest.

Broker read Kit *The Cat in the Hat* twice, sitting in the rocking chair next to the woodstove. After the book, he played a tape of old standard songs and danced with Kit in his arms. Since establishing this routine, he had become familiar again with the songs of his own childhood and now could sing along without missing words. "Red River Valley," "Old Smokey," "East Side, West Side." Kit settled on his shoulder, and her breathing began to lengthen and deepen. Broker spun around his living room, experimenting with flourishes that he would never attempt on a dance floor. As he twirled by the wall he switched off the lights. The lakeshore floated in his bank of windows, a moonlight aquarium of stone, surf and pines. He managed a decent accompaniment of "Waltzing Matilda" in the dark, and when the song was over, he turned off the tape player.

He padded along the windows, scanning the subtle shadows moving in the swaying pine boughs. Quiet, vigilant, he walked guard with a sleeping child on his shoulder instead of a rifle.

The *Hallelujah Chorus* swelled out of the speakers on Duluth Public Radio, making the seasonal argument that humans were the musical instruments of God. Right now, the exuberant choral voices reminded Broker he hadn't bought a Christmas tree, and time was getting short.

He'd looked at trees in town but didn't like the pickings. So he'd brought a Jeepful of poinsettias back from the flower shop. He arranged them along the fireplace mantel and hearth. His dragon now seemed to be rising out of a sea of fire—a sight some ninth- and tenth-century Christians might have seen before.

Broker was deep in a binge of housecleaning. Nina was due home in two days. Kit sensed something imminent. She took shelter from the fumes of Comet and Spic and Span under the kitchen table. For company, she had a wedge of toast heaped with peanut butter and jelly. In trying to lick off the jelly, she managed to plaster the bread flat against her face. Wads of her curly hair stuck to it. Broker picked her up, carried her to the sink, turned on the tap, grabbed a washcloth, and started scrubbing off the jelly.

Toast in one hand, a mangle of paper in the other, she tried to ward him off.

Hey. Wait. Aw God. Patience. Patience. He took a deep breath and stripped, first the toast and then the mashed sheet of paper, from her determined grip. He toed the trip lever on the trash can, raised the top and threw the toast and paper inside.

The paper caught his eye. Columns of type and numbers. Jogged his memory. He plucked it up and smoothed it out on the counter with one hand as he tried to steady Kit with the other. It was the US West printout Keith had brought with him—to accuse Broker of having a phone conversation with Caren. Where in the hell did the perfect little female human find *that*?

Carefully, he wiped most of the jelly from the paper and stuck it with a pushpin, beyond Kit's grasp, on the corkboard over the phone. He was staring right at the phone when it jangled.

"Hello there," said Nina Pryce.

"Hey. Where are you?" Broker's voice surfed between the *Hallelujah* tsunami and Kit's wailing.

"I'll never tell, but it's a big building with more than four corners. Is that Kit? Making that squealing sound?"

"Yep, with her hair full of strawberry jam."

"You sound good, considering," said Nina, with heavy emphasis on the last word.

"What?"

"Caren's death," said Nina.

Broker took a deep breath. "How?"

"Someone sent me an anonymous letter. It's pretty tabloid. According to it, you were fooling around with Caren behind my back. Her husband found out, killed her and was arrested. They included a press clipping from the St. Paul paper for verification. The news story describes a more sinister version of events, involving the FBI and organized crime. But there's enough overlap with the letter to prompt a reasonable person to ask certain questions."

"It's true, she was on her way up to see me when she died."

"Keith Angland really pushed her into that waterfall?"

Broker ignored the question. "Was the letter printed?" he asked. "With a funny address that was also printed, cut out and pasted on?"

"Yes. How did you know?"

"Do you have it with you?"

"Not right now. It's in my quarters."

"Take good care of it. Bring it home."

"What's up, Broker?"

"I got a letter too. Sounds like from the same person."

"Is this some kind of revenge-taking by someone you rubbed the wrong way when you were a cop?"

"I don't think so." Broker weighed his next words. "The person who wrote that letter didn't know me."

Nina's voice brightened. "Well put. You're a die-hard analog cave fish, but not a cheater. I recall I had to hit you between the eyes with a two-by-four to get your attention. So what's it all mean?"

"My analog cave fish deduction is—it's mixed up with Caren's death."

"Hmmm."

"Come home and we'll talk about it."

"Okay. But can we have Christmas first?"

"Absolutely."

"Good. How many teeth does Kit have now?"

"We refer to them as 'teef.' Two on top, three bottom, two in back each side, top and bottom."

Nina gave him her flight information and said good-bye.

Broker rubbed his hands together. Determined not to have Christmas ruined, he looked around the house and announced in a loud thespian voice, "Kit. Where's the tree?"

She squinted at him. Tasted a strawberry finger. Darted her eyes.

"We have to get the tree. Mommy's coming home."

"Tee," she chirped.

"That's right. C'mon, we're going to sneak into the woods and poach a tee."

After giving her face and hands a quick cat wash, he stuffed her into boots and a snowsuit. "Lots of mysterious goings-on around here lately, Kit. Sudden death. Sick letters. The first, last, best line of defense against the big black questions posed by sudden death is the make-work of ritual."

He swung her under his arm and went out the door. "And getting the Christmas tree is way up there on the ritual list." Instead of strapping her in the car seat, he stood her on the passenger side floor. The top of her cap did not quite reach the dashboard. "Keep a sharp eye out for cops." Outlaws, they hit the road.

Devil's Rock was hardly there if you drove fast. It had a post office and a volunteer fire department. But no place that sold Christmas trees. And anyway, buying a tree up here was like buying lake water to fish in.

He drove south, parked off a hardpack gravel road that skirted Magney State Park, and slipped into the forest with Kit under one arm and a bow saw in his other hand. Deep in a thicket of tall spruce, Broker listened for a moment, then, reassured they were alone, felled an eight footer. He dragged it out, threw it on top of the Jeep and bungeed it down.

When they got it home, and had the tree inside, he built up a fire in the Franklin stove and put a Christmas CD on moderately loud.

Once the tree was fixed in the stand, boxes of decorations and lights were opened. Slowly the tree assumed the fantasy sparkle of Christmas. Broker rummaged among the bulbs and candy canes and removed a small, worn, handmade wooden loon. The paint was wearing thin. A frayed ribbon draped the neck.

"Loon," he explained.

"Lew," Kit pronounced in a burst of breath.

He'd made the set of decorations for Caren, kept this one for himself. Patiently, he put it in Kit's hands and assisted her in hanging it from a branch.

Like a preview of things to come, the room had no windows.

Tom wasn't sure what state he was in. It could be Wisconsin, Illinois, or even Michigan. He had seen license plates from all three states on cars in the lot at the last rest stop.

His escorts didn't provide clues.

They had driven the morning on freeways. He based this assumption on constant speed and very little stopping and starting. Finally they did slow down, stop, start and turn a lot. The van nosed down. Parked. The engine quit. He was invited out of the van into an underground garage. Red letters and numerals of the license plates. Wisconsin.

Milwaukee, he thought. He sensed a large body of water nearby.

The cars in the garage didn't look like a government car pool. It could be any building. He was taken up five floors in a service elevator and ushered down deserted carpeted corridors. Room numbers and ID plaques had been masked with tape.

His wristwatch said 5 P.M.

He bet Seymour Hersh never did anything like this.

One of his escorts opened a door. When the door closed behind him tumblers clicked. Locked.

The room contained a conference table and a blank blackboard. An empty cork bulletin board took up one of the narrow end walls. The other walls were bare. Blue shag carpet covered the floor, wall to wall. Three chairs were arranged on one side of the table. A single chair on the other. He figured the single chair was for the person being grilled.

He put down his suitcase. It contained toilet articles, four changes of underwear and socks, two pair of slacks, three shirts and two sweaters, and an extra pair of shoes. The brown parka with the money sewn into the hem never left his hands.

They'd told him he could take up to seven bags. Tom didn't even want the bag he carried. He'd only removed the bare essentials from his apartment when Agent Terry whisked him in on the midnight visit.

Tom smiled and composed himself. Take deep breaths. Be appropriately nervous. Do not overreact. Avoid looking smug. Most people lived their innermost desires as talk or fantasy. He was through talking and dreaming. Being in this room proved that.

He was a player now. And he felt like the man who drew the first circle. Simple and perfect. The only way to commit the seamless crime was with the unwitting assistance of the most powerful government on earth.

Airtight. Mentally, he felt along the seams of his accomplishment, assuring himself that they were snug. He savored the picture of Angland in his cell—soon to be condemned—powerless. Up against that tape, not even his own lawyer would believe his protest of innocence in Caren's death. He was guilty of too many other things.

The door opened. Two marshals entered the room, a man of medium height and a short compact woman. They both wore slacks. The man wore a tie. The woman wore a tailored shirt. Laminated clip-on ID cards hung from their belts along with blocky-handled automatic pistols riding high in nylon holsters.

They introduced themselves. Norman and Sarah were in their early forties and had veteran cop faces, eyes set like tired rhinestones in nests of fine wrinkles. As he had with Lorn and Terry, Tom looked for signs that these two could sense a criminal. Scent an evildoer.

"Sit, Mr. James," said Norman, pointing to the single chair. Tom sat. Adopting a patronizing tone, Norman admonished, "Do you have any idea what you're getting yourself into?"

Tom had been prepared for this by Lorn Garrison, and by his own research. He had also read everything he could find on the Internet about body language and interrogation techniques. Direct, short answers. Maintain eye contact, but don't overdo it.

"Who's the psychologist? Isn't that the first step on an intake evaluation?" he asked.

"Ordinarily, yes. Psych and vocational interviews. But usually we're dealing with scummy criminals. Are you a scumbag criminal, Tom?"

Tom laughed. Incredulous of the charge, frightened by the power they represented, a little uncomfortable because of the healing gunshot wound in his leg.

Norman backed off. "Relax, you don't even have any outstanding parking tickets."

Tom's sigh of relief was genuine. "I drive the speed limit. I don't walk against red lights. Even on empty streets. I read instruction manuals to the end."

Norman and Sarah smiled a little.

"And I know what I'm getting into. I read everything I could find on the Net about you guys. The suicide rate among protected witnesses is fifty times the national average, if that's what you mean," said Tom.

Norman and Sarah exchanged glances. "Okay," admitted Sarah. "You're our first newspaper reporter. How do we know you're not crazy enough to go through all of this just to write a story?"

"If I was going to write a story, I would have already."

"Maybe," said Norman.

"Two people knew about that tape. One of them is dead. The other got shot." Tom smiled weakly.

"And it's worth giving up your identity?" asked Sarah.

"You betcha."

"Convince me," said Norman aggressively.

"How long have you been a marshal?" Tom asked.

Norman steepled his fingers. "Eleven years. Eight years as a detective in Akron before that."

"Uh-huh. And how many times have you been shot?" Tom raised his leg and yanked up the cuff of his trousers to show his bandage.

That backed old Norman off. "Okay, Tom. It's like this. The kind of people we handle don't sit at desks and wear ties, you know what I mean?"

"I think I see," said Tom.

"The jobs our clients wind up in tend to be blue collar. You get your hands dirty."

Tom nodded his head. "You can't take your résumé with you. It's harder for architects than for street hustlers."

"You need to think about that," said Sarah. "And the idea that you won't see anybody you know again."

"Won't see anybody I know again if I'm dead, either," Tom observed.

"Think about it. All alone someplace. Working some entry-level job, or plain labor to start. Could be boring. You really should think about it."

Tom had thought about it.

The beauty of this part was that he had to simply and passionately tell the truth. A thought occurred that was almost touching in its sincerity; if he told the truth, could it be all wrong?

"I'm a forty-one-year-old white guy," Tom stated. "You know what that's like in the newsroom of the late nineties? I have one foot in the tar pits."

"That's a little vague for purposes of evaluation," said Norman without expression.

"They wouldn't let me do the story," Tom whispered.

"Say again," said Norman.

Tom cleared his throat. "When I contacted my editors about the story, when I first got onto Caren Angland, they told me to bring it in and work the phones from the office. They were going to give my story to younger staff."

Sarah leaned back, elbow resting on the arm of her chair and gazed at Tom over her knuckles.

"Biggest story of my life. I got shot covering it. And they weren't going to let me write it."

"Oh-kay," Norman said slowly.

"It's just not there anymore, the newspaper world I grew up in. Maybe that's a good thing. I don't know. I do know I keep getting asked to dance closer to the door."

"What do you see yourself doing if you're not a reporter?" asked Sarah.

"I want to write," said Tom flatly.

"We, ah, kind of agreed that's out," said Norman.

"Wait, let him finish." Sarah came forward, took a second look.

"I mean really try to write. Fiction," said Tom, eagerly, honestly. "It's the thing I've dreamed about doing all my life." He shrugged. "I just never had the guts to go out on a limb and give it a real try."

For all her training and experience, a wisp of sympathy floated across Sarah's seasoned brown eyes. Tom had expected more of a hearing from Norman. Like a barracuda cutting across a fresh blood trail, he turned all his energy toward Sarah.

"And there's something else," he admitted in a flat candid voice. "I can't afford to take time off to try to write. But if I go into the Program I can skip on my debts—my child support, my credit cards."

Sarah narrowed her eyes. "How do you feel about never seeing your kids?"

Tom came a little forward, edgy. "My wife ran off with a guy who sells swimming pools in Arizona and Texas. Business is good. Who abandoned who?"

"Whatever," said Sarah, seeing that it was a can of worms and Tom looked ready to stick every one of them on its own hook.

"So how do you see this dream life of yours developing in real time?" asked Norman.

Tom hunched forward, and a low-building intensity stitched his voice. He wasn't acting. He was projecting himself into the dream:

"The FBI said I could get some help, like a stipend, a good used car, living expenses and office equipment. But that would be like living on the dole. I think I have a plan that would work."

"Go on," said Norman.

Tom nodded, exhaled, inhaled. Tried to keep his voice controlled, but it started to race: "It would involve investing some money. You set people up in business, help with loans and paperwork." He raised his eyebrows.

Norman nodded. "It's been done. Restaurants, car shops, garbage routes. What did you have in mind?"

Tom held up his hands. "I'm a fair handyman, carpenter. I did all the electrical and plumbing repairs on the house when I was married. And I had a well-equipped woodworking shop going in my garage. So . . ." He took a breath. "What if we bought an old wreck of a house and I slowly rehabbed it. I mean, wherever I wind up?" He looked quickly from Norman's face to Sarah's face.

They watched without expression. Tom struggled a little for control because the irony of his words was bringing him close to laughter. He was basically stealing Caren Angland's house hustle for his own. He waited a few more beats and continued.

"By the time I'd totally fixed up a place I'd have the trial-and-error experience to do another one. And I would have a reasonable fallback line of work for a freelance writer. I could tell people I'm a recovering alcoholic. That way I don't have to be meticulous about job history. And—if I attended some AA meetings, I could pick up part-time work as a painter—I did some stories on AA once. It's full of painters. And, I could be working on writing a novel half the time."

"You know, Tom," said Norman, "at the back of any book, there's the writer's photograph."

Sarah shook her head. "If it comes to that. Something can be arranged. So what's your book going to be about? The Witness Protection Program?" Sarah asked.

Tom grimaced. "You think I'm not serious."

"Just kidding. No, what would you write about?" she asked, sincerely this time.

"Ah, I thought, genre mystery. Create a private investigator who'd been a reporter, who maybe had some law enforcement training in the military. There are formulas for writing that kind of stuff."

"Okay, Tom, I think we get the idea," said Norman. He and Sarah stood up in unison. "We're going to have a talk with our supervisor. Sit tight."

Twenty minutes later the door opened, and Sarah came in with two cans of Diet Pepsi and a paper plate of holiday sugar cookies. She handed a Pepsi to Tom.

"Merry Christmas. You're in. The fact is, you were never in doubt, with all the kilowatts Tony Sporta is generating in Chicago. A toast," she proposed, "to your new career."

Broker jockeyed in the chilly holiday bustle at a gate in the Duluth airport. "Frosty the Snowman" tinkled from the public address system in between arrival and departure announcements. He hoisted Kit in his arms to see Nina's plane land.

Broker had done his army time in the first half of the 1970s, when airports were hostile to military green. More to the point, then he'd been the one traveling in uniform, not waiting at the gate with a baby and a diaper bag slung over his arm.

"There's Mommy, there's Mom." He coached Kit when he saw Nina Pryce's lanky athletic stride swing up the gangway. Mommy wore army camo fatigues, boots and a soft cap. She carried a light travel bag on a strap over her shoulder.

His carrot-headed Athena—she of the glancing brow and steady gray eyes—now sparky with an iron grind of fatigue. When she saw them, Nina smiled.

She owned one good black dress, like his dad owned one good black suit. She wore the dress to weddings and funerals. She despised the army's Class A skirt and avoided it whenever possible.

Broker had a feeling skirts weren't in Kit's future, either.

Her field uniform was clean and faded. Her leather shiny but not showy. A black oak-leaf patch was centered on her cap. The black stitched Combat Infantryman's Badge she'd earned in Desert Storm was worn defiantly above the black jump wings over her left pocket. Late in coming. The first awarded to a female in the history of the army.

But the prize she coveted, the crossed rifles of the infantry branch for her collar, still evaded her. She wore military police insignia.

She carried herself with a wary reserve. Nimble and strong, she walked a tightrope in heavy armor. As an ambitious female officer, she had to coolly mask any outward show of femininity, which could be perceived as weakness.

But she had to avoid being too cold, because she could be seen as robotic or mannish. She had to look to the care of her troops, but without any outward shows of affection that could be interpreted as "Mommish."

Nina carried a lot of weight. Broker's job, despite all his misgivings about her career, was to give her a safe place to lay it down for a few days.

They bumped together. They shared the trait of grace in action and being awkward in polite society. She reached for Kit with the happy growl and nuzzle of a cougar for her cub. But Kit drew back and cried. Her teared eyes reached out to "Daa-dee."

Nina bit her lip, stumped. Withdrew back into her armor. Kit scrambled into Broker's arms. "Patience," he said gently.

They kissed chastely. As they always had in public. The chill of the Yugoslavian mountains lingered on her lips.

On the one-and-a-half-hour drive home, by unspoken agreement, they avoided subjects with dead people in them. They would not talk about Bosnia or Caren until after Christmas. She scanned the diary Broker had brought for her, a list of Kit's vocabulary, menus, sleeping schedules, sickness. She read seriously, cramming for a test.

When they arrived, Nina entered a house that was hardly ready for inspection. *So shoot me.* Everything takes longer with a kid. He hadn't cleaned up the living room, which looked like it had been shot point-blank by a howitzer full of toys. The tree was probably overdecorated. Presents were lumpy, amateur-wrapped. "Puf" the scowling dragon wore a huge crimson bow around his bronze neck. Broker had put out a punch bowl for eggnog and hung a sprig of mistletoe from the living room ceiling fan. The turkey dinner in the fridge was catered from Grand Marais.

When she'd left to go back in the service, the big living room was half done, rolls of insulation spilling from the naked studs. Broker had painstakingly completed the finish work himself; sometimes working with Kit slung in a backpack harness, up on the roof, putting in the skylights. Now the room was snug with maple siding, trestle beams, a chandelier.

"This is very nice, but is it us," said Nina.

Broker narrowed his eyes: army brat. She had lived her life in base housing, dorm rooms, barracks and officer billets. "I know what you mean. Why don't I knock out that corner over there; we could have a party, fill some sandbags, teach Kit how to build a bunker, rig a shelter half."

"Asshole." She lifted a plate of her armor, jabbed, explored a weary smile.

"Ah, we don't swear in the house, elephant ears is listening," cautioned Broker.

"*A-S-S-H-O-L-E,*" she spelled. Then she pirouetted, put out her arms and, in an ultimate gesture of trust, collapsed backward into the deep couch cushions. With a freckled grin, she let down her guard, and he saw the jaws of bone-deep fatigue yawn and crunch her. She probably hadn't slept more than two or three hours a night for months. While Kit watched, Broker knelt, unlaced her boots and eased them off. Gently, he removed her tunic, trousers and socks.

Her lidded eyes clouded, then glazed. She sighed, "That's the nicest thing anyone ever did for me in my whole life." Tawny and sleekly muscled in her olive drab underwear, she wantonly molded herself to the cushions.

"There's a king-size bed in . . ."

Too late. She was ten fathoms down, sinking to the bottom locker of sleep.

She slept for sixteen hours, waking before dawn on Christmas morning. Broker, who got up regularly to cover her and Kit during the night—"both his girls"—heard her cautious reconnaissance of the unfamiliar kitchen in the dark.

Coming out, he found her hugging her blanket, stumbling, still groggy with fatigue. But now she smiled more readily. They kissed; a clumsy married embrace, lips off target, lousy footwork.

"God." She made a sound between a giggle and Bronx cheer. "When we courted, you were an acrobat; what happened?"

"Got beyond that physical mastery stuff. How are you doing?"

"Need coffee." She pointed to the cupboards. "You changed everything."

"I organized everything."

"Coffee," she repeated.

While Broker made the coffee, Nina stood over Kit's crib and passed her right hand over her daughter, palm down, caressing a cushion of air. Not quite ready to touch.

The aroma of brewed coffee brought her back to the kitchen. Steaming cups in hand, they crept into the living room. Broker turned off the Christmas tree lights. They sat on the floor, backs against the couch, and watched the dark horizon melt from iron to pewter to nickel until it caught fire with the day.

"Hard to believe I had her inside my body," she wondered.

"Only thing we come equipped to do, replace ourselves," said Broker.

She patted his cheek. "You'd like that, see me barefoot and pregnant in there again." She nodded at the kitchen.

It was the truth. He wanted her out. "You know me: Fuck the army." He shrugged.

"They don't say that anymore, they like the army now," she mused.

"Bad sign. The army should be ugly and dangerous, and they should bitch every minute they're in. If it's a nice place to be, God help us in the next real war."

Nina didn't take the bait. This particular subject tended to get irrational; she had fought tinhorn Panamanians and Iraqis. And won. He claimed the moral high ground, having been beaten by one of the great warrior races of history, the North Vietnamese.

"I'm sorry," Broker apologized. "It's Christmas."

"Don't apologize. Glad to see you still have a few of your old edges." She tweaked an inch of his belly fat between her thumb and index finger.

Indignant, Broker huffed. "You try taking care of that kid and finding the time to—"

"Shhhh, hey dude, I love you."

Broker moved closer, no longer clumsy. "Glad to see you still have a few of your old weaknesses."

"Mmmmm . . ."

"Why don't we just tiptoe to the bedroom," he suggested.

The sunrise forgotten, arm in arm, they had made it halfway across the room when Kit started wailing and started throwing, first her tippy cup and then her stuffed animals, out of her crib.

Clad in bathrobes, they opened presents, crunching through wrapping paper, cardboard and ribbons. Broker's parents called from Arizona, extolling the joys of sunshine. He gave her the latest lightweight long underwear and socks from the Outfitters in Grand Marais. Kit got an old-fashioned wooden sled with steel runners. Broker had bolted on a wooden box to hold her for now.

She gave him an ornate Macedonian dagger from the fifteenth century.

Kit's presents from Broker's mom and dad were evenly split between dolls, puzzles, and videos. The dolls with dresses Nina marched off, out of sight. She approved of the puzzles. And of the box of Winnie-the-Pooh movies.

Broker was thinking of reheating the skipped dinner when Nina emerged from a long hot shower and disappeared into the bedroom. He went in to check. An old T-shirt he'd brought back from New Orleans, black, with a chorus line of alligator skeletons across the front, was hooked in her right elbow. She had fallen asleep again, in the middle of putting it on.

Broker spent an enjoyable hour, walking with Kit on his shoulder, watching his wife sleep. The first night, on the couch, she had curled in a defensive ball, knees drawn up, arms crossed across her chest. A cold scent had seeped off her skin; nerves marinated in steel, solvents, mud and leather.

Tenderized by rest, hot water and lotions, her clenched limbs began to sprawl. Her hard round arms were flung over her head. Tidy breasts pulled taut, faintly webbed with stretch marks. A light sepia stripe of pigment ran from her reddish pubic hair to her navel, intersecting the half moon bikini scar where Kit had entered the world. Modestly, her carved knees were tucked together.

Shadows collected in a scarred whorl below her left hip where she'd taken two AK-47 rounds during Desert Storm. She'd kept the skull and crossbones tattoo on her left shoulder. Maybe it helped win over the grunts when she walked into a tent wearing an sleeveless T-shirt. She wore her copper hair in a practical wash and wear shag; but it was long enough to curl over her ears to conceal the scarred lump where Bevode Fret had sliced off her left earlobe, nearly two years ago.

Nina's rib cage rose and fell. Kit's soft breath bussed his neck. Mommy was a fast ship pointed in harm's way; their marriage was a voyage in uncharted waters. More than once Broker had awakened of a dark night and rehearsed standing at a graveside, next to his young daughter. Practiced reaching out to accept the precisely folded flag.

He faced it straight on. Why she chose him. Amen.

He put Kit to bed.

She and Kit woke in the late afternoon. Nina yawned, moving in one slow languid stretch. Famished, she flung open cupboards, loaded pots, pans, fired all the burners, the oven and filled the table with plates of turkey and trimmings. After they ate, Broker wanted to try out the sled, but Kit let Nina carry her on her shoulder. Soon they were swept away in a conspiracy of baby talk–girl talk. Nina put a Pooh video in the VCR, and constructed an elaborate nest in front of the TV: couch cushions, pillows and blankets.

Broker watched them crawl into this lair, curl up and watch the cartoon. Nina coached: "Now, see that one, Tigger. See the way she moves—"

"Nina," protested Broker. "Tigger is a guy."

"Not anymore," said Nina, snuggling Kit into her arms.

Long after the sun went down, when Kit had fallen asleep in Nina's arms and had been lowered into her bed and tucked in, they turned their backs on the living room, a toy town sacked by a marauding horde of Santa's elves.

And finally, they wound up in the same bed.

When they'd met, she'd been between hitches, a graduate student in Ann Arbor. Broker had never shared a bed with a jet-lagged woman wearing dog tags. She wore the two steel ID wafers taped together with black electrician's tape. So they wouldn't jingle. Like he'd worn his.

Until 1993, all the dog tag blanks for the military had been made at the Duluth Federal Prison Camp. He didn't know where they made them now.

The tags and chain twined, cool steel between the skin of his chest and a cushion of smooth muscle where her ribs met. He was very aware of the tiny notch incised into each tag. The notch was a guide for Graves Registration, to help insert the disc between a corpse's teeth. A swift kick from an army boot drove it into the cold gums, good and tight . . .

Not exactly an aphrodisiac.

But then, they were not a sensual couple. What they were good at was removing each other's armor, layer by layer, without being awkward or giving offense.

They made love like they did everything: directly, unself-consciously, and far better than most people.

**34**

The day after Christmas.

Broker could feel morning light press on his eyelids and smell the fresh brewed coffee. But he kept his eyes shut, squirmed deeper to sniff the covers. Happy armpits.

The aroma of coffee came nearer and he opened his eyes. Nina, hair pleasantly disheveled, lost in the folds of her old voluminous, burgundy terry cloth robe, sat on the edge of the bed. Holding a cup out to him.

"Actually, you're not half bad for an old fart," she yawned.

Broker put the coffee on the night table and swatted at her hard ass, hiding somewhere in the baggy garment. She laughed, danced out of reach and wagged her finger.

He grumbled, "Don't pick on us old farts who tend the home fires while you're out there being glamorous."

"Glamorous. *You* sleep in this warm bed. Sometimes *I* sleep in the snow."

Broker stuck his tongue out, wiggled his wolf eyebrows and mugged a satyr's grin. "Show me where it hurts and I'll kiss it."

"Gawd." ·

"Ha," said Broker. "I made the major blush."

Nina quickly changed the subject. "I told you to stay in the Stillwater house. Hire a nanny. I told you you'd go crazy up here alone with a baby. Especially after your mom and dad went off to Arizona. But no—you were going to give Kit the Old North Woods Launch." She mimicked his deep voice and pointed her finger toward the ceiling: "Orion. The wind in the trees. The sound of the lake. Frostbite. Wolves . . ."

"Yeah, yeah."

Kit stumped in through the doorway, butt naked.

"That's an accident waiting to happen," said Broker with authority.

"Bo Bra," Kit pronounced proudly.

"What's that?" Broker asked.

"All-purpose Yugoslavian; means *good*," explained Nina.

"Great," said Broker.

"Correct, *Do*bra. Now get dressed, and let's try out that sled."

They were returning to normal. But their unspoken pact continued, not to let the world intrude on them until tomorrow. They dressed, went outside and loafed. A rested, idle, unplanned day. They pulled Kit along the shore and through the snow-laden trees. Broker rolled his first snowman in thirty years, positioned it on a granite outcropping, complete with a carrot nose and a blaze orange hunting cap.

The young skiers in the cabin on the point came snowshoeing down the shore, picking their way among the ledge rock. Seeing the snowman, they stopped to introduce themselves.

David something and Denise something, from Chicago. On their honeymoon; fleeing the law firm where they worked. Crisp wind suits. Fancy cross-country skiing gloves and caps; slim physiques straight from *Outside Magazine*. They explained that their office represented the doctor who owned the cabin, so they'd arranged for an extended getaway. David produced a Polaroid camera from his knapsack and offered to record the snowman. Denise had a serious Nikon on a strap around her neck. David was in every way polite, but Broker disliked his carefully tended narcissism, his artfully askew blond hair, the way he watched Nina, to see if she was watching him. Broker and Nina shrugged, positioned Kit between and posed.

The young Chicagoan snapped pictures and handed them to Broker, who held them in front of Kit, to see if she reacted to the images swimming up from the chemical emulsion.

David asked if they could have a few for themselves. Sure. This time Denise did the shooting because David was out of film. She moved in close and snapped rapid-fire, moving in a half circle. She continued shooting, taking in the shore and the house, the cabin where they were staying. Then they said good-bye, Merry Christmas, and they slogged off on their snowshoes.

"Yuppies," said Broker.

"That term is ten years old," said Nina, putting the snapshots into her pocket. For a few beats, she tracked them carefully as they trudged away down the boulder-strewn beach.

When they came in for lunch, Nina inspected all the frozen baby food in the freezer and read the list of ingredients on every package. Broker split some of the dry oak he'd been saving and built the first fire in the tall fieldstone fireplace.

They made hot chocolate. Got out Hershey bars, graham crackers, marshmallows, and toasted smores in the flames. Broker dragged the mattress off the master bed, positioned it in front of the fire, and they curled up and fell asleep in a pile like newborn puppies.

Nina, wearing only her dog tags and drops of water, vigorously rubbed her hair with a towel as she stepped from the bathroom. One hand still working the towel, she crossed the living room to the kitchen and stooped, retrieved the spoon Kit had just hurled from her high chair, went to the sink and washed it off with antibacterial soap. Tag team. Broker went into the steamy bathroom, twirled the shower nozzle and took a long shower, shave and shampoo.

Time to get the letters out.

When he emerged, he cleaned Kit's lunch off the floor, and her face, gave her a fresh tippy cup of milk and carried her to her room. When he returned, Nina had traded her towel for a pair of old Levi's and the black alligator T-shirt. She sat at the kitchen table and read through a pile of articles he'd torn from the Duluth paper and saved for her. They sketched Caren's death, Keith's arrest, James's role in turning over the incriminating tape and the cases against Chicago crime figures that proceeded from the tape.

Broker went to his study, removed the letter from his desk, and brought it to the table.

"Okay, homework's done." She pushed an envelope down the table. "Here's mine."

He took hers, handed over the one in his hand and sat across the table. Nina had poured cups of fresh coffee. The afternoon had turned gray and windy. A fine sleety snow pecked the windows. Superior brooded, humpbacked with black swells.

Broker opened the letter. "The type is the same," he said.

"I make it Courier, ten point," Nina said without looking up.

Broker read:

Dear Ms. Pryce, or should I say Dear Ms. John,

I just thought you should know. While you're over there freezing your famous butt in the Balkans your husband is augmenting his baby-sitting duties by living a B movie behind your back. He's seeing his ex-wife, Caren Angland, and I mean seeing.

Now these kinds of things can go two ways; there's the *Bridges of Madison County* theory of adultery, where nobody gets hurt unless they drop a heavy metaphor on their foot, or there's the *Presumed Innocent* scenario, where they do.

Phil Broker is currently sweating out the latter story line. As the enclosed press clipping will verify, he got caught with Caren by husband, Keith. Keith flipped out and killed her dead.

Merry Christmas and keep up the good work,

An admirer.

Broker looked up. Nina's smoldering eyes were waiting for him. Fast reader.

She asked, "Are you and Kit in danger?"

"No," said Broker.

"Who wrote this garbage?"

Broker pointed to the articles. "I'd say Tom James."

Nina scanned the articles, looked up. "The reporter?"

"The witness," said Broker.

"Why? What's he got against Kit?"

Broker explained the fight in the yard, James and Kit in the workshop, Kit choking on the money, James running. Then finding another hundred in the Subaru.

He pointed to the articles. "What they don't say in there is the tape shows Keith getting a two-million-dollar payoff, in a suitcase. In hundreds. And the suitcase has disappeared."

"So let's go have a talk with James," said Nina.

"Can't, he's in Witness Protection. He used Caren's tape for trading material. Interesting, huh," said Broker. "Caren comes to see me with this tape. And gets killed." Broker held up his left hand and counted off fingers:

"No one has questioned me. She had a reason for wanting me to see the tape.

"Why did Keith crawl down into that pothole. Why not just point down and shoot Caren.

"When they pulled Keith out, he had inch-deep claw marks raked down his left forearm into his palm. Caren's flesh was rammed under his fingernails. Her wedding ring was clutched in his fist."

Nina exhaled. "Trying to save her or pound her in?"

Broker nodded. "Rescue is my interpretation. But he wouldn't say anything. So why's he keeping quiet?"

Nina screwed up her lips, lowered her eyes, needing to deal with something concrete. She placed the letters and envelopes side by side. "If these were run off on the same printer . . ."

"I thought of that; James has been in FBI or U.S. Marshals' custody since he left the Sawtooth Mountain Clinic. If he wrote the letters, he did it on their equipment. But the new laser printers are pretty slick. They don't leave signatures like typewriters or dot-matrix printers."

"A specific machine could have an anomaly that we can't spot. But maybe a forensic documents expert could."

Broker nodded. "I'll give them to Jeff. He can pass them on to the feds. Except the feds are real blind where James is concerned."

"James is a reporter, reporters have editors," said Nina.

"Ah," said Broker.

"So—one of his editors might recognize something in the way these are written, some idiosyncrasy."

"You're pretty smart."

"Nah, just smarter than you," she said. Then more seriously, "You sure this is a spin-off from Caren, not some baby raper you put in jail, coming back on you?"

"I'm sure. Sixteen years I busted people. This is the first time I've got a threatening letter. But there's only one way to be sure."

"How's that?"

"Find James."

Nina got up, came over and patted his cheek. "Poor cave fish. You don't find people in Witness Protection. That's the whole idea."

"Bullshit. This guy lets babies steal his money. He leaves hundred-dollar bills lying around. This is a guy who makes mistakes."

Nina rode at his side, girding, getting ready to go back. Kit snoozed in her car seat. Trees stood at attention on the right. Superior was an endless parade field to the left. Nina wore her uniform. Broker was driving her to Duluth, to catch a plane.

"We never talked about what you're doing," he said.

"We're not supposed to talk about what I'm doing," said Nina.

Broker drove in silence for a few minutes. "Special assignment," he speculated aloud, "they've finally decided to go after some mass killers. You're back here to be briefed."

She smiled thinly. "I envy you your mystery. And a good old-fashioned motive like money."

"What's it like?" he asked.

She smiled wryly. "The Serbs look like people; they talk, walk, laugh, just like us . . ." She glanced in the backseat, to make sure Kit was asleep. Under her breath, she mused, "But they don't eat fish caught in the Sava River anymore."

"What?"

"The Sava runs past my duty station, Brkco. The Serbs established a death camp there. They'd march Muslims out, stand them against a wall and shoot them. You can still see the shot patterns on the wall: AKs, full automatic, pulls up and to the right.

"They threw the bodies in the river. The Sava runs into the Danube, so the bodies bobbed up in Belgrade and upset people having their morning coffee. The word was put out. Hey, stop dumping bodies in the river.

"The Serbs in Brkco, being practical fellows, got out their chain-saws and dismembered the bodies before dumping them in the river. But pieces still floated down to Belgrade.

"Fix the problem, they said in Belgrade. So the local Serbs put away the chain saws and, with workmanlike initiative, took the bodies to the meat packing plant in town. They literally ground them up in the sausage machines. Then they dumped the "meat" in the river. Bodies and body parts stopped floating into the Danube at Belgrade, but nobody eats sausage in Brkco anymore and nobody eats fish out of the Sava River.

"That's what it's like. And while this was going on, I was doing the moral equivalent of watching O.J. or *Seinfeld*, like everybody else. But after you've been there awhile, and hear the stories, see some mass graves and see your two-thousandth rape victim, you get the impression that society is just a scab formed over a nightmare."

She looked him straight in the eye. "In '45, my dad helped liberate one of those camps in Germany, and you know what—between you and me, I really hope some of the fuckers I'm going after resist arrest."

"I asked," said Broker.

"I told you," she said.

At the airport, Nina carried Kit, still asleep, on her shoulder into the terminal, to the departure gate. With her free hand she reached up and touched Broker's cheek. "My dad was overseas half my life when I was little. Do you think he felt like this every time he left?"

"I don't know, I only know how I feel."

They stood without speaking, holding hands. The PA announced that her flight was loading. Carefully, she transferred the warm weight from her shoulder to his. "You're doing a good job with her," she said. Fiercely and gently, she touched the baby's hair, her back, her leg, held on to the tiny booted foot. Let go.

The parting kiss tasted of tears. She shouldered her bag. Just before she turned to leave, she said, "The other day on the beach, when we made the snowman? Those kids from Chicago—the girl taking pictures, she zeroed in on you. Like she was IDing you, she got you full face, three-quarter, and profile both sides. I thought that was a little bit odd."

"Thanks, take care."

They squeezed hands and their fingers pulled apart as she turned and walked toward the boarding ramp.

* * *

To be married to her, he had to section her off, keep her in a separate compartment. As her jet taxied and took off, he shifted his attention back to his own concerns. Her observation about the couple on the beach was curious. He'd keep an eye out.

He left the terminal, walked to the lot, loaded Kit into her car seat and drove north on 61. This morning, before leaving for the airport, he had called Jeff and told him about the letters. They agreed to meet, after Nina was safely off, at The Blue Water Cafe in town.

The streets in Grand Marais were quiet under an unseasonably warm blue sky. Forty-six degrees. You could hear the snow and tourist dollars melt.

Broker went into the cafe, took a booth and sat Kit in his lap. Patiently, she pulled a string of napkins from the table dispenser. He ordered coffee and apple pie. He stared out the plate glass window at a seagull sitting on the tall Amoco station sign across the street.

Two rugged men in worn pile jackets, dirty jeans and Sorel boots pushed up from the counter and stood at the cashier's station to pay their checks. Carpenters. One of them, Lunde, had worked on Broker's house last summer. Lunde nodded. "How's it going?"

Broker nodded back. "Just fine."

"Well, have a good one."

Last summer, as right now, the carpenter treated him with the aloof attitude locals reserved for soft-hand tourists with money. Except Broker had been born here, had graduated from Cook County High, had put his hand to kinds of work the carpenter couldn't even dream of. The new crop of "locals" didn't know him.

His coffee and pie arrived. He picked up a *Cook County News-Herald* that had been left in the booth and was showing Kit the picture of a wolf on the front page when Jeff pulled in.

Jeff, usually placid, looked mildly excited. He sat down, reached over and tousled Kit's hair. "Hiya, Kitten."

"Bo Bra," said Kit, absorbed in Broker's apple pie with both hands.

"How'd it go with Nina?" asked Jeff.

"Good. We didn't have much time."

"Well, you look better." Jeff grinned. He didn't grin for long. Broker handed him the Ziploc containing the two letters. Jeff started reading. Once, he looked up at Kit. He was a solid man sworn to uphold the law. He had deep reserves. But push him far enough and you saw firing squads in his steady brown eyes. Broker saw one there now. When he finished, he folded and inserted the letters in their envelopes, which he returned to the plastic bag.

"You ever have one come back on you before?" he asked.

Broker shook his head. "Couple guys made threats on the inside, but nothing like this."

"This could be—him? James? How the heck did he get Nina's military address?" Jeff raised an eyebrow.

"No clue. But it'd be nice if the FBI could put those letters through their documents section. If it is James, the only access he had to computers and printers was in their custody."

Jeff said, "You can give them to Garrison yourself."

"How's that?"

"John Eisenhower called, after I talked to you. Said he tried to reach you, but you must have left. Seems Keith put you on his visitors list."

Broker came forward. "No shi—fooling." Eyeing Kit.

"Except, the way he wrote you down was, Cook County Deputy Phil Broker."

"Really?"

"Yeah. John thinks it's Keith's way of bossing you around one last time. You aren't wearing a badge, you don't get in to see him. And John says there's a lot of people would love to talk to him."

"Hmmmm," said Broker.

"Yeah, hmmmm," agreed Jeff. "About five minutes after John calls—Garrison calls, all warm and folksy, and says he'd like to chat with you before you talk to Keith."

"Not like the FBI to reach out to a remote outpost like us," said Broker.

"Not like them at all, especially after the way they swooped down. I guess the threat of doing life in a federal joint hasn't impressed Keith into giving up whatever they want," said Jeff.

They both studied Kit as she heaved a fistful of apple pie into her face, some of which actually hit her mouth.

"John said the talk's starting."

"Talk, huh?"

"Yeah, word's out about all the money on that tape. Now every cop in St. Paul is looking at every other cop, trying to figure out who was in this thing with Keith. Now that you're on his visiting list, there's talk it could be you."

"The Russian mob's man in Devil's Rock. I must be in charge of the northern smuggling route." Broker smiled.

Jeff sipped his coffee and leaned back. An amateurish wall mural, configured in the shape of Lake Superior, hovered over his head like an opaque blue thought caption.

"Do you suppose," pondered Jeff, "that Keith is ready to clear his conscience?"

"You willing to badge me up to find out?" asked Broker, reaching for more than one napkin to clean up his daughter.

"Sure. You need to get out of the house anyway," said Jeff.

They left the cafe and walked up the street to the sheriff's office. In his windowless bunker, Jeff pawed in a desk drawer, found a silver badge and slapped it on the blotter. "Okay, raise your right hand and swear."

Broker covered Kit's ears in a loose headlock with his left arm, raised his right hand and stated, "I'll be damned."

"Fine, you are now a sworn temporary deputy with the rank of investigator. You'll only work one case, the death of Caren Angland. I can hire you for only sixty-seven days, after that I need a resolution from the board of commissioners.

"Your salary comes out of the discretionary budget, except we used that up when Lyle maxed out the tranny in the Ranger up the Gunflint last month, so I can't afford to pay you."

"No problem."

"Go over to the courthouse and have a picture ID made. I'll call ahead. And I don't have an extra pistol. County guidelines specify a forty-five automatic. One of which I happen to know you own. Don't really see why you'd need it. Unless you're the kind of hair shirt, bigoted savage who likes to strap iron when you go down to visit the Cities."

"Hmm, have to think about that one."

Sheriff Tom Jeffords, father of three, shook a stern finger in Broker's face. "Sally and I will watch Kit, but you will spend no more than four, five days max, down in the Cities before checking back in. Your kid shouldn't lose total contact with her parents."

"Agreed."

Jeff scratched his square dimpled chin. "And remember, you represent the least-populated, most remote county in the state. Keep us out of the newspapers."

"Absolutely," said Broker solemnly.

"There's a powerful raft of, well—bullshit—in all this. Be nice if Keith would tell us what happened out there that day."

Broker nodded, stood up and handed Kit the badge to play with. "Say good-bye to Uncle Jeff," he said.

"Boo chit," said Kit.

Broker woke slowly from a dream of running wolves. Their howls sounded like sirens echoing down rainy, neon-streaked city streets.

In the dark, he showered, shaved and tucked toilet articles into his light travel bag. One ear was cocked to Kit's slightly congested breathing. He checked to make sure the humidifier was working properly. Then he leaned over the crib and placed the inside of his wrist along her forehead. She sprawled, ravished by sleep, in an orgy of stuffed animals: Cucaracha Dog, Good Night Bunny, Pooh, and Kitty.

The emotion tugged him; never left her before.

He had been with her constantly since the doctor, a woman who wore red rubber boots on the floor of the operating theater of the Stillwater Hospital, had dug and levered in Nina's slit stomach with a tool that resembled a stainless steel spatula. She'd yanked Kit out like a scowling purple potato trailing a tuberous umbilical root.

Nina's hips were more narrow than generous, and Kit's head had been ninety-ninth percentile. Nina dilated, effaced, and it was grid-lock. There were also questions about the wounds in her hip. Bullet fragments could have damaged the birth canal. The doctor waited three hours, said the dreaded word *complications*, examined Nina again and went for her knife.

They wheeled her into surgery for the prep; he paced in a waiting room, clad in a mask, gown and shoe booties. Waiting to be summoned. Alone, he had dropped to one knee and fumbled his first daddy prayer.

*Into your hands*—something like that. The only other time he'd touched knee to ground he'd been a green twenty-one. All around him, Vietnamese troopers were writing prayers on slips of paper and burning them in the predawn darkness. The wisps of smoke summoned the helicopters that flew him to his first battle.

He touched a lock of his daughter's copper hair. *Learned it backward,* all about death before he had any idea about life. He eased the door shut behind him.

With a cup of coffee, he went over his meager briefcase on the kitchen table. Just a spiral notebook, the two hate letters—originals for the FBI agent, Xerox copies for Broker's use—a laminated county ID he'd had made at the courthouse. And the Colt. The .45 caliber automatic pistol made a stumpy steel question mark, snugged in a holster and curling straps.

Shaking his head, he took the pistol back to his study and locked it in the lower desk drawer. This trip was about talking, not rousting people. He didn't see the need for a weapon.

Then he went over the schedule he'd put together on the phone yesterday. Meet with Garrison, the FBI man, this afternoon in St. Paul. Tomorrow he'd visit Keith at the Washington County Jail, then grab a late lunch with his ex-partner J. T. Merryweather at the St. Paul cops. J.T had been cool to him on the phone. Even John Eisenhower had sounded a little distant. Garrison, however, sounded eager to talk to him.

Only one Dr. Ruth Nelson was listed with St. Paul directory assistance. She'd confirmed she had treated Caren and agreed to talk to him very reluctantly.

He'd reserved a room at a Best Western in Stillwater, near the jail. All set.

The morning was mild by local standards, above freezing. He was finishing his coffee out on the deck when Sally Jeffords wheeled up in her station wagon. She got out and waved, a rugged version of Tipper Gore. He went down the stairs to meet her and explained his concern about Kit being a little stuffed up, what time she'd gone down last night and what she'd had to eat. Sally took a thermos of her own coffee from the car—she preferred hazelnut, he drank Colombian—and with a *People* magazine for company, tramped up his steps. After Kit was up, Sally would bundle her off to her house.

Broker put his bag, briefcase, and thermos in the Jeep, drove into town and pulled into the Blue Water for breakfast. Lyle Torgerson's patrol car was parked alone in front. Broker knew it was Lyle because Lyle always backed into parking slots so he could leave quickly.

A tempting mist of sausage, eggs and hash browns dangled over the grill. Lyle sat in the front booth, where he could look out on the waterfront, now shrouded in fog. He was reading the *Duluth News Tribune*.

Broker slid in across from him. A waitress brought a cup of coffee. After eyeing the grease feast on Lyle's plate, Broker ordered, "Oatmeal, whole wheat toast, big orange juice."

Lyle raised his eyebrows over the top of the paper and commented, "Off to the Cities. How's it feel to be back in harness?"

Before Broker could respond, the deputy reached across the table, peeled a square jack-o'-lantern sticker from the sleeve of Broker's parka and deadpanned, "When I go visiting federal prisoners, I learned it's best to leave my stickers home."

Lyle was square, muscular and his uniform looked as trim at the end of his shift as it did when he put it on last night. Twenty and out of the coast guard, most of it driving a cutter on the big lake.

"You never wanted to work down in the Cities, did you?" asked Broker.

"Not once. Too many rats in the cage." Lyle yawned. He was a wilderness deputy. His idea of an adrenaline high was to take a snowmobile alone into a blizzard after a lost hunter. Or a Boston Whaler out into ten-foot waves to rescue some dumbass sailor. He didn't mind wolves, bears, thirty below zero, or drunk hermits stockaded into cabins with deer rifles; but the image of a full moon perched on top a housing project on a sweaty July night filled him with unease.

Broker ate his oats and said so long to Lyle, went across the road, gassed up at the Amoco and checked the air pressure in his tires. Then he pointed the Cherokee south to go see the fallen man who had stolen his first wife.

Broker liked having the North Woods at his back door to disappear into. Living a half-hour drive from Ontario, he agreed with the Canadian perspective of American culture as the "Excited States." Traveling south was a moral plunge. Into the cities of the plain. Broker was not churchgoing, but he held to an Old Testament notion that cities were incubators of temptation, greed, and all the deadly sins.

Jeff and Broker bantered this subject every deer season, and Jeff always pointed out, in his blunt sly manner, that the Ojibway and Cree had never been city dwellers, and they'd concocted the Windigo—the snowbound demon spirit who embraced all the lurid potential of long winters in the great outdoors: cannibalism, incest, and murderous rages of wigwam fever.

Broker was undeterred. He argued that nature, unobstructed by jet planes, freeways, sirens, strip malls, and billboards, was necessary for the normal development of our brains. Human imagination, he insisted, evolved because our ancestors watched the subtleties of foliage playing in the breeze, or studied cloud formations and the patterns of wind and shadow on water. Soon there was Mozart.

Yeah, real serene, Jeff agreed; Mozart would love it up here with the chain saws, snowmobiles, and now we got those Jet Skis.

But Keith was a pure city guy. He'd go to the woods but only to shoot a deer to stuff and hang in his paneled den. The den was his spiritual retreat, with a beer close and the big screen flashing with football gladiators. The sound of cheering crowds fueled his soul. Broker liked loud silences. Big skies and big nights: Orion. The borealis.

To Broker, urban America amounted to lousy working conditions, an anomaly that nature would eventually rub out. Keith, like a spider, gravitated to the center of the humming web of rules that made a city run. He loved the intricacies of organization, of the law. Of man-made things. He loved control and the idea of enforcing. His flaw was his perfectionism. Broker saw the tidal wave of social bullshit coming, made his plans and walked. Keith, absorbed in meticulous detail, read it wrong, mocked it, and it had slapped him down.

And he'd proven more fragile than anyone thought.

*He took your wife.*

*Didn't want her anyway.*

*Didn't want her wooed out from under him either.*

Now Caren was bringing them together.

His senior year in high school, Broker had tested himself against the turns of Highway 61—sipping a beer and trying to puzzle out the lyrics to homeboy Bobby Dylan's "Highway 61 Revisited." Now the road was losing its two-lane charm. New construction widened it. Tunnels pierced the granite shoulders.

The world he had grown up in was slipping away. Once you traveled at a pace determined by the terrain. Now you rushed to keep up.

South of Duluth, the speed limit jumped to seventy and became a de facto seventy-five. Drivers hurtled past, hunched behind their steering wheels, holding cell phones to their ears.

At Toby's Restaurant, the traditional halfway pit stop between Duluth and the Cities, he pulled off to use the john and refill the thermos. Back on the road, now he moved in fleets of traffic. The pines thinned out and gave way to mixed hardwoods and snow-covered farmland. Billboards and chain-link fences lined the side of the road. New tract houses sprouted in the fields, subdividing farms, one by one.

It amused him. Children were still raised on animal stories, still sang "Old MacDonald." But rural grandparents were becoming extinct. Soon nursery rhymes would be set in nursing homes and malls.

Up ahead, the horizon congested into a standing wave of haze. He exited the interstate at Forest Lake and jumped over to quieter highway 95 and meandered through winter woods and farm country along the Saint Croix River.

He drove up out of a cut in the bluffs and saw the church steeples of Stillwater—half of them now converted to condos—and the railroad lift bridge. Three-story wood frame gingerbread homes posed, postcard perfect, on the hills. Even on a late winter morning the antique stores thronged with tourists. He and Nina owned a house here, at the north end of town; he'd leased it for the winter.

He continued through the town, following State 95 along the river, toward the interstate. Keith was up there, on the bluff to his right. In the Washington County Jail. He drove south, approaching Bayport, passed Stillwater Prison. Knew some people in there too.

Rumor was, Timothy McVeigh scouted the St. Paul Federal Building, among others, before he settled on Oklahoma City. The building was therefore spared so Broker could meet Agent Lorn Garrison at 1 P.M.

The first time, they'd met under extreme circumstances, and Broker had not formed an opinion of the man, beyond his being another imperial control freak swooping down on his sky hook. As he watched Garrison come across the lobby he reminded himself to be positive; this guy could actually help him.

Garrison's suggestion they meet casually was encouraging. Feds excelled at playing two-way mirror. They stopped you cold on the phones, or, if they admitted you to their inner sanctum, they met you in teams of three so that the guy you really wanted to talk to had his supervisor breathing down his neck. Choosy. Locked down. Secret. In charge.

But that was the old shoot-quick FBI of Waco and Ruby Ridge. Louie Freeh's new FBI was more in touch. As evidenced by Garrison's easy smile as he came across the lobby and extended his hand. They shook. Lorn's grasp was steady, strong but not too assertive. His blue eyes were watchful.

His garb, however, was old cold war formal; the darkest shade of gray Brooks Brothers made, white shirt, muted red tie. Black leather gleamed from his belt and his wing tips. He carried a heavy olive green trench coat folded over his arm and wore the felt slouch hat.

Broker looked like an ice fisherman meeting his lawyer; he wore cord jeans, scuffed Timberline low boots, a cardigan over a turtle-neck, a blue mountain parka, a wool scarf and a gray Polarfleece cap.

"Deputy Broker, Lorn Garrison; we met up north. You were a civilian then, and I was in a hurry. I've got more time today, and you have a badge."

And, thought Broker, I'm on Keith Angland's visitors list and you're not.

With a few cordial words, the FBI man intimated he'd reviewed every report and personnel evaluation ever compiled on Broker during his prior sixteen years of police work, for St. Paul and the BCA.

Though on the surface Broker was relaxed, on a deeper level he became wary of getting a Clintonesque federal hand job—touch you up, feel your pain; now get lost.

"I know why you're here," said Garrison. "You want to see justice done for Caren. She died on her way to see you." He paused and squinted at Broker. "Consider this; had she not died, you would have been the person to turn that tape over to us, not some reporter."

"I wondered why no one talked to me about that?"

"Hell, we've been busy, putting the Red, White and Green Pizza franchise out of business. And—I'm talking to you now."

Playing me, thought Broker. Reel me into his hoary confidence and I'm going to be so grateful I'll go milk Keith for him. Broker cleared his throat. "I want to question Tom James."

"You know that isn't going to happen."

"Do I?"

"Look. You got a personal stake in this. And I understand. But you don't really get it. What we're dealing with here," said Garrison.

"I got a feeling you're going to fill me in."

"And take you for a ride and buy you lunch," said Garrison. The agent led him out the door to a tan Dodge Dynasty parked in the no parking zone in front of the building.

"Where we going?" asked Broker, getting in.

Garrison grinned sideways. "Across state lines."

The FBI man turned left on Kellogg Boulevard and took it to the I-94 interchange. They drove east. He said, "First thing. I can't help you on James. He's gone. They washed him. That boy's on the other side."

"What about Caren Angland's death?" Broker asked. "We're carrying her on the books as missing."

"Just bear with me awhile, Broker," Garrison appealed. "We're talking way bigger than dead snitches and cocaine deals in Minnesota."

Garrison was not smooth, but he was definitely foxy. Or maybe he was sincere. His tone did not patronize. He was reaching out, lawman to lawman; indulging in none of the bureau's old arrogance. Broker was being brought into the fold.

"Let's start with specialties," said Garrison. "You used to work undercover, St. Paul cops and the state bureau. You were long on balls and short on paperwork, popped the bad guys on dope and weapons, you worked with DEA and ATF. Black market sales, cash and carry."

"Stuff that was too sweaty and dirty for you guys at the bureau to mix in."

Garrison pulled a blue tip match from his trench coat pocket and stuck it between his lips—a reformed smoker's trick. "Let's get something straight. I'm old FBI. But I ain't old dumb FBI. You know the old dumb FBI—they're the guys who'd piss in their pants because nobody authorized them to unzip."

Garrison treated him to a lidded crocodile smile. "And I came into the bureau red hot from the marine corps, not some fuckin' law school."

The agent turned his attention back to traffic, goosed the Dynasty and, going eighty, passed a string of cars on the right. "I swear people in this state all learned to drive in shopping mall parking lots," he observed in a dour voice.

"So," said Broker.

"So, we agree. Policy left over from the Hoover days was to stay far away from grunge details. Especially the tempting stuff. Like all that cash floating around drugs. Times changed. Down in New Orleans we busted that ring of cops selling dope. Helped revitalize the whole department. Fact of life. Now the bureau is down in the cotton, chapter and verse with the homies."

"Right, I saw an example of the new cooperation up in Grand Marais," said Broker.

"Special case. Called for extreme measures," said Garrison.

"What's special? A cop maybe kills an informant, takes payoff money from a dope dealer . . . it's New Orleans all over again."

Garrison replied slowly, rolling each word off his tongue. "I never worked bank squads, I never worked Italians and I never worked dope till New Orleans. Counterintelligence was my thing."

"You lost me," said Broker.

"'Cause I'm such a convincing good ole boy I worked the Klan, and the militias, but I got in a little time with the KG-fucking-B. You heard of it?"

Broker scoured Garrison's features for a hint that the agent was joking, toying with him; Garrison's face was stone solemn. It was silent in the car as Garrison took the exit for 694 and drove north.

Garrison let Broker ruminate. Miles of frozen landscape scrolled past. After several more minutes, Garrison began to sing, almost to himself, in a mournful country baritone.

*"If I had the wings of an angel*
*Over these prison walls I would fly*
*And I'd fly to the arms of my loved one*
*And there I'd forever abide."*

Garrison grinned. "Corny, huh?" He smiled. "Yeah, well, Garrisons come out of Kentucky. We fought on the Union side in the Civil War. And we fought on the union side in Harlan County. My daddy retired deputy chief in Louisville. I got a brother just retired from Secret Service."

His pale eyes snapped at Broker. "Always been more than a paycheck and a pension, if you know what I mean."

"I get the picture," said Broker.

"Don't think so, but it's time to expand your mind, temporary Deputy Broker. Consider this: Who was the guy Keith Angland sold the information to?"

"A Chicago hood named Paulie Kagin."

"Uh-huh. Kagin's *Organizatsiya*—Russian Mafia."

"I read about it, but I wouldn't know," Broker admitted.

"That's right. Nobody does. Including us at the bureau."

Garrison slapped the turn indicator and took the exit ramp onto Highway 5. He retreated into silence again, and Broker watched the cornfields, wood lines and silos of Lake Elmo zip past. Garrison exited onto Highway 36 and drove east past the motel where Broker would spend the night. As the road swept north in a turn toward the Stillwater business district, Garrison jerked his head toward the red brick outline of the Washington County Jail sitting next to the government center,

"He's gone pretty nuts in there. Gave himself a tattoo."

"What?"

"Yeah. Brother Keith has also migrated over. Scratched him a Russian pachuco cross, in blue ink, on his left hand." Garrison tapped the top of his hand. "Don't know what he's using, but in Russian prisons they mix urine, ballpoint ink and ashes from burnt shoe soles. Like jail credentials; for instance, a spiderweb signifies professional drug trafficker. Now a star, that's an assassin. Not sure about crosses."

Garrison sliced him with a thin look. "We offered Angland the usual deals to plead down. Real hard ass. He wouldn't even open his mouth. The second time we met with him, he just laid his left arm on the table, the tattoo on one side, those stitches on the other." Garrison screwed his lips up. "Like he was taunting us with his wife's murder.

"I had a good look at those stitches. He must have taken his time shoving her in. That girl fought. Hard. When we took him to the hospital after we picked him up in Grand Marais, I had the doctor pare the shreds of her flesh out from under his fingernails." Garrison grimaced. "The tattoo is pretty unusual behavior. He's gone spectacularly nuts. He has a real high IQ, you know. My experience is, cops and priests shouldn't be too smart. Gets them in trouble. What they need is big dumb hearts, to soak up lots of suffering."

He swung his slow eyes on Broker. "What did you think, you'd go in there tomorrow and get him to confess?"

Broker was now curious. He leaned back as Garrison shot through the gauntlet of Christmas decorations that draped the light poles of Stillwater. As they turned right and blew across the old railroad bridge into Wisconsin, he wondered aloud, "Keith and the Russian mob?"

Garrison stroked his chin, reached in his pocket and withdrew two horehound hard candies. He handed one to Broker. Garrison sucked on his and began to talk in a slow, deliberate cadence.

"Well, you know, we Americans like to be entertained. We tend to get distracted. While we were having our play war in the Gulf and watching the O. J. Simpson trial some dramatic changes were going on—out there." He cast a big hand at the snow-covered Wisconsin horizon and the larger world beyond.

Garrison chuckled. "We're about to start living some real bad B movies. Remember the old James Bond novels—SPECTER, the international criminal conspiracy from hell. All those suspicious foreign fuckers with accents. Well, they're here. Goldfinger. Dr. No."

Broker frowned.

"You think I'm shitting you? When the whole shebang started to collapse over there in the late 1980s, all these forward-looking appa-ratchiks in the KGB heisted billions of dollars' worth of Communist party funds and pirated them out of Russia. Socked them away in Swiss banks. At the same time they emptied the Soviet prisons to raise an army of thugs. It's the perfect nightmare—veteran intelli-gence agents running nets of hardened criminals.

"These guys have literally hijacked the Russian economy. Now they're branching out. So they're here, where the easy money is. 'Cause we consume so much dope. And we're so fat and stupid."

They turned right on a county road, slowed for a small town named Claypool and followed the twisting two-lane past empty pas-tures, farmhouses, woodlots and the stubble of snowy cornfields.

Garrison continued, "But it isn't the dope, fraud, counterfeiting or gasoline scams I worry about, uh-uh . . ."

They topped a rise. Through a gnarled screen of barren oaks, higher than the nearest silo, Broker saw a golden onion dome crowned by the distinctive silhouette of a Russian Orthodox cross.

The St. Andrews Orthodox Church was tidy red brick with a white slat belfry culminating in the sectioned Kremlinesque dome. Atop that dome, the three-barred cross threw its long unusual shadow across a snow white cemetery lawn. Mature red pines sheltered the church. Arborvitae stood sentinel along the approach road and among the dark gravestones. The grounds were deserted.

Garrison turned in and stopped the car across from the graveyard. The Russian cross was repeated in stubby stonework on the apexes of somber tombstones hewn in gray and black granite.

"A little touch of the Byzantine among the Holsteins and snow-mobile rabble," chuckled Garrison. He swung his door open. "C'mon, stretch your legs."

They walked among the granite slabs: Liwisky. Born 1869. Died 1933. Brusak. Zema. At intervals, drab indestructible plastic flowers jutted from the snow.

Garrison threaded among the graves, stopped, stooped and swept snow away from a headstone—Lorene Angland—1923–1996. He glanced up. "We all have mothers, Broker. This here's Keith's."

"Keith's Russian?"

"Half." Garrison pointed at the two larger grave markers that loomed over the headstone. "Her parents." Boris and Laura Kagin. "Not like he embraced it. Never spoke the language. The pastor told me the only time Keith ever walked into this church was the day they buried his mother. She grew up here. Moved to St. Paul and met Keith's dad."

Garrison pushed on his knees with his palms and stood up. "Buried in July, two years ago." He reached inside his trench coat and pulled out a black and white photograph. The graveyard in summer. Broker imagined heat. Shiny shoe leather among tall blades of grass. Ants. Keith Angland stood among a crowd of mourners. Men with hands like sledgehammers protruding from the too-short sleeves of their dark suit coats. Women in black babushkas. Farmers from around here. Working people. A Russian enclave he never knew existed.

The two men Keith was talking to weren't local clod kickers. One was short, balding, his ample middle wrapped in a double-breasted suit. He was introducing Keith to a gaunt very well-dressed man with short cropped hair. The photographer had caught them shaking hands.

"Did you take this picture?" Broker asked Garrison.

"Hell no. I've got too much time and grade to be low crawling through the woods over there with a camera. We have young guys—and, ah girls—for that. But because of this meeting in this graveyard Keith Angland's name was put on a list."

"What list?"

"They call it the Russia Squad. Not real original, but there it is." Garrison tapped the picture. "The short guy you've heard of, Paulie Kagin, a distant cousin to Keith's mother. Came all the way from Chicago for the funeral. And what's more natural than to introduce another old friend of the Chicago branch of the family. This guy shaking hands."

"Who is?"

"Victor Konic. Worth a couple hundred Kagins. He's an entrepreneur, I guess you'd call him. He runs a couple of banks, in Moscow and Chicago. He used to be a colonel in the KGB. Worked out of embassies and trade delegations, here, in the U.S. He specialized in recruiting American agents." Garrison squinted. "He still does."

"What?" Broker pointed at the grave. "Here?"

Garrison nodded. "Just making the initial connection. Keith is too good a prospect to pass up. And the link with Kagin makes it natural, them meeting."

Broker felt like his carnival ride just left the Wisconsin State Fair and went global.

Garrison blew on his hands, covered his red ears with his palms and stamped his wing tips in the snow. "Now, if you're coordinating a coast-to-coast criminal enterprise in a new country, and you're these guys, you make inroads into the local power structure. You need advice on how the law operates, their techniques and habits. Hell, man, Angland graduated with honors from the academy in Quantico. This was, you know, before he went into . . . decline.

"Okay. You're Kagin and Konic and company—you want to recruit a believer. You want to gratify someone's deepest yearnings. Give them a home. What did Keith Angland want above all other things?"

Broker studied the black tombstones against the snow. "He wanted to run things."

"There you go. But the world took a giant dump on him. Unfair maybe, but it happened. So he starts screwing up, starts drinking, having problems with his wife. Along comes his long-lost relative. Remember me? We met at Lorene's funeral. Just a businessman setting up some new ventures in Minnesota. And they talk.

"And the businessman says, you know, I can help you with these black kids from Detroit and Chicago, the ones running around with guns, who make you so nervous. The ones shipping that nasty crack cocaine into town. Suddenly all these gangbangers get popped, and Angland starts making big busts.

"But then comes the dark side of the deal. Help us or we tell the cops how you got the information. Powder and heroin start mainlining into the suburban market. Almost like the Russians know the local game plan. And they did. Because Angland sold it to them. Then they give him a taste of power, and he likes it.

"I brought in a snitch—Alex Gorski—the only goddamn snitch we have in the Russians—and he got close to busting Angland—he disappeared and the bastards sent us his tongue in the mail.

"The problem is we don't speak the language. We only see the outside. We can't see in because we don't have an informant base inside their organization. And we need one real bad. And in a hurry. Keith fingered the only one we had."

Garrison turned up the collar of his trench coat. "World's coming in on us fast. You got a kid?"

"A daughter."

Garrison nodded. "Then you should know about The Suitcase."

"The suitcase?"

"Yeah, back at Quantico there are floors full of people who worry about nothing but The Suitcase. And when it's going to arrive. We know for a fact the KGB adapted tactical nuclear weapons to be delivered in a suitcase. And right now, the Russian military establishment is not just up for grabs, it's for sale."

Garrison squinted across the cold Wisconsin farmland and mused, "That bridge Clinton wants to build to the twenty-first century won't get there if some Russian scumbag peddles one of those satchels to Hamas or Hizballah. They tuck one of those babies in the parking ramp of the World Trade Center"—Garrison's hands sketched a mushroom in the air.

Broker nodded slowly. It explained the sudden chill on the phone from former colleagues. Keith had gone beyond the pale, and Broker was the only one, besides a lawyer, he'd talk to. His eyes swept the graveyard. "The same old undeclared war with the Russians, huh?"

Garrison nodded. "And Caren Angland was a casualty." In a quieter voice, "You should understand these things, you wore the uniform. You fought."

Broker felt like he'd blundered back through time, into the muscular church of his youth.

"What do you want, Garrison?"

"It seems he wants to tell you something. Possibly he has remorse about his wife. If you can get him to talk about what they did with Gorski, tell him maybe we can work a deal for him. Especially if he can link Gorski's death to someone higher up than Kagin.

"We found Gorski's car in the Saint Croix River, by an old ferry landing near Scandia. Somebody jammed the gas pedal and sent it out through the ice. We want to know if Gorski went into the river, too."

"You and I have similar problems. It's a stronger case if you have a body," said Broker.

"The thought has occurred to us," admitted Garrison.

Broker stared across the gravestones, into the tangle of oak limbs across the road and asked, "Did you ever find the money?"

"No. It was cash, in a suitcase. Easy to transport. Keith had plenty of time to sock it away someplace. Hell, down in Missouri, they're still digging up stashes of old bank notes the James gang buried. We'll probably never find that money."

Since Garrison was in a generous mood, Broker asked, "How did Tom James get on to Caren?"

"That's easy. She called him up from home. We checked the phone logs at the paper. And her phone bill. The time checks out. December 12, 10:33 A.M. James said the caller disguised their voice.

We found a commercial voice changer at the house, in her bedroom."

Broker couldn't see Caren calling a mediocre reporter. More likely, the feds, maybe even Garrison, had sicced the reporter on her to spook her into cooperating against Keith. And things got out of control.

"Okay," said Broker, "I'll give it a try tomorrow."

"Good," said Lorn Garrison. "I thought you'd do the right thing, once you were in the picture."

Over a late lunch at a Perkins in Amery, Wisconsin, Broker handed Garrison the hate letters. Garrison read them, handling them carefully by the edges. When he raised his pale blue eyes, Broker said, "I think those came from the same place that hundred-dollar bill came from."

"Say again?" Garrison squinted.

Broker's turn to narrow his eyes and lean forward. "The bill? We found it in the glove compartment of the rental car Caren drove up north. The Cook County sheriff called your St. Paul office, they said send it certified mail."

"When?" The Kentuckian wasn't faking.

"Before Christmas."

"I was hitting those pizza joints," he mumbled.

Patiently, Broker explained the sequence of events. James coming to his house, not saying a word about the tape, refusing to reveal where Caren was, the fight with Keith, putting James and Kit out of the way in the workshop. The choking incident.

"Why didn't you say something about this?" Garrison asked.

"Because you guys never asked me."

"I'll personally make sure they go over these letters. I know the exact machine to match them to," Garrison promised.

Then, patiently, he answered questions about James—how James had said Caren wanted him along to buffer her approach to Broker. How she wanted advice about how to proceed with the tape.

"Because of what was on the tape, she didn't trust anyone Keith worked with. She didn't even trust us. She wanted you to be her advocate," said Garrison.

And how she panicked when she found out Keith was at Broker's place. So James volunteered to go ahead, to make sure Keith was gone before bringing her forward. So, yeah, he was probably being manipulative, going along for the ride, to get the scoop.

"If he'd a been a trained man he wouldn't have left her alone in that lodge. But he wasn't trained. He was just a reporter, in over his head. Then it went to hell and he got shot. Which scared him shitless. So he made the best deal he could to get free."

Garrison paused, making no attempt to disguise the speck of doubt in his pale eyes. "But he never said anything about a baby choking, or seeing money in the car. And I'd think, for a reporter, that would be pretty hard to forget."

Broker drove to his motel on Highway 36 in the rush hour twilight, anonymous in the stop-and-go accordion of headlights and taillights.

He called Sally Jeffords, who told him that Kit was fine. Jeff wasn't home yet. Was there a message. No. Not yet. Broker hung up and paced. He chewed an unlit cigar. The walls were too thin, he could hear people in other rooms talking, hear the traffic on the highway.

Garrison clearly did not take being left out of the loop lightly. Something was funny, and Broker needed to fill in the blanks. Experience had taught him to trust a woman's powers of observation over a man's. Just that a woman would give him about two hundred more details than he needed. But a trained woman, who'd broke his bed sixteen years ago . . .

He called the St. Paul Police switchboard and asked for Mary Jane Cody's extension. No one answered phones anymore. He got the answering machine. Janey's voice sounded the same, except for a slight infusion of rank-weighted gravity. Captain Mary Jane. And that made it slightly dicey because, like his old partner, J. T. Merryweather, Janey had scored lower than Keith on the captain's test and had been promoted over him.

"If you need to reach me in an emergency," said Janey's recorded voice, "page me at . . ."

Broker hung up and punched in the page.

He paced for a few more minutes. Decided it was a long shot. The phone rang.

"Who paged this number?" Janey's no-nonsense voice sounded

slightly out of place with a tidal surge of classical music in the background.

"Janey, it's Broker."

"Aw shoot."

"What's that in the background?"

"Aw shoot. The St. Paul Chamber Orchestra. I'm at a concert."

"What's wrong with this picture," said Broker.

"Hey, screw you—when we worked the streets, our snitches hung out in bars. Now they hang out in the mayor's office and at the symphony."

"I appreciate you calling back."

"I didn't know who I was reaching. Now that I do, hey, Broker—I can't talk to you. I heard J.T.'s having lunch with you tomorrow, and I advised him not to. This thing with Keith is so dirty, it's got like—yuk—tentacles going everywhere . . ."

"C'mon, Janey, it's me."

"Right. Who is on Keith's visiting list. Look, we arrested a lot of crack dealers after Keith came back from the FBI Academy. Big busts. Now the word is, some slimy lawyers are getting hot to reopen those cases because of the rumors coming out of the U.S. attorney's office—that we went after people based on illegally obtained information. Keith's new pals went around torturing people. They pull tongues out.

"There's another thing, when I got promoted I protested in writing, strictly on the merit of passing over Keith. Now that's been twisted around somehow. Sometimes I think *I'm* under suspicion."

"That's just nuts."

"Broker, there's talk about huge amounts of money being thrown around, everybody is scared and paranoid. We've never had a scandal like this before."

"Okay, what about Keith?"

"What about him, he went nuts. He killed Caren—I'm sorry Broker, I should have said something earlier . . ."

"No, I understand."

"No you don't. We all saw it start to fall apart. She stopped talking to everybody. Should have known when they bought that haunted house in Afton. We knew about his drinking and that she was seeing a shrink. I heard she lost it after her last miscarriage, when she found out Keith went and got snipped."

A vasectomy?"

"Right. Look, he went nuts, okay. Then the booze just made him unstable. He'd be trashing the chief, and Dobbs would be twenty feet away, getting on an elevator. We all started avoiding him. Talk had already started about doing an intervention. But, I don't know, he'd run over so many people—everyone sort of wanted to see him take a belly flop . . ."

"Janey, could we have a cup of coffee, meet somewhere?"

"Sorry, lover. Your name on the visitors list in Washington County gave you galloping leprosy as far as St. Paul cops are concerned."

"What's that supposed to mean?"

"That several million alleged dollars are unaccounted for and Caren was headed for you with a videotape. Some people—like people over at BCA who never did like you and your independent ways too much—have speculated you may be mixed up in this thing." Broker did not reply to that and she said, "I know, it's the new tabloid morality. Whatever. Sorry Broker." A flash of anger. "Dammit, I know why you're digging in this and it just isn't worth it. St. Alban was a long time ago."

Silence.

Her voice changed, less jangled, full register. "God, you're married, I heard you have a baby."

"All true. Girl. Fourteen months."

"That's a nice age," said Janey. "Call me when this is all over. Gotta go."

Broker hung up the phone. Janey was no prude and had never been squeamish, but she had been uncomfortable talking. Nobody really wanted to know what happened to the Anglands. They just wanted it to go away. Instead of *doing* their jobs, people were *worried* about their jobs in a new political climate.

He got up from the desk, crossed to the bed, took out a cigar from a Ziploc and bit the end. On the way out the door he scooped up his hat, coat and gloves.

Looking up, he saw meager stars washed out by the neon smear on the horizon. Traffic grumbled on Highway 36. The parking lot light illuminated a large red wooden horse with a flower-patterned saddle that was fastened to the motel's brick wall. The *Balahast*, a traditional Swedish symbol. Like Broker, an old-fashioned Minnesota derelict, lost on fast-food row.

He remembered something Caren used to say: "Do people change or do you just get to know them better?"

Good question to ask Keith tomorrow.

Washington County, the fastest growing county in Minnesota, was also the site of the main state prisons: Stillwater and the newer maximum security lockup, Oak Park Heights.

People, Broker among them, moved to Washington County for more open space, less crime, better schools—and wound up living with the largest prison population in the state. On humid summer nights you could almost smell the funky weight of all that incarcerated flesh bead up and sweat in the haze that drifted up the Saint Croix River Valley.

The Washington County Jail could have been a tidy brick and glass corporate headquarters. No taint of punishment attached to its clean exterior. Inside, the climate was almost medical in its spotless isolation; movement was remotely controlled by electronically triggered doors, needle-nosed surveillance cameras tucked in corners, baffles of bullet-proof glass, intercoms.

The U.S. Bureau of Prisons rated institutions numerically, from one to six, based on their level of security. The Washington County Jail, like Oak Park Heights about a mile to the south, was referred to as a "seven."

The U.S. Marshals liked the jail because of its advanced security features and gave it a lot of business. Which was good, because it had been overbuilt and it would take a decade for the county to grow enough bad guys to fill it. Sheriff John Eisenhower had developed the skills of a hotelier to keep his beds full.

Broker checked in on the administrative side. A deputy behind a glass bubble recognized him, lowered his eyes and buzzed him into the sheriff's offices. Eisenhower met him in the hall. Broker had been a year behind Eisenhower going through the St. Paul Police Academy. He went to BCA, and Eisenhower ran for sheriff. Working undercover, Broker had reported to Eisenhower on a number of cases. Eisenhower, Broker, Keith, Jeff, and J. T. Merryweather. The old days.

Bluff, ruddy-faced, blond, blue-eyed, and mustachioed, John usually wore a tan department uniform. Today he was in a suit and tie. They shook hands briskly. He asked, "How's Nina and the kid?"

"Fine."

Eisenhower tapped the laminated ID Broker had clipped to his chest pocket. "You went and got badged up over this?"

Broker nodded. "Just walking out Caren's death. Jeff and I don't buy the FBI version."

"Forget it. He won't tell you anything."

"Then why'd he send for me."

Eisenhower studied him. "A lot of people are curious about that. They think Cook County should have left him down in the ice water to drown."

Broker smiled thinly. "Janey Cody in St. Paul called me a leper."

"They're spooked in St. Paul." Eisenhower exhaled, grimaced slightly. "Another thing. It's hard to be around him if you knew him before. He's nuts."

"Some kind of legal ploy? Insanity defense?"

Eisenhower shook his head. "No. He's lucid enough. He"— Eisenhower chose his word carefully—"turned." He shrugged. "Maybe all the stuff he was holding inside all these years came out when he killed Caren. I don't know."

A gesture toward the darkness that walked with cops, step for step.

Eisenhower shot his cuffs, his hands circled his belt, tucking at his shirt. "I've got to hand you over to Dave Barstad. Got this damn meeting with a bunch of consultants." He raised his eyebrows. "Some brilliant mother's son has this plan to hook all the jail toilets up to a computer. Get all the assholes to crap on-line or something."

He shook his head. "We have Keith down in separation; I didn't think it was a good idea to throw him in general population. There could be people he busted in there."

They went down a corridor, got on an elevator and descended

two floors. A stocky blond man in a white shirt and tie met them at the master control station.

"Dave, Phil Broker, he ran some stuff for us when he was with BCA. He's up in Cook County now."

Broker and the jail administrator shook hands. Eisenhower touched Broker on the arm and excused himself. Barstad pointed to a small locker inset in the brushed stone wall, twist-out key in the lock. "You can leave your weapon and cuffs—"

Broker shook his head. "All I have is this." He held up his spiral notebook, which contained the photo Garrison had given him. Barstad took the notebook, indicated the spring spine and left it at the control station. He handed the photo back to Broker, then walked him into a maze of glass partitions and security doors. An intercom voice monitored their progress, unlocking and locking the doors for them on the jailer's command.

They passed the normal visitors' cubicles, went through more doors and down on another elevator. They came out on the bottom level, where new inmates were processed.

Walled off behind glass were large pens—called pods—with bolted tables and guard desks. Tiered cells were built into the walls of these bays. Solid steel slotted doors. The inmates couldn't see out. Broker couldn't see in. He had been through three levels of the jail. He had yet to see a single prisoner.

The disembodied voice of the master control operator sang a cadence back and forth with Barstad. They negotiated the quiet electronic click of locks on thick glass doors opening, then closing. "Leaving such-and-such. Entering Thingamabob."

No Christmas carols. No little decorative trees. No paper plates set out with sugar cookies. It was what the taxpayers wanted today: a seasonless storage locker for hazardous waste. Broker missed the feel of air transfixed by steel bars—the notion of a cage. Even whips and chains and tormented jailhouse cries were preferable to this silence. Too clean. Too orderly—an antiseptic womb in which the lethal injection was conceived.

He had a headache. Had only slept three hours last night. Strange bed. Strange task.

They exited the large reception area and walked down a corridor. "I've got him waiting in Transport. You'll have the most privacy there."

Broker nodded. Transport was a small holding pen where prisoners were picked up or dropped off when they had business outside the jail.

"Open Transport," said Barstad to the eyes and ears in the walls. Click click.

The door opened, and Barstad said, "I've had them turn off the audio but I have to keep the video on. It's policy. Just signal at the camera when you're through."

Broker shook Barstad's hand again and went in.

# 41

Keith smelled like spoiled meat washed in disinfectant. He sat in a blocky ModuForm armchair. The large dense blob of furniture was molded from a pebbly rubberized substance that looked, in color and texture, as if Barney the dinosaur had been run through an auto compactor and turned into a seat. The chair, designed for prisons, weighed two hundred pounds.

He wore loose blue denim jail utilities and blue slippers. His shirt-sleeves were rolled up, showing biceps. Frankenstein stitches in his left arm twisted like centipedes sleeping in the packed muscle. Yellow disinfectant discolored the seamed forearm. He'd lost fingernails on three fingers on his right hand to frostbite, and they were scabbed over, blackened. His left hand was clamped in a fist in his lap. His hair was short, sidewalled and bristly. No sunglasses allowed here. His yellow eyes were hard, clear and shiny as frozen ball bearings. In them, Broker felt the icy embrace of the Devil's Kettle, and, possibly, the fixed stare of mental disorder.

Despite his present circumstances, Keith held his powerful body with the erect bearing of a mad warrior monk.

On the top of his left hand, a patch of infected skin puffed up a blue tattoo of a three-barred Russian cross. Crude, self-inflicted; probably with the straight end of a safety pin and ink from a felt tip.

Self-laceration.

What happens to a perfectionist who loses his rule book.

He opened his curled left hand. And Broker saw that he wore Caren's wedding ring on the little finger. What was left of the little finger. The first joint had been amputated, and the stub closed with stitches. The skin under the gold wedding band was swollen, marbled with purple bruising. He wore his own ring on the next finger. His fingers twitched, and the gold bands jingled.

Keith stood up. Instinctively, they circled each other in a sort of preliminary dance. They did not shake hands. The room was wedge shaped, with three holding cells built into one wall. The cells were empty, and the doors were open. A guard podium was on the other wall. The camera peered, bracketed in the corner.

Broker evoked it all with the sound of his name: "Keith."

Keith laughed soundlessly. His eyes roved the walls. "This place is really something. Last night I smelled cigarette smoke. It's been bothering me all day. How the hell did someone sneak a cigarette in here. You quit, didn't you?"

"About six months ago."

"What made you do it?"

Broker looked straight in the icy eyes. "Well, the baby."

"Uh-huh. Maybe I only imagined I smelled smoke. My taste is all screwed up since . . ." He held up his hands. His eyes continued to travel the walls. "You know, I never even smoked a joint in my life. You did, though. You had to, working undercover."

"Yeah, Keith."

Keith shook his head. "You think they'll legalize drugs?"

It was an absurd conversation, but Broker was carried along. "No, I don't think so."

"Me either. It's job security. Like the buffalo. They support a way of life—cops I mean, and corrections, the people who work in and build places like this."

"What the hell happened, Keith?" The hang-fire question cooked off.

Keith avoided eye contact. "What happened," he savored the words. "Who is owed an explanation." Again, the soundless laugh. The dead eyes crawled over the monotonous brick pattern. "Maybe I'm the one that's owed an explanation." He raised the damaged hand and felt along the stone wall. "These walls won't last, not like, say, an Inca wall. I saw this thing on *Nova*. I could spend my life staring at an Inca wall. But this . . ."

He let the thought get away, pressed his forehead against the bricks. "Maybe I got tired of fat cop faces. You ever notice how many fat cops there are." His disfigured left hand explored the unyielding brick. "Maybe that's what happened."

"Why'd you put me on your list?" Broker asked.

"Why'd you ask to be invited?" Keith shot back. A muscle in his left cheek jumped under the skin. His fingers jerked, clinking the wedding rings together in a nervous tic.

"Thought you could tell me what happened out at the Devil's Kettle." *Clink-clink-clink.*

"What happened is I never intended for her to get hurt. She just had to stick her nose in." *Clink. Clink. Clink.*

"That doesn't answer my question." *Clink-clink-clink.*

Keith spat on the floor. "Uh-uh. C'mon." He jerked his head at the camera. "The FBI is listening to everything we say."

Broker held up the picture Garrison had given him. Keith shook his head. "You? Carrying water for the feds? I smell that fucking Garrison."

"He took me to Wisconsin yesterday. We stood over your mother's grave and he told me what a bad motherfucker you are," said Broker.

Keith grinned, took the photo, ripped it in half and let the pieces fall to the floor. "Did you check out the Russian cross, with the three bars?" He raised and twisted his left hand, turning the palm in so the tattoo confronted Broker. Stepped closer. "See the little one on the bottom that's crooked?" His fingers squirmed. Nerves. Gold circles clicking.

"Keith? You want to talk or play games?"

"I am talking. The reason it's crooked goes back to a dispute in the early church, in the second century. This faction insisted that the cross should remind people that Christ really was human and he really suffered." The rings clinked. "That little bar represents the footrest, where the condemned braced their weight. See? Crucifixion was all about muscles giving out, the chest cramping the lungs. Slow asphyxiation. The pain gets more and more excruciating. They writhe and twist the footrest . . ."

Keith smirked. "I learned that on the History Channel."

"Was it like that when Alex Gorski got it?" Broker asked in a low voice.

"Excuse me, did I hear right?" Keith cupped his hand to his ear. "Got it? The death of? The problem with 'the death of' is—we're fresh out of bodies."

Keith sneered and rubbed his chin with his gruesome black fingertips. "Give me a break, you were never a detective. Go back to the fucking woods. Pretend life is a show on public television. Get used to it. Old cop dilemma—you know who did it, but you just can't prove it."

He was changing, like a diver going deeper. His face altered, distorted by the pressure. The lips pulled tighter, creating a ruthless mask wiped clean of illusions. He was getting ready. He would go to federal prison where strangers would try to kill him, on principle, because he was a cop. Broker started to turn away from the willful madness, the jingle of the rings. To the camera.

Keith raised his left hand, blue infected tattoo, nightmare stitches, stumpy little finger and ring finger beating out the demented rift. *Clink-clink-clink. Clink. Clink. Clink. Clink-clink-clink* . . . His voice boomed in the cell. "Hold it. I didn't say you could leave. I brought you here for a reason. You owe me an explanation."

Broker tensed at the contemptuous tone of command.

"Were you fucking my wife, you shit?" hissed Keith, exploding forward, driving Broker off balance, back through the open door to one of the cells. They smashed into the tight masonry pocket, tripped over the stainless steel combination sink and toilet. Keith's hand at his throat smelled like rotting flesh.

"Think fast. Cells aren't miked," Keith rasped.

Broker's reflexive defensive left hook glanced off Keith's face. Felt like hitting a pig, hard gristle. But very alert now. They clinched. Keith's voice, low, sinister in his ear: "*Find James.*"

"Wha—?"

"In your yard, James said Caren took the money."

The outer door burst open. Incoming shoe leather. Keith continued to whisper, "Check Afton. False wall under the antelope. Key, garage light."

Three guards dove into the cell, tackled Keith. He swung as they tangled him up. Broker took the punch on his arms. With manic strength, Keith wrenched free, charged. Broker saw the stinging left hand coming, a glitter of gold rings that snapped his head back. Stunned, he got off a wild right hook, which connected with Keith's nose. They clinched again. Went down. Keith's hot sour breath taunted, low, "Catch me a thief."

Broker saw it was two deputies and Lorn Garrison piled on Keith. This time, breathing heavily, they bore down and cuffed him. "Outside, Angland," panted a deputy. They hauled him to his feet. Keith shrugged, his nose was bleeding. He smirked at Garrison.

"How's it feel, Lorn, to have spent your whole career in law enforcement peeking through keyholes?"

Garrison shoved Keith aside and went to help Broker to his feet.

Keith grinned again, and his gaze locked on Broker's eyes with icy traction. He hurled his voice like a curse: "*You owe me, fucker . . .*"

The last Broker saw of Keith Angland was his broad denim-covered back as the deputies dragged him, yelling, from the transport room. His voice carried crazy off the brushed stone walls: "*Owe me . . .*"

The shout ended in a collision of flesh and bone on brick.

"Watch your step there, Keith," a deputy sang out.

Without a word, another deputy handed Broker the two halves of the torn photograph and escorted Broker and Garrison back up to the master control bubble.

The deputy said, "You want a first aid kit for your face? See the doctor?"

Broker shook his head.

"We told you he was fucking nuts," the deputy said in a tired pitiless voice. He turned on his heel and slipped back into the maze, his outline shimmered, then swam away through layers of soundproof, armored glass. Broker and Garrison exited the locked perimeter. Garrison retrieved his weapon from the wall vault, and they left the building.

Garrison dabbed a handkerchief at Broker's right cheek. "Got you a little mouse out of the deal."

Gingerly, Broker took over the hankie and moved his jaw around. He was grateful for the shock of the fight, and the blow to the face. It disguised his rising excitement.

*Keith, you devious creep, what are you up to?*

In a bruised voice, he said, "He's not exactly feeling remorse about his wife."

Garrison shrugged. "Had to try."

"So," said Broker. "I tried. What about James?"

The sympathetic Garrison of yesterday had changed into a practical horse trader.

"I can't bring him back, even if I could, shoot—not like I got a lot of incentive. Keith didn't say anything new in there. Just accused you of banging his old lady. You, ah, weren't banging her, were you?"

Broker flung the bloody hankie at the FBI man's face. Garrison plucked the cloth in midair, squinted. "Didn't think so. But what'd he mean, about you owing him?"

Broker shook his head. "You never meant to cut me in on James."

Garrison's shrugged again. Not arrogant, just realistic. "You know how it is."

"Yeah," Broker quipped bitterly, "it's tough poop." A concept he was preparing his daughter for.

Garrison smiled, sad, wise, cynical. With a trace of mournful music in his voice, he admonished, "Now you put some ice on that cheek, hear?"

**42**

It *was* the money. James and the money. But now it was something else. From the climate-controlled purgatory of the jail, Broker drove south into a picturesque Minnesota snowstorm.

*You owe me.*

Of course, Keith had always been nuts. Driven, single-minded. Like the Wright Brothers were nuts.

There was the time Keith—in his gadget phase—had this insane notion he could get all the Homicide squad guys to wear these beepers that would send a signal to a tower and the tower would relay to his office at the station, where he could plot the position of all his men, at every moment, on a wall map.

Just like that character in *Catch-22*, somebody had joked, wiring the platoon together so they'd march better. And Keith had shot back, "I know that book, it mocks authority."

*Owe me.*

Broker pummeled the steering wheel. Keith would never bring that up. Had never mentioned it. Unless . . .

His hand searched for a cigar in his jacket, found the cellophane bag, pulled one out and stuck it in his mouth. Okay. Break it down. Keith wouldn't give a straight answer about Caren. But he would link James to the money.

The "owe me" part—Broker grimaced.

God, we were young that night on St. Alban:

*That night Broker had been reminded that heroes are like the rest of life, a come-as-you-are party. They can be unbearable assholes—*

*And still save your life.*

*How it had happened at St. Alban was like this: Jimmy Carter was the president and Keith was a sergeant; Broker, J.T., John Eisenhower, and Jeff were patrol grunts. They got the call. Eight in the evening on an inky soft June night. Man with a gun, threatening his family. Little house on St. Alban, on the East Side. When Keith arrived, they had the house secured. The SWAT team had been called. Guy had the family in the kitchen. Wife. Three kids, all under ten years old.*

*Broker—young, dumb and full of come—crouched at the back door with a shotgun. Could hear the guy raving in there. This one didn't want to talk. This one was working up to it. And that's what he told Jeff and Keith. What he yelled to J.T and John in the front. Can't wait for SWAT to tie the laces on their spit-shined jump boots. No time.*

*"He's gonna do it. We gotta go in."*

*So he went, figuring angles, slamming off doorjambs. Airborne. Ranger. Veteran of house-to-house close combat in a forgotten place called Quang Tri City. Dived on the tacky linoleum, shotgun sweeping on target as he hit the floor. Jeff scrambling to cover him. Saw the guy right there, skinny, runt-of-the-litter redneck piece of shit. Should have been drowned at birth. Saw his mad rabbity eyes, bad teeth, thin lips screaming, saw the wife screaming, kids screaming. Then a shot and the wife wasn't screaming and Broker sighted the shotgun at the guy who was barricaded behind the cowering fetal shape of the woman. She was down, bleeding profusely from a messy head wound. The guy hid in back of his kids, all three of them pulled tight to him, human shield fashion, with one arm, while he extended his other arm, and the pistol at the end of it, straight at Broker, who was lying in the prone position, on the kitchen floor, ten feet away.*

*Broker could still remember those kids. Towheaded, terrified cornflower blue eyes in sugar-diet faces. Two little girls and a boy. Them screaming. The mother bleeding. The guy yelling. No way he could take the shot. Not with the kids in the way.*

*Then, so fast Broker never even shut his eyes, the guy pulled the trigger. Except someone moved over him, put their body between Broker and the round. The bullet blew the back of Keith's right shoulder all over the dirty dishes in the kitchen sink.*

*Keith just kept walking. Slow. Hands up, talking calm, taking the bullet. No gun. Threw the guy off just enough. His next shot went wild and Keith smothered him, grabbed the gun. The kids were all right. The mother made it. Keith, the college quarterback, never threw a football again.*

*And Keith, the asshole, wrote Broker up for recklessness.*
Think fast.

Everyone tended to forget how fast Keith could think on his feet, how slippery his mind worked, how he could adapt and innovate . . .

Broker had to stop at a convenience store and check a phone book. He didn't know where Keith lived. When he had the address he checked it in the *Hudson's Street Atlas* he carried in the glove compartment. He located the road and continued up Highway 95, through Afton.

Gentle snow. Kids in colorful mufflers and mittens toting sleds. He turned off Highway 95, onto the back roads.

The house would look great once it was fixed up, but right now, with so much trim missing and patchy from sanding, it had warts.

The key was where Keith said it was, embedded in a wedge of snow under the decorative rim of the garage light. He went up the steps and let himself in. The heat was turned down, cold enough for his breath to cloud.

Two steps into the front hall he looked into the barren living room and. . .

The footlocker lay on its side on the dull, dusty maple floor. It had resided in Caren's closet when they were married. Every Christmas . . .

Strewn around the trunk, he saw the set of decorations, minus the loon, he had turned out on a jigsaw the first winter of their marriage. The room was empty, no furniture, so he slid his back down a wall and sat on the floor.

The wooden baubles caught a random moment in Caren's life. The house was like a blueprint of her hopes. Roomy enough for a big family. Miles of yard to run in. Near the water. Swimming and sailboats and canoes. But also a shambles.

He heaved himself up and went into the kitchen. On the counter, filmed with dust, he saw a perfectly preserved lump of chocolate halved by the neat incision of teeth marks.

The kitchen drawers were tidy but contained no tools. He backtracked to the breezeway and found drawers where the tools were kept. He took a WunderBar and went down the basement stairs. A musty veil of dust hung over the den. A discarded pair of rubber gloves lay on a pile of siding torn out of the wall. The feds hadn't cleaned up after themselves. They'd brought the dog in. The dog trained to sniff out money saturated with particles of cocaine. The dog had found the stash.

Like Keith said, under the antelope. A hidden niche was built around an old chimney base.

Empty. So it wasn't where Keith hid it, and the feds didn't have it. If they did, they'd be posing with it on TV. And Keith had been exact about one thing—find me a thief.

In a bathroom, off the den, he found a box of Band-Aids and put a square patch over the bruised cheek. Then he sat down on the couch. The stuffed twelve-point white tail and the antelope peered down with glass eyes from the wall over the hole in the paneling. Two armchairs, the couch, a coffee table. A desk that served as a storage platform for Keith's trophies. Pistol. Skeet. Golf.

Connect the dots. Caren found the money, took it, along with the tape. Had it on the trip north. Did something with it. Hid it. James knew. Then it all happened and—not like James *stole* it. Nobody asked him about it.

But proving it? His eyes roved over the musty basement.

Jeff had said this was where Caren set up the camera. Keith must have been brain-dead to bring the bad guys and a suitcase full of money right into his house.

Why would he do that? Caren would have to know . . .

Caren knew. He knew Caren knew.

Conventional wisdom: The control freak went out of control.

Broker pictured it, working a nervous rhythm with his palm on his thigh. Keith the perfectionist, spurned. So Keith the racist. The drunkard. The dirty cop. Wife beater. Murderer.

People were pleased to see him go down. Almost like a group of siblings getting back at their tormenting, stronger, smarter older brother. Love and hate tangled tight. "And he did this and he did that and he . . ."

The only hot-button sin Keith had neglected on his suicidal plunge was drowning puppies.

When he was good, he was very, very good. When he was bad, he did it perfectly.

The wall clock said twenty to twelve. He was going to be late for lunch with J. T. Merryweather. As he let himself out, he debated whether to go in the living room and collect the strewn tree decorations and pack them. Her father had died, but her mother could still be living in Williston and might want them.

But he could not act on the impulse. This was still Keith's house, and he was very aware of trespass. Broker turned away from the living room, walked out, closed the door behind him, put the house key back where he'd found it.

He got in his truck, fastened his seat belt, turned the key and drove west, toward St. Paul.

U.S. 94 formed a moat in front of the cement bastille that was St. Paul Police Headquarters. Broker grabbed an exit and parked in the visitors' lot.

A beefy cop behind a bullet-proof bubble in the lobby squinted at Broker's badge and ID, called up to J.T., and pointed to the elevator. Broker knew the way to Homicide.

J. T. Merryweather was a really black man with fine Carib features and pouchy lavender circles under his eyes. He had given up the cigarettes and had put twenty pounds on his hips that he disguised with expensive tailoring. Coming into the Homicide bay, Broker noticed that J.T. was spending twice what he used to on suits and shoe leather. J.T. was a captain now. He had his own alcove and desk.

J.T. spotted Broker and reached for a ringing phone. "Be right with you. I'm up to my ass, putting this new gang task force together."

Officious. Not making solid eye contact.

A chubby detective waddled by. Broker quipped, "Hey, Reardon, still keeping Sara Lee in the black, huh."

Expressionless, Reardon said, "Nothin' personal, Broker, but fuck you." He shouldered by.

The treatment. Janey had called it right. Keith was a plague carrier. Broker had touched him. The dismissive distance set a boundary, implied in J.T.'s gesture and the brush-off from Reardon. And the other Homicide cops in the room—most of whom knew him—barely acknowledged his presence. None of the old horseplay or lurid jokes.

No bitching. Always a bad sign.

*Not one of us anymore.*

Broker found himself on the receiving end of the tribal cop stare—suspicion and disapproval. Guilty until proven innocent. Either way—unworthy.

J.T. finished his phone call, got up, grabbed his overcoat and walked Broker past the cold-eyed Homicide cops, out of the bay, into the hall, toward an elevator.

"Keith do that to your face?" J.T. said offhand.

"How—?"

"Deputy out in Washington told us. Word's out Keith was yelling something about you owing him." J.T smiled, and it wasn't a smile at all.

Broker, blindsided, stopped and stared at his old partner.

J.T. shrugged. "You don't have a whole lot of friends here right now. But that shouldn't bother you, you always liked to operate alone." They entered the elevator and rode down in silence.

At ground level, on their way out of the building, they passed the chief. Prester Dobbs was skinny and balding. An import from San Francisco. His loose neck flesh and big popped-out eyes reminded Broker of an ostrich.

Head in the sand, the street coppers agreed privately. Keith had said it out loud. Among other things.

Dobbs's blue button eyes struck Broker's and glanced away. They knew each other, not well, but enough to chat in the hall. The chief turned away without a greeting.

J.T. said from the side of his mouth, "Chief don't even want anybody saying Keith's name in the building anymore."

J.T. grabbed an unmarked car from the lot, and they shot through the downtown loop, turned left and parked in front of a hydrant next to Galtier Plaza. Broker followed J.T. into an overdecorated Italian restaurant.

Too loud, too many people. Tables too small. Triple canopy hanging baskets of ferns. Going in, it was clear they knew J.T. They were seated immediately.

Away from his colleagues, J.T.'s manner relaxed. His world-weary gaze became more curious than suspicious. But still at a distance. There was no small talk. No catching up. No congratulations on J.T's promotion or showing pictures of Kit. Ten years ago they'd got off on foxhole camaraderie, taking chances for each other. Wrestling ass-holes full of PCP down to the cuffs on the pavement.

J.T. scowled at him, like he read his thoughts. "Look," he said, "you picked a loser to come back on. Being out to Washington County having prayer meetings with Keith. Not saying it's fair, but there's this shit-rubs-off thing. Some of the guys think you need a bath."

"What do you think?"

"I'm listening."

Broker took a cigar from his pocket. The ferns about wilted as he clipped the end. J.T.'s eyes enlarged with disapproval. "You can't do *that* in here."

"Not going to smoke it. Going to chew it."

"Man, that's disgusting."

Broker rolled his stogie in his mouth to the dismay of a waitress who informed him that, even unlighted, the cigar upset other customers, who had complained. Broker put it out of sight and they ordered. Lasagna for Broker. J.T. had the fettuccine.

J.T. took a piece of fresh baked bread from a wicker basket and dipped it into a small bowl of olive oil and nibbled. He chewed, swallowed and let his smoky gaze settle on Broker. "So, what do you want."

"I need some computer time, a credit work-up on Tom James, the reporter who was with Caren."

"Not my area. Put it through channels," said J.T. crisply.

"You're a lot of help," said Broker.

"Don't give me that, go talk to the feds. They're all over this thing. Check out bad-ass Agent Garrison. We call him the Lorn Ranger," said J.T.

Annoyed, Broker drummed his fingers on the table. "Okay, let's get right to it. Why did Keith turn?"

"Ask the feds, they made the case."

"I want to hear your opinion."

J.T. occupied himself with fastidiously straightening his silverware. Keith Angland was not J.T.'s favorite topic in the best of times.

"You want to know what I think, huh?" he said.

"Yep."

J.T. squinted. "How do you want the race card? Face up or face down?"

Broker shrugged. "Up, wild, I don't care."

"Okay. The last thing Chief Sweeney did when he left office was send Keith to the FBI Academy . . ."

"Uh-huh."

"He was different when he came back from Quantico. The consensus was, the management courses went to his head."

Broker nodded. Keith's attendance at the prestigious FBI academy spanned the former chief's term of office. The new mayor appointed a new police chief.

J.T. continued. "So Keith comes back and thinks he's going to set the world on fire. He locks horns with Dobbs right from the start. At first, they like, tried coexistence. Keith still ran Narcotics."

"Pretty successfully, I heard," said Broker.

"Yeah, that's why Dobbs wanted him there, he had all this good shit he could get from his new fed buddies after being the honor student out there."

"Sounds good so far. Where's the problem?"

"The promotion board comes up. Dobbs skips Keith and promotes Janey to captain."

Broker said, "Back when I was in patrol, I knew Janey. She's sharp."

"No one disputes that. But Keith had the higher score. So he started a serious rumor that Janey banged the chief to get her promotion."

"The usual department bullshit," said Broker. His stomach churned, and he had that tiresome sensation of rowing through clotted human forms in an iron boat—office politics. "Okay, I can see where this is going. The next promotion test, you make captain and he doesn't. So what'd he say then? You screw Dobbs too?"

J.T. fired back with precision, "Keith Angland made public remarks that were reported in the media. Racist remarks. He tried to racially polarize the department."

"You're giving me a speech," said Broker slowly.

J.T. carefully shuffled his razor blade features. "You asked." He looked away. "I hate this goddamn thing," he whispered. "If *he* could do it, anybody could do it. That's what's got everybody on edge. And all that fuckin' money . . ."

Broker came forward in his chair, on the verge of detailing Keith's strange behavior in the transport room. The whole James scenario. But no—what happened in that holding cell, beyond the range of the microphones, was meant to be private. His alone. So he said, "When this started, Caren called, left a message on my machine. Said Keith was in a lot of trouble. Know what my immediate reaction was?"

"Sure, you thought 'good, couldn't happen to a nicer guy.'"

Broker exhaled. "Was he really that bad?"

J.T. inspected a forkful of pasta. "Nah, he was that good, but he was a prick. What the hell did Caren see in him?"

"He was going to be mayor . . ."

"Governor," quipped J.T. In a softer voice, "Is it true, about the claw marks on his arm? The skin under his fingernails?"

"Yeah," said Broker.

"Hate this thing," said J.T. He reached across the table and placed his palm, flat down, on Broker's nervously tapping fingers. "Quit that. Here, eat your food. It's getting cold."

**44**

The snow sifted down, fine as salt, and turned to vapor when it touched the shiny black interstate. After saying good-bye to J.T., Broker drove north, then west, on the freeway loop that belted the Cities. Exile in a cabin with his baby had strengthened a weak spot in his personality. He had been forced to learn patience.

Patience suggested: Go deeper.

So he drove and thought. He'd written Caren off as a frustrated country club Republican. Wrong.

He'd thought that Keith, buried under a landslide of federal charges, would come clean about Caren, describe a messy confrontation on the icy rocks. But Keith had taunted him, and the eavesdropping feds, about the missing bodies of his alleged victims. Taking credit.

He massaged the dull ache seizing up in his left shoulder. Didn't bounce as well as he used to. Why stage a fight and *whisper* about James and the money.

Why was he wearing her ring? What was that sermon about the Russian cross?

The early afternoon traffic was almost lulling; tires turned like prayer wheels. He fell into the shifting rhythms, cruising through the northern suburbs on U.S. 694: New Brighton, Fridley, Brooklyn Center. At the 94 interchange he turned south through Minneapolis, jogged east to 35 and took it to the bottom leg of the loop, turning east on 494 in Richfield.

Broker thinking, thinking, tapping his right hand on the wheel.

Trying to decipher Keith. The broad shadow of a commercial jetliner drifted over the freeway, flaps down, on approach to Minneapolis–St. Paul International. Broker drove through the sweeping shadow, looking for the trapdoor that descended down into Keith's mad thoughts.

He saw Keith's mind as a labyrinth of austere stonework. Like a Gothic cathedral, it had tortured figures imprisoned in stained glass, relentlessly vertical buttresses. Gargoyles.

God and Satan. Right and wrong. No middle ground to take up the slack.

The road turned north, curving around St. Paul. He left the freeway at Highway 5 and took the road to Stillwater.

Didn't tell J.T. what happened in the cell. Would he tell Jeff?

He pulled into his motel, parked and walked into the lobby. The desk clerk handed him two messages. Jeff had called. The second note was from the Washington County Jail. He went to his room and called the jail.

A deputy had called Cook County and received this number. He told Broker that Keith Angland would not be receiving visitors other than his attorney. The assault earned him a move to lockdown status. Did Broker want to press charges?

No charges. The deputy thanked him and hung up. There would be no more communication with Keith. Before calling Jeff, Broker took off his coat, lay down on the bed and stared at the uniform pattern of holes in the ceiling tiles. Nothing emerged Rorschach-like from their monotony.

He heaved off the bed and reached for the telephone on the desk. Jeff would have to wait. This was between him and Keith.

"How's Kit?" he asked when Jeff was on the line.

"Coming down with a cold. What happened?"

"Keith baited me, practically admitted to the murders of Caren and Gorski and dared everyone within earshot to prove he did it. Then he accused me of having an affair with Caren and jumped me. It took two deputies and Garrison to wrestle him down and cuff him."

"How are you?"

"Sore. I'm getting too old to grapple with psychos."

"That bad, huh?"

Not lying. Omission. "He's wearing her wedding ring on his frostbitten little finger. They took off the first joint. It's pretty gruesome."

Jeff said, "Garrison did some follow-up after talking to you. Two Duluth agents picked up the Subaru this morning. They filled me in on their theory about how the Russians made their approach to Keith. Didn't know his mom was Russian."

"Yeah. Garrison walked me through it. And I gave him the letters. But we'll never see James, they're too taken with themselves and their big case."

"Maybe," said Jeff. "Maybe not."

"How's that?"

"You've got a sympathizer out there. Got a call with a message specifically for you, to use at your discretion. Looks like the feds might trip on their trench coats. That fake bomb with the tongue in it? Widely reported in the press to be the property of a missing FBI informant. That tongue?"

"What about it?"

"It's a woman's tongue."

"What?"

"No kidding. A person called me, who shall remain anonymous because I gave my word—but they could work in the state crime lab—they heard it from somebody in the Hennepin County coroner's office, who got it straight from a big mouth at the FBI lab at Quantico. The feds ran DNA tests on the tongue and guess what—it had two of these DNA markers—amelogenin markers, I think they're called. Males only have one. They mislabeled the report and put it out."

Broker touched his bruised cheek where Keith had hit him. "That could play hell with their case."

"You bet. My anonymous caller also said the tongue was pickled with formaldehyde, like they use in a medical school. The feds probably have a hundred agents checking med schools for missing tongues."

"Being real thorough about it too, I'll bet."

"There you go. The caller also suggested this is the kind of bone Layne Wanger at the St. Paul paper might like to chew on."

"So, it's a gift," said Broker.

"Spend it wisely," said Jeff. "What do you want to do?"

"Depends. Is Kit holding up?"

"Sure. She's graduated from Pooh to the hard stuff. Sally had her watching *Mary Poppins* last night."

Broker smiled, keeping it in separate compartments. "Okay, then I'd like to poke around a few more days. See if I can turn up something on James."

The ebony marble art deco gallery of the St. Paul City Hall reminded Broker of the set for an old Flash Gordon serial. Any minute he expected Ming the Merciless to rise up out of the floor mosaic on a dais surrounded by fakey smoke and overweight spear carriers. What did rise on a dais in the dark, pillared concourse, and did in fact rotate, was *Onyx John*, a thirty-six-foot statue of an Indian with a peace pipe crafted from Mexican onyx.

Layne Wanger was the only newspaper man he'd ever trusted. Wanger would screw you, but he'd tell you first. They hadn't spoken in two years, but the St. Paul reporter agreed immediately to meet with him.

Wanger stood in front of the statue like a temple guard dog in charge of the past. Hardy as crabgrass, he looked like he was wearing the same suit and tie he'd worn the day he cast his last vote for Richard Nixon.

"You got your knife," asked Broker, deadpan.

Old joke. Years back, when Wanger was fresh out of the marines, a shiny new cops reporter, he'd bought a shiny new hunting knife. And he'd brought his shiny new knife up to Broker's cabin, joining Broker and John Eisenhower for deer season.

Never took that prized knife off. Wore it when he went to the outhouse, where he fumbled it down the hole. They'd spent a hilarious day drinking, grappling for the knife with coat hangers and sterilizing it in successive gasoline fires.

"Very goddamn funny," said Wanger.

They shook hands. "So how's it going," asked Broker.

"Not too bad, considering the new cultural weirdness. Damn near afraid to say 'bullshit' in the newsroom anymore, worried some split tail is going to accuse me of offending cows."

The smile washed quickly off Broker's face.

Wanger's eyes briefly touched the Band-Aid over Broker's bruised cheek. More serious, he said, "So what's up?"

Broker brought his hand from his pocket, palmed the badge. "I'm back on the job, temporary with Cook County."

"The Angland mess," said Wanger.

Broker nodded. "We'd like to get a statement out of your former colleague, James, so we can close the case on Caren."

"Never happen," said Wanger. "They washed him. The feds screw up a lot of things. Witness Protection isn't one of them. Unless he wants out, you'll never find him."

"So I'm learning. What kind of guy was he?"

Wanger shook his head. "Last person in the world you'd expect to get shot and wind up as a protected federal witness."

"What's the word that sums him up?"

Wanger, a man of exact descriptions, squinted. "Gambler. In the worst sense."

"How so, worse?"

"It ate him alive. Destroyed his marriage. Almost lost him his job."

"Who'd he hang with?"

"Nobody. Everybody. He was good at that, drifting in and out of any situation." Wanger frowned. "He couldn't settle for being a fair-to-good reporter, he kept reaching for the gold ring. He'd always get close, then he'd get lousy breaks. Bad luck, you could say, an interesting affliction for a guy addicted to the casinos. Last year he wandered into Mystic Lake between assignments and got lost. Lost track of time, missed his deadlines. Problem was, some busybody supervisor in Circulation was at the casino on his day off and saw James drowning at the blackjack tables.

"Problem was, he faked the story he was supposed to be covering. Word got out. He was suspended and demoted."

"Maybe his luck changed," speculated Broker.

"Not exactly the way I'd characterize getting shot," said Wanger slowly, narrowing his eyes. "What you got going here?"

Broker shrugged and dangled a sentence. "Could be I have something on the case against Keith Angland."

"Hmmm." Wanger feigned boredom, but Broker saw his jaw muscles tense, ready to bite.

"But first, I'm curious how James got onto Caren. I need somebody who can help me get to know him real fast."

"Ida Rain," said Wanger. "The East Neighborhoods editor, his boss. I detect a little heat there. She took it hard when he disappeared."

"What's she like?"

Wanger composed his face, searching for a word. "Interesting woman, independent, reserved. Classy dresser. She must have thought James could be saved. She does that every couple years. Plays medevac. Reaches down and pulls some fuck-up out of the glue and fixes them."

"What did she see in him?"

Wanger squinted philosophically. "You ever meet a woman who's pretty impressive. Has her life very together in all respects, except she keeps making this one mistake over and over."

"Yeah," said Broker. Caren, who kept marrying cops.

She agreed to meet thirty seconds into the call. "There's a coffee shop catty-corner to city hall, around the block from the paper. I'll be wearing a scarf," she said in a husky voice.

The muted autumn colors of the scarf were quietly understated in everything she wore. She stepped from a sudden snow squall wearing a slim gray wool skirt down to high-heel boots, a raw silk blouse and a bulky beige sweater. He guessed forty, with a complexion that stopped aging at thirty, lustrous reddish brown hair, smoky brown eyes, the fresh posture of a young Lauren Bacall . . .

And a chin that rescued her from a life sentence of beauty.

He stood at the door, pointed to her scarf. She extended a cool hand, long white fingers, tipped with burgundy-lacquered nails. "Phil Broker, wife of Nina Pryce, hello."

He cocked his head, let the playful jibe whistle past. Shook her hand. Ida lowered her eyelids a fraction. "I just mean that Nina is a headline. Some people are headlines."

Broker took a closer look at her and understood she could throw sex across a room like a ventriloquist. If you were in a mind to play catcher.

Which did not occur to him.

They sat down, ordered two cups of expensive coffee. "Do you know where Tom is?" she asked straight off.

"He went into Witness Protection."

"I know that. But where is he?"

"I was hoping you might have some idea. I need to find him," said Broker.

"So do I," said Ida with a droll smile. "To hang up on him. He left without saying good-bye."

Not missing sleep over James. Not even bitter, he decided. Disappointed and . . . curious and maybe a little intrigued, talking to a cop about it. "The conventional wisdom is, you can't find them once the feds disappear them."

"But you don't believe that, or you wouldn't be here," she said, leaning forward. "Why do you need to find him?"

After you looked at her awhile, the flaw in her face became less odd and more of an artistic exaggeration. She had a definite undertow. Broker wondered if her skin was that smooth all over. He thought of the snowy, nude Dresden figurine his dad had brought back, as a war souvenir, from Germany.

He unzipped his satchel and placed a photocopy of the hate letter on the table in front of her. "I think he sent this to me."

Her eyebrows bunched as she scanned it, her lips curdled once. She slid it back to his side of the table. "Sick," she said. "The person who wrote this was having a bad Stephen King experience. Why do you say Tom wrote it?"

"I have a fourteen-month-old daughter," Broker said. "Tom James spent two minutes alone with her. The next thing she did was almost choke to death on a piece of a hundred-dollar bill. Then he ran away before I could question him. An hour later Caren Angland was dead."

His words levered her back, erect in her chair.

Broker smiled thinly. "Stuff they left out of the news stories." Now that he had her full attention, he said, "You were his editor, so I wondered if anything about the writing was familiar?"

She shook her head, a trifle too quickly. "Tom was more like Joe Friday in the old *Dragnet* series. Just the facts. Strictly old-school AP style. He was *not* a creative writer, believe me."

"I believe you. Just one of those grounders you have to run out." But he left the sheet on the table between them.

She crossed her arms, caught herself, unfolded them. Her eyes perused the sheet. "Why would he write that? He doesn't even know you." More than curious. She was trying to solve a puzzle in her mind. Good.

"Maybe he's angry at me because I accused him of hiding something. You know about the scene at my place up north?"

"I read all the stories."

"Tom came alone, he left Caren down the road. By herself. If he'd brought her along, she'd be alive today. And, like I said, when I confronted him, he ran."

Ida twisted her lips in a half smile. "He saw his big chance to run out on everything. And he took it."

"Really?"

She nodded. "Left his job, his debts and . . ."

"You," said Broker.

"Correct."

"Ida, who is he?"

"He uses people." She took a measured breath. "He can't help it. It's not . . . malicious. He does it naturally. It's the kind of gift that made him a good reporter. In his time."

"Why 'in his time'?" Broker asked.

Her shoulders shifted in a subtle shrug. "Things changed. New management arrived, went on a retreat and played spin the newsroom. Currently we are in the grips of team theory. Are you a team player, Mr. Broker?"

"My stomach gets upset every time I go in an office," he admitted.

Ida continued. "The new atmosphere favors the young. Tom was no longer young. He also tended to get ahead of his facts, sometimes." She sniffed. "Nothing a good editor couldn't correct."

"I hear he gambled," said Broker.

"Blowing off steam. I may be wrong on that."

Broker wondered aloud, "What did he want most?"

She cut him with a precise look. "That's easy. He wanted to be someone else."

A custom-fitted aura of loneliness surrounded her, as carefully chosen as her attire.

Broker came forward in his chair. "How, someone else?"

She pulled back. "I'll have to think about that. Do you have a card?"

Broker reached into his wallet and gave her one of Jeff's Cook County cards. He crossed out Jeff's name and wrote in his own. On the back, he left his name again, his home phone and the number of his motel. "I'll be at the last number for the next two days," he said.

She narrowed her eyes. "I researched every angle of the Caren Angland story. I even saw her, briefly, when she picked Tom up, in front of the paper. You were married to her."

"Didn't work out," said Broker.

"So this is personal?" she asked.

"You could say that." He was thinking more of Keith than Caren.

Ida inclined her head. "You were a detective for the BCA. Before that, St. Paul. Two years ago, you took medical leave and went on your 'adventure' with Nina Pryce . . ."

"Really," said Broker.

Ida hid her chin behind her knuckles. The effect was devastating. "Really. My job is checking facts. You traveled to Vietnam to find Nina's dad's remains. Which you did. The Vietnamese government awarded you something like half a million dollars in gold because you and Nina also unearthed a national treasure. There's a rumor that you smuggled a lot more of that gold to Thailand and sold it on the black market. That you have these interesting foreign bank accounts. You quit the BCA and moved up north. You tell people you look after a bunch of lake cabins, but your folks really do that."

"Hmmm," said Broker. "How'd you put all that together?"

"I'm real good," she stated boldly. "That part about the hundred-dollar bill, your daughter? Mr. Broker, Tom was broke as a church mouse, unless he won it gambling."

Broker smiled. If there was a key to James, she was it. "Maybe we can talk about it some more," he suggested.

"I'll think about that," said Ida. "And I'll take this"—she picked up the letter—"and read it again."

He tapped his finger on the business card lying on the table. "Do that. Then call me."

Ida picked up the card, put it and the letter in her purse, and thanked him for the cup of coffee. He watched her walk from the coffee shop, hearing the two-inch heels on her boots strike the tile floor. A snappy rhythm to her walk. Like castanets. Like . . .

Ida faded into the headlong snow streaming between the buildings, but Broker had tripped into a rabbit hole of memory and was thrown back more than twenty years, to a torpid summer day, sitting in a classroom at the army signal school in Ft. Knox, Kentucky, listening to dots and dashes beep from a sweaty pair of earphones. A crash code course, for Special Operations.

Ida's heels. The rings on Keith's horrible licorice fingers.

Slowly, stunned, he tapped his finger on the table. Dot-dot-dot. Dash. Dash. Dash. Dot-dot-dot. Only the most well-known Morse code signal in the world.

Keith had been sending S-O-S, with their wedding rings.

*Help.*

The plummeting snow drilled straight down, each flake individually aimed. Broker stood in the street next to his Jeep, car keys in hand. Unmoving. A white crown of flakes slowly built on his hair.

*Help me.*

*Help you do what? Asshole.*

Lips moving. Crazy man playing statue in the snow, talking to himself. He shook it off. Locked it in its own compartment, checked his wristwatch, dusted the snow off his head and got in the truck. He had to see Dr. Ruth Nelson, Caren's shrink.

Heavy snow churned the streets of St. Paul to white canals. Cars floated through turns, slid sideways. Broker dropped the Sport into four-wheel, left the downtown loop, climbed the hill and passed the cathedral.

Dr. Nelson maintained an office in her home, a shambling white elephant in a herd of Summit Avenue mansions overlooking St. Paul.

She opened the door and asked to see his identification. Somewhere in the echoing gymnasium of the house, Broker heard preschool-aged children being nannied.

She was about Broker's age, midforties, with strong features, a large nose, healthy circulation and short black hair. Her handshake was firm, her brown eyes direct and the calves trim below the hem of her casual denim jumper.

In her second-story office, tall windows looked out on bare oak branches that swam off into white schools of snow. A gas fire jetted discreetly in a small fireplace with artificially sooty bricks. The walls were a barricade of shelved books, and an invasion of blunt Eskimo stone seals and walrus overran the place. Three large photographs of European rooftops, probably Paris, were prominently positioned. Broker wondered if the patients were supposed to notice there were no people in the pictures.

He had once dated an FBI profiler who had trouble keeping her clip-on holster fastened to her miniskirt. When they broke off, she described him as a fugitive from modern psychology.

Broker was leery of therapy. Under the high ceilings of this room, it looked to be a game of let's pretend to be intimate in an atmosphere of scholarly reserve and quietly paraded affluence.

Two comfortable armchairs were arranged in front of the gas fire, but Dr. Nelson did not invite him to sit down. Instead, she asked, in a challenging tone, "How did you find me?"

"I read your name on a pill bottle."

"Are you wearing a gun, Mr. Broker?"

Broker smiled. "I hunt Bambi too." She had him typed: cube of beefcop with a holster for a truss. He had not formed an impression of her, which meant he had more distance than she did going into this situation. Her cliché about guns, given the neighborhood and her title, was a liberal conditioned response, like lighting a cigarette. He ignored it.

"I'd prefer you leave it out in the car, actually."

"Sorry. This block looks nice, but I hear it has a high burglary rate. But the answer is no, no gun." He smiled again and looked around the room. "So, this is where it happened?"

"I beg your pardon."

"Where you met with Caren."

"Don't play cop tricks with me, Mr. Broker." She crossed her arms across her chest. Miffed, looking down her beaky nose. Big eyes and black hairdo. Heckle or Jeckle with a medical degree.

"I mean, you actually sat here and talked. I thought you guys just wrote prescriptions for drugs these days. Fifteen minutes per patient."

"Does this look like an HMO?" Cool. Expert on defense.

"No, it looks expensive. How'd she pay for it? Police lieutenants don't make that much."

Getting a little sanguine around the cheeks, she said, "She had her own money. She did quite well when she sold their last house."

"Of course." Broker pointed to one of the chairs. "May I sit down?"

"No."

"Would you show me your file on Caren?"

"No."

Broker took his small notebook from his parka pocket. "When was the last time you saw her?"

Dr. Nelson walked behind her desk and flipped open a thick leather-bound organizer. "December twelfth, ten to eleven A.M. She was always prompt." She flipped the book shut.

Broker jotted the information. Spoke without looking up. "Did she look agitated? Mention being in danger?" When he glanced up her eyes burned at him. He raised his eyebrows.

Dr. Nelson recrossed her arms. "The morning of the day she died, he, Keith, called my office, early. He was looking for her. He said they'd had a fight. He thought she'd come here."

Broker jotted: *Keith thinks she needs shrink. Caren thinks she needs me?*

He looked up. Dr. Nelson shook her head. "Just routine questions? Taking notes. You were *married* to her once. She talked about you. She died on her way to see you."

Broker shifted his weight, leveled his eyes. "Caren and I divorced almost fourteen years ago. I hardly spoke to her in that time. I literally haven't seen her for five years. I'd love to know exactly why she was coming to see me . . ."

*What the hell?*

Broker covered the distance to her desk in two brisk strides. He spun her appointment book around. Opened it, leafed through the dates on the pages. Verified the name and time written in the doctor's tidy printing: *"Caren. 10 a.m."*

"Hey," protested Dr. Nelson.

His voice canceled hers: "Did she leave early?"

Dr. Nelson narrowed her eyes. "No. She always stayed the full hour. Sometimes longer, we'd talk . . ."

Broker raised his hand, a plea for quiet. Started to take a step, halted, changed direction, another half step, stopped.

"Maybe you *should* sit down," said Dr. Nelson.

Broker shook his head, thumbed through his notebook, checked something, looked up at her. "Did the FBI—anybody from the U.S. attorney's office—contact you about Caren?"

"No." She hugged herself. Not body language games. Real. "Why?"

"No one confirmed the time of her last session?"

"No."

"I would like to sit down," said Broker. He lowered himself in the nearest chair. He engaged the concern in her eyes for several beats, asked, "What was your professional opinion of Keith?"

"Keith?" She masterfully controlled her distaste. "He *killed* her, that's my opinion."

"I mean, did he come here? Did you observe him?"

She looked at him with this amazed expression. "Twice, at the beginning. His beeper was constantly going off, he kept asking to use the phone."

"You didn't like him."

"We don't have the luxury of personal preferences."

"Bullshit. You disliked him."

"I recognized him for what he was," she said.

"Which was?"

She spun, took two steps, reached for a hefty maroon book in the bookcase behind her desk. "You want to understand Keith. He's right here." She thumbed the pages and thrust the heavy book at Broker.

He took it and read where she tapped her finger. "Obsessive-compulsive personality disorder." Under the subheading Diagnostic Features, he scanned: "The essential feature of obsessive-compulsive personality disorder is a preoccupation with orderliness, perfection-ism and mental and personal control at the expense of openness, flexibility and efficiency."

"Add anger, mix with booze and you get a witch's brew," she said.

Broker rubbed his chin. "Did you point out, to him, what you just told me—give him a few shots, you know, in the back and forth?"

Back to the folded arms. "I may have told him he had some classic control issues."

"Uh-huh." Broker stared at her.

"I mean—he systematically killed the relationship. When he didn't get promoted, his obsessiveness went from mild to full-blown. They had put off having a child until he became a captain. When he didn't get the rank, he privately had a vasectomy. Then the drinking started. And the abuse. Every day he was on her, drip, drip, drip, like weather torture. The belittling, the silent anger. When he finally destroyed her, there wasn't much left."

Slowly Broker stood up, carried the book to the desk and set it down. He wrote the title in his notebook: *Diagnostic and Statistical Manual of Mental Health. Fourth Edition.*

"So, basically, her problem was Keith."

"Her problem was an irrational decision to stay in a destructive situation."

"She was loyal," Broker said.

"Don't play word games," said Dr. Nelson.

"I'm not," he said with a flash of rising anger. "She *was* loyal. She took an oath. She tried to live by it. When Keith violated the oath he lived by, she decided to do the right thing, and it got her killed."

"That's morbid."

Broker looked around the posh office. "She came here because if she went to the HMO, people she knew would see her. You gave her privacy, and drugs, for a price. If I'm morbid, what's that make you?"

"I don't have to listen to this."

Broker pressed on, "Did you try to warn her?"

"Of course," Dr. Nelson stated in an icy tone. "She said the one thing she knew about Keith was that he'd never lose control. But she was wrong. He did lose control. First he hit her and then he killed her."

Broker shook his head, said slowly, "Keith Angland never did anything spontaneous in his life. He always has a reason."

"Amazing. You're protecting him. He killed a woman that was once your wife, and you're making excuses for him. What a bunch of sexist crap. Next you'll tell me she asked for it."

Broker smiled. "May I use your phone?"

"You may not. Now, if you're through, I have a patient coming in a few minutes."

Broker wheeled through the storm, looking for the nearest phone booth. Mental note. End his rustic Luddite phase. Buy a cell phone.

The first booth he found was glyphed with gang symbols. When he got to it, he found the receiver cord cut. Turning, he noticed the grayish brown Ford Ranger pickup, black tinted windows, parked across the street, trailing a plume of exhaust. Did he see it in front of Dr. Nelson's home?

Broker had to drive a block over, to Grand Avenue, to find a phone outside a 7-Eleven. As he dropped in a quarter, he saw the butternut-colored truck drive by and turn the next corner.

Madge in Grand Marais accepted charges. "Jeff's got my house key in his office. Have whoever is patrolling north of town stop by my place. There's a crumpled copy of a phone bill pinned to my bulletin board in the kitchen over the phone. Can't miss it. Has strawberry jam on it. Have them call me at my motel. I'll be there for the rest of the day."

Madge had the motel number. He thanked her and hung up. Then he called J. T. Merryweather. Two minutes later, he stepped from the booth and made the truck, idling half a block down the street, reflecting the confetti swirl of the stormy sky in its opaque windshield.

*Who was he? Was he Danny yet?*

He was in the program, they said; but for a week his jubilee was put on hold. The Marshals Service was skeleton-staffed for Christmas and New Year's. He had once written a story on Tibetan Buddhists that required some research into the *Tibetan Book of the Dead*. Tibetans believed that souls languished in a void known as the Bardo zone between incarnations. The description fit his current status, somewhere after Tom and before Danny, spending Christmas sequestered in a room in a Ramada Inn, in a bombed-out blue-collar neighborhood in Milwaukee, Wisconsin.

His window overlooked the empty parking lot of a defunct beer factory, the dingy, red brick housing of the departed workforce and the dreary Lake Michigan sky.

His guards changed daily, sometimes twice a day. He started demanding that they show their ID. The phone connected to room service but not to the outside.

"It's the holidays," a marshal explained. To compensate, they plied him with all the food and drink he desired. And VCR videos.

On Christmas day, he ordered a porterhouse steak, a fifth of Chivas Regal, and chose three movies. The films were calculated to indulge his current predicament—stories about Witness Protection, or about people who changed their identity.

*Eraser* with Arnold Schwarzenegger was a hoot—WITSEC on steroids for the popular culture, which was to say, teen-agers. Tom laughed, drank, turned down the volume on all the gunfire and explosions.

The second movie was appropriate. *The Passenger* with Jack Nicholson was somber and European. Nicholson played a reporter who escaped his life of quiet desperation by impulsively switching identities with a dead gunrunner. But Jack got in over his head and wound up murdered. Bummer, because old Jack hadn't thought it through, like he—Tom, almost Danny—had. Which figured, Jack's character was a TV reporter, therefore light in the ass. But the chick, Maria Schneider—the one Brando stuck the butter to, in *Last Tango in Paris*—looked great in a cotton dress against the background of the African desert.

Lascivious on Scotch, he saved the best for last. One of his all-time favorite movies: *Apartment Zero.* Another foreign film, natch—had to be, it had character development. This time the protagonist, a mild Buenos Aires landlord, Colin Firth, rented a room to a psychopathic killer-mercenary. Drawn in by the killer's dark charm, Firth finally overcame his wimp personality by murdering the psycho and absorbing his scary persona.

*That* was more like it.

Tipsy, he hit rewind and played the last scene over. Colin Firth, transformed, walked out of the art film cinema he owned, which was showing a James Dean retrospective—James Dean see, a subtle cue there in the background, brooding from the movie posters. Now Firth had exchanged his conservative suit for a leather jacket. Smoked a cigarette. New hair. Rugged, ballsy, a killer who got away with it. And, yeah—cultivating the look of James Dean.

You know, Tom thought. If you took away the glasses . . .

He stood, weaving slightly in front of the mirror over the dresser. Took off his glasses, experimented with combing his hair straight back, no part. Danny Storey could look like James Dean. Get contacts, some muscles. Put a dab of gel in his hair.

He poured another drink, rewound the movie and watched it again.

The holidays ended and Tom checked out of the Bardo Motel. Another blacked-out van was waiting. This one opened in front of the Northwest baggage handlers at the curb of the Milwaukee airport. Two new marshals, in the young, taut, military mold, met him.

They introduced themselves as Dennis and Larry. Their job was to escort him to "orientation."

Dennis and Larry were correct but uncommunicative traveling companions. They said about five words apiece all the way to Richmond, Virginia.

Another hearse was waiting in short-term parking. Tom guessed that his destination was Washington, D.C. In keeping with WITSEC's clandestine nature, the marshals never flew point to point, they always traveled at a remove.

Tom spent three hours in comfortable isolation. They stopped once at a Holiday station on an interstate exit, to use the bathroom. The marshals parked the van literally three feet from the bathroom door. Tom was out and back in, not seeing more than a slice of bare trees. Cloudy sky. The air was cold, wet, damp. But still some trace of green lingered to the exhausted grass. No snow.

The ride ended in another parking garage. Tom went up another elevator and was admitted to another quiet floor of an office building with unmarked doors and thick carpets.

His escorts unlocked a door and told him to go in and wait. Tom carried his bag into an efficiency apartment appointed with clean, plain furnishings. A sliding door led to a small balcony that faced brick walls on three sides. He heard voices, Spanish vowels slid off Asian tones. Cooking smells hung on the stale enclosed air. People were living all around him. A child yelled, then another.

He was in a warehouse of protected witnesses and their families.

There was a knock on the door. Tom opened it and faced a tall slender prematurely gray man in dark slacks and a light blue button-down shirt. No tie, black loafers. He looked less military than the escorts. He looked tired.

"Tom, my name is John, and I'll be handling your processing." He pointed to the telephone next to the bed. "That's an internal line that rings in my office."

"So we're self-contained?" asked Tom.

"Completely. You won't even see other people going through the process."

"How long will it take?" asked Tom.

"Not that long for you. In fact, very fast." John handed Tom a manila folder containing a menu and schedule of daily activities. Most of the regular schedule had been Magic-Markered out on his copy.

"All the testing except routine physical and dental has been waived. And your file is green lighted—which means you're being processed quicker than anyone I can remember."

John rubbed his eyes. "Actually, while you were in transit, we came up with a workable plan to reestablish you. Basically, we're waiting on minimal redocumentation."

Tom grimaced. "I've read about people going years before they get new Social Security cards and birth certificates."

John wrinkled his nose. "They didn't deliver Tony Sporta."

"So how long?"

"Just weeks. Less."

The last item in the folder whipped Tom's pulse. A map of northern California. Tom grinned. "I wanted warm."

"San Francisco and the immediate Bay Area are full. But we have an inspector-handler on the coast, south of San Francisco who has a ready-made situation that is perfect for you." He pointed to the map, below San Francisco.

Tom scanned the map. California. Hollywood. Earthquakes. El Niño. And Charles Manson.

John's finger stabbed a place-name where the coast notched in south from San Francisco Bay. "How does Santa Cruz strike you?"

Something about the name snagged in his memory. Something he'd read. Something exciting.

*Santa Cruz.* He recalled it was the epicenter of the big quake in 1989. But that wasn't it.

Pondering, he acted merely curious and apprehensive. John smiled and said, "It's perfect for you. A laid-back college, tourist town. With San Jose and Silicon Valley just over 'the hill,' that's what the locals call the Coastal Mountains."

"Mountains and the ocean," said Tom happily, and it was like a dream.

"And redwood trees," added John. "A slice of Berkeley preserved from the 1960s. Real tolerant people."

John placed a pile of books on Tom's bed; they were a mix of travel manuals and locally published nonfiction about northern California. He glanced at his clipboard.

"You've expressed a preference for a new name: Daniel Storey."

"Is it all right?" Tom asked.

"No one in your mother's or father's family is named Storey, are they?"

"No. I didn't borrow it. I made it up. From the sound of it."

"Storey," said John. "It could be a corruption of a Scotch, Irish or English name."

"James is English, and my mother's maiden name was Higgins."

"No problem." John shuffled some paper in the folder and handed Tom a legal form. "Fill this out. It's an application for a legal name change. We'll hand carry it to a federal judge."

"Quick," said Tom.

"Absolutely. Now, is there anything else to start?"

"Contacts," said Tom eagerly. "And a haircut."

John nodded. "Get you to an optometrist tomorrow morning. For now, take it easy. Anything you need, just pick up the phone. The TV is full cable, all the movie channels plus pay per view. You understand you can't leave the room without an escort."

John left and Tom inspected the room service menu. He picked up the phone and ordered grilled pork chops, baked potato, green vegetable and a salad. The refrigerator in the kitchenette was stocked with soda and water. A shopping list form stuck to the front with a magnet. Cupboards were stacked with dishes, drawers with towels and dishcloths. Coffeemaker. Dishwasher.

Back at the table, he perused the map of California. What was it about Santa Cruz? He picked up the phone and heard John's voice answer immediately.

"John, there is something about relocating to Santa Cruz I'd like to discuss."

"Sure, give me about twenty minutes."

Tom opened a Diet Pepsi, carried it to the table on his balcony, and sat down. Below him, the voices of a family, male, female, whining child, rebounded off the brick cocoon. The enclosure resonated with the hive smells and sounds. But furtive. Out of sight.

The unmistakable scent of fish sauce drifted up from a lower gallery. A half dozen cable television stations and radios competed. The different languages. The Witness Program had been conceived for the Italian Mafia. Now it sounded like the UN. Tom smiled. The multiculturalism of the drug trade.

Santa Cruz?

John knocked. Tom got up and let him in.

"I'm trying to remember something I read about Santa Cruz, something that made the place stick in my head. Was it ever the site of a big story? I mean, besides the big quake in 1989?" asked Tom.

John grinned. "The UCSC mascot is the Banana Slug. Is that it? Just kidding. Does serial killers ring a bell?"

"Wait, yeah," said Tom. "In that book by the FBI profiler."

"Sure. Douglas's book. In the early 1970s, Santa Cruz had the reputation of being the Serial Killer Capital of the World. It's where Ed Kemper went on his rampage—he killed six coeds, then his mother and a friend of hers. At the same time, a guy named Mullin was killing people in Santa Cruz, apparently at the direction of inner voices. Also, a hermit named Frazier came down from the hills and slaughtered a whole family, claiming to be defending the environment."

"Real fun place to put a college," said Tom. S*erial killer capital of the world*. Where the United States government, in its wisdom, was relocating him.

He savored the irony. Thanked John. After the marshal left, Tom turned up his collar, whipped a wet comb through his hair and viewed himself, minus his glasses, from different angles in the bathroom mirror.

Tom had his hair cut, received an eye exam and ordered his contacts. And he took a full physical. The doctor told him his leg was mending well, he could begin light exercise. He settled into a routine. "The facility" had a small gym. He visited it two hours in the morning and two hours in the evening. Faithfully Tom began to perform Agent Terry's road exercises.

The red streak of scar tissue on his calf stung as he jogged on the treadmill. Liking the pain, he ran harder. In the privacy of his room, he stood naked in front of the mirror. His glasses were now a backup system. The marshals had fitted him with contact lenses. His hair was shorter, but it wasn't there yet. He experimented, combing it back, turning for different angles. What would he look like with ten pounds of belly hacked off.

He was not quite pudgy, but he was definitely doughy. His breathing was shallow, and he tired easily. It seemed as if his lungs and circulation only serviced the outer layer of his body. No blood or air getting deep down inside.

His new self waited beneath that layer of flab. He began to drill through the fat. Searching for Danny Storey.

And he practiced being more assertive, aggressive. He mimicked Robert De Niro in *Taxi Driver,* standing in front of the mirror, pointing, demanding:

"You talking to me?"

He paid attention to his diet. *I will never go to McDonald's again.* He passed on the butter, the cheese, the ice cream. The salt. More chicken, fish, turkey, and steamed vegetables. Rice.

An hour every morning and evening on the running machine. A half hour rowing. The first time he struggled through thirty push-ups in a row, he cheered out loud. *Yeah, Danny, yeah.*

**48**

He was Danny now. John had started using his new name. They were changing him too fast. He was getting ahead of himself. Requesting the movie had been a mistake.

Danny paced his balcony, trying to shake off a creepy reaction to watching the movie *Jeremiah Johnson*.

Dumb, going back into things, *she* said.

Pretty dumb movie too, mountain man horse opera, right up until the part where Jeremiah, played by a young Robert Redford—clefts, no wrinkles yet—set out to wreak bloody revenge on the Indian band that killed his family.

Fucker running through the trees. Relentless.

Broker's favorite movie. Watched it over and over, Caren said.

Out there. Him and his bug-eyed kid. Never quit.

Calm down, Danny. Deep breath.

He forced himself to draw the oxygen down into the bottom of his lungs. Couldn't do it right, not all the way. But soon he would master the technique. Was going to master a lot of things. Not just the casinos. Golf. The piano.

He sucked in deep breaths and pictured emerald California fairways, movie stars trundling past in golf carts.

It seemed to work; he felt calmer, centered.

Orientation was over. He'd assumed it would take months to change into Danny Storey. Not weeks. Hell, they were booking him on a flight to San Jose. He wasn't even used to his contact lenses yet. He'd be totally dependent on his inspector in Santa Cruz.

He shut off the light and stared into the dark, into his future. His nightly ritual began with visualizing the desolate patch of woods where his fortune was hidden in the snow-covered cistern. Sometimes he imagined animals creeping around—foxes, squirrels, even unsuspecting hunters. But hunting season was over.

After he thought about his money, he, and his right hand, conjured Ida Rain. Then, usually, he was ready to go to sleep.

But tonight Broker's fat kid was waiting in the dark, reaching for his money. And she stayed there, off and on, all night

The document was called the Memorandum of Understanding. It specified the conditions of Danny's acceptance into WITSEC. If he abided by the rules, the Marshals Service pledged to support and protect him. If he violated security, he was out on his butt.

After he signed the agreement, John handed him a Photostat of a Michigan driver's license with a phony address in Warren, Michigan.

There was his new name. Daniel Storey.

"We kept your day and month of birth but took a few years off your age. Turn it in when you apply for your California license," said John.

"That was fast," said Danny, studying the picture next to his new name. In the picture he still had Tom James's hair, mustache and glasses. That would change in California.

"Danny, we think you're going to be one of our more low-maintenance clients," said John. He really was Danny now. His new legal name-change papers and new birth certificate had been mailed to his handler in California.

Danny's meager belongings lay spread out for one last inspection on the kitchen table. All the clothing had been combed through to make sure that there were no labels that originated in Minnesota. The procedure was brief because Tom only had the one bag.

As John checked through everything again, Danny shifted from foot to foot. He tensed as the inspector perused the parka label, turned the pockets inside out. He handed the jacket to Danny and went on to another item. Danny hugged the jacket and let out a breath.

Basic security. He could not contact anyone from his past without permission from Travis, who was his inspector in California, and then, he could only initiate supervised approved phone calls on a secure line. He could never receive calls. Mail, such as holiday cards to family, would be handled by the marshals, who would post them from a secure mail drop.

"I won't be sending any Christmas cards," said Danny.

He had to practice "unlearning" references that would identify him as someone from Minnesota, hereafter known as the "danger zone."

"Forget snow. Forget winter," advised John.

"No problem," said Danny.

"Forget the Twins and the Vikings."

"Who?"

Danny could tell John enjoyed working with him. Or was relieved. The rare exception. The "innocent" witness.

As with Norman and Sarah, Tom vacuumed every moment for a hint that John scented a killer in his presence. Nada.

Referring to Norman and Sarah's extensive notes, John went over the phony background. They used Warren, Michigan, where Tom had spent childhood summers with an aunt. They expanded it to include classes at Wayne State University in Detroit. He'd had a life-long drinking problem and was now sober for three years. They agreed, the ruse would paper over his job history. However, John cautioned against attending AA meetings. "Too many questions. Too many experts on drinking behavior in those meetings. You may not fit the profile over a long period and might arouse suspicion."

When his checklist was completed, John extended his hand. "It's been a pleasure, considering what's waiting for me down the hall."

"Which is?"

"Believe me, not a reporter. Good luck," said John.

The night before Danny was to fly to San Jose, which was one mountain range away from his new home and life, he violated his no-red-meat rule and ordered a steak, french fries and a bottle of red wine.

Later, he couldn't settle on an Ida Rain fantasy. Usually he pictured her in a mask, naked. Sometimes no mask, in the light. He went back and forth. Could *not* decide. Then. What if—

What if, when the time was right, he went back for the money *and* Ida. Brought her to California and, with his new wealth, turned a plastic surgeon loose on that chin.

God, she'd be unbelievable. Gorgeous.

The power of it nearly threw him off the bed.

He took the last of the wine and went out to his courtyard. His eyes moistened with emotion, imagining how it would be, slowly removing the bandages from her face.

How grateful she would be. How smooth her new chin would feel, sliding between his naked thighs, as her sweet auburn hair tickled his belly . . .

*Thank you, Danny. Thank you.*

And she'd cry, she'd be so happy and she'd raise her face to him and the hot salty tears would trickle down her perfect chin.

**49**

Late afternoon in the motel room off Highway 36. Last light leaked through the cheap venetian blinds and streaked the wall over the desk. Broker sat, eyed the telephone, sipped from a can of ginger ale, confronted the blank notebook page in front of him, fingered the message that had been waiting for him at the motel desk: Call back Ida Rain. Her work number. Put down the message. Stared at the phone again.

He picked up a ballpoint pen, twirled it, clicked the plunger.

Keith sat in a jail cell buried under an avalanche of lurid allegations, moral condemnation, and some solid evidence. The federal grand jury would indict. He would be charged. He refused to defend himself.

He wanted people to think he'd killed Caren and Alex Gorski, had tried to kill James. No remorse. Defiant. Strutting. Dabbling in jailhouse tattoos.

Wanted people to think he was crazy

*Everyone except me.*

Broker's hand dropped to the sheet of notebook paper. He drew a vertical line. Near the top, he added an intersecting horizontal line. Below the first line he added another horizontal, wider, parallel to the first. Farther down the vertical, he drew the short bottom bar. On a slant.

Bottom line.

The bottom line on the Russian cross represented suffering.

*What do you want me to see that has to stay hidden from everybody else?*

Broker stared at the symbol on the notebook page for a long time. He finished his can of ginger ale and opened another. He reached for a cigar, rolled it lightly in his lips. The phone rang. He reached for it.

"Broker? Dale Halme. I'm at your house." Halme was a Cook County deputy.

"Hi, Dale, you get in all right?"

"Sitting right here at your kitchen table with one crumbled phone log, shows call information for the eleventh and twelfth of December. Kind of smeared up, but legible."

"Strawberry jam. Can you make out any calls made between ten and eleven A.M. on the twelfth?"

"Right. Okay. Lessee, there's one. Made at ten-thirty-three A.M. Short, less than a minute. You want the number?"

"Yeah." Broker copied it.

"That all?"

"Yep. Thanks, Dale."

Broker hung up and immediately entered the number. A woman answered. "Barb Luct, East Neighborhoods."

"Hello, this is Cook County Deputy Phil Broker. I'm down in St. Paul cleaning up some details on the Caren Angland case. You're familiar . . ."

"Yes, of course; but you want the City Desk, not Neighborhoods," she said.

"No, I think I'm in the right place. Did Tom James pick up his calls on this extension?"

"He doesn't work here anymore," she said stiffly.

"But this was his phone?"

"Yes, this was his direct line."

"Thank you, you've been very helpful."

Broker chewed the cigar, was tempted to light it. The FBI had dug into the phone log, determined a call went from Caren's house to the newspaper. And then they had rested on their shovels. No one took the basic step to verify whether Caren was home.

A ghoulish configuration arose out of Caren's death and Keith's silence. Broker had always had a gift for timing, for seeing into people. He moved in step with things, so when life accelerated, became tricky, or monstrous, he didn't trip. Whatever came his way, he accepted it at its own speed. With equanimity, the world produced malignant cancer and beautiful children, like Kit.

These qualities made him a natural for working nights in Vietnam. He'd been the best deep undercover cop in Minnesota. In his time.

*If the job was merely charging the Gates of Hell with a bucket of water, send a young dumb guy. But if you needed to penetrate all nine rings, and get down past the sulfur, to the bottom, where Judas Iscariot was buried in the lake of ice—send Broker.*

If you can't send Broker to hell, send Keith.

The second call came as anticlimax.

"Broker? Yeah, J.T. I checked the phone logs with Dispatch. Keith signed out to his home number between ten A.M. and noon on December twelfth. And the feds never ran a tap on his home line."

"Thanks, J.T., and ah . . ."

"Yeah, yeah; we never talked. So long, partner." Captain Merryweather hung up.

Broker placed the phone back on the cradle and rubbed his eyes. Then he studied the Russian cross he'd drawn on the notebook page. Remembered Keith, holding up his left hand—and now he thought: as if the wounds, the tattoo, the rings, were a shrine he kept to Caren. Broker said it out loud, "Caren didn't call James. You did. You crazy sonofabitch, you're . . . *working.*"

*And it got all fucked up.*

Broker only had one move. He called Ida Rain.

"Is this business or pleasure?" she asked in a wry tone. Broker caught her still at work.

"If you've something for me, I have something for you," he said, being deliberately coy. As he spoke, he wrote in the notebook, under the Russian cross—Question: *Help me?* Answer: *Find James. Tongue story!*

She answered with wry ambiguity, "Gee, and we've only just met."

"You'll love it, what I've got," he predicted.

"I will, huh? Give me a hint?"

"An embalmer's syringe full of hot ink, straight in your heart."

Instantly practical: "Where shall we meet?"

"Someplace private, your house."

She gave him directions. She left work in half an hour.

He worked his way back toward St. Paul, took the Cretin exit off of U.S. 94, continued south down Cleveland Avenue and turned on Sergeant. Ida lived across from a junior high. Kids made bright blurs in the dusk, walking home in those absurd baggy pants. No snowball fights. No chasing and yelling.

Computer kids. Weak arms—different from the kids who climbed trees. Then he saw a suicidal skateboarder zoom on the ice.

Maybe not so different.

He checked the address she'd given him, found it, parked in front, got out, walked up the steps and knocked.

Ida swung open the door, looking fresh in a long, reserved burgundy dress after eight hours in the office. She ran her hand through her hair. "I just got home. Come in."

He entered. She took his coat and hung it in the hall closet. "Ah, watch your step," she cautioned.

Crossing the living room he had to detour around a large—as in six by five feet—jigsaw puzzle laid out on the carpet. About a quarter of the tiny pieces were assembled, framed by loose corners. A constellation of colored cardboard filled the surrounding room.

"What is it?" Broker asked.

"The Tower of Babel. It's a Ravensburger."

"How many pieces?",

Ida shrugged. "Nine thousand."

Except for the puzzle, Ida's house was neater than he could imagine living. The old rambler was dense with ribbed curlicued woodwork that insurance companies won't insure anymore because the replacement value was off the charts. She collected knickknacks. Teak elephants, Asian brass, pre-Columbian stone figures—probably souvenirs of world-trotting vacations. An old walnut-paneled Philco stand-alone radio sat in the corner of her dining nook.

A female bachelor's house. Orderly, free of dust and just shy of severe.

"Is coffee right? Or tea?" she asked.

"Tea sounds good."

Her body swept like a sensual wand through her immaculate kitchen. Like the knickknacks on her shelves, her clothing was perfectly arranged, every crease and fold deliberate.

"Should I call you Mr. or Deputy?" she asked.

"Broker's fine."

"Sit down, Broker." She pointed to one of the two chairs at the small table.

Broker sat and watched the teakettle. And her. Being married to a prodigy of Title Nine, he now noticed women who grew up forbidden to sweat. Ida was tremendously physical but in no way athletic. She'd wear blue jeans, but never get them dirty.

When the kettle boiled, she poured water into a teapot and placed the pot, two cups, two teaspoons, napkins, two tiny ceramic wafers to hold the used tea bags, a creamer and a sugar bowl on the kitchen table.

Then she brought her purse from the counter next to the stove, sat down and steepled her fingers. "I'm willing to share information with you. This puts me in a ticklish ethical situation. I'm a very private person."

She pulled a folded sheet of paper from her purse. The copy of the sick, one-page letter he'd left with her.

"I resisted doing this because, frankly, I don't like where it goes." She placed her hand, palm down, fingers spread on the letter. "Tom could have written this. This part." She tapped a stanza toward the end. "About the rats. There's one particular grisly image. The gnawed bones. The marrow."

"Go on."

Ida nodded. "Two years ago, I worked the copy desk when Tom was general assignment. He covered an ugly story about an abandoned toddler locked in a basement in a condemned house. She'd died of malnutrition and animals got to her. He was working on a tight deadline and I edited his raw copy.

"He wrote a straightforward story until he described the condition of the baby's remains. Suddenly his language went into this over-the-top fascination with a single image. I remember it almost verbatim— along the lines of, 'in the harsh glow of a naked light bulb, the tiny wrist bones had been snapped and the marrow methodically scooped out.'"

Ida made a face, sipped her tea. "He can't help himself. It's like his signature. He writes a straight news story and then gets caught on one detail that he inflates with runaway similes and metaphors. The first thing I'd do with his stories was go straight for the overwritten item." She leaned back in her chair and folded her arms across her chest. "Just my opinion. Not exactly proof."

Broker disagreed. "That's how they caught Kaczynski; his brother recognized the phrasing in the Unabomber Manifesto and called the feds."

Ida exhaled. "Tom is feeling sinister all of a sudden."

Yesterday, Broker might have agreed with her. Today, James's desperate motives were overshadowed, and he was reduced to a flawed little man who had blundered onto a huge chessboard. But Broker couldn't say that to Ida. Or Jeff. Or even Nina. He only glimpsed the barest outline himself.

"My turn," he said.

"Wait." Ida rotated her teacup in her long fingers. In a cool, wagering voice, she asked, "You don't like journalists, do you?"

Broker shrugged. "You know how it goes. The dog that bit me."

"Be more specific," she said.

Broker explained, "You don't tell the truth. Two of you can read a police report and come up with two different versions of the crime, neither of which are completely faithful to the original."

He picked up the tea cup and studied it in his hand. "The newsie comes and asks the cop what's going on. The dumb cop says it's an empty blue and white teacup with little flowers on it. The newsie goes back to the office and turns real life into a story with his name on it. Has to jazz it up. Find somebody to balance the facts from another perspective. Say they remember the cup when it was full once. If it's a big story, they'll grab at anything." He looked straight into her eyes. "Real life doesn't fit into tidy stories, Ida."

"Real life doesn't even fit into most lives, Broker," she replied, boldly holding his gaze.

Slowly, her slim hand reached across and gently disentangled the teacup from his fingers. She placed it flat, picked up the teapot and poured it half full. Her eyes swept his face. The cup was no longer his literal example. Now it was that powerful cliché: half full or half empty.

Broker asked, "How did you wind up with James?"

She touched her hair with her right hand and looked away. When she faced him again, her eyes registered the faintest glisten. "Maybe I can't compete with the Nina Pryces of the world for guys like you." She composed herself. "All I try to do is *improve* things," she said simply.

Broker waited a few beats, for the air to clear. Then he got up. "I'd appreciate it if you'd give what I'm about to tell you to Wanger. We go back a way."

"Sure." She bounced back from vulnerable fast as a speed bag. Stood up.

"Probably the place for him to start is the Hennepin County coroner's office. Apparently they have a direct line to the horse's mouth at the FBI lab in Virginia." He smiled.

"Tease." She lifted slightly, forward. Up on her toes.

"The famous tongue, that was mailed to the federal building? That they announced in a news conference as being a male tongue. And hinted it came out of a missing FBI informant . . ."

"Well?" She kind of twitched. A full-body, news-junkie twitch.

"They screwed up on the forensics. It's a woman's tongue. Probably from a medical school."

"No."

"Yes."

"That's a great tip. We'll try to get it right."

Broker nodded, they walked to the closet, carefully skirting the puzzle. She gave him his coat. As he pulled it on, his eyes swept the living room, and sitting on a cabinet shelf, he saw a framed photograph. Tom James's sincere face, glasses, longish hair and mustache. A regular "Minnesota Nice" poster boy.

"You have an extra copy of that picture?" he asked.

Ida shrugged, crossed the room, plucked the picture off the shelf and tossed it to him. "He's all yours."

Danny, wearing his new contact lenses, his hair combed back, made money plans at thirty-five thousand feet.

The problem with cash was it attracted attention. Even relatively small amounts consistently deposited in a bank would arouse suspicion. Most successful laundering schemes involved other people. Setting up a cash-and-carry business, falsifying books.

Danny wasn't interested in trusting other people. Or lugging "twenny bricks" to the Cayman Islands.

He would fix up houses. He would write. And slowly. SLOWLY. Very slowly, he would take weekend trips to casinos. He'd just play the slots at first. The long-odds megajackpot slots. He'd invest thousands of quarters and dollars. Until he hit a jackpot.

It might take years. But once he did, he'd have a legitimate income. He'd pay taxes. He could invest. He'd become known as a professional gambler who was expected to deal with large amounts of cash.

How long did it take to drive from Santa Cruz to Tahoe, Reno, Las Vegas?

Danny smiled and hugged his worn brown parka.

Twenny bricks. Flying with the sun. He pictured the barren cistern in the woods, above Highway 61, under a featherbed of fresh undisturbed snow.

He shut his eyes and imagined walking through the doors of the Sands. The sounds, the smells, the coin-song of the trays.

From the window seat, he watched the great plains pucker into the steep, shadowed wrinkles of the Rocky Mountains. Two more deputy marshals, who had taken vows of silence, escorted him to San Jose. The jet wallowed down through about a mile of clouds and landed with a splash in rain puddles under an overcast early afternoon sky. Sunny California had the El Niño flu.

In the small terminal, the escorts turned him over to a tanned man with a confident smile. Early thirties, he was part bodybuilder, part cowboy, in a lightweight sports coat, black T-shirt, faded jeans, cowboy boots and sunglasses. One of the escorts said, "He's all yours, Travis." And they ambled away.

Travis smiled, displaying perfect California teeth. A tiny stud twinkled in his left ear, and his styled hair had been irradiated to the color of ash by the sun.

"Inspector Joe Travis, pleased to meet you," he said, holding out a brown muscular hand. Danny saw a strap when the collar of Travis's coat shifted. Wearing a gun in a shoulder holster.

"Danny Storey," said Danny, shaking confidently.

"Prove it," challenged Travis, tightening his grip.

Danny froze, explored Travis's merry prankster smile and resolved to show no fear. "Hey, what is this?" he demanded.

"Ground zero orientation. Survival lesson number one coming up—where is the center of gravity in your new world?"

Danny studied this young, assured, armed weight lifter. Caught the drift. "You are the center of gravity."

"Good," said Travis. "You feel the slightest vibration, the tiniest temblor, you get on the horn to Travis. Got it?"

"Got it."

"Hell, pardner." Travis slapped him on the back. "This is going to go off slicker than whale shit."

They were walking out of the terminal toward the parking lot. Danny asked, "You're from the West, right?"

"Snowflake, Arizona."

Danny took a Power Bar from his pocket and tore off the wrapper. Made a joke. "Are there any marshals from, say, the Midwest or East?"

Travis's hand shot out and intercepted the energy bar wrapper. "Gotta watch that out here. You can't litter or smoke anywhere anymore. Not even beer joints. You drop a butt or a wrapper anywhere outside and it's a two-hundred-dollar fine."

"Jesus," said Danny, as he devoured the Power Bar.

"Fine his ass out here too, they catch him littering in public. You're in California, man," quipped Travis. After several steps, he asked, "Now, what were you saying?"

Danny shook his head. He had just discovered how wonderful the blasé air tasted. Under luminous clouds he strolled through an open-air greenhouse. "When's the last time it snowed here?"

"Oh, that's good, I like that."

Travis led him to a mud-spattered Chevy pickup. Under the thick coat of dirt it might have once been maroon. New tires, though. The box was piled full of sawhorses, scaffolding and several large plywood, padlocked boxes.

They got in, Travis turned it over and the engine purred. "Like the ad says. Like a rock." He wheeled from the lot into traffic and onto a freeway. A small portable cooler sat on the seat between them. Travis popped it open and took out a can of Diet Coke. "Help yourself," he said.

Danny selected a Sprite and leaned back while Travis dodged through lanes of congested traffic. They passed an orange Kharmann Ghia, a mustard Volvo, an eggshell blue Saab; makes and colors more exotic and expensive than Danny was used to seeing on Minnesota highways.

"Trying to beat the rush to the hill," Travis explained. "All this around here is Silicon Valley. Right over there." He swung his pop can at a jungle of vegetation and buildings. "That's Cupertino, where Steve Jobs did his thing. You into computers?"

"Sure," said Danny.

"Only way to go. Everywhere you look it's Startup City, people out in their garages working on the next software coup so they can be bought out by MicroSquash.

"Problem is, a lot of the gearheads work here but live with the potheads, over the hill in Santa Cruz. And there's only one road over the mountains. Highway seventeen. Accurately nicknamed the Highway of Death."

Travis wasn't exaggerating. The tortured road snaked through cuts in the hills. A steel guardrail fortified the center line. There was no shoulder. And no room to escape between the rail and the stark rock, both of which were scarred with auto paint. Tiny galaxies of shattered glass sprinkled the edge of the pavement.

"See what I mean," admonished Travis. "I was you, I'd stay put on the other side of this damn mountain."

Crossing the peak, Travis identified where the San Andreas fault came through. Then they started to descend into the Pajaro Valley. Danny had a contact high—hot metal, gasoline, cooked rubber, rain-plump vegetation, all marinated in the delicious air.

Travis interrupted his travelogue. "Hey, you're a college graduate, right?"

Figuring he was being tested, Danny responded, "Nah, I went a few years at Wayne State in Detroit."

"No. I mean really. You graduated."

"Really?"

"Yeah."

"University of Minnesota. Journalism."

Travis grinned. "I've handled twenty-three people, counting dependents, in WITSEC. You're my first college graduate. Also the first one who had a workable plan for their future. I'm fucking amazed."

They were winding through rolling foothills, and soon the land broadened out. The air thickened, spongy with mist. There were orchards, fields, and more swarthy people in jeans and straw Stetsons. Mexicans. Mexicans with muddy boots. The Pajaro was soggy this season. Travis stopped for a red light and then put on his left turn signal.

"This is Scotts Valley. I know a guy here. We're going to get you a haircut."

Not suggesting. De facto. Danny shrugged. They pulled off in front of a rundown strip mall of storefronts. One had a crude barber pole painted on the plate glass. Inside there were two chairs, both empty. A short Mexican guy in a white smock was sweeping the floor. A quick smile creased his brown face when he saw Travis.

"*Buenos días*, hair ball," said Travis. "Those papers come through yet?"

"Hey, Travis. Good, man. Finally got it."

They shook hands ritually, locking thumbs, cupping fingers, then clasping both hands.

"Great. Ah, this is a friend of mine. Danny Storey. Meet Hector Sanchez."

Danny took the guy's hand. After a more conventional hand-shake, he discreetly wiped a patina of Vitalis off on his pant leg.

Travis said, "Danny needs a haircut. He looks like he just crawled out of a blizzard. Fix him up so he looks at home eating fish and chips on the Municipal Wharf."

"Could you cut it like James Dean?" asked Danny.

Hector squinted. Vacant. But he winked and said. "Yeah, sure, sit down." Travis laughed and said, "I'll do my best to stage direct." Hector unfurled an apron like a matador and whipped it around Danny's neck as he sat in a chair.

Travis gave pointers as tufts of Danny's hair collected on his shoulders and tumbled down into his lap. Hector massaged some fix in Danny's new hair and worked him over with a hair drier.

Travis paced, arms folded, squinting. "Yeah, I think so. James Dean for the 1990s."

The chair spun and Danny studied his new head in the mirror. His hair was full on top and short on the sides. Kind of lightning-struck.

"Get you some sun, maybe a little body piercing, you'll look like a native," approved Travis.

"I'll skip the earrings," said Danny.

"No problem, I just do it to blend in with the gazelles up in Frisco." Travis handed Hector a roll of bills, they did their elaborate routine with the hands again. Then Travis and Danny left the shop. The soft late afternoon light was a cool haze around Danny's ears. They got back in the truck.

"So what do you think?" asked Travis.

"He's one of your success stories," said Danny.

Travis gave him an appraising look. "You got it. I'm trying to help, but he's sucking wind, one day at a time. Maybe I can swing him a better location in town, that'd help. But basically he's fucked. He's an almost illiterate Mexican dude who sold dope all his life. And now he's the one thing he was raised to hate: a rat, a squealer. Guy never heard of James Dean." Travis sighed. "What are you gonna do. Most of my clients are up north in the Bay Area. I don't get down here a whole lot."

"You put him through school to cut hair?" asked Danny.

"Nah, he picked that up in the joint."

"Life is not fair. And anything that can go wrong, will," he observed.

"A-fucking-men," said Travis. They drove in silence for a while, entering a built-up area. Travis whipped into another strip mall, but this one was broad, paved, landscaped, full of late-model cars and devoid of Mexicans.

"What is this?" Danny balked as Travis walked him into a tanning salon.

Travis spun on his Spanish heels. "Hector just got his new birth certificate. It took nine months. Yours is in the glove compartment of the truck. Along with a new Social Security card. Tomorrow when you get a driver's license, they take your picture. Right now your face looks like veal. *Comprende?*

"After you get your temporary license, we go to the bank and you open a checking account. Then I sell you this truck and the tools in it. Then we take you to look at the house you're going to buy from us on a land contract. You're getting it at a steal because of a stipulation we write into the contract, that you rehab it. You with me so far."

"What about the computer, printer, modem?"

"In the works. The best money can buy."

Danny pushed past Travis into the salon and walked up to the receptionist. "How long is the wait to get into a booth?"

An hour later they were strolling past an open fish market on the Municipal Wharf that jutted into Monterey Bay from downtown Santa Cruz.

"You don't need that jacket, it's warm," said Travis.

"That's okay," said Danny, hugging his jacket.

"See that." Travis pointed at a large mound of fish flesh on ice. "That's a bonito, that fish rode El Niño from Hawaii. Everything here is upside down this winter."

Danny smiled; the idea that things were upside down put him on top for a change. Soon they were, as Travis had predicted, sitting outside at a picnic table, eating fish and chips.

Lassitude wrapped Danny. He watched the twilight play on his newly grilled arm. His reflection in the restaurant window stared back at him. Tanned, the contacts, the shorter, swept-back hair. Eerie.

"See that big hotel over there on the boardwalk," said Travis. "That's where we'll stay tonight. Tomorrow I'll take you to the house."

Danny swung his eyes, saw a lot of hotels. Yawned. There was a beach, but nobody was swimming. And the Coney Island fretwork of an amusement park. And sailboats. Some tourists, Japanese maybe, were tossing shreds of hot dog buns off the pier to sea lions that roared hollowly below them among the pilings. A pelican perched on the railing in back of Travis, and behind the pelican the setting sun smelted the smoky sky and the ocean into a sheet of burning amber chrome.

He had been trained to ruthlessly excise clichés from his writing. But right now, he couldn't improve on: today is the first day of the rest of your life.

Danny woke early, windows thrown open to the swoosh of Pacific surf, and went slowly at the day, one cup of room service coffee at a time. He took the carafe of coffee and the little silver creamer out to the small table on the balcony that overlooked the fog-soaked board-walk. Wet cement tickled under his bare feet. Mist. Dew. Everything was jeweled. He could make out the ghostly shapes of palm trees and pine trees side by side, and the white tufts of the tall lollipop grass that Travis called pampas grass. Red tile roofs and squared-off hacienda architecture.

The gourmet air smelled like rising tropical dough. Dank. Humid.

People came here to start over. They had to. No more land to run away on. Me too, he thought.

The fantasy returned. Warm in his lap. As the first blades of dawn stirred the mist he pictured Ida Rain sitting across from him in a silky little bathrobe, kind of a kimono thing. Saw it draped open to show the one perfect crease that marked her smooth stomach. They'd have hidden the scars on her new face. Tucked them up under new chin. Her wide expressive eyes would be brimming with gratitude.

*If I did all this, I can make that happen, too.*

The kind of generosity that could make amends for the death of Caren Angland. Yes. Exactly.

Purposefully, he glanced back over the California Rules of the Road booklet Travis had given him to study last night. An hour later, when Travis called his room, he was showered, shaved, and upbeat.

At breakfast Travis presented him with a new wallet containing a

Social Security card, and, nestled between the clean-smelling leather folds, four hundred dollars in cash. And he handed over the Photostat of his new birth certificate. He also gave him an index card on which were written three more pieces of his new identity.

His address: 173 Valentino Lane, Watsonville, California, his phone number, and his employer, Acme Remodeling.

"Which is basically me, Joe Travis, Doing Business As," said Travis.

They had a full day. Travis seemed to genuinely enjoy himself. He grooved with quiet glee at being able to move behind the scenery at will—to effect deft custom alterations of reality.

First they stopped at a State Farm office, and Danny purchased auto insurance, which he'd need at the Santa Cruz County Building on Ocean Street, their next stop. Travis preceded him into the license bureau to put the fix in. Then Danny went in and waited in line, then waited in another line with a lot of people talking Spanish. Then he sat in a room with a lot of these people and took a multiple-choice test about the rules of the road in California.

An hour later the test was graded and he stood in a third line. Travis had arranged for him to skip "behind the wheel" to save time. He surrendered his fake Michigan license Photostat, used his new contacts to read the optical chart, and stood, short haired and tanned, for a photograph.

Then he completed his first transaction as Daniel Storey, paying for his California driver's license. The clerk filled out a temporary form good for thirty days and told him his license would be mailed within two weeks.

Then they got back in the truck and drove Highway 1 out of Santa Cruz. Travis joked, calling it Highway 911. "More fact than joke, you get 'down below,' that's what they call fuckin' L.A."

Soon they were out of town, into the country. The fog had drifted up to baste the low-hanging clouds. Danny began to sweat.

"Welcome to Steinbeck country, the Pajaro Valley," waxed Travis. "Strawberries, artichokes, apples, blackberries, lettuce and celery. This, and the Salinas Valley down south, is the stronghold of the United Farm Workers."

Danny was too drowsy to pursue it, so he nodded and took in a road sign. They'd turned off the highway onto a secondary road named Freedom Boulevard.

"Freedom's the town this side of Watsonville," said Travis.

Danny smiled. Took it as a good omen. Another turn onto Varni Road, then a right onto Amesti Road. They were out in the sticks. Danny liked that too.

Then Travis turned one last time, onto Valentino Lane, and passed a sign: DEAD END. And that's where they went, past tidy one-story white stucco homes with fanatically manicured cactus gardens, until they ran out of road and stopped in front of a six-foot-tall slat fence overgrown with bushy vines. A whitewashed hacienda was about a hundred yards to the right separated by a corral. But no horses. Danny did see about five cats lolling in the muzzy shadows of the fence posts. The next nearest house was almost five hundred yards away.

Travis got out and turned a key in the padlock on the gate, which was barely visible among the overgrown shrubs. Pulled the gate open, returned to the truck and drove in.

The house was a simple box, flat roof, painted dark brown and tucked under the leaves of a tall spreading tree in the backyard. The picture windows along one front side were smoke streaked. A corner of the trim was buckled and charred. The fire had flashed in the kitchen, shot through the doorway into the attached garage, and burned a hole in the garage roof before it was contained. Plastic sheeting was tacked over the mangled garage shingles.

Once there had been extensive gardens surrounding the place, but they had reverted to thick brush. Tall yucca cacti poked through here and there, and he saw a few smaller prickly pears.

"Are there snakes?" he asked Travis as they got out.

"Nah, bull snakes maybe."

Travis unlocked the door, and they went into a dirty empty living room that reeked of lingering smoke damage. The hideous orange shag carpet was tinged with soot.

"This end of the place is shot," said Travis, walking him into the kitchen, where a black slash up one wall revealed charcoal wall studs. A cheap GE electric range and refrigerator were plugged in at the edge of the living room. Neither had smoke damage. Used. Recent additions. The tour continued. "But back here it's not bad." They came out of the kitchen onto a broad screened porch that overlooked a tiered redwood deck that fitted around a gnarled spreading oak.

Travis led him down a hall, pointed out the working bathroom and the two bedrooms at the end. One was empty. The other was stockpiled with furniture, boxes of bedding, utensils, dishes, mattress and springs. It looked new or, at least, not fire damaged.

"We brought all this stuff in to use in a pinch if we have to hide somebody." He folded his arms and perused Danny. "You sure you want to do this? It's going to be hot sweaty work."

Danny grinned. "Hey, I eat this shit up."

Travis squinted and cocked his head. "You sure you used to be a reporter?"

"What's that?"

Grinning, they went out the screened door, down the deck. The back lawn was knee deep in weeds and ended in an extensive oak woods.

"What's that way?" Danny pointed past the oaks.

"Just fields. It's pretty isolated here. That's what appealed to the asshole who used to own it. Remote. Good place to set up a meth lab. Except he was an idiot who flunked basic chemistry and he burned down his kitchen when we busted the place. We seized the house as assets. Same way we came into the truck out there. We were getting ready to auction them off when your case file came across my desk. And I got to thinking. We sell it to you on paper and you fix it up and sell it back to us—you'd have a legitimate paper trail to fall back on. Plus, you get a quiet place to work. Like in the proposal you put together during your intake interview."

Danny smiled. "It's perfect." He pointed to the white house next door past the corral. "Who lives there?"

"Couple of women."

"Oh yeah," said Danny, making a long wolfish face.

"Forget it, they're lesbians. This is Santa Cruz. Five percent of the county population is registered lickers."

"That can't be right?" Out of reflex, Danny questioned the statistics.

"Didn't say it was right, but those are accurate numbers. C'mon, we have some serious shopping to do."

Travis was on a tight time line, so they made whirlwind rounds. Danny opened a bank account in Watsonville. A $6,000 money order from Acme Remodeling signed over to Daniel Storey launched the account. The money was combination living stipend and business expenses to get started on the house. Then Travis sold him the truck and the tools in it for a ridiculous $1,000. They transferred the title and registration in the bank and had the deal notarized. Danny was the legitimate owner of a 1989 Chevy truck. He had a bank account, driver's license, house, and a phone number.

And the money in his coat.

Danny drove his new truck, feeling his way down the unfamiliar roads back to Santa Cruz to drop Travis at the hotel. Travis left him with a county map unfolded on the front seat and the route back to Valentino Lane marked in yellow Magic Marker. "Okay. I'll call every day and be back in a week. Give you time to settle in. Then we'll go shopping for a computer. Slightest problem you call Travis." He waved, turned, and walked away.

Danny put the truck in gear and drove from the hotel, turned up Ocean Street and traveled under mingled palm crowns and tall evergreens. El Niño was taking a lunch break. The sun peeked out and rolled a blue cobalt sheet of sky in back of the scattering clouds.

People crowded the streets. Aging hippies on skateboards with sparse ponytails, tourists, cyber millionaires, and Mexican lettuce pickers. And students showing lots of brown California skin. Shorts. Sandals. The clean air had been rinsed in the rain and mist, now the sun cured it. Dizzy on his freedom, he missed the turnoff from Highway 1 and had to backtrack. He stopped at a corner liquor store and bought a six-pack of Coors.

*Follow the yellow Magic-Markered twenny-brick road.*

He found his way back to the locked gate at the end of Valentino Lane, got out of the truck, held the keys to the truck and the house over his head and shook them in his fist. Like he'd been handed the keys to all the locks in all the prisons in the world.

Find James.

*How the hell do I find James. I'm going home to change diapers. Goddammit.* Broker drove north, away from St. Paul, staring ahead into a Minnesota sky that could inspire Sibelius. He cocked an eye to his rearview mirror to see if any butternut-gray Ford Rangers with tinted windows were behind him. All clear.

On his right, a flock of ravens descended on a snow-covered field like a shower of black arrows. Reflex thought. Something dead over in those trees.

He continued his argument with Keith.

*So you decided to play Holden Caulfield. Catcher in the Russians. Intercepting suitcases? You assigned a role to Caren. The battered wife. She would tattle on you to a reporter and end your career. You didn't confide in her. Can't confide in anyone, can you? But she stuck her nose in.*

Then James had bounced weird.

So why find James?

*The money is an excuse. James knows what really happened at the Devil's Kettle. He can blow your cover. So use me.*

*So maybe I find a thread to follow. Maybe I find James. Then what, Keith? Your new Russian "buddys" kill him. More credit accrues to your mole account.*

*Do I owe you that much?*

Broker shook his head. He was running out of separate compartments in which to store things.

*    *    *

"You don't look so hot," said Jeff.

They sat in Jeff's office. Kit hugged the Beanie Babies moose she'd acquired from Sally Jeffords. Broker debated whether he should turn in his badge and ID. He nodded his head in agreement. "Didn't sleep much last night. Motel bed."

"Well, it's up to the FBI now," said Jeff. "Maybe they can tie James to those letters." His desk was piled with paper. Petty crime and nuisance complaints go on. Jeff had other things on his mind. He didn't mention the badge, so Broker kept it.

He reached down and wiped Kit's runny nose.

"Cold going around," said Jeff.

Broker went home and called Garrison's office to see if the FBI had made any progress on the hate letters. An agent informed him that Garrison wasn't working there anymore and gave no forwarding information. No one in the office knew anything about the letters. Good-bye.

His eyes drifted south, to the cabin on the point. The glow of a TV screen illuminated the windows. Come all the way up here and watch TV.

The next morning he watched the snow melt.

Saber-toothed winter was supposed to keep the riffraff out. But January slogged into the North Shore like a muddy green tramp, reeking of April. In town, piles of snow dwindled to humps of black cinders.

The second day he was home, Kit woke up coughing, nose plugged. He spent a sleepless night holding her in his arms, fearful she couldn't breathe lying down. In the morning he called the clinic, made an appointment and took her in. Ear infection. Amoxicillin, three times a day.

After another sleepless night, he looked out on a damp morning and saw more ground than snow. The next day it was mud.

Kit's illness gave his mind a rest from thinking about Keith. A powerful urge to go buy a pack of cigarettes befriended him in the middle of the night. He put on his bathrobe, sat in the kitchen and fought back with frozen yogurt.

Refilling his bowl, he opened the thick volume, *DSM-IV*, he'd purchased at a Barnes and Noble on the way out of St. Paul. He turned to the section on obsessive-compulsive personalities.

*   *   *

Four days of antibiotics reduced Kit's infection, and Broker bundled her up to go grocery shopping. Returning home, as he flicked his right turn signal coming up on his driveway, he noticed the truck.

Hidden in the trees, a hundred yards down the road. Right on the edge of his property. New Ford Ranger 250. Tinted windows. Confederate brown-gray. He grimaced, glanced at Kit, who was doing her windshield wiper exercises half-speed in the car seat.

He slowed and passed the vehicle. Damn. No plates. Dealer's sticker in the window. He hurried into his turn, gunned the Jeep and nearly rammed the porch because he was reaching over in back, unbuckling her seat straps one-handed.

He swept her over the seat, and she squealed, thinking it was great fun. Up the steps. Plunged in his house key, turned the lock, was inside and reaching into the closet.

One hand in behind the coats, the other high, reaching for the box of shells. Kit stomped at his knee, a tiny Samurai figure armored in Patagonia fleece. Broker loaded the twelve-gauge with double ought buck.

Now what.

With no place to put her, he did the unthinkable, checked his house with her in one arm and the shotgun poised in the other, like an ancient dueling pistol. Satisfied the house was secure, he strapped her in the high chair, put the chair in the laundry room, and closed the door.

Just for a minute, honey. Promise. She was screaming before he was out the back door.

Broker checked the garage, the workshop, and then ran into the trees. Winded. Even without the cigarettes, he hadn't really worked out for months. Then he slowed. The truck was gone.

Boot prints led from the tire marks, down the slight slope into the trees. They stopped above the cabin the Chicago couple rented.

Okay. Get home. Breathing heavily, he dashed up the porch, heard her wails as he unlocked the door. Setting the shotgun aside, he freed Kit from the chair, pulled off her coat and tried to console her.

"I promise, I'll never do that again."

After he put Kit down for her nap, he tried to write a letter to Nina. *"Kit's coming out of her ear infection. Breakfast: oatmeal, vitamin, bananas, milk. Reverses spoon and holds scoop for handle and shovels it in that way. Progress? Still sleeping three hours for nap. And averaging eleven hours at night. 8:30 to 7:30 A.M. Has settled on Bedtime Bunny as her sleep toy. Cucaracha Dog gets tossed out of her crib every night."*

Broker kept the letter to providing information about Kit. Nothing about Keith. Nothing about snooping Ford Rangers. Nothing about his curiosity about his new neighbors to the south. Nina had enough to worry about.

In the evening, after supper, Kit stomped back and forth waving a shotgun barrel swab that looked like a cattail. "Puf" the Dragon loomed over her like a member of the monster chorus line in *Where the Wild Things Are*.

Then she dragged her two favorite blankets, Bedtime Bunny, Cucaracha Dog, Kitty, and her tippy cup over to the fireplace. She set them down on the hearthstones, returned to the kitchen, seized the short step stool, pulled it all the way across the living room and positioned it in front of the fireplace. After recollecting her stuffed animals and blankets, she precariously mounted the stool and peered up at the Puf. Worry wrinkled her brow.

"Oh oh, Daa Dee, Oh oh," said Kit over and over.

Broker waved at her and went back to cleaning his .45 automatic at the kitchen table.

Ida Rain called after Kit was asleep. "The Wanger story runs tomorrow morning. I can fax you a copy . . ."

"Don't have a fax."

"Well, then I can E-mail it as an attachment."

"Don't have one of those either."

"You don't have a computer?"

"Everybody says that."

**54**

From mud-swept Cook County, Broker watched and read as Wanger broke the tongue story.

*A source in the Hennepin County coroner's office . . .*

*A source close to the BCA Crime Lab confirms . . .*

*A well-known Twin Cities forensic pathologist, who prefers to remain anonymous, told this reporter . . .*

Then Wanger challenged the FBI to disprove the allegations.

The feds held a press conference. Faces washed out in the camera lights, backs against the wall, they stood for questions like candidates for a Pancho Villa firing squad. No Lorn Garrison in the lineup.

They stonewalled. The second day, they waffled. The third day, Wanger flew to Virginia, to Quantico, and filed a story that forecast an official FBI correction about the "evidence." The next day the media rep in the Minneapolis office read a brief press release: DNA testing proved conclusively that the tongue in the bomb hoax delivered to the federal building came from a woman.

"Does this change the government's case against Keith Angland?"

"No comment."

Keith Angland's high-buck criminal defense attorney held his own news conference in front of the Washington County Jail. He said he was encouraged by recent favorable turns in the discovery process. Cryptically, he predicted a jury might divine more than one interpretation for the events depicted on the famous FBI tape.

Broker watched Keith's lawyer plant the first seeds for reasonable doubt.

But it didn't solve Broker's—or Keith's—problem about James. He was down to one idea; he had one story left to leak to Ida Rain. But it was much thinner than the tongue exposé.

The FBI would not report back on the hate letters, and soon they'd trace the tongue leak to him. Then there was the Ford Ranger lurking around. And the Chicago kids in the cabin down the shore.

He was cool. No big thing, walking around with a toddler in your arms and a loaded .45 stuck in the back pocket of your Levi's. People up here did it all the time.

That night, he rocked next to the woodstove and read passages from the *DSM-IV* to his innocent drowsing daughter.

"Check this out: 'Displays excessive devotion to work and productivity to the exclusion of leisure activities and friendship.

"'Emphasis on perfect performance. These individuals turn play into structured work.

"'Reluctant to delegate tasks or to work with others. Stubbornly insist that everything be done their way.'

"Narrowly applied, that could be Uncle Keith," Broker admitted.

Or any overworked, underpaid, strung-out copper.

Nowhere in the thick manual did they list the symptoms of, or a diagnosis for, hate, greed or lust. Or the laziness that led to criminal shortcuts. The book could excuse as much evil as it could trap. He yawned, shook his head and mused out loud: "Smile for the camera, say victim."

At two in the morning, Broker got up to pee. Walking past Kit's crib he encountered a minefield of toys he'd neglected to pick up. Tiptoeing carefully, almost through—but then, ah shit.

*Dada dah da!*

*Dada dah da!*

Cucaracha Dog. Stepped right on it. Immediately Kit bolted up and wailed. It took an hour to get her back down. They both overslept, so Broker was still in bed when the phone rang. He fumbled. Picked it up. "What?"

"Hello, Broker, it's Ida Rain. How about that Wanger, eh?" In good humor, she perfectly mimicked the Far North argot.

"They sure made a pretty pasty-faced bunch of suits on TV," agreed Broker. "Ah, Ida, can I call you back, I have to change my kid."

"Girl, right? What's her name?"

"Kit."

"That's it? Kit?"

"Nina named her Karson with a *K*. I thought Karson Pryce Broker sounded like a department store. So—Kit."

"Gotcha. You have my number?"

"On caller-ID." He rang off, attended to Kit's diaper, got her a tippy cup and then called Ida back. Her voice, still relentlessly upbeat, picked up right where she left off.

"We blew everybody's socks off. We're going national with the story. We want more."

"Well," said Broker, "there is one thing." He played his last card. And it was mostly bluff. "Angland put me on his visitors list at the Washington County Jail. He had a complaint. They'll do that some-times. They can be wrong straight down the line, but they cling to one thing, a perceived quirk in procedure or a fact they think the cops or the press got wrong."

"The fact being?"

"That day, before Caren died, Keith and James had a shouting match up here. Keith told me James goaded him, said: 'She took your money.'"

He could almost hear her connecting the dots long-distance. "Tom disappears. The money disappears . . ." Ida's voice trailed off.

"You're the one who said he wanted to be someone else. Well, he is. And maybe he's better off than we know?"

"Hmmm. And everybody was looking the other way."

"You want to write that story?" asked Broker.

"It's not a story. It's hearsay. But Wanger might do some digging, considering you give such good tongue."

Broker's wince was almost audible.

"Sorry," said Ida. But she wasn't. She was having fun. "I'll run it by my boss and see what he says."

Broker hung up the phone, went to his desk, took the photo of James out of his briefcase, then removed the picture from the frame. Then he picked up Kit. "C'mon. Let's get dressed and go to Duluth. Daddy's got an idea."

**55**

Monday morning. Ida Rain called in the middle of *Sesame Street*.

"Broker, I'm sorry. But there's no story. Keith Angland won't talk to Wanger. His lawyer painted you as a nut up in the woods with a personal ax to grind. The editors backed off for now."

"Well, thanks for the try." A pause on her end stretched to awkwardness. "What is it?" asked Broker.

"Probably nothing. I'll let you know. Just wanted to touch base."

They said good-bye and hung up. He popped a piece of toast out of the toaster, buttered it, added jam, trimmed the crusts, sectioned it into wedges and placed it before Kit.

The phone rang again. The store in Duluth, saying the delivery truck was en route. Broker thanked them and hung up. Kit's spoon clattered on the floor. He took it to the sink, scrubbed it under hot water. Came back, removed the jelly from her face and had just managed to get one spoon of oatmeal into her when the phone ran again.

"You got coffee?" asked Jeff, rumbling cell phone connection.

"Sure."

"I'm coming over."

You could never tell when Jeff was really upset. Broker had seen him jam a Muskie lure through the loose skin between his thumb and forefinger without as much as an ouch. Just asked calmly, "Ah, you got a little tin snips in that tackle box?"

Just as calmly now, Jeff sat at Broker's kitchen table and took three sips on his cup of coffee before he said, "You know how the

U.S. attorney and the state attorney general don't necessarily get along?"

"Uh-huh."

"Well, they found something they can agree on. Namely, that you are a grain of sand under their blankets." The sheriff took a pull on his coffee. "I know this because the AG's office just called Pete over at the county offices and read him the riot act. Said how this loose cannon part-time deputy in Cook County has gone off half-cocked and stepped in a cow pie. Said you were interfering in an ongoing federal investigation for personal reasons."

"They found out where the tongue story came from."

Jeff took another pull on his coffee. "Be my guess. They also suggested that, if this is the kind of police work we condone up here, it might be a waste of taxpayers' money to add another patrol deputy next year."

"Your Clinton cop?"

"Yeah."

"What'd Hustad say?"

"Well, Hustad's a Democrat, and the AG's a big-cheese Democrat who's running for governor. So Hustad, being a new guy, is going to toe the party line."

"And you came over here to take the badge back?"

"Humph. Citizens of Cook County elected me, not the AG in St. Paul. They can keep their Clinton cop."

"So I can still try to find James?"

Jeff screwed up his lips. "The feds are not exactly forthcoming. And now . . ."

"I've been thinking of making the leap from analog to digital," said Broker. He told Jeff his latest idea.

Jeff scratched his hair, mulled it. "I don't know if anybody's ever done that before? Is it even practical?"

"Doesn't have to be. It's news," said Broker. "That's why they won't be able to resist putting it in the paper. They get enough bad press, they just might cough up James."

Broker and Kit drove to Grand Marais and went into the print shop and picked up his order. The picture of Tom James had been made into an old-fashioned wanted poster. Type at the bottom announced: *WANTED FOR QUESTIONING IN THE DEATH OF CAREN ANGLAND. If you see this man, immediately call Deputy Phil Broker at the Cook County sheriff's department.* The relevant phone numbers were on the bottom. There were a hundred of the posters. He left most of them at the sheriff's office. Tonight, after school, Jeff's oldest daughter, Allison, and her friends would plaster them all over town.

The truck arrived from the Circuit City store in Duluth at noon. As arranged, it contained one tall, ponytailed, young computer nerd named Steve, who agreed to set up Broker's computer for a fee of fifty dollars an hour and unlimited quantities of pizza and beer.

Steve and Broker unloaded the cardboard packing crates that contained the computer package Steve had sold him. Computer, monitor, modem, printer, assorted software manuals and a program to connect with America Online.

Broker cut doorways and windows into the cardboard boxes so Kit could crawl in and out. Jeff arrived with a case of beer and two deep-dish pizzas.

Steve's eyes, obviously cured in cannabis smoke, worked nervously over Jeff's uniform. "Ah, what is this?"

"Relax," said Jeff. "I'm the pizza man. But if I was you, I wouldn't pull any fast moves." He pointed at the all-purpose leather Mantool Steve wore in a small holster on his hip. "You have a license for that?"

It turned out like Tom Sawyer painting the fence. Steve spent most of the time eating pizza and swigging on a beer and giving directions to Broker and Jeff, who sifted through piles of manuals, cellophane bags full of screws, and tangles of cables.

Drinking beer and getting wired.

By the time the pizza was gone they were hooked up. Steve sat at the keyboard and created a Web site. "Easy, comes right with the software." He turned to Broker. "You get that picture J-pegged onto a disk at Kinko's?"

Broker handed him the disk he'd had made at a Kinko's in Duluth. In a minute Tom James's face appeared on the screen.

Broker handed him one of the posters. "Let's put in this type."

"What size?"

"Big."

"What color?"

"Loud."

Steve bumped the type way up across the top of the page:

**WANTED for questioning in the death of Caren Angland**

Then Broker sat down at the keyboard and typed, below the picture. *Local law officers could use some citizen help in locating this man. The government has hidden him in the Witness Protection Program and we would like to question him about a murder he witnessed. Since the government won't cooperate with us, we are turning to the people. If you see Tom James please contact Deputy Phil Broker, Cook County sheriff's department, etc., etc.*

Jeff maintained a hearty front throughout, but Broker could tell—the sheriff thought he was grabbing at straws. Jeff said good night and went home first. Steve departed with a wedge of cold pizza in his hand. The Pentium glowed in the twilight in Broker's study, exuding the factory-fresh tang of upholstery in a brand-new spaceship.

Broker called Ida Rain and left a message on her machine.

"Check me out at broker@aol.com. Tell me if you think *this* is a story?"

Then he gingerly removed his sleeping daughter from her nest of blankets and pillows among the cardboard boxes. With all the activity, she hadn't had a nap, and now she'd be off her schedule for the next few days. With Bedtime Bunny and Cucaracha Dog clutched in her arms, Broker moved her to her crib and tucked her in.

He went outside to stretch his legs and chew a cigar. Staying within earshot of the house, he picked his way through the ledge rock down to the shore. A thin knife-edged drizzle shot down. Thick mist mushroomed over the lake. The air had ice in it.

Something moved a few yards away. Broker instinctively dropped to one knee, his hand moving to the grip of the .45 in his belt.

The blond kid. David. From the cabin down the beach. A skier robbed of his snow, he clambered through the rocks.

Broker stood up. David stopped, startled. He wore a running suit and carried a hiking pack over one shoulder. The pack cover was open and had been hastily stuffed with a blanket, a thermos and a smaller cylindrical shammy bag from which protruded collapsible tripod legs. A Leupold logo was stitched in the material of the bag.

"Hi," he said. "Lousy weather, huh."

"Not much skiing," said Broker.

David grinned. "And we took the place for the whole month; dumb."

"It could change," said Broker.

"We can only hope," said David. "Well, have a good one." He continued on and Broker watched his outline disappear in the mist. It was difficult to see this pretty boy brat as a threat. But the small drawstring bag sticking from his bag was familiar. Broker had one just like it in his closet, with his hunting rifles. It contained a high-power spotter scope.

Days took on a routine. Danny rose early and went for a two-mile run down Valentino and out Amesti. Then he did sets of push-ups and sit-ups. After a shower and a shave he brewed coffee and had a light breakfast of yogurt mixed with oats, raisins, and bananas. Then he started in to work. It took a day to remove the moldy carpet and carry it, like hunks of whale blubber, out to the trash cans by the gate.

He found a serviceable hardwood floor under the carpet, but it was impregnated with rubbery glue and staples that he had to lever and pry out one by one with a pliers and screwdriver.

On the third day he heard a knock on his back screen door. Through the mesh he saw a tall, willowy beach blonde. She was around thirty. The taut flesh of her thighs and the tight denim of her shorts looked to be the same surface painted different colors. Her eyes were aqua colored, dreamy. Fluffs of blue soapsuds.

She held a platter in both hands, which supported a bottle of wine, a loaf of bread and a saltshaker.

"Hi," she said as he came to the door.

"Ah," he said, moving his hands awkwardly to apologize for his sweat-drenched T-shirt, his dirty arms.

"I live next door. Ruby."

"Oh," said Danny. "Daniel Storey. Danny. Hi." He opened the screen. Tentatively, they shook hands. She balanced the tray in one hand expertly. Self-consciously, he yanked off his cowhide work gloves.

"Danny," she said.

It should have been a defining moment. A good-looking woman was calling him Danny. He'd had to roll Ida Rain's orgasms uphill like Sisyphian boulders to get her to call him Danny, and that was in the dark. But the tribute coming from Ruby's lips was curiously unmoving.

"I, ah, brought you a housewarming gift," she said.

Remembering his lines, he smiled, "I'm afraid I don't drink. Anymore."

"Oh, no, it's . . . a custom. See, you're supposed to carry the tray through all the rooms of your house before you spend the night, to appease the former residents. A kind of offering."

"You mean ghosts." Danny's voice went flat as a shadow sat up in his mind.

"Welll," she drawled playfully. "It's not *that* serious."

"I'll give it a try," said Danny. He opened the screen door and started to take the tray, then he looked around. No place to sit it down. He motioned outside, to the deck chairs and the small round table between them.

He placed the tray on the table and offered her one of the chairs. "I appreciate the gesture. But I already spent a couple nights here."

"We know," said Ruby. "At first we thought you were a cop." She lowered her eyes. Shy. "Are you. A cop? I mean."

"Why do you ask?" He drew it out in a slightly neutral voice, playing the drama, enjoying it.

"Well, there's been a lot of cops here since the fire."

"No. I bought the house from the cops, they auctioned it off. The guy who used to live here was cooking speed, they said. Turns out he wasn't such a good cook." Danny shrugged. "It was pretty cheap." He hunched his shoulders. "Needs a little work."

"I'll say. Well, just wanted to drop by and say hello. My partner is Terra. We have a lot of cats."

"I noticed."

"We try to keep them home, but they stray. You don't mind cats?" She raised a slim eyebrow.

"Nah," he said, almost visibly excited. Not by her. But by stage fright. His first real conversation from inside his new identity.

She waved, walked down the deck and disappeared around the side of the house. Danny marveled at how Ruby was, well, perfectly manufactured. And how utterly without sex appeal.

In the long shadow of Ida Rain.

That night, for the first time, he woke up with his ears plugged by the roar of rushing water. His eyes tracked across the dark porch to the tray of offering presents, and he had a piercing memory of Caren Angland falling away, shrinking, tiny—gone in the thrashing pit.

The next night, after a microwaved supper, Danny opened a can of Coors and strolled his fence line. Ruby and Terra had their CD player turned up. Gurgles of whale music belched, groaned and farted on the evening air. Obscene. Cows fucking. Them fucking. Disturbed by the sounds, he went home and shut his doors.

He sat on the bare floor, sipped his beer and studied Ruby's tray with its burden of offerings. The wine, the bread and the salt.

He did not believe in presences that needed appeasing in old houses. He did not believe in ghosts. What he did believe in, powerfully, was the potency of secrets. There was an old cop adage: getting out isn't as hard as staying out. It was easier to escape than to avoid detection on the run.

There were so many opportunities to talk, to reveal oneself. To explain yourself.

To confess.

After an interval, he went back outside and determined that the awful racket had stopped next door. In the dark, faintly, he heard Ruby calling. "Here kitty, kitty."

The dream was just that. A dream. Not a nightmare. In it he clearly saw Broker and his baby girl. She of the big eyes and thick eyebrows. She was watching him grab the money off the floor of the workshop. Her eyes getting bigger and bigger.

That's all. Then he woke up, slick with sweat. And for a while, he felt around the mattress he'd laid out on the back porch, to establish its reality. His own.

He got up, shaking. Fumbled for his contacts. Too much bother. Put on his glasses. The air clung like wet sheets. Mist fumed in the porch screens. Monet painting with a steam hose. The yard light looked like a smear of Vaseline.

The rumpled covers plucked at his sweaty skin, turbulent waves he might sink in.

Barefoot, he picked up the tray containing the wine, bread and salt. As he carried them through the rooms of his new house he pretended that his life also had rooms that he was making clean, and he was moving through them as well.

**57**

A sultry orange rain came down for days. And every day, Travis called to inquire how things were going. Then he came in person, driving through the gate in a late-model, black Ford Expedition.

"Nice wheels," Danny said, going out to meet the inspector.

"Came from a bust in Menlo Park." Travis walked into the house. The floors were clean, barren of carpet, glue, and staples. All the floor and window molding had been removed.

"You've been working. Looks great," said Travis.

"I'm going to rent a floor sander, called in an order," said Danny. He glanced at the dripping sky. "But I was hoping for a letup in the humidity."

"You, ah, wanted a computer, right?"

"It was part of the deal," said Danny.

"Just so happens we stumbled onto one." He marched out to the shiny Ford and opened the rear hatch. In the cargo bay, piled haphazardly in mismatched boxes, in a tangle of cables, was a computer, monitor, keyboard, modem, fax and copier, a printer.

"Where'd you get this?" asked Danny.

Travis grinned. "Same place we got the Expedition. Reparations from the war on drugs. This is nothing. The guy had a stable of racehorses." He tugged one of the boxes toward the hatch and raised his eyebrows. "Pentium 233, you like?"

"Definitely."

"There's an America Online kit in there too, thought you might need it. And this." Travis reached for his wallet, selected a piece of plastic and handed it to Danny.

A VISA card. "How'd you do this?"

Travis shrugged, like what the hell. "Consider it a little bonus. It's drawn on the incidental fund at my office. We put you on as an authorized user until you get your credit rating up. I'd prefer you keep it under two hundred dollars a month. Any big-ticket items for the house, you clear it with me first. But, you know, there's a lot of little shit"—he pointed to the computer—"like hooking up on-line, you can do over the phone with plastic. Otherwise it's a hassle."

"Thanks," said Danny.

Travis adjusted, but did not remove, his sunglasses. "No. I'm thanking you. Usually when I launch a witness, even if they don't have a family, I have to hold their hand every day. Sometimes I have to stay with them, sleep on the couch, around the clock until they adjust to being inserted."

They carried the boxes inside, and Danny decided to set up in the cleanest room in the place, on the screened porch. The humidity wasn't good for the machine, but the only way to escape humidity in the shadow of El Niño was to leave the state. The dust in the house would be worse.

"So, is there anything else you need offhand?" asked Travis.

An impulse leaped. Unplanned. "There is one thing, kind of a tangent," said Danny. He thought of it as pulling the tiger's whiskers. "I've been reading the books they gave me on Santa Cruz. One of them referred to the town being the murder capital of the world in the early 1970s."

"*Serial killer* capital of the world," corrected Travis. "Yeah, there were three killers active, two of them at the same time. Ed Kemper, he's up in Vacaville; he got the most ink."

"He hung out with cops, didn't he. I mean, when he was doing the killings."

"Yep. The original cop wannabe. A theory the FBI fell a little too much in love with. Ask Richard Jewel in Atlanta."

"I hear you," Danny grinned. "I was wondering, have you ever relocated a killer?"

"Hell yes. What do you think we do? Handle nuns? That's why you're such a walk in the park."

"What's it like, being around a killer? I mean, are they different?" He wished he could see Travis's eyes.

"Well . . ." Travis leaned back, again the furrows on the brow. He ran his square hand through his styled hair. "Depends. There's the high-up ones and the soldiers."

"I mean, do they feel different, being around them. You know, this close."

"These guys, they only think of one thing. Getting their way. it's like—'I'd never do anything that wasn't absolutely necessary, so obviously Louie had to get whacked.' Like that. Ego maniacs. Mob guys I mean. But most of them had been in the joint by the time they got around to me, so they had old-fashioned prison manners. Now, the new ones we get, the druggies, who the fuck knows about them."

Danny pondered, then brightened. "I was wondering. Is there any way you could hook me up with a local cop who worked the Kemper case."

Travis's forehead furrowed above his shades. "Ah, hmmm. What I could do . . . is talk to a guy I know who teaches criminal justice at UCSC. He's been around for a while. Maybe he could find one for you. That way I don't have to get involved." Travis nodded, took out a slim pocket organizer, a pen and made a note to himself. "Anything else?"

Danny shook his head.

Travis slapped him on the arm. "Look. You've been busting your balls all week. Take a break. Set up your computer. Go see a movie. Buy some new clothes. I'll check in a couple of times next week . . ."

"Uh-huh?"

"I mean, call you. And try to drop by in six, seven days. You all right with that?"

"Sure." Danny felt like a witness remembering his lawyer's advice. Simple concise answers.

"Great. I have a new pile of people to process, so, if you're doing all right, just get in touch with me if you need something. You got the number?"

Danny patted his hip pocket. "Right here." He tapped his forehead. "And here." He made a mental note to call Travis, thank him for the computer. Sound grateful.

Travis walked back through the living room. For a moment he paused and tipped down his shades. He was facing away and Danny couldn't see his eyes. But he was looking at the tray, which sat in the corner of the barren living room on an upturned cardboard box. The faint astringent scent of ripe mold insinuated from the mossy green bread sitting next to the unopened bottle of wine and the saltshaker.

Three half-burned candles jutted from a formation of wax that had spilled over the side of the box and reached to the floor. Travis pushed his sunglasses back up on his nose and kept walking, out the door, across the overgrown front yard, got in his confiscated black Ford Expedition and drove away.

Danny spent the rest of the day hooking up the computer and situated it on a makeshift desk made out of an old door and two end tables he had found in the junk room. The software was Windows 95, which he'd never actually worked on. He played with it, ran the AOL disk and called in to start an account. That took another hour.

By the time he had it all hooked up and running smoothly it was getting late. He drove into Watsonville, ate Mexican, had a few beers and drove home in a steady rain.

The next morning was Saturday, so he slept in. Floating onto the day, opening his eyes to a damp fluffy cloud of fog, his head ached pleasantly from the beers.

He saw the silly shrine he'd erected in the corner and laughed. He padded over in his bare feet and picked it up.

"Tough shit, Casper," he said as he dumped it all in the trash.

He yawned and scratched his stomach. Put water and grind in the Mr. Coffee and went to take a shower. Later, after he'd shaved, the phone rang about three sips into his first cup of coffee.

"Hello."

"Dan Storey?"

There was that second when the name flew by. Then contact. "Speaking."

"This is Arnold Templeton. I teach at UCSC. We have a mutual friend. Joe Travis."

"Sure Joe," said Danny.

"Joe said you do some writing and you're kicking around Santa Cruz picking up atmosphere."

"You know," Danny said expansively.

"Sure, well, about the good old days, when the ravines were full of bodies. I know this retired county sheriff's deputy—Harold Wicks—I've had him in to talk to a few classes. He's a sound guy. He was on the job then, with Kemper and Mullin. He said he'd meet if you buy the drinks."

"That's great"—his memory spun without traction for a beat, then caught—"Arnold."

He took the name and number and called the man immediately. Wicks was the only person left in America who didn't have an answering machine. The phone rang nine times until a gruff voice, slightly breathless, picked up.

"Hold on, hold on," said Harold Wicks.

And then. "Yeah sure, Arnie Templeton over at the college talked to me. Writer huh? Okay. How's tomorrow. Say two. You want atmosphere? There's this place called the Jury Box Bar on Ocean Street. Across from the courthouse. That's where Ed Kemper used to hang out with the cops. You know. Him buying the drinks and asking us how the investigation was going."

"Sounds great."

Dead acorn husks and rain dripped on the flat roof. Danny had slept a full eight hours and had not dreamed. It was too foggy to run, so he showered, shaved, and fooled in front of the mirror with the hair drier, fluffing his new haircut.

When he emerged from the bathroom, the new coffeemaker he'd bought had his coffee waiting, and he took a cup to his computer on the screened porch overlooking the backyard.

Coastal fog basted the foliage, drifting like a cloud through the screens; he had to wipe down the computer. First day in his new office. A little rustic, but that would improve.

His video monitor cut a crisp black rectangle in the morning mist. The screen saver was a flowing star scene that created the sensation of traveling through deep space—the view from Captain Picard's command chair on the *Enterprise*.

He sat down, sipped his coffee, and logged into the net. The whole world just a click away. Cruising.

Old habits. He'd started the *San Francisco Chronicle* and the *Santa Cruz Sentinel*, but they hadn't shown up on his stoop yet. No problem. He'd peruse the St. Paul paper's Web page. He typed in the address. The awesome Pentium gobbled up the bytes, constructing the site.

When the page was intact, he selected the weather icon and waited for the display to come on-screen. The familiar forecast symbols marched across the page. White dots sprinkled from a cloud on a blue field. Snow today. High 31. Low 13. Snow turning to sleet tomorrow . . . sounded ugly.

Through the screened mist he heard Ruby's voice, "Here kitty kitty."

Danny grinned. The voice came again. "Dan . . . can I come over. I'm missing a cat."

"Sure," yelled Danny back. "I'm on the back porch." He clicked off the site.

She materialized out of the vapor in shorts and a blouse tied in a loose square knot above her navel. No shoes. Flossy white hairs coated her brown stomach. The idea of touching her was as sexually appealing as hugging a bundle of cotton sheets fresh off the wash line.

Looking at her. What? Nothing happened.

*Ruby. I'm sure. I'll bet your name was a solid Lutheran Emily or Gertrude back in Iowa before you came to California and were reborn in Licker-ville. Was she the pitcher or the catcher? Which one strapped on the dildo?* Some night he'd drop over for a peek.

"Hi, Ruby. Want some coffee?" he said pleasantly.

"Thanks," she said. "You haven't seen any of the cats have you?"

"Nope." He got up and went into the kitchen. As he poured a cup he called out, "You take anything?"

"Some two percent if you have it. You've really been fixing this place up. Pentium. Nice box," she added.

He poured in a dollop of half-and-half and returned to the porch. Ruby took the cup and sat in a wicker chair he'd brought in from the deck. Her smooth thighs would feel like tennis balls if you squeezed them. Or if you got squeezed by them. He pictured Terra, her butchy partner, whom he'd only glimpsed, caught in a choke hold between those thighs. Fat zapper tongue, he bet—like the frog in the Budweiser commercial.

"Cats are independent. It'll come back," sympathized Danny.

"It's not that simple around here," she said.

"Why's that?" Curious.

"Do you believe in precursor events?" she asked seriously.

Danny gnawed his lip. Hmmm. Some New Age mumbo jumbo?

Seeing his lost expression, she explained, "I mean to earthquakes."

"Oh." He leaned back to listen. As he did, he discovered that if he looked at Ruby and thought about Ida Rain, he started to get excited.

"Dan, you're living in the footprint of Loma Prieta," she announced in hushed tones. "I was in downtown Santa Cruz, at work, when it hit. And I never want to go through that again."

"What's that got to do with cats?"

"Well, that was before I . . . met Terra, and I only had one cat. And before the quake, my cat vanished. When I met Terra she told me she had two cats, and both of them ran away two days before it hit."

"Cats," said Danny, looking at her flawless delineation of inner thigh, remembering the clasp of Ida's legs in the dark. *Here, pussy pussy.*

"Terra explained it to me. Abnormal animal behavior is common before seismic events. There are scientists who keep track of lost cats. When the cats run off, watch out."

"Ah huh." Playfully, Danny moused into accessories, pulled up networking and dialed the 800 number for the St. Paul paper. It was about eight o'clock. Ten in Minnesota. Ida Rain ran on strict time. Sunday mornings, she went out to breakfast and then grocery shopped for the week. It was safe to assume she wasn't logged on to her computer at home or in the newsroom.

Still thinking Ida, he watched Ruby cross her legs. Ow, that was nice.

The network marquee came on the screen. Under user name, he typed in Ida Rain. Password—one of the first things he had learned about Ida was her password. He'd just watched her type it in until he had the sequence of keys. It was Burgundy, her favorite color. He toyed with the notion of reading Ida's E-mail, getting seriously kinky and voyeuristic as his eyes tracked south of Ruby's belly button. The computer screen shivered, repixelated. He was in.

Ruby sipped her coffee and went on. "It's something to do with their ears. There's a mineral in a cat's ear—magnetite? You ever hear of that?"

"Ah, no." He opened Ida's E-mail box.

"According to this theory, when the tectonic plates down in the earth grind together, the pressure on all that rock acts like a transmitter . . ."

Danny started to scroll down the menu of Ida Rain's messages. Memory Lane. Going-away party for Howie Norell. Bye Howie. Internal memo about company cell phones. United Way Appeal.

". . . and the magnetite acts like a receiver for these low signals—like a dog whistle. It vibrates the magnetite in the cat's ears, and they take off because they know . . ."

Danny's eyes scanned past and then whipsawed back on the message tag; *BruceNote*, the metro editor; Good old Bruce, the prick. He clicked on it. It opened. Began to read:

Ida,

We're holding the Wanger's story idea on Tom James you proposed. Wanger contacted Angland in jail, and Angland denied that James ever told him anything about the money. So we have questions whether this Broker, who is just a temporary deputy up there, is pressing a legitimate investigation. I put the story back in your basket. Let's talk—B

". . . an event is coming."

"MOTHERFUCKER!" he screamed. He shot to his feet, his chair and coffee cup flew in different directions.

Ruby went rigid, terrified, speechless. Coffee slicked her bare thighs and shorts. Her empty cup spun in hollow circles on the tile floor.

"FUCKING NO GOOD BITCH . . ." Danny seized the upturned chair and slammed it down. When it fell over again he hurled it through the screens, it smashed into a collection of brittle, empty terra-cotta planters on the deck.

Ruby was on her feet, backing away with her hands extended, palms out, but turned sideways, not defensive, more like pleading. "Pleaaase," she whispered. And the nightmarish expression on her face bespoke a fault line all her own, a terror of men rammed deep within her. Seeing it brought Danny to his senses.

His smile came too suddenly, still quivering with anger, and that also terrified her, as if she'd seen it before.

"No, no," he said in an embarrassed voice. "It's . . ."

But she was going through the screen door. Her pretty face froze in profile. One flat wild eye splashed on features jagged as a piece of broken glass. Her bare feet made fast slapping sounds on the paving stones as she fled the property.

God. He touched his forehead, which felt like hot paper ready to combust. His eyes locked back on the monitor. But the screen saver had kicked on. Black panel. White dots zipping like blizzard snow pelting a windshield.

Like a bad night in Minnesota.

God. He felt like he was going to puke. Unsteady, he walked

toward the bathroom. He even managed a sickly smile. His rubber knees duplicated the shock of a quake. God. I could lose it all. That thought went down like a plunger, and he felt a wave of stomach acid froth in his throat.

He barely made the bathroom, knelt before the stool and projectile vomited. Immediately he felt relief. He rose to his feet, wiping away hot strings of spittle.

The shower curtain moved.

Someone in the shower.

A fast low shape shot past the cheap plastic curtain. Gray. Sleek. Oriental black boots on the gray paws. Ruby's cat.

Her missing fucking precursor cat.

Rage networked a million miles of nerves and assembled, red hot, in his hands. He ripped the toilet seat from the stool and in one powerful, flawless spin, turned and smashed the wooden oval down on the animal's head.

He dropped the seat and kicked it and kicked it and . . . it died a kind of floppy miniature animal death somewhere between a small dog and an insect.

Squashed. Blood on its tiny white needle teeth.

Calmer now, with matted blood and fur on his bare feet, he walked back through the house to the kitchen, got a fresh cup and poured coffee.

Think. Clean up the bathroom. Hard to think. Fucking Broker again. Got to Ida somehow. *And I would have bought her a new chin*. He grimaced at his gory feet as he walked back into the bathroom. Bloody footprints on the tile. Splashes on the wall. Jesus Christ, he giggled. Looks like a goddamn slaughterhouse in here.

Then—holy shit!

Almost as an afterthought, he saw his whole new life crumble. The folly. So obvious. *She knew his name*. Had whispered it in the dark for months. Those pages in her desk . . .

He stooped, picked up the dripping cat-thing and said to the smashed head, "We'll have to do something about that!"

Then, practical: Wash the floor, Danny; get rid of the damn cat. With a pail, some Comet and a rag he sopped up the tracks and the mess in the bathroom. He placed the toilet seat tentatively back on the stool.

Stupid damn thing to do. Got to be careful now. This is when you make mistakes.

He wrapped the dead cat in the ragged cleaning towel and carried it to his truck. A light rain hissed from the warm tangerine sky, strange low clouds, air thick as jam.

He consulted his county map, drove through the flooded strawberry fields and orchards until he found the road to the nearest beach. Good. The parking lot was deserted. With the leaky cat wrapped under his arm, he went up the plank walkway through the dunes and crossed the beach toward the Pacific Ocean. Rain threaded down. He could barely make out the silhouette of the power plant to the south in Monterey.

Slow gray rollers flopped over and foamed lacy surf across the beach. Coils of fluted gray kelp protruded from hummocks of damp sand. Looked like dead worms from Mars.

Fucking Jeremiah Johnson running through the trees, tomahawk out.

He'd zeroed in on Ida.

She knew his name. But she didn't know she knew it.

The fear washed through him faster than his eyes could process or conscious thought could catch. And there, like his fear manifest— thirty feet away, where the waves tumbled in the first breaker line— a long supple shadow broke the surface, glided. Fins.

Had to be twelve, thirteen feet, the distance between the dorsal and the tail. Just—right there. Then silently gone into the wide endless Pacific.

He lobbed the cat overhand, a lazy layup. It splashed just past the first breakers. He waited to see if the shark would strike. If it did, it happened below the surface where he couldn't see.

Like he would. Silent.

Some fishermen in hip waders with very long poles were walking up the beach. Short men with black hair. The tonal mystery of an Asian language cartwheeled in the sound of the waves. He watched them take huge lures with ferocious curved hooks from their tackle box and string them to their leader. Calmer, composed, Danny walked back to his car.

These events disrupted his timetable. He'd have to take risks. It infuriated him that Ida Rain had repaid his compassion with betrayal. The bitch could have had it all.

*The best goddamn face money could buy.*

Then he looked at his watch. Shit. He was supposed to meet the retired cop at that bar in Santa Cruz this afternoon.

The sky over Monterey Bay sagged in rainy streaks of aqua, orange and lime like a bleeding South American flag. He parked, got out and walked, nibbled the sweet California air. Passed a girl in cutoff jeans with beach bunny legs and safety pins in her face.

She looked at him funny. He glanced down, saw he had a wad of gooey cat-hair-stickum on his arm. Rubbed it off with spit.

The bar was wedged between an insurance office and a small strip mall. Across Ocean Street, the county building looked faintly colonial behind a screen of tall palms and pine trees. Sunday. Except for cop cars, the parking lot was almost empty.

In testimony to the new antismoking ordinance, four patrons stood outside the bar, furtively smoking like high school kids behind the field house. Inside, the Jury Box was black as a cave. A partition faced the door like a blast shield to defeat the light of day. The interior was cramped and made smaller by dark paneling. A pool table was covered with garish red felt.

Custom street signs adorned the header over the bar. One said BULL-SHIT PLACE the other spelled out ASSHOLE ALLEY. In the corner a video game had a large green *Creature from the Black Lagoon* swimming on its side. The creature appeared very much at home in the darkness.

Danny ordered a Sharps nonalcoholic beer and sat at one of the small tables next to the pool table. He checked his watch. Early, 1:45; 3:45 in St. Paul. He eyed the pay phone on the wall. The urge was palpable, treading in the dark. Like the creature in the corner, silently swimming to and fro.

He tried to imagine Kemper filling the space of this room. A really big man, six nine. Kemper, according to the literature, hated his mother and finally killed her. Danny did not hate his mother. He was glad she was gone because she was a bother. He'd always dreaded the long haul across the rickety ministrations of some nursing home. But he never hated her. Sometimes he wished she had been someone else. Someone with better genes. Better looks. More goddamn money.

Danny eyed the phone again. Imagined hearing Ida's unsuspecting voice and jacking off.

He had to get rid of her of course. Not effortlessly, like Caren. This time it had to be done with authority. Some fear and pain to mark the arrival of Danny Storey. Trauma. Not unlike birth.

The sunlight oscillated on the other side of the partition, and a square medium-size man in his late fifties shouldered into the gloom. Danny squinted and held up his loose leaf binder. He rose and extended his hand.

"Harold?"

The man nodded curtly. Came forward. His handshake was forceful, casual retro macho. Danny winced a little and did not try to compete.

"Dan Storey?" he asked.

"That's right," said Danny. They walked to the bar. Wicks ordered a Scotch and water and asked for an extra glass of water. Danny dropped a five to cover it. When Wicks had his drink, they went back to the table.

"So Arnie says you're interested in old Santa Cruz, back during the serial killer epidemic," said Harold.

"I was curious if you had a theory why it happened here."

Harold shrugged his shoulders. "Why not here? Those guys were like bad weather. You know it exists, but you don't think it'll come ashore where you're having your picnic. But there it is." He was philosophical. A Big Thing, but at the same time, in the long view, no big thing.

He took a sip of his drink and studied Danny. "It's not like there are rules that govern these things."

Danny cleared his throat. "Well, the FBI studies them, the killers."

"Common sense," said Harold.

"How's that?" asked Danny, polite.

Harold gestured offhand. "Most of Kemper's victims were coeds.

He picked them up hitchhiking. Who keeps hitchhiking in Santa Cruz when somebody's killing female hitchhikers?"

"I hear you," agreed Danny. He probed his cheek with his tongue. "The thing that got to me was, he used to sit in here with you guys."

Harold nodded. "I remember one night he was at the bar with a bunch of deputies." Shook his head, grinned. "They were trying to *recruit* him for their basketball team. He was this big guy. Meanwhile pieces of missing people were showing up in the ravines. Had a foot wash in on a wave with a surfer up toward Monterey." Wicks sighed. "I went out and picked that one up."

Danny leaned forward and studied the lines in Harold's face. "What I mean is, you were sitting this close to him and you didn't know."

"Hell," chuckled Harold. "I was just a copper, a patrol grunt." He shifted forward, and his face creased with a rueful smile and his blue eyes twinkled with elfin mischief. "You know about what he did to his grandparents?"

Danny nodded.

"Naturally, the state of California in its infinite wisdom let him out of the nuthouse. He had to go in for regular sessions with a shrink. You know, a college-educated liberal fruit the state of California employs to look after its wayward children. Well, Kemper goes in for his therapy and convinces the shrink that he's a well-adjusted example of rehabilitation. And you know what?"

Danny cocked forward. An eager audience.

Harold continued. "During this interview, Kemper's got a victim's severed head in the trunk of his car out in the parking lot."

"Why?" asked Danny. Fascinated.

Harold shrugged. "He was taunting us. Part of the thrill, I guess."

Danny laughed in Harold Wicks's face.

They studied each other philosophically. Finally Harold pronounced, "You never fuckin' know."

"Ah," Danny glanced at his wristwatch. "Could you excuse me, I gotta make a quick call." He rose and picked up his empty beer bottle and eyed Harold's almost dry glass. "You want another one?"

"If you are," said Harold.

Danny took Harold's glass and his bottle to the bar, ordered another round and got change. Then he walked to the side of the room, picked up the pay phone receiver and dropped in quarters, got long distance and asked for Ida's number in Minnesota.

He watched smoke shift through the rays of balmy light splayed to the side of the partition while the phone rang on Sergeant Street in St. Paul.

"Hello?"

He gripped the receiver and experienced a pleasurable squirm of muscles low in his abdomen.

"Hello?" her voice was husky, busy, practical. Not concerned. Just inconvenienced.

Danny waited another beat and then hung the phone up. He went back to the bar, paid for the round of drinks and returned to the table.

"Do you think he wanted to be caught?" asked Danny.

Harold sipped his drink. "Guess so. Called up the city cops and confessed. At first the dispatcher didn't take it seriously. Their old drinking buddy, Ed."

"So he had a shred of conscience?"

Wicks shook his head dubiously. "Him? Nah, I think he was expecting to be famous or something."

Danny felt no such urge. He just wanted to be left alone.

Right under their noses. He was cruising right under their fucking noses and they couldn't see. Smooth as that shark off the beach.

Old Harold Wicks was on the job, just inches away, and he didn't see anything. None of them did. Except Broker. Still hanging on. Some hick resort owner playing cop.

Danny tore the wrapper from a Power Bar and wolfed it down. It started to rain again. He slowed down, hit his indicator and turned off on the Freedom Road exit. Waited at the light. Turned and picked up speed.

He had not planned on going back for a while. He tossed the wrapper out the window in an explosion of nerves, steadied, passed a slow station wagon in the right-hand lane.

There was the question of how to get it back here. He couldn't just fly in a commercial jet with a big suitcase. Money would show up as a suspicious blob on the X rays. The kind they were trained to look for. Transporting the money was a problem. If he took a jet back to the Minneapolis–St. Paul International, he could rent a car. Drop in on Ida, zip up north, pick up the money and drive the rental back to San Jose and pick up his truck in the airport lot. Have to show ID to rent a car. Not good.

Be nice to visit Broker. Just up the road from where the stuff was buried, but that would be too many coincidences. He had to silence Ida Rain. Had to. Had to—

*Had to be careful.* She had that damn little gun in the dresser drawer right next to her bed, or in her purse. Knew how to shoot it.

A loopy shriek interrupted his thoughts. Behind him, the red flasher flooded across the wet pavement like a liquid sound wave. One turn of the siren. He checked the rearview.

Aw shit. The cop car was right on his bumper. Danny pulled over. He pulled out his license certificate and watched the side view mirror. The county deputy came forward from his green and white cruiser. Cautious, hand on his pistol, approaching from the blind side.

"What's the problem, officer?"

The cop accepted the license form and placed it on the clipboard he held on one arm. Pen in the other.

"When you turned off the highway onto Freedom you sailed a candy wrapper out the window."

"Aw Christ," Danny sagged. It was an expression of guilt. But also relief.

The cop went back to his cruiser to write the ticket. About five minutes later he returned. "You can mail it in or stop by the courthouse and pay it. Otherwise you've got a court date if you want to go that route." He handed the license back.

Danny studied the ticket as the cop got back into his car and pulled into traffic.

Give me a fucking break. He groaned—$240 for *littering*?

## 60

Like a joke, the next morning, his new California driver's license came in the mail.

Danny sat at his kitchen table studying a *AAA Road Atlas* of the United States. Rain sluiced down the windows.

The most secure way to sneak back into the "danger zone," without leaving a trail, was drive the truck; burn cross-country, sleep in the cab, no motels, nothing on record. There and back. He turned to the map.

The United States was shaped like a clumsy dinosaur with a pea head in Maine and Texas and Florida for feet. Road net for arteries. Big cities the vital organs. And it looked like Interstate 80, depending on the weather, was his best route, through Salt Lake, Cheyenne, Omaha, and into Des Moines, then shoot up into Minnesota.

Okay. He got up, meaning to flip on his new TV and check the Weather Channel when he saw his front gate shimmer in the rain. Swing open. Joe Travis wore sunglasses even in the gloom and rain, also a long brown oilcloth raincoat. He climbed back in the black Ford and pulled it closer to the house.

Shit. He hadn't expected Travis for five, six more days. He met the inspector at the door.

"Hey. Travis, how you doing," he said, smiling slowly, apprehensively, looking past Travis at the downpour.

"Yeah, it's a bitch driving, but I had to come down. Mandatory security call when there's a violation."

*Violation?* Danny shifted nervously. "What?"

"Take it easy. Just a quick visit. Have to get back up to the city. This is strictly pro forma. You had a traffic stop last night by a Santa Cruz deputy sheriff."

"How'd you know that?" Danny was really getting nervous.

"Anytime a protected witness has an encounter with law enforcement, he's identified under his new name. You presented the new driver's license, right?"

"Yes I did."

"The copper ran it on NCIC. Protected witness names are flagged in the system. Washington notifies the on-site inspector that one of his people has had a run-in with the law. We have to come right over and investigate. Log it."

"I tossed a candy wrapper," said Danny glumly. "Two hundred forty bucks."

"Yep. I saw the complaint. I warned you, huh." Travis grinned.

"Now I know."

"Good. It's bullshit in this case, no problem; inside the county, could happen to anyone. But if you were a felon-type witness, say— and you got stopped in L.A., in a high-crime neighborhood, could be suspicious. But it's a rule. So . . ." Travis glanced around. "Hey, you got the computer up and cooking."

Danny smiled. "Nice box." He snapped his fingers. "Fast."

"Cool. Hey, I'm going to use your john and be out of here." Travis walked down the hall toward the bathroom, went in and closed the door. The toilet seat clattered on the tiles. Danny prayed a soggy piece of dead cat didn't attach to Travis's boots. The toilet flushed. The door opened. Travis emerged. "You need a new seat for the shitter, man," even white teeth curved in a smile below the sunglasses. "See you in about a week." He walked out and he was gone.

Danny flopped back on a kitchen chair and wiped sweat from his forehead. Goddamn, if Travis hadn't popped in he'd have packed a bag, tossed it in the truck and headed out to drive day and night cross-country. Scratch that.

He tried to remember. Stories he'd done about the airlines. He recalled they were stingy with their flight information. He'd have to present a driver's license to board a plane. But his name in a Northwest computer would not be shared with the U.S. government short of a subpoena being issued.

He pulled the atlas out again. He wasn't sure how far his "danger zone" extended in a radius around the Twin Cities. But then he slammed the manual shut. Screw it. Take risks. Fly right in under their noses. To Minneapolis–St. Paul. Cab to Ida's. Take *her* car up north. *Yeah*.

The Money.

Traveling on the airlines was out. A constant stream of drug couriers moved through airports. Airports used random luggage checks by dogs trained to sniff out cash. They'd spot it going through the X-ray machine.

Danny paced the kitchen, ducked under a loop of electrical conduit.

Mail it.

Why not. Again. Right under their noses. Another old story came to mind. Postal inspectors reacted to problems; they dealt with too much volume to scrutinize every package. Better yet, send it commercial carrier. As long as it didn't look overtly suspicious, it would go straight through. Overnight express, from Duluth. Bundle it up good enough to disguise it. Take it to a Wrap and Ship. Let them do a professional box job. Tell them it's books.

These things decided, Danny leafed through the local phone book for airline numbers. He'd have to pay for the ticket in cash, couldn't use the marshals' VISA card. And Travis's procedure probably called for auditing the checking account.

Time to take some high-stake risks.

Danny, on approach to Minneapolis–St. Paul International, heard the pilot put the ground temperature at thirty-one degrees, with softly blowing snow. He deplaned, moved through the familiar airport, went to the men's room, used the toilet, then washed his hands, dried them with a paper towel and studied his appearance in the full-length mirror on the wall. Unafraid of winter, he wore a new, reddish leather bomber jacket and a black T-shirt. Hair combed back. Shoulders squared. Could be Colin Firth stalking out of the movie theater in *Apartment Zero*. New short haircut, contacts, his tan and, modestly, his new muscles—he could probably walk through the St. Paul newsroom and no one would recognize him.

Not walk. Stalk, baby, stalk.

He turned sideways and thumped his gut.

Abs still needed work.

Soon he wouldn't have to suck it in. Soon it would be like a washboard. More crunches.

"Let's go get paid, Danny," he said, grinning at the mirror.

His light carry-on bag contained a change of underwear, a sweater, a toothbrush, toothpaste and a pair of latex gloves he'd bought at a sporting goods store in San Jose.

He had a little under twenty-four hours until the return flight to San Francisco tomorrow at 4:15.

Off the concourse, he stopped at a store fussed up with Minnesota bric-a-brac and bought a black wool ski mask, a pair of warm gloves and a pair of Snow Pac boots. Too cold in those woods for his California tennis shoes.

He inspected a stout canvas carry bag. Loon decal. Hefted it, felt inside. Should be big enough to hold the stuff. He bought two.

Local time was 4:30 P.M. On a Tuesday. She'd be home at six. Came home after work during the week like clockwork.

Catch her in the shower, like *Psycho.*

Outside. Now for a cab. He gave the cabbie a street intersection for a destination. Cleveland and St. Clair. Close. Walking distance. He settled back in the seat. His main worry was that her car could be in the shop.

Nah, she scrupulously kept up the maintenance on the Accord.

The main problem was—and he'd wrestled with this the whole flight from California—just what was he going to *do* with her. His thoughts yelled back and forth like the cohosts on *Crossfire.*

In one scenario he became her protector and patron, generously forgiving her betrayals, flying her off to a new life, and a lot of expensive cosmetic surgery, in northern California. That pact got sealed with great sex.

The other method was less charitable. The pistol came out of the drawer of her bed table and Bang. End of story.

But the gun would make noise. He needed another way of *dealing* with her.

His mind still balked at the word *kill.* At intrusive techniques that broke the skin and let stuff leak out.

Overpower her. Use a garbage bag and duct tape. Wrap her head. No mess to get on him. Wear the rubber gloves.

The hard part would be talking to her. And not touching her. No sex, he told himself. NO SEX. Christ, that was a hardship after almost two months. But it couldn't happen. Fluids, fibers, body hair. Too risky.

Get the draft of the story in her desk.

Never take the gloves off.

Could propose to her.

Or kill her.

The Rainbow Cab lunged through the snowy night as Danny gave Ida her life, took it back, gave it over again.

Either way, around midnight, he had to be on the road to Lutsen. It would take four hours to get to the money pit. Another hour to dig it up. Get back to Duluth in the morning. Pack the money, then take it to a Wrap and Ship, have them repack it. If they asked, say it's books. They wouldn't ask.

Here he paused.

Four, five in the morning, when he came out of the woods. Broker would only be a few miles up the road. Sleeping.

No. He had to be absolutely disciplined on this point. But God, it would be nice to be rid of the man. And his brat.

Back to his schedule. The other reason not to dally up on the North Shore was because there was only one road in and out. Highway 61.

He leaned back and fantasized about her fragrant hair, slightly sweaty, tickling, spread on his bare thighs . . .

No. No. Think about the money. This was about the money. She had to go. Bury the money in his small oak woods—except for a few packets that he'd take to Reno—to celebrate.

This time next week he'd be taking a break from sanding the floors, having a cool Coors and looking forward to his first trip to Las Vegas.

So. Stick to the schedule. No detours. And drive the speed limit. A routine traffic stop would sink him.

His eyes had become accustomed to foggy nuances of green growing things. And rain. The snow-swept outskirts of the Twin Cities looked foreign. Unfriendly. A billboard whisked by. "AT LEAST YOU CAN STILL SMOKE IN YOUR CAR." WINSTONS. Danny laughed.

He felt like a visiting ghost. Thought of Ruby, the neighbor, her gifts of bread, wine and salt. Uh-uh. None of that shit.

Focus on Ida. She would clean her desk, put on her coat and take the elevator down to the second floor, where she would get off, enter the skyway system and walk a short few hundred yards to the drafty, creepy Victory Ramp where she parked.

When she entered the dark ramp she would slip her right hand in her purse and clutch the can of mace in her coat pocket. Unless she was packing "Roscoe." In her other hand she would hold her keys so the longest one protruded between her knuckles, as she'd learned in a self-defense class.

She would approach her car from the rear and check the backseat. Then she would check the surrounding area, the shadows, the contours of the other cars. Only when she was satisfied there was no threat would she release the Mace and open the car door.

He'd seen her do it dozens of times. He depended on her being a strict creature of habit. She'd be there. The house key would be there, hidden under the flowerpot near the garage. The car would be there.

They wouldn't miss her until after noon tomorrow. By then he'd have ditched her car in Minneapolis. Be in another cab on his way back to the airport.

It was going to work.

Every minute was another mile closer. No talking. Just go in fast and get it done. Best to not even let her see his face.

Do it and be free. He thought of the ocean and fog and palm trees. Ruby and her damn dead cat.

No other way. Ida was a loose end that someone like Broker would tug at until she started to unravel and . . .

They crossed the city limits of St. Paul.

Melancholy, nostalgia—he dared to call it love—informed his thoughts about Ida. Not enough to deter him but sufficient to serve up images of their relationship. Sadly, he realized she would be glad to see him. She'd think he'd come back for her. He shook his head. Probably why she tried to help that bastard Broker. See if she could get him back. He shook his head. The world was going to lose one great piece of ass.

They were making good time on clear main streets. Unplowed side streets looked treacherous. *He'd have to drive carefully.* Fog had preceded the snow. The branches were cased in exquisite sleeves of ice. Stalactites of ice drooped from eaves. Quaint, but after California, how could anybody live here.

Deep into Highland Park now. The driver pulled over to the intersection. Danny gave him a fifty and told him to keep the change. Big spender.

Checked his wristwatch. 5:30 P.M. It was time. He turned and walked to Sergeant Street. Walked right to her house. Dark, except for the light she always left on in the kitchen.

Go in now, or wait?

No hesitating now, go straight for the house key and get in. Standing around would draw attention. But it was doubtful anyone would be watching the street. The homes presented the posture of snowbound fortress, turned inward, hunkered around their hearths.

His tennis shoes went silent in the snow. The air shocked his Santa Cruz contact lenses. The sidewalk, front steps and driveway were cleanly shoveled. A flower bed ran along the side of the house, and at the back, where it turned into the backyard, a terra-cotta pot was turned upside down. He reached down and—shit, the damn thing was frozen solid. Danny kicked the pot, shattering it. The key ring caught the slick side door light.

No wasted motion now. Quick to the door. The key slid in, the tumblers turned. He was inside. He set his bags on the floor. Took off his shoes, so he wouldn't track snow. Then he went into the bag and took out the ski mask, slipped it on. Kept it rolled on his forehead for now. Put his stuff in the broom closet by the door.

A tidy cinnamon warmth circled his senses. The clean bewitching spoor of Ida. Everything in its place. Fighting off the memories, he crossed through the kitchen and entered the living room. Stepped on? One of her goddamn puzzles. Pieces stuck to his socks. He kicked them free and continued to the all-season side porch where she kept her computer and writing desk.

The computer sat on a table like the family shrine. Motion on the screen lent a votive flicker. Her screen saver swam in the darkness. Coral, oranges, purples—a lazy, turning cyber jellyfish.

He tested the drawer on her antique writing table. Unlocked. Thank you, Ida. He eased it open and by the shifting light of the screen at his elbow, picked through the stacked folders. Underneath her 1997 income tax folder, he found the familiar black cardboard jacket. Squinting at the label he himself had immodestly pasted on the cover. *"Untitled. A novel by Tom James."*

As he closed the drawer, his hip jarred the computer table. The screen saver jittered off and was replaced by a blue field on which huge hot orange type screamed:

### Wanted for questioning in the death of Caren Angland

Wonder—surprise—slowly withered into shock.

What the fuck?

Then disbelief. Right there, staring at him. His old face, shaggy hair, glasses, quiet smile, liquid blue eyes behind the glasses frames. Gushing sweat, growling, spitting; he noted the page's address:

*Broker@AOL.com*

His eyes whipped down the screen, reading the copy block. If you have seen this man contact the Cook County sheriff's department in Grand Marais, MN. Phone numbers.

No, he thought. No.

Then. *Broker.*

Stealth deserted him. He kicked at the computer and, fortunately, only tangled his stocking foot in the chair, which spun across the room on casters and smacked against a tall, potted dwarf pine.

His heart pounded in his throat. Acid sweat burned his eyes.

Bright light pinned him to the wall. Shadows. Like jungle vines, flashing across the living room, his body. Headlights. A car pulling into the drive. He dropped to a squat. Not ready. A muted sound of a car door closing. Not ready for this. Not now.

Needed time to . . .

Key turning in the door, the slight groan of the hinges, and he felt the draft of cold air as the door opened. He was moving, his veins seething with battery acid, muscles on fire.

"What the hell?" Her surprised voice, instantaneous with the flick of the kitchen light.

**62**

Ida froze, a bag of groceries in her arms, overcoat collar turned up, crushed tam cocked on her head. Shock made her long face into a noirish shadow-catcher. The whites of her oval eyes enlarged—processed—man coming at her—

"What have you done?" he hissed, bursting out of the dark living room, scattering puzzle pieces into the kitchen light.

She was halfway to a startled scream, dropping the groceries, reaching in her purse—then: "Oh my God." Horrific recognition on her face. "Tom?"

Cans popped and rolled on the floor. Desperation took the chilly scent of damp celery, the skitter of burst coffee beans on waxed linoleum. He stooped, swept up a can and threw it, through the kitchen doorway, across her living room, into her porch. It slammed her computer table, shaking off the screen saver. The lurid wanted poster glowed in the dark.

He faced her, leaner than she'd ever known him, more dynamic. A force to be reckoned with. He pleaded, "I would have done anything for you. I would have given you a new face. And you betrayed me."

After her first fear, seeing who it was, she stood her ground. Coolly assessing him, she fired back without missing a beat. "You sonofabitch, you never called."

He flipped the light switch off, then on again. "How do you want it, Ida, off or on? You always like it off. Let's leave it on, okay?"

So she could look at him. He couldn't help opening his wallet, showing her his new California license.

"I was right," she said in a dull voice.

"What's that supposed to mean?"

"That it was you; I recognized you, because of your voice," she said evenly.

Danny puffed a little. "I look different, don't I?"

"Yes." Same even voice. Trying to put him at ease. Up to something.

He pointed to the computer. "Explain that."

Still very cool, as if they were discussing a story in the office, she asked, "How did you get on to this?"

Danny grinned. "I hacked into the newsroom network with your password and read your E-mail."

"Not bad," said Ida.

"So what's he up to?"

"He wants to talk to you. He thinks things like that"—she jerked her head at Broker's Web page—"will make the FBI give you over. He thinks you took some money . . ."

But she was just making conversation to throw him off. Look at her, backing against the sink, inching toward her purse.

"Uh-uh." His hand shot out, faster than hers and stripped the purse from her grasp and—holy shit—closed his hand around the small compact pistol with the recessed hammer, jammed it in his belt.

"Tom, it's me," she stated. He wanted her to be more scared.

"Don't call me that," he said emphatically.

"Okay, Danny."

"That's better."

"Did you take some money?"

Like she was working or something. Ida, get a clue.

"You don't want to know," he said frankly.

"C'mon, you can tell me," attempting the old cajoling voice, her alley cat voice.

"Believe me, Ida, it's better you don't know."

"Tell me, Danny."

"How much is it worth to you to know? How much would you pay?"

"We could work it out," she said. And for a moment it was like the old days, their secret sharing.

*News.*

"Oh, for sure, we'll work it out. But how much?" Looking at her. And her opening her coat, shifting around, sending out a fleet of little sex gremlins.

"How much do you want?" smearing the tense air with hormones.

"All there is."

"You got it." Putting that great lilt in her voice.

"That's fair," he said leisurely. "Okay. I hid the money, I'm going to get it when I leave here. No one knows except you . . ."

"Real smart, I'm impressed," she said.

"Nah, that was just logical. I'll tell you what smart is. Killing Caren Angland was smart. Yeah." He relished her eyes getting wide. Now there's some NEWS for you. "*I* pushed her in. Why in the hell Angland hasn't told somebody, I don't know. He tried to stop me. That's how I got shot."

"That's a hell of a story," she managed to say in a dry husky voice.

"No it isn't. It's a secret. There's a difference." He took a step forward, so their bodies brushed. Felt the squirm of passion. Sadly, because that was definitely out. Fluids. Hair.

Eloquently, her eyes noticed the latex gloves.

He half turned. "The thing about a secret is—they only work as long as the person who hears them lives to tell about it."

Her face composed a scream. But no sound. It was a diversion, because her sharp left knee pistoned up and caught him—almost—in the balls. He took the attack mostly on his right thigh. Enough to knock him back. Pawing for balance, he ripped a shelf off the wall over the stove. A scatter of tea bags flew across the counters, the floor. But then he lunged forward, caught her as she dashed for the door.

His hands shot out to beat the real scream to her throat. He felt it like water inflating a thick hose. Had to choke it off with both hands. All those weeks working the hand springs really paid off now.

"You?" she managed to gasp. Swinging with her free arms, pummeling his outer arms. Fighting back. He whipped his right elbow as hard as he could and felt the sharp pain as it connected with her cheek.

Now the left side of her face matched her chin. She went loose, flopping. The body going slack inside the thick coat, twisting, thrashing. Her legs went out from under her and he forced her down, clamping one hand over her mouth. With the other he felt for something to use as a weapon. Felt a hard cylinder. A can.

Between a skewed lock of her hair and the back of his left hand he saw a wedge of her cheek and one cloudy eye. Pinpoint bright in the overhead light, he saw her long lashes, individual hairs, the liquid in the corner of her eye. Smelled the hair rinse she'd used in the shower this morning. Body lotion. Her sharp animal scent. Finally, here was fear, a forest fire of it boiling out of her armpits.

The thick crush hat was still on her head and that's where he brought the can down with enough force to split a round of spaghetti elm.

Ida Rain arched once and collapsed.

Danny straddled her, gasping for breath. Not thinking. Just pictures. The side door was open, and he could see through the open door, across the driveway and into the neighbor's kitchen windows.

See her keys still hanging below the doorknob.

Finish the job. Like someone who criminally misunderstood CPR, he kneeled on her chest with both knees and pumped his crossed hands down on her mouth and nose, clamping off her breath, he kept this up for minutes as her strong body fought back independent of her unconscious brain.

Finally she stopped. Everything stopped.

He tore her blouse away, and needing to touch her, to feel her, flesh to flesh, he ripped the bra to shreds, snapped off the rubber glove and placed his right hand, palm down, on the calm silent chamber of her smooth chest, between the swell of her breasts.

Felt. Listened.

Nothing. Slowly he pulled the latex glove back on. Never this close to Death, he paused to study it. The writer in him, perhaps. Her lips looked like raw meat. Her teeth imbedded like stones in the clay gums.

Too much. He shuddered, panicked, scrambled to his knees, reached up and turned off the light.

The real thing. Not shoving someone off a slippery rock.

Okay. Now what.

His eyes swept the dark interior of the house and encountered the innocent perpetual motion of the screen saver looping itself. He literally watched his reason leave, a toy helicopter flying off the top of his head. Thus unencumbered, like a true denizen of WITSEC, he could argue that the sonofabitch Broker was to blame for this. If he had left Ida alone, she'd be alive today.

All Broker's fault. Danny got up. His hand closed around the handle of the stubby pistol on his belt. More bad luck for Broker. *Now I got a gun.* He stooped among the cans, boxes and vegetables on the floor, found the slim manuscript he'd dropped. Tucked in his belt, in back.

Remembered kicking over the chair in the study. Returned there, righted the chair. Picked up a can of soup that he'd thrown. Now.

The keys still in the door and the strewn groceries sketched a desperate scenario. He could leave the door untouched, ajar. A smash-and-grab robbery gone sour. In thirty seconds he found the spare set of keys she always carried in her purse.

So. What would a dumb junkie do? First, he wouldn't take off his shoes and figure out where the house key was hidden. Danny retrieved his tennis shoes and coat from the hall broom closet and put them on.

He slipped outside, walked back along the side of the house and stamped his feet in the snow beyond the throw of the house light, next to the garage. Then he walked back and stomped into the house, leaving distinctive sneaker treads on the linoleum. He continued this little routine around the kitchen, reenacting his fight with Ida. Throwing in a few extra moves. Victory dance.

Then back to the purse, tore through the contents and pulled out the wallet. Standing up, he took a quick inventory. Had the manuscript. And the gun. Without looking down, he stepped over the sprawled form and exited the house, careful not to disturb the door. The dangling keys.

Like complicity, a heavy fog cloaked the street. Lights were smears of jelly in the soft gloom. With his shopping bag and travel bag, he got in Ida's car and backed into the street. Turned on to Cleveland Avenue and rolled down the window near the crosstown bus stop.

He pulled the currency from the wallet and the VISA, Dayton's, and Neiman Marcus credit cards. Twenty yards from the bus stop, he tossed the wallet into a frost-painted hedge. Since all the gang kids started shooting each other on the streets, cops made jokes about the bushes being full of guns. They always checked the shrubbery near a crime scene. They'd find the wallet.

Free of the wallet, he checked the gas gauge. Nice of her to leave him a full tank.

Real deep in the "danger zone." Driving a stolen car, with a loaded handgun, on his way to visit two million bucks. Master of Life and Death. So this was what it was like, living in real time. One of Joe Travis's clients for sure, now.

He toed the gas. The muscular snow tires surged and carved a sidewinder pattern in the slush. Behind him, back on Sergeant Street, a cold draft knifed through the ajar inner and outer side doors. It ruffled a strand of sticky hair that coiled in a tiny trickle of blood on Ida's cheek.

The trickle stopped. Seeped. Stopped.

Slowly, her powerful heart failed, fought, failed, fought. Until. Lubdub. Lubdub. Through the firestorm in her brain, a red push rallied to whip the sluggish blood; a wispy spark fired the slack lungs. The tiny bubble of vomit swelled at the corner of her mouth. Popped. Ever so slowly, another bubble started to form.

Unseen in heavy fog, Danny drifted north, up the deserted lanes of U.S. 35. Cooler now, he took the long view.

A difficult task. Ruthless necessity. Like a killing in wartime. Tying off the loose end. She had to go. Living privileges revoked. Air stopped. Lights off. Her magnificent snatch and her cockeyed face stuffed in a hole in the ground like any other dead animal.

His thoughts swelled until he blundered on Profundity. Like slavery and killing the Indians, her death was the regrettable, but necessary, price of admission to the American Dream.

The thrill propelled him miles and miles up the foggy empty road. Time elongated. Contracted. Stood still. *Why,* he marveled, *don't more people do this.*

South of Duluth, he stopped at a Holiday to gas up. He saw a display of kids' plastic sleds, marked down. Bought one. Might need it to pull the suitcase out of the woods, if the snow was bad. He also bought a flashlight and a thermos. Duct tape, to wrap the canvas bags.

On impulse he got a half dozen jelly donuts. Filled the thermos with black coffee.

Back on the road, he gobbled the pastry, licking jam and sugar off his fingers. Driving the ghostly highway was retracing his journey with Caren Angland. A pilgrimage.

Watch it. Don't flirt with being caught.

The profilers counted on that. Gloating in the crime. Why Ed

Kemper had frequented the Jury Box bar and hung out with cops. He was dangerously close to the profile, baiting Broker.

Had to watch that. "Control that," he said out loud because, as the miles rolled beneath his tires and he drew closer to Cook County, he could feel the urge to settle it.

Creep into his house. Scamper around in the dark like the Manson disciples. Press the pistol against his sleeping head. Surprise ending for *Jeremiah Johnson*. This time, the Indians win.

A night like this. One shot, then disappear into the fog.

He softened the hard thoughts. Self-dramatic. Spare the child— no—pardon the child. Noblesse oblige. Hey. He wasn't a monster.

But then her eyes would still be there. Bugging him at night.

Have to think about that.

Focused, he drove past the red and orange blur of the Black Bear Casino sign without so much as a nod. God. Where'd all this fog come from? Duluth was out there, someplace. Superior.

The distance narrowed to Cook County. Discipline was important now. He removed the nondescript pocket calendar card from his wallet on which he'd carefully copied the directions to the money stash from one of his old business cards. When he was in the Orientation Center.

Flashed on Ida, sprawled, a broken doll among the vegetables. Shook it off. Never could have changed his life this much, this fast, without shooting through the keyhole of opportunity Keith and Caren Angland presented.

He'd still be going into debt playing the quarter slots at Mystic Lake. Be Ida's latest goddamn rehabilitation project.

Ida. Past tense. Concentrate. The mileage and the map. He literally had to navigate by them because his vision was so limited.

The road he wanted was represented on the map as a black and white checked line. A secondary gravel road. The number in a square marked it as local as opposed to county. Number 4. Just past Lutsen.

Then he had to turn 3.7 miles up that road and turn right onto the property of Keith Angland's father.

Tension pounded a wedge of pain between his shoulder blades. He had to force himself to stop clenching his latex-gloved hands on the wheel. In the last forty-five minutes he had not encountered a single car. Only his low beams, pushing at the thick fog.

He barely saw the road sign for Lutsen. No hint of what lay off the road to either side. Solid cotton batting, opaque, white.

In first gear now, driving this slow, he was begging for a rear end accident. Some tanked-up Jack Pine Savage speeding.

And then, his road sign blurred in the mist. Number 4 on it. Danny stopped. Had to get out of the car and walk across the road to see the turnoff. He returned to the Accord and edged forward a few yards to make his turn.

A wet red shadow blinkered the mist. He jumped and then laughed out loud. Out of habit, he'd hit the turn signal.

Take it easy.

Carefully, he drove the road, his eyes constantly dropping to check the speedometer. He passed three miles and began counting off the tenths. Six rolled up and then seven. He stopped and got out again to scout on foot.

A chain. A chain. Linking two trees. In December, with no snow, there had been a rutted path filled with orange pine needles. Not much snow down on 61, but up here, in the woods, there was plenty of snow. The trees looked like faint black girders joining the white mist to the white snow.

He'd backtracked less than fifty yards when he saw the ragged horizontal line draped between two trees. Remembered the small yellow metal sign hanging in the middle. PRIVATE.

Feeling in the snow for the key. Tin box under the rock, by the roots of the tree. He laughed again. It was turning into a night of hidden keys.

He stopped his searching. Peered into the solid wall of white. The obvious. Ida's city car couldn't make it through even this wilting snow.

And with no tracks to go by he could go off the path. Get stuck. Better to use the plastic sled, walk in. It meant leaving the Accord on the road. Had to risk it.

He returned to the car, backed up and parked. He pulled the sled from the backseat and exchanged his tennis shoes for the new Sorels. Took off the leather coat, put on his sweater, pulled the coat back on, a hat, gloves.

Hauling the flimsy sled, sweeping his flashlight before him, he set off through the drifts. No way the Accord would have made it through this. Couldn't get lost, just follow his tracks back out. A hundred yards into the pines, he had his bearings. The shanty, the birch tree. The place was still engraved on his memory.

He figured his direction and set off into the pine thickets.

At first he couldn't find the cistern in the snow. So he walked a circle and crisscrossed it until he hit the mound, knocked through the surface snow and found the tangle of rusty tin debris.

Calmly, taking pride in the way his muscles warmed to the work, he removed the layer of junk, and soon the black plastic peeked through the snow.

He brushed it off, shoved, pulled, yanked, and lifted it out with his new muscles. No work at all, with the sled. Almost wanted to run; that's how greased he was with the physical high, coming off of Ida.

A few minutes later he was huddled in the front seat, coaxing the heater to warm faster. Catching his breath. Checked his watch. Just past 2 A.M. What time did it get light?

He forced himself to drink a cup of coffee from the thermos. Had to calm down before he got back on the road.

Chill out. Formed the phrase in his mind. Curious usage under these circumstances, freezing.

Okay. Very carefully he turned around, fearing unseen ditches in the snow and drove back toward Highway 61.

When he got to the intersection, he stopped. Slammed by waves of impulse. Broker to the left. Freedom to the right.

Discipline. Think of everything he'd achieved. Can't take the chance of blowing it. Stick to the plan.

But he knew that, in the house where Broker lived, a computer was turned on, the Web site the hick ex-cop had concocted. Up there, glowing in the dark.

Mocking him. And causing problems. They'd probably move him from Santa Cruz because of it. Stick him in some trailer court in Idaho.

Reached under the seat, checked the cold shape of the pistol. What if he wasn't there. Nah, he'd be there, with the brat.

The big-eyed brat who haunted his dreams.

It was wrong. Stupid. But Danny knew he was going to do it anyway. Because of who he was now. Because he was through taking shit off people. His foot released the brake, stabbed at the gas and turned left.

**64**

Broker had stayed up late, had consumed too much coffee. He watched for trucks. He had even crept through the woods, up to the cabin next door and peeked in the window. David and Denise were fused together on a foldout couch, a carnal pretzel illuminated by the glimmering TV screen. Stacks of video cassettes piled the coffee table.

Chastised, cursing himself for a paranoid, he came home and headed for bed. Caffeine limbo waited, a dehydrated shadow of sleep. At 2:30 A.M., his kidneys prodded him and he got up and padded to the bathroom. On the way back to bed he saw the bright display of the video monitor suspended in the dark, Tom James's face under the garish orange type.

He and Ida Rain had missed each other. She'd communicated remotely, leaving a message on his voice mail. She thought the Web site, while novel, was desperate—if *he really wanted to find James.* Like she was promising something.

No reaction from the FBI.

Wouldn't be, either. He was out of moves. It was over.

Out the windows, fog slowly crept into the chinks and crannies. Broker never sighed.

He sighed.

Too much thinking. What he needed was sleep. He went into Kit's room and checked on her in the soft spill of the night-light. She lay as if flung headlong, limbs willy-nilly, in a clutter of stuffed animals. Her head was thrown back in a nest of sweaty curls, one arm twisted out and ended in an upturned hand. The tiny fingers continued to reach. A miniature detail from Michelangelo.

The mystery of Peace made simple, in the undisturbed sleep of a healthy child. Everywhere, always, the same. Softly, he touched her chest, sensitive to the tiny rise and fall, felt her warm forehead, said one of his wordless daddy prayers.

Back in the covers he drifted in shallow tangles. Fatigue marched over him, an ant army of tiny distractions. The fog turned to rain, which lulled him. But then the rain turned hard, a sleet downpour. Eventually he sagged in a hammock of consciousness, just below the surface of sleep. A muffled drawn-out crash shot him bolt upright. Up, looking out the windows. A whole row of pines had keeled over against the roof, their branches weighted down with ice.

Ice storm. Like they were getting up in Canada. Nothing for it tonight. Back in bed, his last snatches of wakefulness recorded the ominous scrape of ice-burdened branches against the roof and eaves. The steady thud of icy rain. The crash of trees falling in the woods.

His muscles snapped to while his mind was still blind with sleep. A tinny musical reveille insinuated through the groan of the wind and ice-tormented trees—Cucaracha Dog.

*Dada Dah da*

*Dada Dah da*

Kit's cry, simultaneous to the calliope weirdness of the toy. Then—the scramble of feet in his house. *In Kit's room.*

Broker sprang off the bed in a gymnastic movement at combat speed. The twelve-gauge came off the floor and swung comfortably into his hands before his eyes opened. *KARAA-CKKK* went the steel slide, chambering a load of double ought buck.

Lizard brain pushed the mammal brain, then cerebral cortex, the civilizing membrane, but way out front and absolutely ready to kill— was the new daddy brain. And the daddy brain propelled Broker through the dark. Seeking the threat in a cold rage, thumbing off the safety on the shotgun, heading for his daughter's cries, filtering out the sound of the toy.

Someone in the house. Stepped on the toy?

How? Figure it out later.

Without thought of caution or strategy, he went immediately to the crib and scooped up the bawling child. He backed from her room—Kit in one arm, the weapon ready in the other—to his room, and as he dropped her in a plastic hamper in his closet and closed the door and heaved the dresser in front of it, he realized—

No yard light.

No night-lights.

No light over the stove.

Just ice glowing in the luminous mist. He proceeded to search his house. Room by room, corner by corner, closet by closet. Finally he backtracked, pausing in Kit's room. Found the musical toy at the foot of her bed. She could have tossed it out, that could have set it off.

But he didn't believe that. He heard somebody. He crept out on the back porch on planking slick with ice. Ice was everywhere. Trees dipped in it. Every branch and pine needle was sheathed. His driveway was a transparent sheet.

Then he saw the power line and the phone line, sagging to the ground under the heavy whiskers of ice. An ice-stricken pine had toppled with them, the snowy crown punched in a basement window.

Immediately, he went inside, down the basement stairs. Found tiny pools of dirty melt on the steps. Led to the broken window. That's how they got in.

Back up, outside. An engine growled up on the highway. But, before dawn it was routine, even in this weather—truckers ferrying supplies to the casino at Grand Portage.

He squinted at the fog. Went in, picked up his phone. Dead.

No cell phone. Just as well, Jeff would have his hands full on a night like this.

One last check to make. Forgive me, Kit. He slithered through the woods again. And—the Audi was gone from the blacked-out cabin. Deserted.

Okay David. We're going to have a talk.

Whatever happened, it was over, and now he felt dumb waving around a loaded gun.

The barrel of the Remington arced down from alert, his thumb clicked the safety back on. He went back in, the shotgun in the crook of his arm, got a flashlight and liberated Kit from the closet.

Her discomfort was aggravated by a mighty pants full of poop. Broker changed her by flashlight. Then he lit candles, took her into the kitchen and bribed her with a tippy cup of milk and a plate of animal cookies.

Great formative memories, eh kid? The books said they didn't remember things from this early. So he hoped she wouldn't fix on the image of a plateful of cookies by candlelight, on the surface of the maple table, next to a loaded shotgun.

**65**

A fucking kid's toy!

Unbelievable. Find a window broken, like fate had opened the way. Got all the way into the house. All keyed up. Had the gun out, and he stepped on some damn kid's toy. But that other sound he'd heard, over the brat's screaming—heard very clearly—like the jaws of hell clashing, steel on steel. *No-shit shotgun being loaded,* and all he had was the puny woman's .38, and suddenly his Billy the Kid rampage was over. No way he was going to face off with an armed awake Broker in his own house.

Uh-uh.

Danny had turned and sprinted back down the basement stairs, crawled super fast out the window and over the downed pine tree, tripping on wires, terrified he'd be electrocuted.

But he wasn't and Thank You God for the goddamn fog.

And that he'd pulled the telephone line before he went in. More the ice storm than him. The line was halfway down when he tugged on it.

Slipping and sliding. Amazing. The snow had hardened to glass. Took his weight. Like a huge water spider, he scooted over the crust. Through the trees, toward the highway. Looked back once, at the shadowy mass of the darkened house.

Nothing.

Like he never was there.

He'd pulled the car off the road, into the shadows of some trees. Now, inside, engine on, in gear—and damn, the tires whined, clawing for traction on the ice.

Goddamn fucking Minnesota, never come back to this no-good place. Finally, he began to move. Running like hell, doing about eight miles per hour.

Can you believe this shit?

Giddy. Nervous. Hilarious. He drove south. Then: sobered. Quit when you're ahead. How far to the county line? He had to drive through Grand Marais. Broker could have a cell phone. Only the one road in and out.

When he saw the red flashers flare in the gloom up ahead, he almost screamed out loud. God. No. A roadblock. Then, no, it wasn't. Slowly he came on a truck, off the road, on its side in the ditch. A county deputy appeared, swinging a flashlight.

Oh Christ. Now what. Danny reached for the pistol in his belt. He'd fight for the money. He would.

But the deputy just waved him on. His strong ruddy face jogged Danny's memory. The mustache. He laughed hilariously. The same guy who had bandaged him up at the waterfall. Small world, motherfucker.

Expecting any second to be pulled over, he drove real slow on glare ice into Grand Marais. Red and blue rotating flashers slapped the shuttered buildings. Emergency vehicles. Phone company trucks. The ice had collapsed the lines.

The whole county was without communication.

Mist to rain and then the temperature dropped. Like it only can up here. Cryogenic cold snap.

Ice City.

Hell. If he was this lucky, he should stop at the Black Bear Casino. But—no more detours. Keep moving. Toward California. Toward his hideaway on Valentino Lane.

Like a shadow, he crept through a landscape transformed into white coral reefs. Every surface hackled, feathered. White trees from Mars. And him the only thing moving.

When he'd passed out of Cook County, he stopped at a rest area that overlooked the lake. Had the whole place to himself. First, he threw Ida's gun into Superior, then went back to the shelter of the car. Methodically, steeling himself against the temptation to break open the bundles and frolic in hundreds, he sat in the backseat, opened the suitcase and packed the tidy wads of currency into the canvas bags. Taking care of business. Nothing but focused. He buffered the money with newsprint, wrapped them with duct tape.

Tried to make two symmetrical bundles. Twenty-two pounds apiece. Then he stuffed the wrappings from the trash bags in the suitcase, carried it down to the beach, filled it with round cobbles, walked out on a boulder and flung it into the lake. One last thing. Burn the manuscript in a frozen camp grill.

Now. Wait for stores to open. Back on the road. In Two Harbors, he found an open restaurant, ate a huge breakfast and renewed himself with coffee.

And did what he did every morning. Read the paper.

In Duluth, at 9 A.M., after consulting the Yellow Pages, he walked into a Wrap and Ship office with his packages. Watched the lady behind the counter pack them in sturdy boxes. No questions. No problem. Was given a tracking number. He filled out the return address as B. Franklin on fictitious Pampas Street, Duluth.

And sent them to Danny Storey at 173 Valentino Lane, Watsonville, California.

*Yes.*

At 10 A.M., he was making good time on the sanded freeway. Heading south.

Through the whole thing he had faithfully worn the latex gloves under his winter gloves. No fingerprints on the car. His hands were turning to liquid from the sweat. Not much longer.

The rest of the drive was uneventful. Clear roads. Not much traffic. He drove into Minneapolis, stopped at a gas station and used a vacuum hose to clean the upholstery and carpet. Stuffed the sled into a trash can. Then he continued on to the downtown loop and parked at the bus depot. Generously, he handed the new boots, the hat and the gloves to a derelict standing outside the Greyhound station.

Then he walked Hennepin Avenue until he flagged a cab. Under way, he threw first Ida's credit cards, then the rubber gloves out the window. He arrived at the airport with hours to spare. He passed through the metal detectors, checked his flight information on the monitors, turned up the collar of his leather jacket and walked down the green concourse to celebrate in an airport lounge.

Not a bad day's work.

**66**

The morning after the ice storm, Broker strapped on his sidearm and checked the cabin on the point. Still no one home. Kit, adjusting to being abandoned, gave herself an oatmeal facial, strapped in her high chair, and didn't cry. He drove into town and dropped her with Madge at the sheriff's office. She wandered between the legs of harried dispatchers who were fielding cell phone calls from stranded motorists and alarmed tourists in remote Gunflint cabins. Broker put on a Cook County deputy's parka and helped out.

With a gum ball stuck on his Jeep roof, he four-wheeled back roads, collected stranded people and drove them to Trail Center, the lodge halfway up the Gunflint where emergency services had set up.

Midafternoon, Jeff overtook him in his Bronco, waved him to the side of the road. The sheriff walked slowly, up all night, red-rimmed eyes. Broker rolled down his window. Jeff leaned, resting on his forearms, said, "Bad news," in a tired, flat, official voice.

"Some phones are up. Tommy Reardon, St. Paul Homicide, just called. They found that newspaper woman you've been talking to, Ida Rain, damn near dead, in her kitchen three hours ago."

"Shit." Broker took a sledgehammer to the chest. The cliché poised on his lips: *I just talked to her the other . . .*

"Bludgeoned, strangled, robbed, took her car. Her house keys were still in her side door. Neighbors spotted them and called 911. Looks like somebody jumped her carrying in the groceries, her wallet was missing from her purse. Probably had a spare set of car keys in there."

"How is she?"

"Fractured skull, broken nose, comatose; in ICU at Regions."

"How'd you get the call?"

"Tommy spotted your card—or my card with your name written on it—tacked up on her refrigerator. He wants you to check in with him."

Broker nodded. "They establish time of the attack?"

"The receipt in the shopping bag logged 5:47 P.M. So sometime after that. Guy whacked her with a can of minestrone soup, Tommy said, then smothered her. Probably to stop her from screaming. Looks like a botched mugging. Didn't know what he was doing. Left her for dead."

"Shit," Broker said again. "Tommy say anything about her chances?"

"The docs say she's strong. Have to wait and see."

"Broken skull for twenty, thirty bucks, that's a bummer," said Broker. But he couldn't shake a bad feeling about the timing. Still hadn't told Jeff about the break-in.

"Yeah, well, anytime I can wreck your night, just let me know."

They watched a column of olive-camouflaged Humvees, National Guard out of Duluth, slowly snake into town. Jeff said, "Finally, these guys can handle the back roads better than we can. And their radios work. Why don't you hang it up, take Kit home."

Spirited Ida Rain, randomly chopped down. His sadness produced the image of the huge ambitious puzzle on her carpet—unfinished. Fluky? His night visitor. Ida. Broker didn't rule out coincidence. But he was suspicious. Back at the sheriff's office, he shouldered his way to a phone, grabbed at Kit as she scurried past, missed, got through to St. Paul Homicide.

Tommy Reardon came on the line fast after Broker identified himself. "What you got going with this Ida Rain?"

"She was Tom James's boss. I talked to her about how he got on to Caren."

"Women have bad luck with you lately, huh, Broker? First Caren, now this one." More ill will than suspicion snickered in Reardon's voice.

Not funny. He ignored the dig and asked, "You have any leads?"

"Nah. Looks like smash and grab. The asshole wore gloves, no latents on the soup can he used. We have everybody looking for her car. Maybe something will show up on her credit cards. That and the car's our best bet. Until she wakes up. If she wakes up."

Broker shut his eyes. C'mon, Ida. "So, just in and out fast?"

"Yeah, probably followed her home from the grocery store."

"Okay, thanks, Tommy. If anything comes up, appreciate it if you call Cook County."

"Yeah, sure, good-bye."

Broker watched Kit play with Lyle Torgerson's flashlight. Amazement glowed in her eyes as she moved the switch with both tiny thumbs and the light came on. Then off. Ida, turned off that abruptly? Lyle collected his flashlight. "You all right, Broker?"

"Yeah, tired."

"Everybody is. Damn storm."

He heaved to his feet, took Kit, left the fatigued synergy of the sheriff's office and crept north in four-wheel low. The crystalline world, enchanted in the light, became melancholy with sundown. Trees bowed under the icy yoke, their green dreams of spring turning to nightmares.

Ida fighting, screaming. Which compartment could he check her into? He was full up.

Broker eased down his driveway, edged around the turn, cleared the trees and—

The butternut Ford Ranger 250 had a new camper box up back and was parked right in front of his porch.

Broker threw into reverse, fishtailed back behind the garage, apologized to Kit for leaving her alone again, and rolled out; county police radio in one hand, .45 in the other.

He approached the Ford, still no license plates, keyed the radio, about to ask for some backup when he peeked through the cracked driver's side window and saw the classic, felt, porkpie brown hat perched on the dashboard. He took his thumb off the transmit button and clicked the pistol back on safe.

Garrison.

The porch window presented a view of the man, sitting in the dark flickering living room. Definitely Garrison. In out of the cold. Building fires in Broker's fireplace. A minute later, with Kit dozing on his left shoulder, Broker mounted the porch and heard the mournful voice warble through the ajar door.

> *"As I walked out on the streets of Laredo*
> *As I walked out in Laredo one day*
> *I spied a young cowboy all wrapped in white linen*
> *All wrapped in white linen and cold as the grave . . ."*

Lorn Garrison, calm as can be, in a red Pendleton wool shirt, jeans and hunting boots, sat in front of a roaring fire. A lined Levi's jacket hung from the back of the kitchen chair. A section of the *Duluth News Tribune* spread on the floor, by the hearth, under his boots. Wood shavings littered the newsprint.

Broker carried Kit into the living room and saw that Garrison delicately held an old Randall pocketknife in his right hand. Firelight flickered on the sweat-cured walnut handle, the pitted shank and the razor-sharp wink of the blade. In his left hand, he turned a flitch of basswood that was becoming the comical head of a six-legged insect, complete with feelers. Garrison cleared his throat,

"Hope you don't mind I let myself in. Got a little weathersome in the back of the truck when this storm hit."

"Am I under FBI surveillance?" asked Broker, very alert, fatigue forgotten. His mini–Ice Age, north of Grand Marais, was suddenly crowded with possibilities: first the break-in, then the news about Ida, now Garrison.

Garrison grinned, folded the knife with a flick of his fingers and stuck it in his back pocket. "Sit down. Relax. I'd offer you a cup of coffee, but you haven't made it yet."

"Answer the question. I picked up that truck on my tail over a week ago in St. Paul. Saw it again, right out there in my woods. You might as well be driving a fire engine."

"Beauty, huh? Cost a big chunk of my early retirement bonus."

"Retirement?"

"Yeah." Garrison raised his elbows and gyrated his hips. "No badge, no cuffs, no gun. I don't work for uncle anymore. Some bean counters at headquarters are cooking the books for the budget, clearing off as many old-timers as they can. So I signed up. Cashed in a couple days after pulling Keith off you in that cell." Garrison shrugged. "Maybe I'll write a book about President Clit's love life and go on *Larry King Live* like everybody else. But first, I figured we should talk."

"I'm listening." Broker walked to the kitchen, took candles from the cupboard and set them on the counter. He filled a teakettle with bottled water and put it on the stove. He had propane. No lights. No water. Checked the phone. No phone.

Garrison stood up. Without a suit coat, he looked like an aging wrangler, barrel chest, heavy shoulders, narrow hips. He squatted and handed Kit the carving. "Hello, little girl, this is for your daddy." He rose slowly, favoring his knees, and joined Broker in the kitchen.

Kit stared at the carving, at Broker, at Garrison, then back at Broker. "Bring it here," he said. She darted under the kitchen table, sat down and hugged the carving to her chest.

"Smart move, kid," said Garrison.

"So, what—?" Broker started to ask.

Garrison cut him short, raising a finger to his lips. He smiled, reached over, plucked up the pen off the magnetized notepad refrigerator door and scrawled on the pad. Broker read in the failing light: "You got cooties!"

Garrison roved his eyes over the living room and drew a little bug on the note for emphasis.

Broker took the pen from Garrison and wrote: "Talk in the workshop." Garrison nodded, picked up his coat.

Five minutes later, Broker had instant coffee in a thermos and candles. Garrison had moved his truck into the garage. By candlelight, Kit was banging the carved bug on a bench in the workshop.

Broker snapped trim pieces of maple, shoved them in the woodstove with handfuls of wood shavings. He took a matchbook from the bench, lit a crumpled piece of newsprint. The stovepipe creaked as the tinder ignited. He turned to Garrison.

Garrison said, "I started out following you. After your session with Keith. I wound up following the guys who are following you."

A slow wave of heat melted the chilled puff of Broker's breath. "What guys?"

Garrison crossed his legs. He sat in a distressed rocking chair, sipped his coffee, rolled a blue tip match in his lips. He'd brought a heavy plastic briefcase in from his truck and balanced it across his knees.

Whack. Whack. Kit laid about her with the carving.

"Three guys, one dolly," said Garrison, "in a VW van, a gray Saturn and a blue Plymouth Horizon." Garrison rubbed his chin. "You talk to Keith in jail. People start following you. Gotta be a reason. So I don't sleep for a couple days, drive a lot and get a lot of parking tickets. You had lunch with Captain Merryweather. You tooled all over the freeway system. They're on you. They put you to bed at your motel and stayed on you when you got up. You talked to a guy in St. Paul City Hall, they drifted past, stood around chatting, listening. You met that woman in a coffee shop across the street, they sat at the next table. They followed you up to the big place on Summit Avenue, back to your motel in Stillwater. Then to Sergeant Street in St. Paul, where the woman you met for coffee lives.

"The Saturn followed you when you left the Sergeant house, but the Horizon and the VW stayed. So I hung with them. In the morning, the woman left for work. The young guy and the chick in the

VW van broke in the house. The Horizon stood watch. They came out, split from the Horizon, drove the VW to the Maplewood Mall, left it, got in a black Audi. I followed the Audi up here." He pointed out the window, south along the shore to the cabin on the point.

"Did you take pictures of them going in her house," asked Broker. That impatient stamping sensation was back in his chest.

"I always take pictures; got my Nikon in the truck," said Garrison. "Just costs more now to get them developed." He popped open the briefcase. It was custom-fitted to hold a cordless drill, screwdrivers, electrician's pliers, coils of wire, screws, staples, other stuff Broker couldn't identify. A stack of glossy, black-and-white, eight-by-ten photos slid out. And two VCR recording cassettes. The labels were dated and numbered—two days last week.

Broker picked up the top picture. David and Denise, the "lawyers" from Chicago. They were using Ida Rain's storm door for cover as they worked on the inner door. The next picture showed then coming out.

Seeing Broker eye the case on his knees, Garrison explained, "I paid a visit next door. Nobody home. Picked up this kit. Thing is, there's no recording equipment. Just a TV, VCR and lots of tapes. I don't know how he's doing it."

Broker said, "The woman in the Sergeant house is Ida Rain, she's an editor at the St. Paul paper and Tom James's girlfriend . . ."

"Little shit James never mentioned a girlfriend," said Garrison with a salutary nod.

"I get the feeling it was discreet. And you never checked," Broker said pointedly. "Ida Rain is in intensive care at Regions. Somebody beat her head in last night. Left her for dead. St. Paul Homicide called. She had my card on her refrigerator. I've been talking to her."

Garrison rocked, exhaled, reflected, "Knowing Tom James sure is hard on women, ain't it." After a pause. "You think she has a line on him?"

"She's the kind of woman who gets under a guy's skin. It's possible. She's my best bet."

Garrison nodded in agreement. "Good call. It's the most likely security lapse, James gets lonely. Phones. Writes a letter." He stabbed a finger at the picture in Broker's hand. "I don't think they did it. That blond kid isn't in the bone-breaking end of the family. He's an electronics freak. I figured he wired you and Rain."

"Family?"

Garrison palmed another photo, one Broker had seen before, in the cemetery in Wisconsin. Keith shaking hands. The distinguished guy with close-cropped hair in an expensive suit. Garrison pointed to the lean gentleman. "Nice Chicago family. There's miles of insulation between Victor Konic and the Paulie Kagins of the world. Got this monster brownstone on North Lake Shore Drive. Banking. Imports. The blond kid is his son, David; degree in computer science, Stanford. The apple of his eye."

"This Russian Mafioso sent his kid to bug me?"

"A bunch of weight lifters with blue tattoos on their hands would kind of stick out up here. But they're exactly the guys who could have worked on the Rain woman." Garrison shook his head. "If she knew anything, they know it now . . ."

"Maybe," said Broker. "She's tough. Another thing, if these guys are such pros why'd they make it look like a shivering junkie with a claw hammer did it? Why's she still above ground?"

Garrison glanced out the window, toward the cabin down the shore. "If they come back, we'll find out."

Broker ignored the dark undertone in Garrison's voice. "So the bureau finally is taking me seriously about James and the money."

"Well, it's tricky, isn't it. Someone in the bureau actively discouraged my attempt to investigate your questions about James. I got used. On both ends. James hustled me. And the bureau kept me in the dark. I don't like being used. So I walked. Now *I'm* taking you seriously. And I'm here to tell you you're going about this all wrong."

Broker studied the FBI man. "Who are you, the Good Fairy?"

"No. And neither are you. You're the guy who went to Vietnam, dug up a pile of lost gold and smuggled it out of the country. You find things. That's why Keith put you on his list."

Broker engaged the weary knowledge in Garrison's eyes. "What do you want?"

"Same as Keith, same as the people he's got following you." Garrison grinned. "Stop playing cop. Be yourself."

Kit barged into Broker's knee, looked up, thrust out the carving. He picked her up, tousled her curls, smelled her innocent breath. He had been a happy exile in babyland. Hiding out, up here in his smuggler's cove. Now, here was Garrison, making sense. Kit would have to go into a compartment for a while.

"How do I know you're alone?" asked Broker.

"You don't. But we both know who is. Way out there, deep, alone." Garrison squinted. "Don't we?"

Broker went with his gut. "Yeah," he said.

Garrison nodded. "To get Keith off the hook you need a motive these Russian bastards can understand. Like making a few bucks off his misfortune."

"Are you that smart? Didn't you tell me cops need big hearts and weak brains." Broker grinned.

Garrison shrugged. "Well, you know—you work the edges long enough, you come to a place where your edges intersect with someone else's edges . . . and you feel your way along the new edge and suddenly you've poked your foot into this little Manhattan Project."

Broker met the ex-FBI man's serious gaze, held it.

Garrison rocked back in the chair, swept stray wood shavings off his lap. His voice was quiet, resigned. "You may owe him. But clearing that debt don't mean you can trust him. Not the way he is now. The only person you can trust is me."

**68**

On the way into the house, they paused and studied the cabin on the point. Twilight pooled under racing Appaloosa clouds. Rollers thrashed the granite shore. No lights. No wood smoke. No black Audi. A phone company truck pulled down the drive. Too weary to even wave, the lineman patched the down wire and left.

Kit, trussed in layers of Polarfleece, resembled a ball of yarn with a tiny visor between a wrapped scarf, her cap and the hood of her coat. Alert little eyes peered out at the sudden, violent cold. Her lips emitted tiny burp-scented jets. Broker's own breath made a starched spinnaker in the rising wind.

Hatless, ears turning red, Garrison shook his head. "Somebody should have told Keith the trouble with fucking heroes is they get people killed."

"Watch your language," said Broker. Habit. But he nodded, agreeing with Garrison's assessment. He raised his chin toward the cabin. "If they come back I'll roust them. I'm going to nail the guys who messed up Ida," said Broker, hugging Kit.

"Do that," quipped Garrison. He pointed to the moose in the Cook County insignia on Broker's parka. "You got the badge and you're wearing the outfit. Just walk in there, read them their rights and give them the protection of the legal system?"

"Not what you had in mind."

"We're playing with Konic, we need some life insurance. I was thinking more along the lines of taking hostages."

"Well talk about it. What about this bug? Think we can find it?"

"They can afford the best—and the best is wafer thin, half the size of a playing card, receiver and transmitter. Let the guy who put it in find it."

"If he shows up."

They went inside, Broker peeled Kit out of her layers and opened a can of kids' pasta rings and veggie franks, heated it on the stove. Half of it went on her bib, the other half made it into her mouth. Stranded at the sheriff's office, she'd missed her nap. She was beat. He left Garrison in the kitchen opening a can of Hormel chili.

By candlelight, he dressed her for bed, then filled a tippy cup with milk. Kit stood at the window, staring, perplexed, at the frozen grill of stalactites. The bird feeder where she watched the chickadees was deserted, cased in ice.

"Dees?" she passionately wondered aloud.

He picked her up. "No dees, and Daddy needs a hug. It's tough poop out there, kid." As he rocked Kit, he pictured Ida Rain, turbaned in white, laced with tubes, IVs, hooked to machines. Her suffering was a direct result of talking with him.

He squirmed in the rocker, trying to get comfortable. It was the first time he'd put Kit to sleep wearing a .45 strapped on his hip.

When she was asleep, he came back to the kitchen, tried the phone, heard a dial tone and called Regions Hospital in St. Paul. After a few minutes working through another goddamned automated phone system, he reached a human, a nurse on ICU. He identified himself. The nurse told him that Ida Rain was stable but still comatose. Her pupils were equal. She showed faint responses to sounds and light.

The prognosis was optimistic but guarded.

Broker hung up. Garrison had retreated to the chair by the fireplace, where he meditated under the flickering dragon's head. He turned his knife blade, testing it against his thumb. A damp split of oak hissed in the flames.

He put the knife away, came forward off the chair, stooped and stabbed a hooked iron poker at the burning slabs. Sparks boiled up against the sooty fieldstone. The firelight played in the dents and wrinkles of his face, the kind ones and the sinister ones.

Broker brought two cans of Grain Belt from the fridge, they put on their coats, went out through the studio, down the stairs to the beach and hunkered in the lee of a large boulder. Six-foot waves dotted them with spray. A groan twisted on the wind, then a long splintering crash echoed as another ice-loaded tree toppled in the woods.

Garrison turned his collar up, sipped the can, shook his head. "What kind of people sit out in the winter and drink cold cans of beer?"

"Been doing it all my life." Broker put an unlit cigar stub in his mouth. Chewed.

Garrison asked, "How'd you figure out Keith went on the mother of all undercover operations?"

"Everyone assumed Caren called James. But she was at her doctor's office when the call was made. I checked with Dispatch at the St. Paul cops. Keith was signed out to his home number. He set it all in motion."

"See. Like everything. We never checked. Off chasing the big case."

"What about you?" asked Broker.

Garrison said, "Hell. Go figure. They put a guy who's three months from retirement on a complicated case like this. They told me it was another dirty cop hunt, and they picked me because of my work in New Orleans and Atlanta. Look at me, Broker."

Broker looked.

"Fifteen years ago, I went undercover in Meridian, Mississippi; had me a little store, barbershop in front, used furniture in back. I fit right in with those good old boys in the Klan. I know my way around that scene. But Russians? What do *I* know about the Russian mob?"

"They brought me up north and gave me Alex Gorski to run into St. Paul as a snitch. Right off, he suggests my bad guy is Keith Angland. I didn't know this Gorski, his habits, his weaknesses. I did know he couldn't get anything hard on Angland, just rumors, hearsay—then boom—he disappears, and this tongue is sliding around on the floor. I know a few people at Quantico. I found out that tongue didn't go through normal channels. The lab work-up went straight to the director's office. Same place the money you found went, and the hate mail. We didn't investigate Caren's motives"—he held his bottle up in a salute to Broker—"or James's motives, even after you raised some interesting questions about the missing cash. The case against Keith was designed at the very top to slowly fall apart. Maybe get him a little jail time."

"Then Caren comes in from left field and . . ."

"And gives him the break he really needs." Garrison swatted his hand at the air in disgust. "Don't matter how she did it—don't mean to sound cold—Hell, guess I do—this is a cold business. Don't matter how he did it either, drinking, calling the chief names, abusing his wife—point is, he did it masterfully, and everybody believed him. Konic believed it enough to recruit him."

Broker nodded. "He was trying to get her clear. She didn't run for her therapist or a divorce lawyer, like she was supposed to."

"Doesn't matter. What matters is, before Caren died, Keith was building a legend as a corrupt cop who might kill a snitch—'cause, hell, we can't prove he killed Gorski, and the Russians can't prove he didn't. It's still suspicious, could be a setup. But *everybody* knows he killed Caren, right. Because James, the eyewitness, said so. Suddenly he's got lots of credibility, and it's more believable he killed Gorski too."

"Where's Gorski?" asked Broker.

Garrison shrugged. "Probably going through WITSEC orientation in D.C., with James."

"It all comes down to what happened at the waterfall," said Broker.

Garrison hunkered forward, gestured with his bottle. "Could be Keith overreacted. They fought. Somehow James took one in the leg. She fell in, Keith tried to save her. James freaked. But he knew about the money, so he sees a way to escape from his messy little life. He exaggerates, makes it into a war story. Hell, he probably believes Keith pushed her in."

Broker recalled Keith, his icy rage, strutting in the cell. "Keith . . . improvised. He's taking credit for her death to give himself better cover. Almost like he piled her corpse on a barricade, to hide behind. Which only leaves him with one problem."

"Yeah," said Garrison. "James knows what really happened. James can burn him. Keith reached out to you, didn't he?"

Broker nodded. "He staged the fight in that holding cell, told me James had the money, to find him."

"He's using you. You know that."

Broker thought of gold wedding rings jingling on Keith's purple, swollen fingers. On the same hand with the claw marks, the tattoo. *Help.* That felt more personal than finding money. Something between them. About Caren. He glanced up at the glow of the night-light burning softly in Kit's window. His safe place. It wasn't protecting himself that worried him; it was protecting the space where he stopped and Kit started.

Garrison was saying, "I like to read old Civil War journals, stuff written by the actual soldiers. In one account—I think it's a Union soldier writing about the fighting in the cornfield at Antietam—the word *translated* is used to describe surviving the point-blank fire. Well, Keith has taken up residence in hell, those wounds on his arm are his permanent passport. He's been *translated*. He's different now. This isn't law enforcement, where you catch the bad guy and provide him a lawyer."

Garrison picked up a smooth cobble and threw it at a breaking wave. "Keith's at war, and in a war there are acceptable casualties. Caren was one. Ida Rain might be another. And you could be the next. If you do find James and lead these bastards to him, you won't be coming back. And that pretty little girl sleeping in there is going to be out one daddy. That's why you need some insurance. You roger my last, soldier?"

They finished their beers without talking. Broker listened to the anthem of the surf tossing against the ancient stones. There were no ethics in nature, no impossible missions, no heroes.

Just survival lessons.

It was an old-fashioned patriotic tragedy, playing to an empty auditorium in the land where Jerry Springer rated number one. The players rose above themselves, tried to do the right thing, and walked straight into the propellers of history. Caren, doomed, ironically, by her husband's love, died blind to his real motives. Broker's attempt to fill in at shortstop could still cost Ida Rain her life.

All because Keith had climbed on his Russian cross and decided to go out there and try to save the goddamn world.

They took four-hour shifts, watching the cabin down the beach. The next morning, still no electricity. No black Audi. Routine kicked in. While Garrison slept on the living room couch, Broker put breakfast out for his daughter. Kit called yogurt "aga." Possibly related to her word for spaghetti, which was "spaga." Broker noted the new word in the journal he kept for Nina.

He heard a vehicle up on the road, glimpsed the mail truck through the trees. Early. Catching up after the storm. He carried Kit out to pick up the mail. Maybe there would be a letter from Nina.

When he opened the lid to the rural route box he found no letter from his wife. Just junk mail, a phone bill and a manila envelope.

After reading the neat angular printed name on the return address, his stomach churned, sweat popped on his temples: Ida Rain.

He tore open the seal and pulled out several paper-clipped photo-copied sheets. A note attached on a memo under the logo of the St. Paul paper. FYI was printed across the top. Then Ida's vigorous slanting penmanship:

Broker,

I should have given this to you before, but I was a little embar-rassed by what it reveals. But, what the hell. The notion of Tom's writing being a link to recent events intrigued me, so I dug out an old manuscript he played with last year.

When you read the first few paragraphs it's clear he was projecting a personality along the arc of his fantasies, not to mention fine-tuning his narcissism.

The rude part is that he insisted I call him his protagonist's name in bed. And I confess, I did on occasion. And when I did, it enhanced his performance. Which was never more than B minus, top end.

I called the local FBI media representative and asked if people entering Witness Protection can choose their new names. It's common practice that they do, as long as the name is "secure." I thought you might find this interesting.

Regards, Ida

Broker checked the postmark. Mailed on the day she was attacked. He flipped up the memo and studied the typed pages below.

UNTITLED

by Tom James

There were first-time suckers and forty-year Vegas Strip alumni at the table, the bejeweled wife of a man who owned the casino sat elbow to elbow with a $500-a-night call girl. What they all had in common was fascination for the tall man with the cold blond hair and steady blue eyes as he blew in his fist to warm the dice. More money was riding on this toss than he had earned last year. Oblivious to the envious eyes trained on him, and to the chips heaped before him, utterly without hesitation, Danny Storey threw the bones.

There was more, but Broker went back and reread the first paragraph. He did not read literally, he listened to the language. The cry of it.

Disliking the clarity of his imagination, he pictured Ida Rain locked in a carnal embrace with Tom James.

He squinted at the typed paragraph again.

*Danny Storey.*

Hugging Kit, he said, "I take everything back I ever said about newspaper people."

Running on the ice, taking the steps two at a time, kicking open the door.

"Garrison!"

*  *  *

"Hiya, Madge."

"What's up." She looked up as Broker came into Dispatch. Since the National Guard arrived, the pace had slackened. Madge was alone in the office. Kit had been handed off once more to Sally Jeffords, who said she was going to claim the kid as a dependent.

"Need a favor."

"Shoot."

"Let's run this name—Daniel Storey." He handed her his notebook, with the name scrawled across a whole page. "And all spelling variations they come up with—for a new driver's license . . ."

"In Minnesota I'll need a middle initial and date of birth."

"Skip Minnesota, run it on every other state in the country."

"Alaska and Hawaii?"

"Yep."

"And here I thought your brief return to law enforcement was winding down," said Madge, squinting. She turned to her keyboard and ordered, "Get me a date of birth." Her terminal routed to a state computer in St. Paul that could talk to all the systems in all the states.

"Working on it," he said as he picked up a phone and called the Sawtooth Mountain Clinic. Thinking the feds would alter James's DOB, but maybe not that much. Experience taught him that people falsifying ID changed the year of their birth but frequently hung on to the real day and month.

The phone rang. Calling this number made him think of ear infections. A receptionist answered, he asked her to get Doc Rivard. She said he was in emergency with a patient. Broker left a message for Rivard to call him at the sheriff's office.

"How's it going?" he asked Madge.

"Zip for Alabama."

Broker nodded, looked down a list of emergency numbers on the wall and called Regions Hospital in St. Paul. It took five minutes to get a straight answer out of a nurse on ICU. Ida's signs were improving, but she wasn't "out of the woods" yet.

Another phone rang, Madge took it, spoke, shoved it at Broker. He hung up on St. Paul, took the receiver.

"Broker, Frank Rivard."

"Yeah, Frank, need a favor."

"Uh-huh?"

"Our big scene before Christmas, Tom James. You treated him for a gunshot wound. The Kettle thing. Caren, right. Ah, I need his date of birth."

Patiently, Broker sat still for a lecture on the confidentiality of medical records. "Frank, it's urgent."

"You owe me, I'll get back to you," said the doctor. He hung up.

Broker tapped his pen on his spiral notebook. Looked around. "Where's Jeff?"

"Conducting a sweep with the border patrol. There's a party of winter campers missing out by Saganaga. He and Lyle took gear for three days," said Madge.

"Uh-huh," he said. But he thought, Good. He didn't want Jeff and Garrison locking horns. He pictured Jeff and Lyle snowshoeing up the Gunflint, staring across Lake Saganaga into the Canadian mist.

Madge handled a few storm calls. Used the radio to reach a deputy patrolling the ritzy West End around Lutsen. Then Doc Rivard called back.

Broker wrote down: November 22, 1956. "What do you have for a physical description?" He wrote: five feet ten, 180 lbs., hair, brn, eyes blue. He thanked Rivard, hung up. Turned to Madge. "How's it going?"

She whistled. "I thought we'd need middle initials and DOB, but I'm getting hits without it." Her fingers pounded the keys. "Alaska, Robert Store, that's o-r-e, March 15, 1941."

"Nah," said Broker, "too old." He pushed the DOB note to her.

"Arizona, no record. Arkansas, no data. California, hello: Three hits: Arthur Story—not your spelling, but the second one is right on the money. Daniel Storey."

"Date of birth?"

"Eleven. Twenty-two. Fifty-eight."

"Is there a physical description?" Broker had a pleasant déjà vu sensation from high school hockey, set up at the net and Jeff passing the puck right to him.

"Brown hair, blue eyes, a hundred and seventy-five pounds, five ten."

"Address?"

"One seven three Valentino Lane, Watsonville, California." She gave the license number. "Just issued last week." She looked up. "Happy?"

"Very. Thank you, Madge." Broker wrote the address on a notepad and stuck it in his pocket. Briefly, he slumped in his chair. Shut his eyes. C'mon Ida.

Could be you found Tom James, girl.

He got up, walked to the bookcases, selected a road atlas, thumbed to the map of California, and checked the index. Watsonville was below San Francisco, inland from Monterey Bay, near Santa Cruz . . .

Madge waved, pointed to a glowing light on the phone. "Hit line one," she said.

Broker tapped the extension. "What?"

"We got company," said Garrison.

"I'm on the way," said Broker, having full-blown predatory thoughts and intending to act on them. He hung up, turned to Madge. "Where's the key to the evidence closet?" He pointed to his head. "I got a jacket but no duty hat."

Madge opened a drawer, threw him a key marked with red tape. Broker went down the hall, ducked in Jeff's office, found a used paper coffee cup and plastic spoon in the trash, took them, went back down the hall. He opened the closet, picked among the hangers and shelves, found a winter cap with ear flaps. Then, quickly, he stooped to the footlocker where Jeff kept evidence seized and tagged. He thumbed through plastic bags, found the one he wanted—a piddling amount of cocaine. Eased one end open around the staple, inserted the spoon, scooped a pinch and put it in the cup; folded the cup and stuck it in his pocket.

When he returned the key to Madge, she observed him in his new headgear and pronounced, "You look like Elmer Fudd."

"The girl is with him," said Garrison. He was looking through Broker's spotting scope, which he'd set up on a ledge in the casement windows by the bathroom. Aiming through tangled birches. "Looks like they got stuck on the road, coming in. They're carrying stuff into the cabin. The chick don't seem too happy."

Broker banged cupboard doors, opened drawers, found a box of Ziplocs. Dumped the grocery bag in his hand. Five amber plastic four-ounce bottles rattled on the table. He grinned. "Just cleaned the local Health Food Coop out of inositol."

"What is that stuff?"

"Inositol. B vitamin supplement. Back in the Stone Age, when I was on the job, they used it to cut coke." Another lupine grin. "Right, you never worked narcotics."

"I worked narcotics," defended Garrison.

"Yeah—Jax beer and moonshine." He spun bottle tops, shook white powder into the Ziploc. Weighed it in his hand. "About twenty ounces," he said to Garrison. "If this was coke, what's it worth these days?"

"On the street?"

"No, man, in jail time."

Garrison rubbed his forehead. "Ah, I think seventeen ounces can get you five years mandatory."

"I plant this on him and threaten to take him in. But we really want to talk to his dad." Broker winked. "Maybe Ida Rain found James."

"No."

"Yes. Now I don't intend to leave a mark on this punk; but I definitely am going to fuck him up. You with me?" Broker felt his voice speed up, his whole body lighten. Eager for contact.

Garrison's face, more suited to the lumpy sorrow of his country songs, split into a sly smile. He pulled on his jacket. "We'll kidnap his ass."

"Not exactly, we'll let the girl go, give her a message for Konic."

"The girl could be for banging or she could be heat. Or both. I'm not armed."

Broker stuffed the Ziploc in his parka pocket, went to the closet by the door, pulled out his Remington twelve-gauge, and tossed it to Garrison. He reached to the upper shelf for the shells. Threw them over. Garrison pushed in shells, racked the slide. Broker checked his .45. Put on the Cook County sheriff's department winter cap.

Feeling good. Like a racehorse who'd slipped a plough harness. They got right to it. No stealth, straight ahead. Cut through the woods—CRASH CRASH—stomping holes in the armored snow. The sound of incoming doom.

The waxed Audi was skewed in a dipping turn on the slick road a hundred yards from the cabin. The right tire was buried to the wheel well in snow that looked like crushed glass.

"I don't know where you fuckin' learned to drive." Unpleasant female voice, heavy with accusation. The trees parted. Broker and Garrison could see them, started down.

"Cool it, my cell phone's in the cabin, we'll call a tow truck," said David Konic. He wore dark slacks, a full-length black leather coat and sunglasses. He was lifting a bag of groceries from the trunk of the car.

"Great, first the lights go out, now this," said Denise, exasperated. They could see her now, blonde hair, white headband, trim in a navy blue nylon wind suit and ankle boots. Hands on hips, in back of David. She spotted them the moment they saw her. "Ah, David . . ."

"Oh, hi," said David, removing his glasses and putting the winning boyish smile on his face.

"Hi yourself," said Broker. Coming down a slight rise, Garrison moved off, balancing the Remington casually on his shoulder.

Denise, not David, reacted instinctively to the shotgun. "So what the fuck is this, hunting?" she asked, eyeing Broker's official parka askance as she moved a step back, hands loose at her side, and Broker thought Garrison might have called it. She was the dangerous one. He veered toward her. Reflex and experience took over.

"So, you're a cop, huh?" said David, amiable, still smiling. "Think you could get us a little assistance. We're stuck."

"Shut up, David, get down," ordered Denise. Cut-mouth tense. Right hand starting to swing back. Making her move.

"Think fast," yelled Garrison, bringing the Remington around.

Broker rushed her, building momentum on one running step and planting the toe of his left boot in a short vicious kick into her right shin. She grunted in pain, went off balance as the black automatic pistol came up from the waistband in the center of her back. Broker stepped in, grabbed the pistol and twisted it from her hand as he body-checked her. She made a hollow thunk against the side of the car. Limbs spraddled, she rag-dolled to the frozen ground.

"Nobody fuckin' move," yelled Garrison, covering David with the shotgun.

David froze, hugging his bag of groceries. He didn't look afraid, merely inconvenienced.

Broker stuffed Denise's Walther P5 in his pocket. Then he advanced on David, grabbed him by the shoulder, roughly spun him around and threw him against the car. The grocery bag fell and burst. Oranges tumbled, Van Gogh bright, on the mean ice. Broker removed the Ziploc from his pocket and let it fall among the orange parade.

He growled at David. "You broke into my house, you little shit. What were you doing in my . . ." Then Broker stopped in feigned surprise. "Hello? You dropped something."

David glanced down. Shook his head. "Is that lame. That's pure bush. God."

Garrison hauled Denise by her jacket collar over next to David and let her fall. She moaned, rolled over and struggled to sit up.

"Denise, look at this, Andy of Mayberry is trying to set me up," said David.

"Motherfuckers," hissed Denise, enunciating every syllable.

Broker placed his boot heel on her shoulder and propelled her back against the car. "Watch your fucking language," he admonished and almost laughed, getting his worlds mixed up.

Garrison picked up the Ziploc of powder. "Ah, David, do not pass go, do not collect two hundred dollars, go directly to jail. You heard of federal sentencing guidelines?"

"C'mon, David," said Broker, "we got work to do." He pulled him to the front of the car. "Hands on the hood." David leaned forward and spread his legs, assuming he was going to be frisked. "No, no," said Broker. "You're going to push." He turned to Denise, whom Garrison was helping to her feet. "Denise, honey, you through trying to kill people? You think you can drive?"

Regarding him with viperish brown eyes, she stated, "I got the right to defend myself, and him, like I get paid to do. And I have a license to carry. And you're not a straight cop, that's what I think."

"Of course he isn't a straight cop," said David, still smiling. "I don't know about the other one."

"I'm a member of AARP," said Garrison.

"Here's the deal," Broker said to David. "It happens I am a temporary deputy in this county, so I can run you in on the dope, which I'll say I found in the course of investigating the house invasion you pulled on me. You with me so far."

"But you don't really want to do that, do you?" said David, still smiling.

"What's going on, David?" asked Denise.

"He wants to talk to Victor," said David. "We're cool. I told you about this guy. It's business."

"Smart kid," said Broker. "C'mon, let's push this car out of the ditch. Lorn, there should be a shovel around the cabin." Broker removed the floor mats from the Audi while Garrison went to the cabin, poked around outside, went in, and emerged with a snow shovel.

After digging out, Broker stuffed the floor mats under the bogged tire. Denise got in, started the Audi. Broker, David, and Garrison pushed. The tire bit into the mats, spit them away but picked up the traction to climb back on the road.

"Now what?" asked Denise.

"Take off. Tell your employer to call me. I'm in the book. And no rough stuff, or David here will be decorating the bottom of Lake Superior."

She looked at David. Totally self-assured, he nodded. "Okay," she said. Then to Broker, "You have some of my property."

"Sorry, I'll hang on to the Walther."

Lurching, brake lights jarring, she backed up the driveway, turned on the access road, and accelerated toward Highway 61. Broker turned to David, who was still smiling, up from North Lake Shore Drive to slum among the jack pine savages. "You're pretty sure of yourself, huh?"

David shrugged, continued smiling. They walked him back to Broker's house.

71

The lights were still out in Broker's house, but the propane furnace kept the grayness a comfortable sixty-eight degrees. They stripped off David's coat and sat him down on a kitchen chair. Garrison placed the electrician's briefcase in front of him, opened it, showed him the pictures, the videotapes.

David yawned.

Broker and Garrison signed with their eyes. Garrison stepped back. Broker took a deep breath, composed himself, gave Daddy the afternoon off, popped the lid on a crypt in one of his compartments, and invited his old self out to play.

He held up the picture of David and Denise breaking into Ida's. "The woman who lives there? Did your people work her over? She's in intensive care. She might not make it?"

"I wouldn't know," said David.

Broker tapped the briefcase. "Did you bug her place?"

David held up his hands, wondering. "Not a clue."

"Did you sneak in here the night of the storm, put a bug in *my* house?"

David smiled and ran his hand through his thick blond hair. He cocked his head. "Do you know who my dad is?" he asked sincerely.

Garrison removed a wooden box from under his coat and placed it on the table. A scrolled crest graced the cover. Cigars. David came forward, protesting, "Hey, those are mine." He reached. Garrison smacked his hand with the butt of the Remington. David winced, withdrew his hand.

Broker opened the top and perused the ornate logo on the inside of the cigar box. *Fabrica de Tabacos de H. Upmann* and *Habana*. And if that wasn't enough, in smaller letter, in English: *Made in Havana-Cuba*.

"We owe it to ourselves," said Garrison.

They both grabbed a Corona. Broker bit off the cap on his. David watched in horror, as if Broker had just chewed the head off a kitten.

"My dad gave me those," he asserted. The slight tremble in his voice encouraged Broker. Garrison struck one of his blue tip matches; they lit up and blew a thick cloud of smoke into David's face.

The Havana seed shagged Broker's palate like the burning manifests of Spanish galleons. He stepped back to let a million taste buds die happy deaths. Assessed David. "You aren't going to tell us who beat up Ida Rain, are you?"

"Who's Ida Rain?"

"He's not going to tell us," said Broker.

"What are you going to do, beat *me* up?" David smirked, shook his head. "Look, guys. I grew up here. But my dad—he grew up over there." David curled his Adonis eyebrows: "He killed a whole province in Afghanistan once."

A little dizzy from the Havana, Broker turned, opened a drawer, pulled out a roll of duct tape and threw it to Garrison. "Wrap him tight to the chair."

"Hey, wait a minute." David started to get up. A sharp ripping sound. A loop of tape lassoed his neck. Garrison yanked him down, whipped the tape around his arms, feet, and thighs. Pinned him to the chair.

As Garrison trussed David, Broker took the Ziploc from his pocket and plopped it on the table. "Hey, David, let's get high."

"Sorry, don't use it." Hand it to the kid, he had some nuts. So far.

Broker opened the Ziploc, wet two fingers, dipped and rubbed the white powder on his gums. Touched his tongue. After the Havana, the vitamin was sacrilege. Smiled. "Mount Everest, you sure?"

"Positive," said David.

Broker turned his back, fiddled with the Ziploc to disguise removing the folded paper cup from his pocket. Carefully, he swabbed up two fingers with the real. Slipped the crushed cup back in his parka pocket and faced David. "Hold his head." Garrison locked David's head in place. Broker gently dabbed the powder into David's nostrils. David fought against Garrison's restraining grip, blinked, sniffed. His eyes watered slightly as the tiny ice picks of cocaine stabbed his sinuses.

Garrison released his hold. Broker mussed David's hair. "God, he's so pretty. He looks like that kid in *Titanic,* don't he?"

"Yeah," said Garrison. "What happened to that kid?"

Broker smiled. "You know, he drowned like a fuckin' rat."

David squirmed slightly, but maintained his haughty sangfroid. His father's son, braced for a beating. Broker opened a cabinet, withdrew a glass quart-size orange juice canister, selected a tin one-cup measure from the rack over the stove and began to shovel white powder into the juice container. When he'd put in three cups, he held it up, squinted, juggled it around. Then he opened a plastic bottle of spring water, filled the container, screwed the top back on and handed it to Garrison. "Here, shake that up, would you?"

While Garrison shook, Broker took a wet dishcloth from the sink and filled a glass with water. He placed the cloth and the glass on the table. A touch of color crept into David's cheeks. Controlled fear. Curiosity.

Broker returned to the counter, hunted in another drawer and found a large plastic funnel. He placed the utensil alongside the other items on the table. Kitchen trip.

His Havana had gone out. He chewed it, hands on his hips. "I've never been to Afghanistan. But I can show you a trick I learned in Vietnam."

He came around to David's side, turned him and tipped the chair back until David was at a forty-five-degree angle against the table.

"For some reason, this works better when you're tilted back," said Broker. "Maybe it adds to the disorientation." He slapped the damp dishcloth over David's nose and mouth. After a moment, David started to squirm. His blue eyes swelled. Broker sympathized, "Little trouble breathing, huh? The idea is to give you just barely enough air to stay conscious. It really messes with your mind."

David coughed and sputtered, tried to thrash his head, but Garrison's viselike hands returned and held him immobile.

"Now," said Broker, "we can sit here while I add water, drop by drop; but you have to come from a culture with four thousand years of history to develop the patience for that. This is the 1990s, so we're going to speed things up."

He removed the cloth. David gasped, coughed, sputtered, "You . . . guys are . . . crazy."

"Absolutely," said Broker. "Lorn, is the cocktail ready for David here?"

"Right you are," said Garrison, picking the juice canister off the table and handing it to Broker.

"Um good, nice and thick." Broker nodded. "Hold David there, will you." Garrison wedged the chair against his hips, grabbed David's head in both hands. Broker picked up the funnel. David, eyes swelling in recognition, clamped his mouth shut. Broker pinched David's nose until he had to open his mouth to breathe. "Thank you," he said, jamming the funnel between his perfect teeth and deep down his throat. David writhed, gagging against his bounds as Broker explained, "You ever hear about the body packers, David? The dummies who swallow balloons full of cocaine and carry it through customs in their intestines. Sometimes those balloons break . . ."

"Oww," Garrison grimaced.

"Yeah," said Broker, rolling the Havana in his lips. "Massive over-stimulation—the big *O*, I mean"—Broker snapped his fingers—"that fast. Seizure. Your ticker maxes out. You, ah, ready to blast off, you snotty little punk."

Broker picked up the canister and splashed white malt into the funnel. David, eyes bulging, neck veins pumped up red, put out a pint of sweat and trembled with a mighty effort to wheeze it back out. The funnel bubbled. His eyes signaled frantically, going from side to side. Broker withdrew the funnel. "Yes?"

David spit the residue from his mouth. Gagged, trying to make himself vomit. Broker cupped his hand over David's mouth. "Now, you going to answer some questions?"

David nodded furiously, smothering. Broker lifted his hand. "Didn't bug the woman on Sergeant . . . just checked for mail, address books, diaries . . . Dad figured this James dude is too smart to use the phone."

Broker let some of the liquid spill on David's cheek. He cringed away. "What about beating her?" asked Broker.

"Not us, not us," David gasped. "Honest."

"Okay, so where's the bug in here?"

"I feel sick," wailed David.

"You didn't get that much. But your pupils are starting to dilate." He turned to Garrison. "Maybe we could get him to the Clinic, have his stomach pumped. Whatta you think?"

Garrison nodded. "Sure, we could do that. Where's the bug? How come I didn't find a tape recorder in your cabin?"

"Nauseous, really . . . Okay, not a mike: a wireless discreet camera . . . fish-eye lens. Transmits over normal radio waves." His head jerked toward the living room. "Behind the dragon's eye, aimed at the telephone in the kitchen . . . set to a TV channel nobody uses up here. We picked it up on the set next door. Taped it."

Garrison crossed the room in long strides, climbed on his whittling chair in front of the hearth and pulled a black object from behind the sculpture. The camera sprouted a small antenna and was the size of a cigarette pack

Broker glanced at his dragon, furious. "You were watching me on TV?" He raised the juice canister. "Die, you Communist."

"I'm not a Communist, I voted for Dole!" David protested, convulsing, huge tears spilling from his eyes. "My dad was a Communist, but only because he had to."

Broker timed David's sobs, inserted the funnel, bore down, and poured half of the white liquid down his throat. They watched him try to hold his breath, to fight it. Broker tickled his throat. Finally, choking, he swallowed.

They sat the chair up and turned it around facing the table. He was hyperventilating, eyes swollen; strangled puking sounds hiccuped deep in his throat.

Then Broker raised the container and drank some of the mixture. When he finished, he smacked his lips so he left a white mustache on his upper lip. David watched, gasping. Broker reached in the cupboard, removed one of the supplement containers, sifted some residue through his fingers for David's edification. Then he held it in front of David's bulging eyes until he quieted enough to read the ingredients.

Broker smiled and patted David on the head. He was almost certain now that David's crew had not jumped Ida. Garrison took David to the bathroom to clean up. Broker called Halme's North Shore Travel Agency in town; Gretchen, wife to Dale Halme, the county deputy, answered.

"Hi, Gretchen, Phil Broker. What's the quickest way to get to Santa Cruz, California?"

He waited while the tap of computer keys plotted a solution. Gretchen said, "There's an eleven A.M. flight to San Jose tomorrow—but I've had those get canceled if they're not return booked on the other end. Safer bet is a Northwest daily flight to San Francisco. Leaves four-fifteen our time, gets into San Francisco six-forty-five Pacific time."

From looking at the Atlas, he figured a two-hour cab ride from San Francisco to Watsonville.

"Get me a seat on the flight to San Francisco tomorrow," said Broker. He finished up with Gretchen, gave his VISA numbers and expiration, thanked her and hung up.

He had a strong notion who'd hit Ida. Also, who might have been in his house. And what Keith meant. The signal of the rings.

"Papka—they're not cops. They're crazy, no, I mean, they're *psycho*." David, somewhat recovered, sat unbound in the chair and clutched the phone with both hands. His knuckles were white pennies under the skin and the air was thick with Garrison's cigar smoke. David handed the phone to Broker.

"Hi, how you doing," said Broker.

"If you've harmed my son . . ." The controlled urbane voice conveyed great resources of retribution. A slight rumble of accent had been filtered through layers of education.

"You mean this weasel who's been spying on me? It's not what we did, Mr. Konic, we just spooked him. He's a little pussy, is all. It's what we'll do." Broker frolicked briefly in the undercover biker persona he'd used ten years ago. He felt loose, ready. He used to excel at this kind of thing. Fast, developing, dangerous.

"So," said Victor Konic.

"So, you stuck your nose in my business in a rude way," said Broker. His voice changed, less confrontational, more businesslike. "If you want something. Ask."

Konic answered directly in the same tone of voice, "Did you find James?"

"Yes."

"What do you want?"

"You know, I need to question him about Caren Angland's death," said Broker.

"Right," said Konic, settling in, enjoying the negotiation.

"Okay," said Broker, "we want the two million dollars we suspect he took, but you won't let us have that, will you?"

"No. The money must be returned to its rightful owner. It's a matter of . . . business. And reputations."

"I have a reputation too. Half," said Broker. Across the table, Garrison curled his forefinger into his thumb in an "okay" gesture.

"We know about your reputation, and it's only worth twenty percent and you get to live," said Konic.

"Forty and David gets to live."

"Thirty," said Konic indifferently. "Take it or leave it. I have other sons."

"Thirty," Broker said to Garrison. Garrison shrugged and tugged the brim of his brown hat down over one eye, drew on his Havana.

Back to Konic: "I want to talk to him alone. I'm serious about taking his statement."

"What a hypocrite. But agreed. Provided you are not recording."

"I need an excuse for going out there."

"And where is that?"

"You know what I look like?"

"We had pictures made."

"I'm arriving in San Francisco tomorrow at six-forty-five their time. There should be regular flights to San Francisco where you are. I'm flying Northwest flight one-eight-nine from Minneapolis. We had pictures made too. I want to see you personally. But not before I talk to James. Understood."

"Agreed."

"When I get back, we let David go."

"Fine. What about the money."

"We don't know where the money is, that could get complicated. We'll have to convince James to tell us."

"Fine. Give me the flight again," said Konic.

"Flight one-eight-nine. Call their automated flight information and check the gate. I'll be wearing Levi's, a Levi's jacket"—Broker paused, reached across the table and plucked the brown Mickey Spillane hat off of Garrison's head and put it on his own. It fit just fine—"and a brown felt hat, narrow brim, you know, the kind the FBI wore in the 1950s, chasing Commie spies. You think you can spot that one?"

"Are you trying to be funny?"

"I'll tell you what's funny. We have some waterfalls up here. People go in, they're never seen again. My partner'll put your kid in the Devil's Kettle if you cross me, Konic."

"Take it easy, we checked you out. We know you. A deal's a deal."

Broker glanced away from the table, across the living room at the twisted tenth-century dragon. *Hello, Keith. Shake hands with darkness.*

They had a deal. The unspoken part of the deal was that James was going to die.

Broker had not shared the story of the rings with Garrison. But Garrison had called it. Women have bad luck around Tom James.

Tom James wasn't going to die because Konic's people wanted revenge on a rat. Or because he could endanger a deep FBI undercover operation by telling the truth about Caren Angland's death.

*You know who did it, but you can't prove it.*

Keith had missed. Broker wouldn't.

He drove to Duluth to catch the shuttle to Minneapolis and his connection to San Francisco.

The trip carried him back into that zone he'd tried to escape, where ordinary life became so many silly commercials you passed though on your way down to the basement to bang on the backed-up human plumbing. The public wanted Asshole Control. Keep the shit moving in an orderly manner through the pipes. Out of sight, so they could pretend life was like *Prairie Home Companion*. Like public TV.

So here he was again. Learning more than he'd ever wanted to know. And not the kind of knowledge that necessarily makes you wise. More like vampire droppings you cleaned off your shoes after working sundown to dawn, marching up dim stairways into the mystery of other people's lives.

Eventually you found it all out. Who the mayor was sleeping with. The governor. Even the archbishop. You kept a list of the guilty ones you couldn't quite catch. You kept your weapon clean and your traps baited.

The strain got to her, Keith had said. Back at the beginning. Same thing he'd said fourteen years ago. The strain got to her then, too—except that time, Broker was the one working undercover.

Broker preferred a window seat, to watch the plains coil up into the Rockies. But he had the aisle. Two teens with California tans sat between him and the window. They wore T-shirts with splashy logos that advertised an amateur bowling tournament in Bloomington, Minnesota.

They both had cassette player plugs screwed into their ears. They both played the same handheld video golf game. They were ignorant of, or bored with, the Rocky Mountains.

He landed in San Francisco on time, carrying nothing but a light overnight bag with a change of underwear and toilet articles. An intense muscular young man shadowed his arrival. He had curly dark hair, a gold chain around his neck, wore a green running suit, Nikes and did not hide the blue star tattoo on his left hand. He had touched Rasputin eyes. A poet-priest who kills people.

Without acknowledging each other, they walked slowly through the terminal. Broker sensed there were others. He yanked on the brim of his brown hat and followed along to the cab stand.

Rasputin walked to a waiting cab, spoke briefly to the driver and then got in the second cab in line. When he was sure everybody was on the same page, Broker climbed in the first cab and gave the address in Watsonville.

The cabby smelled of patchouli, an unsuspecting ponytailed escapee from a time capsule. He was pleased with the long fare and chatted amiably about the weather. Rain, seventeen out of the last twenty-one days. "El Meno" he called it, played hell with his landscaping business.

Broker fingered one of David Konic's Havanas. Carefully, he clipped the cap with his cheap guillotine cutter, stuck it in his mouth and lit up.

He rolled down the window and inhaled the mildewed, gasoline-scented freeway air. Pink clouds sweated over the coastal range, gamey as mold on a spoiled peach.

The house smelled like a runaway wood-burning set.

Danny was drenched in sweat and clinging sawdust. His hands took the shock off the handle of the heavy floor sander and distributed the violent vibration up his arms into his chest and back. Grit filtered through his face mask and ground between his teeth. Bulbous ear protectors muted the grinding racket.

He was nothing but happy.

The money had arrived the day after he did. Two packages. Just sign here. For the interim, he'd removed a ceiling panel and tucked it into the narrow space between the rafters above the closet in the back storage bedroom.

He'd returned without a hitch and never looked back. Three days now and not even a call from Joe Travis. He expected a call. That Web site nonsense might filter up the chain of command, and they'd have to decide. Danny's position was that his appearance had altered so much that the threat of identification was minimal.

The computer was packed away, under plastic sheeting in the back room to protect it from the dust. Not looking back meant not even checking the St. Paul paper Web site for news of Ida Rain's death. His scary retreat from Broker's house had chastened him. He wanted nothing to do with the "danger zone." No communication. Telephone, computer. Nothing. Like Tom James, Minnesota had ceased to exist.

Keep it low profile. Day trips to Tahoe and Reno. Take the first one in about two weeks. And something else. This small born-again desire to find his way back to writing had come forward. Danny smiled fondly. But right now he had work to do.

He tipped the sander and hauled it back to start another course of floorboards, paused to adjust the heavy cord over his shoulder, glanced at the TV going in the corner. Under a thick film of sawdust, CNN was "investigating the president." New scandal, breaking news. Danny had been following it since this morning. Couldn't hear with the sander going, but he loved the action. Old Bernie Shaw and Judy Woodruff with fever charts tracking the polls behind them. Wolf Blitzer out in front of the White House. Sniffing the presidential crotch.

It was high fun. To see the slavering reporters from the outside, as it were. As a just plain Joe.

Danny switched off the sander, untied the floppy white dust bag from the exhaust tube and walked through the dismantled kitchen, out the garage, and dumped the contents in his garbage can. Clouds hugged the Santa Cruz hills, the air was dank bubble bath. A moist tickle of drizzle streaked his dirty arms.

Turning back to the house, he saw Terra, Ruby's partner, drive past in a vintage Volkswagen minivan. Danny had to start the process of making amends. So he waved. Friendly. Terra had black, stringy romp-hair and this amazing flat face, like she'd grown up wearing a jar on her head. Wonder what *her* story was. Probably a six-inch pro-lapsed clitoris.

He laughed aloud at his own joke, went back in and opened a Coors. As he stooped to the sander he listened to the press feed on gossip.

His hands set to the work of loosening the steel drum with a T-wrench. He removed the worn sheet of sandpaper, bent a fresh sheet to the drum jaws. He was on the medium coarse. By this time tomorrow he'd be finished with the fine. Be ready to start on the sealer. That stuff put out a stink. And PCBs. Hydrocarbons killed brain cells. Spend the night in a motel. Charge it to Travis's VISA. Business expense.

He grimaced, glanced at the cloudy twilight through the screened porch. One day of sunshine would be nice. To help it dry. Air the place out.

As he fitted the new sheet of paper to the drum, he was struck by the clean power of his hands. Physical labor was toning him up. He studied the network of prominent veins, the subtle play of tendon and muscle. Ennobled, almost, by the fine wood dust and sweat. By honest work.

Saw his hands clamped on Ida Rain's face. Shook his head. Every time the memory leaped up, he revised it, stripping the thrill away. Cleaned it up. Like the sander stripped off the old paint and carpet glue on the floor. There had been no perverse joy, no sexual quickening. If anything he had experienced a melancholy dredging feeling. Hard goddamn work. Necessity.

"I take no pleasure in this," he mused aloud.

On the television someone said, "Twenty-four hours into the White House scandal and the president's approval rating has only dipped two points . . ."

Danny pulled the mask up around his nose and mouth, adjusted the ear protectors, and flipped on the machine. The torque curled sinuously up the handles and corded his arms. Hooked deep into his chest. Had to be good for the abdominals—

The sander shut off. Danny jerked, shucked the ear protectors. Heard a weary voice say, "Hi, asshole."

Not from the TV. Behind him. Danny turned and saw—impossibly—
Phil Broker standing with the power cord plug in his hand. Standing
in a relaxed stance and wearing jeans, tennis shoes, and a Levi's
jacket. The brown hat with the brim pulled down over one eye gave
him an Indiana Jones swashbuckling quality and emphasized his
black eyebrows and his shadowed, tired eyes.

Numb, not tracking, Danny blurted, "How the hell?"

Broker feigned surprise. "You remember me?"

"How—" Danny stopped.

Broker smiled. "It's not important how I found you."

Danny's mind reeled with the power of secrets. Dumb North
Woods hick. *I was just a few feet from blowing your brains out.* Three days
ago. Now—like an Atlas rocket blasting off in his living room!

*What* was he doing here?

Danny's eyes darted. There was a problem with the color on the
TV screen. Bernie Shaw's face bloomed in livid fuchsia. He cleared his
throat, tried to stabilize his voice and said, "Talking to somebody
from the 'danger zone' puts me in violation. I have to call Joe Travis,
he's my inspector. You can deal with him."

He peeled off the mask and started for the phone. Broker blocked
him. "Sorry."

"Hey, what is this?"

"You tell me?" said Broker. He pulled a folded sheet of paper from
his hip pocket and handed it to Danny. It was shopworn, creased, the
futile subpoena Jeff had issued back at the start, for Tom James to
appear before a Cook County grand jury.

Danny handed the paper back. "There is no Tom James."

Broker nodded. "Right. Fuck a piece of paper." He tore the paper up and tossed it aside.

Okay, thought Danny. Deep breaths. Be cool. You know he's on to the money. The E-mail between Ida and Bruce discussed it. Ida discussed it. He had a theory. But no case, otherwise he would have shown up with local cops. These were all things Danny wasn't supposed to know. What the hell was he doing here? What if he knew about Ida? He had to know . . .

"What are you doing here?" Danny demanded.

"Somebody I used to work for sent me," said Broker.

"Who?"

"Keith Angland."

This time, Danny bolted for the door. Broker cut him off with an easy step and gave him a deft, deceptively violent shove with both hands. Broker hardly moved. Danny bounced off the wall, hard, and wound up in the corner. Trapped.

"You're holding me against my will. That's against the law," he protested.

Broker said, "This all began with a call, a tip. Who called you at the newspaper?"

Danny fidgeted. "The FBI checked the phone records. The call came from Caren Angland. She had some kind of gizmo that disguised her voice."

"Half right, the call came from Caren Angland's house. But at the exact time the call was placed, she was in her psychiatrist's office on Summit Avenue in St. Paul."

"What the hell?" Danny's curiosity briefly overcame fear.

"Keith made that call. He figured you'd be useful, you'd already met Caren, so you could do the story about how he'd come apart, beat her up. Like when he bad-mouthed the chief. It's called building a legend. He'd been meticulously putting it together ever since he attended the FBI Academy. There wasn't supposed to be a videotape."

"What are you talking about."

"The Suitcase," said Broker.

"I don't know anything about any suitcase. I want to call Joe Travis, he's my inspector," Danny insisted in a queasy voice. He blinked rapidly, each blink making his head jerk. Broker's every word—blink, jerk.

"You were being used, dummy. In a deep solo undercover operation to penetrate the Russian Mafia. You still are."

Danny stared, not getting any of this. Slowly, he got to his feet.

Broker went on. "They left Lorn Garrison out of the loop. To give it a real feel down at the grass roots. Keith made two mistakes. He tried to push Caren out of his life. And he underestimated you."

"You're crazy," said Danny, back against the corner, going from foot to foot like he had to pee real bad.

"What happened at the Kettle?" asked Broker patiently.

Danny suddenly realized he was in the stronger position. All Broker had, behind his bluff, was questions. Danny raised his right hand to his mouth, twisted his thumb and forefinger as if locking a key in his lips, and then he threw the imaginary key away. Kid's game. *I got a secret.*

Broker shook his head. "You dumb shit. The way it is now, not even the truth can save you. They're not going to believe anything you say. Keith's not going to let you get away with it. You see, you're still useful. Because you took their money. So tell me, what happened?" Broker stepped closer. Danny shied away from the steady North Woods eyes. "Was it like what happened to Ida Rain? Somebody you had to shut up?" asked Broker.

"Ida?" Danny whispered. *Broker knew.* For some reason, he relived kicking the cat to death. But it was his dreams.

"She isn't dead, Tom." Broker smiled that weary smile again. "Unlike you, she's going to survive."

Car doors, opening and shutting outside. Danny, vacant in the eyes, dry-mouthed, tried to rally. Hard to see. His vision popped. Flashbulbs going off in his head. "That's Joe, try this crazy rap out on him," he prayed.

"Don't think so," said Broker. "They followed me to the airport in Minneapolis. And they were waiting for my flight when it landed in San Francisco. They followed my cab here."

"Who?"

"Pros. With enough resources to put someone on the ground in San Francisco to meet my plane on a few hours' notice. Could be the FBI. They know I'm looking for you," said Broker.

They heard rubber soles scurry across the deck in back, coming in through the front door.

Broker watched James smile his deluded smile and fantasize rescue. Watched the shudder of relief go through him when the two men rushed in from the porch. They wore running suits and sneakers. One of them had short cropped hair and a military stoicism to his sunken cheeks. The other was Rasputin.

They carried pistols. Slender automatics with silencers.

Which James may or may not have known would be very unusual sidearms for FBI agents to carry. But that was academic, because James challenged them: "FBI?"

The gunmen shrugged at each other. With the droll expression of a homicidal clown, Rasputin slapped James in the face, unleashed a tirade: "*Slyshay vasya, ya pyshy tebya, govnyuk. Na korm moyem sobakam!*"

"What? Huh?" James blinked, confused, too off balance to track small crucial details, like the blue tattoos they had on the tops of their hands. Rasputin's five-pointed star. The thin military-looking one wore a snake.

The Snake placed the silencer tube of his pistol firmly against Broker's forehead and forced him two steps backward. "Stop," said a voice behind him. The same precise English he'd heard on the phone yesterday. "Put your hands behind you, Broker."

Broker did. Carefully, pinned in place by the pistol barrel. A tearing sound. Then his wrists were efficiently wrapped with duct tape. Once his hands were bound, the Snake lowered his weapon and frisked him. Found a billfold, badge, picture ID.

"Turn around," said Konic.

Broker turned and saw a lean man with short iron gray hair and a fading golf tan. Everything about him was quiet, expensively understated; his build, the statement of his casual clothes—rain jacket, sports shirt, khakis, loafers. The Snake handed Konic Broker's ID. Konic inspected the items like a meticulous clerk who adds and subtracts lives.

"Broker, are these guys FBI?" Surging fear distorted James's voice.

Konic uttered a remark in Russian. The Snake heaved a phlegmy laugh and cracked James across the teeth with his pistol barrel. James sagged to his knees.

It was not pretty. War never is. James looked like a broken piece of meat forked into the tiger house. But Broker felt remarkably calm. All his life he'd listened to his body, and now, his body told him he was not in danger. His experience told him he was in the company of professionals.

Konic gave directions in Russian. The gunmen tripped the now hysterical James and shoved him down onto his freshly sanded floor. Beige sawdust blotted his dirty cheek, his sweaty T-shirt.

Konic took Broker by the arm and led him to the kitchen table. He motioned for Broker to sit. Then he said, "How's David?"

"David is fine."

"You know each other?" James screamed.

Konic said, "Excuse me." He walked to James and said, "Mr. James, Keith Angland sends his regards. He apologizes for being such a bad shot."

"Hey. Just a minute," protested James. "You have this all wrong. Broker, tell them. Angland's a cop. He set this all up, but his wife meddled and it got all twisted."

Konic smiled. "Some cop. He kills his own wife to protect his comrades."

"No. No." James tried to struggle to his feet. "*He* didn't kill her. Don't you get it? *I* did it. I did it. For the money and I knew he was after her. See. It was perfect. So I pushed her and he saw me. Hey. Listen . . ."

Konic smiled. "Of course, you'd say anything right now. But a better choice would be the Our Father."

Broker shut his eyes. So he'd been right, but he took no pleasure in it—not now, being a witness at this ironic execution that was indirectly sanctioned by the U.S. Justice Department.

"Where's the money, Mr. James?" asked Konic.

James whined. "It's mine."

"Where?" Konic could load a single syllable full of menace.

The gunmen positioned James on his knees. A European legacy of feudalism, Broker supposed. The victim must be seen as subject to authority. Even complicit in his destruction.

Broker resented and admired Keith Angland. A problem he'd always had with powerful men on missions, who crafted their plans out of human flesh.

Konic snapped orders. The gunmen tore off James's tennis shoes and yanked off his dirty jeans. They manhandled him into the corner. He pressed his back into the crack of the wall, squirmed. His jockey shorts were damp with sawdust, gray sweat. His white legs trembled. His eyes sought Broker's, pleading.

Konic speculated in a patient didactic voice. "I used to be an advocate of sleep deprivation. Drugs are useful. But in Afghanistan, the mujahideen pried our tanks open with their rifle barrels and killed us with rocks. I learned that techniques are secondary, if the will is present. So. We use what is at hand."

Curtly, he spoke to his helpers. They immediately went to the belt sander and began to loosen the drum.

James pleaded with Broker. He was sitting in a puddle of urine now. "Do something. You're a police officer."

Footnotes, thought Broker. *History.*

James started to scream. The Snake immediately began to kick him into the corner, raging, vicious.

Konic walked to the TV and turned the volume up to the maximum to drown James's screams. Irritably, he hectored Rasputin, who struggled with the unfamiliar machine, folding a sheet of the heavy coarse sandpaper into the drum. *"Oy Blyad!"* Rasputin swore. Sucked a knuckle. Skinned himself on the sandpaper.

They hunkered down side by side. James screamed, drowning out Bernie Shaw's TV voice. Rasputin's and the Snake's practical conversation as they tried to master the unfamiliar mechanism. Drum sanders were tricky, keeping the tension on the sheet of sandpaper while you tightened the drum.

Finally, they had it crimped in place. Rasputin, his eyes merry with experiment, rolled the heavy sander toward James. Blubbering, James drew his knees up and wrapped his arms around them.

Then Rasputin made the mistake of hitting the switch before he had a firm grip on the sturdy cross-T handle. The slack dust catcher on the exhaust inflated with the shock of an air bag. The machine roared and charged. It was an old model Clark, with an eight-inch drum and as thick as a squat fender off a stainless steel tank. They'd put the coarsest paper on. Looked to Broker like number sixteen—black rock grits.

The runaway sander hit James's right ankle and ran over his foot cranking around five thousand revolutions per minute. His scream was lost in the snarl of the drum. A fine spray of blood, shredded skin and tissue spattered the wall. His foot shook violently.

James catapulted beyond fear, swallowed his screams, racked by sick-dog shivers.

Delighted at this serendipity, the two thugs got the sander under control and turned it off. Ignoring James's screams, they commenced a spirited discussion in their native language on the merits of the tool, pausing to point to various portions of James's twitching body.

Konic intervened, dropped to one knee and spoke to James in low tones. James jerked his head, shouted, "Closet, in the ceiling, bedroom."

The two gunmen pulled him to his feet and hobbled him down the hall. A squashed-bug smear of blood soiled his sanded floor.

While they were gone Konic noticed the two cigars in Broker's Levi's jacket pocket. Pulled one out, read the label, tucked it back.

"They're your son's. I took the liberty," said Broker.

"Cuba," said Konic fondly. "Good women; unforgettable cigars."

They brought James back, far gone in shock. They carried two cardboard boxes, and when one of them tipped slightly, Broker saw it was full of banded currency. He didn't know how James got it back. Didn't matter.

Konic pointed to the boxes. "What's your idea? You can't carry it. We'll tie you up and dump you on the beach."

"Alive," specified Broker.

"Of course." Konic smiled. "How about the beach at Haiphong Harbor? I have some old friends in the Hanoi Politburo who would love to find you in that fix."

"Let's save that for another time." Broker removed a slip of paper from his pocket. "Deposit it in this account; you know how, without attracting attention."

Konic viewed the numbers written under the name of the Hong Kong bank. "No problem. They won't be fussy. *'Pecunium non olent,'*" he said, smiling thinly.

Broker nodded. Latin—basically: "Money doesn't stink." Swiss banks chiseled the motto over their doors.

Konic put the note in his pocket, moved to the corner, stooped and squeezed James's bloodless cheeks between his fingers. "You only made one mistake, when you thought you could do it in the first place. You can't steal from us. We can't allow it. If you can do it, anyone can."

Then he heaved James back into the corner and nodded to Rasputin, who grinned and switched on the sander. This time he had a good hold on the handle. A grinding roar chewed up the floor-boards. Inched it forward. The churning sawdust caused James's thighs to pucker and quiver. Shut it off. A test.

The gunmen took a stance, one to either side, bracing, holding the handle and the steering column. Their bodies moved in unison, counting down. One. Two . . .

James slobbered, "All I ever wanted was to go to Las Vegas."

They hit the switch for real.

From being in a war, Broker knew the action eye is a high reso-lution camera of contradictions; the lens is a geyser of adrenaline, and pictures come in slow motion. His only thought was of Keith, desperately trying to pull Caren to safety. Looking into her eyes. Feeling his strength go by inches. How long had he held Caren above the crashing cataract before she slipped from his grasp, leav-ing him to soldier on.

And Ida.

The roar changed from a gritty snarl to a clogged whine. As it bit into James's groin, the gunmen grunted. Rasputin seized the steering column and lifted. The machine drove a red swath up James's mid-dle, threw chips of sternum, bit into the hollow of his throat. When the drum caught his chin his neck flapped like broken film on a reel.

They tried to dodge the mess, the machine tore from their grip and twisted out of control. It raved in the corner, chewing the wall, caught in a jerky danse macabre with James's legs.

Someone yanked the cord out of the wall. Cursed. Then just silence. A nauseating rug-burned stench. And the steady patter of El Niño on the roof. Konic turned to Broker.

"What can I say? They are contract men, they'll be on a plane for the old country before midnight. They delight in savagery." He shrugged. "One of the enthusiasms Russia is going through at the moment. A growth spurt, not unlike your wild west. But I can tell— you think we're crude, huh."

Broker didn't respond. He had spent worse nights.

But not in recent memory.

Communication with Victor Konic ended. They wound more tape around his eyes, but sloppy, so he could see. And bound his ankles. Then they threw him in what felt like a van. They drove. After an hour, they stopped. Hands grabbed under his armpits. Took his feet. And heaved.

The rain had stopped. But it was wet sand where he fell. A beach, because he could hear the deep, regular emptying and filling of surf. Smell the salt. The damp soil seeped into his bones. He ached. Old wounds, old injuries; the doors to all his compartments came unlocked. His living and his dead promenaded in the dark.

The tape cut his wrists and ankles as he slowly, methodically, warred against his bonds. Sometime during the night, animals, dogs he hoped, sniffed near in tall grass. His movements scared them away.

All night he listened to the pounding of surf. There was a fullness to it, a long roll. More resonant than the crash of freshwater on granite.

It did not rain.

Drenched with sweat and dew, it took him until dawn to work through the tape on his ankles. Finally, he freed his legs and stood up. A breath of light nudged the darkness. Like black fog, it drifted out to sea, toward the west.

Sand dunes, tall wind-bent grass. Ancient rounds of rusted barbed wire. And a vast horizon. Superior made the same picture for the eye. But Broker smelled the sweep of Asia out there.

Kit would still be sleeping in Minnesota. He hoped Nina was well. And that Ida Rain was still with us. He wondered if his daughter, if all the sons and daughters, would ever know about Uncle Keith.

Going deep.

Broker started to walk off the beach, out of the Shadow of Death. Into the thin sunlight. Stumbling, hooded with the tape, hands still tightly bound behind his back, he tried to get his bearings. Grids of soggy green fields stretched inland. There was a road. And an old house. Once elegant, now its shutters were rotted, the tiles falling from the roof, walls bleached of color by the salt air.

As he approached the dwelling, El Niño marshaled the clouds. His shadow gradually faded on the gummy road, then vanished. A Mexican woman with four kids stood in the yard, behind a rickety fence rigged from wire and driftwood.

She looked hopefully at the sky, debating whether to hang her basket of laundry on the clothesline. The tall Anglo walking toward her gate looked desperate, but it didn't seem to bother her.

Broker stopped at the edge of the fence.

"I need to use a telephone," he called from his mask of tape.

She gathered the children to her, glanced around awkwardly. Alone out here. No car in the drive.

"Telephone," he repeated.

She shook her head.

"Nine one one," he said.

"*Qué?*"

A lost pilgrim from the Boreal Forest, he struggled at Spanish. "*Nue-vo uno uno?*"

"*Qué?*"

The sky grumbled. She looked up with a resigned expression, and it began to rain.

## 77

Twisting gladioli formed a lavender-blue arch over Ida Rain's hospital bed. Dreamy from medication, she leaned back against her pillows with a noseguard of bruises plastered in the center of her face. Like Broker had imagined, bandages made a white turban around her head. Tests would determine if she'd suffered long-term memory loss. The doctors didn't think so.

Ida licked her dry lips, talking was still difficult. Broker held a sippy cup to her mouth. She drank from the straw.

"How'd it go out there? I mean, afterward?" she asked.

"You waking up and IDing James as your attacker helped a whole lot," said Broker, not real keen about reliving being grilled by the Santa Cruz cops, the Marshals Service, and the FBI.

"Did you see the stories?" She pointed to copies of the Minneapolis and St. Paul papers on the bed.

"I read them on the ride in from the airport."

"Not often a guy like Wanger gets to use a line like: 'Real life is stranger than fiction.'" Ida attempted to smile.

Broker took her hand, and they were quiet for a few beats. Then she looked around the ward, at the curtains, machines, patients, and staff in green gowns.

"Reminds me of *ER*," she said.

Broker shook his head.

"I expect to see Doug Ross or Dr. Benton show up any minute." She stopped. "You don't know what I'm talking about?"

"No."

She tugged for him to come closer. When he did, she whispered in his ear. "I have this little secret."

"You should rest," said Broker.

"No," said Ida. "It's important I get this straight before I talk to any more cops."

"Okay."

"Tom—Danny—him; he told me *he* killed Caren Angland. He was curious why Keith Angland didn't contest his story."

Broker nodded. "That's a secret, all right."

"But it has nothing to do with why he attacked me?"

"Not directly."

"Indirectly?" She attempted to narrow her cloudy eyes. Couldn't.

Broker figured: no memory loss, still sharp. The nine-thousand-piece puzzle would be completed.

"Something's going on, huh?" she asked.

Broker nodded again.

"But you won't tell me?"

"Can't. Don't know myself, for sure."

"Give me just a hint?" Same old Ida.

Broker rubbed his chin. "How's your World War Two history?"

"Try me. You might be surprised." Beaten to a pulp in a hospital bed, Ida sounded like Mae West.

Broker said, "In 1942, Eisenhower briefed the press corps about the landings in North Africa—before the troops hit the beach. He assumed they wouldn't say anything because everybody was on the same side."

Ida leaned back and smiled painfully. "Journalists aren't supposed to take sides . . ."

"Right, for objectivity's sake, they should have solicited a reaction from Hitler," said Broker.

"You, ah, have an example that isn't from the Stone Age?" Ida asked.

"Maybe we're working on that now," said Broker.

Slowly, she picked her words, "You'll tell me someday, when it's more just a story than a secret."

"Deal," said Broker.

"Okay, my selective memory loss has wiped out that part of Tom's conversation. Now we have our stories straight."

"My turn. St. Paul Homicide is after me on this. How did Tom know we were working on those stories?"

"Easy. He hacked into the company office network and read an E-mail about it."

Broker shook his head. "I knew there was a reason I put off getting a computer."

A nurse approached and told Broker that was enough. Ida had to rest.

She touched her puffy upper lip. "You may kiss me good-bye, here, on this bruise."

Chastely, Broker did.

Lorn Garrison, waiting in the hall, asked, "How is she?" He didn't mean her medical condition.

"She's cool," said Broker.

They parted in the parking lot after making tentative plans to hunt together next fall. Soon, bounty money would start trickling into a Kentucky bank account.

"So what did you tell them?" asked Nina over the long-distance connection from Tuzla. She referred specifically to Tommy Reardon at St. Paul Homicide; but she meant them all.

"Same thing I told the Santa Cruz sheriff's department, the Marshals Service, the FBI, and the reporters. They wouldn't listen to me when I tried to make an argument about James being involved with the missing money. So I went on my own to find him. Except *somebody* was listening. Probably bugged the house. When I got the lead on James from Ida, they were right on top of me. Those guys wrapped me up the minute I knocked on the door."

"So they *were* watching you?"

"Must have been. The BCA had a crew up to check the house. They never found a bug, though."

"Did you mention the couple down the beach?"

"You know, they slipped my mind."

"Sometimes I don't like talking to you when I can't see your eyes." Broker didn't respond. She didn't push it. They both reserved separate compartments to store bodies in. So she asked, "Does James change the case against the husband?"

Broker smiled. "Jeff just heard through the grapevine—that Italian Mafioso, Tony Sporta, the feds' key witness—well, after seeing how well they guarded James in Witness Protection, he's changed his story. He's refusing to testify. So the case is getting more circumstantial all the time, and Keith has a sharp lawyer."

"Can of worms," said Nina.

"Yeah, well; I'm through sticking my nose in other people's business," said Broker.

"Can I get that in writing." They laughed, and then Nina asked, "How's Kit doing?"

Broker watched Kit perform her peculiar stomp dance under the dragon. "You know. Normal kid things. It's a beautiful clear night. We're going out and learn some stars."

They stood on Broker's favorite rock while the big water beat a rolling cadence at their feet. Six breath-stopping degrees filed each star to a point. The night sky was sharp enough to bite.

"Ars," puffed Kit, echoing Broker's coaching. Muffled in Polarfleece bunting, only her eyes showed, specked with diamonds.

He held her up, face to the south, where the mighty hourglass of Orion blazed. The constellation was a night anchor running back through time, to the first humans who raised their eyes above survival in the dirt.

"See. The three stars in a row. That's the belt. And the big one down to the right, that's Rigel."

To honor the advent of his daughter's new century—and for her mom and Caren and Ida—Broker pronounced, "That's Orion, Kit; she's a hunter."

```
FIC          Logan, Chuck,
LOGAN           1942-

             The big law.
```

$24.00                    11/11/1998

| DATE | | | |
|---|---|---|---|
| | | | |
| | | | |
| | | | |
| | | | |
| | | | |
| | | | |
| | | | |
| | | | |
| | | | |
| | | | |
| | | | |
| | | | |
| | | | |